Under the Heartless Blue

Under the Heartless Blue

Allyson Stack

FREIGHT BOOKS

First published 2016

Freight Books
49-53 Virginia Street
Glasgow, G1 1TS
www.freightbooks.co.uk

ISBN 978-1-910449-86-8
eISBN 978-1-910449-87-5

Typeset by Freight in Plantin
Printed and bound by Bell and Bain, Glasgow

the publisher acknowledges investment from
Creative Scotland toward the publication of this book

Allyson Stack holds a BA from Yale, an MFA from Arizona State University, and a PhD from the University of Edinburgh, where she is currently a Lecturer in English Literature. She lives in Edinburgh with her husband and their two children.

For T

I want to remain nocturnal and find
my night, softly luminous, in you.
                              —Luce Irigaray

Prologue

Why tonight, after all these years? Why trouble my sleep with this dream of desert rain? You arrive unseen. Just a hard bare arm that curls around my waist so deftly accurate, pressing me up against you – there in the rain-soaked dust, embracing. You are all heat and breath. No sight, no sound. Just a feather-scratch of beard against skin, warmth of your breath in my hair.

Until I jolt awake, heart hammering out its tired backbeat in the breast. Awareness shuffles over me. Blankets twisted. Ache of chilblained hands. Sleep-sounds of the other nurses: air passing softly between dry lips, creak of a bedspring. And as I lie on my side and wait for sleep, the girl I once was rises up before me. Wind-whipped hair without a hint of grey, she is striding down a railway platform beneath a wide arc of sky. Ruddy-faced women turn and stare, eyeing her slim-waisted jacket and lace-trimmed sunshade. A dark knowingness in their eyes. As if they sense something in her gait, her attire, her air of urban worldliness that marks her for failure. Some flaw hooks their gaze, holding it fast.

In the years ahead, the memory of these women will come back to her. Their sun-weathered faces shadowing every doubt and disappointment, haunting her every loss. But on this, the final day of her journey, she gives them little thought. Elbowing her way through the crowd, she is shaken by the rough clamour of the place. Stock-pens, freight cars, shouting cattlemen. Animals bellowing on the load-ramps. Slam of ore carts, the scent of raw timber.

She draws a long breath, choking on dust and smelter fumes. Throat burning, chest billowing like a sail. And there, beneath the sour steam, she can taste it. Something fresh and strange rising from the earth like smoke.

She keeps walking. Down the platform, past the roundhouse, through the town's dusty streets until she is striding through open desert. And as she walks, she thinks. Of days spent inside a Pullman car, of mile upon mile of forest and wide open prairie unfurling behind cold glass. Of nights passed in that narrow coffin of a bed as the tidal rhythm of the rails rocked her to sleep – black and mercifully empty.

An entire continent divides her from the only life she has ever known. The weather-beaten rowhouse where she was born and raised, the ailing dockyards of her youth with their stink of tar and moldering rope. That patch of earth where, at the age of twelve, she watched her mother's coffin slide into the ground. Then, four years later, her father's too. It would take a five day journey to carry her back to the office where she once worked keeping accounts, until a geology professor with a warm smile and straw-coloured hair took a fancy to her. Courted her, then proposed. They married. Moved into a small rented house, where they lived in contentment and quiet ease until Henry died of an illness no doctor could diagnose, leaving her a widow at twenty-three.

Vera scrambles up a graveled slope, breathing hard. Her hem catches. She bends to unhook it, sparing no thought for rattlesnakes, scorpions, black widow spiders. Never thinking to draw her hand back from a thorny tangle of mesquite. For she knows nothing of this place. This land of heat and rock. Knows nothing of the tyrannical passions that accompany a certain kind of love. Its aching doubts and savage joys. Promise of rhapsodic surfeit that never arrives. She knows nothing of you. The one who lies in wait. Even now.

Of all this she remains blissfully ignorant as she stands beneath a sky so big it hurts. Air fragrant with things she cannot name. In this moment she knows only the sun on her face, the dry wind in her hair, sight of distant mountains rolling on and on under a cloudless blue.

She feels a throb of excitement. A delicious shiver stirred by this vast expanse of land. Every breath ripe with briny promise. Salt of something so close you can taste it. Some wild, undiscovered sweet lying just within reach, just barely ahead—

Shout after her. Warn her. The way someone should have warned these nurses who slumber on around me, naïve and unsuspecting. Never guessing where the real danger lies. Never wondering: what will happen when the war ends and every drop of my youth has been drained away?

In every one of them, I see her. That girl staring across a ceaseless sea of dust, gaze locked on the horizon – as if its very expanse were a test of her resolve. A challenge to be met and conquered.

I want to cry out to her. Warn her.

But a soft wave of sleep rolls over me. And when I surface, she is gone.

Chapter 1

France, 1918

A voice calls out my name. *Vite, Vera! Dépêche-toi!* I throw off the blankets, shiver and sit up. Mind-whirl of rising too fast. Grope about in the dark for apron, stockings, rubber boots. Not noticing the silence. Not yet. Just a blade of light slicing through the room and that voice, yanking at me like a chain.

I fumble with collar, clasps, and cuffs… fiddly starched bits that never fail to frustrate me. Uniform by committee. The same one that keeps ignoring my pleas to improve our hot water supply.

Hurrying down the dim corridor of the old château, I hear the uneven rumble of the guns. But it is distant. Chandeliers are still. No dainty tinkling of glass. No mad rush of orderlies, doctors, and nurses. No kettles on the boil fugging up the rooms. All is quiet. Busy, but quiet. A thought burns through the sleep-fog: I have been wakened to perform some menial task. Unclog a drain. Boil water because there is no power to run the sterilisers. I vow to send another letter to the committee. Tell them we cannot keep relying on this faulty back-up generator every time a shell damages our wiring.

The *Directrice* intercepts me in the high-ceilinged hall. Tall with arrow-straight posture and a basset hound sag to her cheeks, she grasps my arm and leads me towards the back-stair. Her words roll over me in a roily wash of half-swallowed syllables. My French is never sharp right after I wake up. Even after eighteen years of living in Paris, I still dream in English. Part of the problem. That dream. It keeps ringing through me, a dissonant chord refusing to resolve and fade.

'Vera,' she snaps.

I nod, grasping the last bit. I am to assist one of the surgeons.

'Qui?'

'Mademoiselle MacNeil.'

I know her well enough. Young, British, female. Studied medicine in the States. Upon learning I was American, she sought me out in the mess-hall and regaled me with tales about her time in Philadelphia, a city I have never laid eyes on.

'Elle vous attends là.' The *Directrice* waves at a door that leads belowstairs to a disused kitchen, which confuses me – surgical *equipés* scrub in the old cloakroom, just down the corridor.

I stammer something about a mistake.

She draws a breath, bosom rising formidably, then releases a long sigh. The same one she reserves for brass-buttoned inspectors who linger in the wards, making endless jottings in their penny notebooks. She tightens her grip on my arm, giving me to know she will brook no discussion. No questions, no protests. Not a word in front of Armand, who is hurrying by with a stack of towels. Lips pressed tight, the *Directrice* projects an air of haughty annoyance. As if the entire war were nothing but a great personal inconvenience. Then I catch something in the dart of her eye. Not panic, no. The *Directrice* never panics. Not even when we run out of antiseptic or lose electricity during a push. But it is something akin to panic. Her hands keep falling to her apron, smoothing it with a fretful twitch. And the furtive flick, flick of her gaze betrays a nervous haste that I have never glimpsed in her before.

Then she gives a brusque nod and walks away. Doctor MacNeil. Is this some mad notion of hers that – for whatever reason – the *Directrice* feels obliged to indulge? And Doctor MacNeil does have her notions. *It is silly to separate officers from enlisted men, back me when I speak to the CMO. Vera, where is your WSPU badge? I shall get one sent over. We must all band together.* Her egalitarian views do not strike me as radical, or dangerous, or even wrong. What disturbs me is the ferocity of her passions, and her insistence – no, presumption – that

6

the rest of us must share them. *Could we equip the light medical ward with a gramophone? Ask the committee, Vera. Would they fund a bacteriological lab to help us research and treat gas gangrene? Write to them. Find out.* Whenever we dine together I depart with a long list of tasks. And yet... I find myself drawn to her. Charmed by these plucky displays of defiance. Her refusal to be carried along by the prevailing wind. And she insists, against all military protocol, that we call her Tosh.

I descend into the cellar, thoughts snagging on the Directrice's words. *Assistes la chirurgie.* No. I misheard. Summon an aging volunteer who has done no real nursing since training ended? My duties are entirely clerical. I pitch in during ward rushes, yes. An extra pair of hands to snip bandages, give morphine, read tickets, record vitals. But assist a surgeon? With what? A delivery of sterile cotton that must be inventoried in the middle of the night?

Rounding the curve in the stair I catch a whiff of paraffin. Long twists of shadow gloam across the far wall. Shuffling from one worn flagstone to the next, I bump into a sack of coal for which we paid dearly during the last *crise de charbon*. And there, on a table where servants used to eat their meals, lies a young girl. Flat on her back, legs splayed. Her sharp white knees jut up into the air. Blood drips down, pooling in a hollow on the old stone floor. Tosh is bent between the girl's pale legs, her gloved hands slick with blood.

I draw in a breath and let it go. The air smells of mice and lime-dust.

She orders me to scrub, do TPRs, and I force my body to obey. Careful to keep every thought pinned to the here and now as I plunge my hands into the greasy froth. Dry them. Sterilise the thermometer. Clasp the bottle of mentholated spirit. Set it back down. Because if you inflate each passing moment, make it big enough, you can smother the rest. Snuff out every spark of recollection before it flares.

I approach. Muddy *sabots* and wool stockings lie heaped

7

beneath the table. The girl's hair hangs off the edge in limp greasy strands. She turns at the sound of my footfall, and at the sight of her face – thin and pale with ink-well eyes – I feel something spring loose inside. I look away but it does not stop, this sensation of something unspooling wildly.

It is the refugee girl who works at the *estaminet*, serving drinks in exchange for room-and-board. Last summer she would come to the hospital and sell flowers for half a sou. Lavender, lilacs, phlox, red hawthorn. Whatever bloomed along the bye-roads. I always bought a bunch, to the great consternation of the charge-sister, who made no secret of what she thought about a grubby refugee hanging about the wards.

I take up her wrist and search for a pulse while Tosh kneels by the smoky lamp, picking through a pile of blood-soaked towels. She holds each one up to the light, face pinched in concentration. I look away. Fix my gaze on the dial as the needle leaps and dips. But it's no use. All the old unhappy visions come swarming back. The bony limb, rubbery and damp with blood. Wrapped in rags, handed to me in a bundle. Swaddled oily mess that I must carry to the back lot and burn to ash as dawn explodes across the sky. It is all here. Right now. Flooding through me in the shadowy dark.

I unwrap the pressure-cuff and swallow hard. '82 over 40.'

'Fetch morphine. Tell Félix to prepare a bed for abdominal surgery.'

Upstairs, nurses and orderlies shoot me inquisitive looks while the *Directrice* sweeps through the wards in an endless loop, as if the sheer force of her presence will stifle any gossip. But it is a slow night and rumors fly: the girl entertains officers then reports back to the enemy... *non*, she was raped... *ces sales Boches... Pas du tout,* she is a whore *tu te souviens,* we examined *cette fille* during the last health inspection... Tsht, she was poisoned for selling military secrets... Filthy little spy!... These Belgians are a shifty lot... Remember the ones they arrested near Soissons?

My own speculations run a different course: a young officer sits alone at a corner table. It is late. *Madame* has gone to bed. Clearing away the empty glasses, her fingers brush his hand. A delicious half-accident. The officer lingers. Orders another brandy. And one for yourself, *ma petite*. It is the first kindness from anyone in months. Candle burning low, they talk. Laugh a bit. The brass buttons of his uniform are shiny, his beard freshly trimmed. The following night, he returns.

The charge-sister arrives to unlock the drugs-cabinet. She hands me the ampoule with a disapproving cluck, then whispers the cost in a low hiss. Her figure is wrong. The price of morphine rose three weeks ago. But why correct her? It will not earn the girl any friends.

Downstairs, Tosh has lit a cigarette. While I prepare the *piqûre*, she smokes and talks. The girl walked uphill from the village with bar towels stuffed into her drawers. She broke a window, snuck inside, then hid behind the cellar-door. When Tosh passed by, the girl grabbed her.

'I tried to get her into surgery, but she bit me.' Tosh extends her arm.

We will drug the girl and strap her to a gurney. It's what we do when a soldier resists. Tosh exhales a long stream of smoke. The paper of her cigarette is stained pink. 'Is there some old wives tale I ought to know of?'

'What?'

'Maybe the French think it's bad luck to go under the knife on a full moon.'

'She's Belgian.'

But Tosh just keeps talking in her nervy flight-of-the-bumble-bee sort of way. 'Never done much of this sort of thing, you know. Had obstetrics in school, but that was years ago. For heaven's sake don't breathe a word…' she lifts her eyes to indicate upstairs. 'I can hear them having a go at me already. Woman doctor who doesn't know how to birth babies. Not that we'll get a baby out of this.'

'We?'

'You're to assist.'

I shake my head.

'Standard abdominal surgery.' Tosh flicks her fag-end to the floor. It lands in a pool of muddy water and goes out. 'No shrapnel. No gangrene. Stitch it up if she's lucky. Remove the whole package, if not.'

There are times when Tosh sounds vaguely American. Not her accent, which is English to the core, but the way she gives orders. Offers diagnoses. It's different from the other surgeons. Direct, pithy, a bit too fast. She spent eight years in the States and her speech betrays her sometimes.

I watch the dark liquid empty into the syringe. 'Get one of the more experienced nurses.'

'You've no choice, I'm afraid. Muriel was adamant.'

I realise, with a start, that she is referring to the *Directrice*. The very thought of calling her 'Muriel' makes me cringe. I feel guilty of insubordination just by listening.

'You're the only one she trusts.'

'To do what?' I press the piston into the barrel to expel any air. 'Mess it up?'

Tosh laughs. 'To keep quiet.'

I give the needle a quick tap. 'You know what this is, right?'

'Morphine, I should hope.'

'I mean the girl. You realise what's happened.'

'Ruptured ectopic gestation.' Tosh waves at the heap of bloody rags. 'I examined the discharge. Some decidua.'

So that's what they call it. The jellied bits, the bony limb. Blood-soaked bundle tossed on a rubbish-fire in the back lot. Decidua. Dead leaves. Nothing more.

Ruptured fallopian tube? No, Tosh is wrong. This is not an ectopic pregnancy. But a nurse must never contradict a doctor, especially an ill-trained war volunteer whose days are spent counting supply-stores and filing recapitulary reports. I do not treat patients. I number and docket them. Four forms for every patient admitted. Six more if he is discharged alive. Seventeen for a death. At this, I excel. And yet... after five decades in this world you learn a thing or two. I step towards the girl. She is moaning. Mouth full and round, lips plump as a grape. I kneel down and ask her name.

'Estelle.'

This will ease the pain, I say. You will feel a swift prick, then relief. But first you must tell me what has happened. Her lace collar, visible above the drawsheet, is askew. When I reach out to adjust it, she flinches.

'Go on,' snaps Tosh. 'She's lost a lot of blood.'

The girl is staring up at the needle, eyes wide. I shake my head. First she must confess. It will be our little secret, I say. But we must know, *le médecin et moi*. How did you injure yourself?

The girl turns her face to the wall. Eerie shadows flicker over the chalky white. Her pulse is thready, cheeks pale. Hands wandering over the sheet in that restless way of someone in such pain that it is impossible to keep still. I put my lips to her ear and tell her what I think: the missed menses, the exhaustion and the nausea, a tiny ghost tad-poling its way to life inside – her attempt at eviction.

This way, she need not speak the words. Only offer her assent, which she does. A slight nod. Eyes damp with unshed tears.

I swab and stretch a patch of skin, slip the needle in and press. You can see it start to work. Muscles in the face soften, eyes go glassy. My movements are swift, but sure. I withdraw the needle and hold the bowl by her head, in case she vomits.

'What is it?' Tosh asks, snapping on her gloves.

I turn and tell her.

We emerge at daybreak. Beyond the tall arched windows of the refectory, the sky is growing pale. I shovel down forkfuls of eggs, sausage, potatoes. Buttered toast, more eggs. While I eat, Tosh smokes and talks. Fond reminiscences about her time at Women's Medical College. Idyllic afternoons in Fairmount Park. A grove of Elm trees that used to remind her of Devonshire. Tales about 'Nursey' – the woman who cared for her when she was young, scolding her so often for making up stories (tosh, tosh, you silly girl!) that her younger brother took to crying out *Tosh Tosh! Wait for me, Tosh Tosh*. Remember this, she throws back her head and laughs and I feel my face break into a smile.

Her vigour astounds me. After the night we have passed, it is all I can do to sit upright. I try blaming my age, but plenty of professional nurses in their fifties work the night-shift. I drink a cup of coffee in three swift gulps. Then another. Still, I feel sapped. Empty. As if nothing can replenish me.

The refugee girl is alive. Asleep in an old cloakroom, which now holds a bed. As the anaesthetic wore off, she talked. Sometimes these ether-fringed ramblings make no sense. Other times you can piece things together. *Madame* told Estelle that a baby was not possible, the refugee charity would not pay her a larger subsidy for it and what good is an *estaminet* with a baby crying behind the bar? So when *Madame* left her knitting in the parlour, Estelle saw her chance. She smuggled a needle into her room beneath the eaves along with a pile of bar towels. She was prepared for the blood, but not the pain.

It could have been worse. We managed to staunch the bleeding. She did not go into shock. Her uterine wall was intact, though the cervix was badly lacerated. She must have used a mirror, Tosh guessed, something (or someone) to show her where to aim the needle, how to poke and thrust. She was not just stabbing away blindly. If she'd done that, Tosh said, she'd be dead.

She still might die. Lost a lot of blood, risk of septicemia. After all, Madame's nine-inch needle was not sterile. But for now, she lives. Asleep in the old ladies cloakroom, because the *Directrice* refused to have her in post-op partitioned off by a screen. How she plans to keep the girl's presence here a secret

I cannot imagine. But Tosh and I are under strict orders to say nothing. A mistake, I fear. Whispers will rustle through the village: a foolish refugee girl taking up space in a military hospital! A civilian consuming precious supplies! Concealing what happened will be impossible, and once it comes to light, we'll have even bigger problems with the committee. I said as much to the *Directrice* but she was adamant.

The refectory is filling up. Nurses, doctors, and orderlies shuffle by, bringing with them the smell of the wards. Bedpans, soiled bandages, idioform, paraffin, and pus. The fat *Gestionnaire* emerges from the kitchen to announce there is no fresh milk. *Sucre?* asks Tosh. *Non. Pas du tout.* Sugar stopped last week and will not resume. We are foolish, his tone makes clear, to even hope for sugar. The news makes Tosh sullen. Each of us has a small indulgence that we rely upon. For Tosh it is a proper cup of tea; for the *Directrice* an elegant coiffure. No matter how late the hour or unexpected the circumstance, never once have I seen her looking *mal coiffée*. And me? I find solace in the sable cloak Louis gave me for my fiftieth birthday. After a day spent struggling with thin ink and faulty nibs, I can throw it over my shoulders, step outdoors, and feel revived.

I finish the dregs of my coffee and push the cup aside.

'A bit of air.' Tosh slides her arm through mine, and moments later we are striding down the pebbled drive. The cold bites at my hands, skin raw from harsh soap and scalding water. I ball them into fists, thoughts swerving back to the refugee girl. I try to imagine the long trudge from Belgium into France. Find myself wondering about her parents. What has become of them? Any brothers, or sisters…? I imagine her asleep under the eaves, alone. Behind the bar at Madame's *estaminet* day after day for three long years. Her hunger for companionship, for love.

Tosh fingers the hem of my cloak. 'Aren't you afraid someone's going to nick this?'

I shrug and say nothing.

Her eyes flash with amusement. 'Yes, quite. One ought to look one's best for the war, duh-ling.'

I smile and she pats my hand, as we draw to a halt beside the huge stone fountain, dry but for a murky soup of fag-ends and dead leaves. Tosh pulls a crumpled pack of Gitanes from her pocket, and as the silence between us lengthens, my mistake becomes clear. Out here, far from any eavesdroppers, I can be questioned. Probed for details about how a lowly office clerk can spot an abortion gone awry.

I cast about for some excuse, but Tosh is too quick. 'A surgical school is being established five miles from the front.' She knocks out a fag, strikes a match and inhales. 'It will train doctors just out of medical school for field hospitals and aid posts. I have been pressing this venture for months, and it's just been approved. Resources are slim.'

'A shoestring budget.'

A confused look crosses her face.

'It's an American expression.'

Tosh nods, fingers worrying a frayed belt-loop. Her hands are never idle. 'I would like to put your name in for a transfer.'

'Me?' I shake my head. 'Ask a professionally trained nurse. Someone younger. What about Julia? Or that new one. With the dark hair. She'd leap at the chance.'

'Most nurses are volunteers. Why train doctors for conditions that don't exist?'

'You want me because I'm inept?'

She pauses, exhaling a cool ribbon of smoke. 'I need someone who can convert donations from abroad into French currency. Calculate expenses, secure supplies. Negotiate with local authorities. You speak French. You are good at sums.' Propping her foot on the lip of the fountain, she waits. Smoke curls up from her cigarette as we regard one another through a blueish haze. My reluctance surprises her. But my duties here are not over-taxing. Some are downright pleasant. Every month the *Directrice* sends me to Paris to meet with the committee and review our accounts. My leave requests are always granted, and the *patron* at the *table d'hôte* in the village never fails to give me a table by the fire.

'Most nurses would be thrilled at the prospect.' She stubs her fag-end against the sole of her boot and tucks it into her pocket. Buttoning the soiled flap of her greatcoat, she regards me with cool nonchalance. 'If you do not want to serve near the front, where proper medical care is most crucial, then why are you here?'

All my life people have asked me this question. What brings you here, Vera? Why? I stare at the fierce, bewildered look on her face. Isn't life just one rash act after the next? An impulse flares and off you go. To war. Out west. Into a man's arms. Are there ever reasons, really? Isn't there just the story we learn to tell ourselves, shaping the welter of existence into what we need to believe?

'I am here,' I say at last, 'because eighteen years ago a man asked me to join him in Paris. Because I am an old-fashioned ninny who knows no better than to stumble blindly after a man and marry him.'

'You're married?'

'Was. Until he died.'

'I'm sorry.'

I shake my head. 'It happened years ago. Three weeks before the war began. We were married after he became ill… Louis was a Frenchman of the old school. We disagreed on many things. Things that did not matter before, but came to matter very much here. In France.'

She waves at me to go on, and for some reason, I do. 'Towards the end of his life, Louis' faith became important to him. He wanted to marry. It made him happy to formalise our relations in this way… the request of a dying man.'

For a long moment Tosh says nothing. I can feel her brown eyes flitting over me, straining to sketch a new image over the old. 'It all sounds rather romantic.'

'I assure you it was not.'

'Well, that explains your file.' A smile tugs at the corners of her lips. 'When I was hunting down your contract, there was nothing under 'Palmer'.'

'Dumont,' I explain. 'Officially, I am Vera Dumont.'

'Yet you go by Nurse Palmer.' She shoots me a sly wink, which makes me bristle, because she is wrong. I know what she is thinking and she is very wrong. I am no revolutionary. No blue-stockinged suffragette. My decision was purely practical. If someone were to shout 'Nurse Dumont' across the ward, I would never respond. I might even flee in a panic fearing the ghost of my mother-in-law had risen from the grave to inform me, once again, of the precise measure of my inadequacy.

I stare at Tosh's wild mane of curls, her smooth unblemished cheek. 'Am I being transferred?'

Tosh throws up her hands. 'Tell me what you want!'

What I want…

To smell the desert after rain? To awake each morning beneath a soft Cheyenne blanket, skin still heavy with his scent? To rip out the flawed cog inside of me that brought it all to a screeching halt, then wind back through the years and do everything all over again. Perhaps that is what I want. A different ending.

Chapter 2

Arizona Territory, 1884

Whenever I spool back through the years, untangling the knot of roads, trains, and cities that has come to comprise my life, I stumble inevitably upon her. She is always there: striding down that planked sidewalk, searching for a street-sign. Some indication of where she is, how much farther she has to go.

She stops. Circles back. Past the same row of hotels, banks, harness shops, and feed stores. Foot-sore and weary, still, she would rather retrace this strip of sidewalk forever than ask another sun-bonneted woman for directions. 'Sixth Street?' she'd chirped each time, only to watch their wind-chapped faces contract in suspicion and mild scorn. And for what? Some breech of local etiquette of which she, fresh off the train, was ignorant? This town was notorious for harbouring outlaws, cattle rustlers, even murderers – a tolerance that did not extend, apparently, to confused young women from Connecticut. Fine, then. *Fine.*

Chin held high, she marches back past the low-slung buildings with an air of feigned assurance. Ruched skirts snap and swirl about her ankles, which are sheathed in soft kid's leather – a new pair of boots of which she is terribly proud. But this portrait is misleading. For if you were walking beside her on that narrow shelf of sidewalk, you would not see this fashionable outfit. You would not see it, because of the wool cloak she wears clasped tight against the grit and the wind. And you would certainly not see the precious piece of paper that lies, carefully folded, beneath her corset.

Discovered six weeks ago among her late husband's papers, this document describes a patch of land with a vein of silver running through it. And because of Henry's 'recent demise' (to use the sterile words of her lawyer) the mineral rights now fall to her. It is this piece of paper, now pressed to her ribs, that has lured her to Goose Flat.

She scans the storefronts – Bootmaker, Dry Goods, General Store, Saloon – face set in a hard glaze of resolution. But deep within she trembles. At the half-finished buildings. At the way trash catches on cactus-spines to be slowly shredded by the wind. At the splintered walls and open trash heaps. Stink of outdoor privies, tallow, kerosene, hot grease and dirt. Whiff of a hog-pen. She halts. Miners in leather brogans shove past. Smell of rock-dust and mules pressing in with the dust whipping up from the street.

It is here, where the raised sidewalk ends, that she keeps turning back. Certain her destination could not possibly lie amid those mud-brick shacks and vacant lots. Then she sees it, lying in the dirt – a sign for Sixth Street toppled by the wind. She hurries down the gullied road, dodging manure heaps and sink holes. A cattleman at the hitch-bar stares, gaze boring into her like a spark on cloth. A look no man back East would dare turn on such a respectably dressed woman. But that, she suspects, is the problem. Lace-trimmed sunshade, ivory shoes… everything marks her. *New arrival. Tenderfoot from back East.* All she wants is to pass unnoticed. Find her new home, take refuge there. Sadie Blair's Boarding House for Girls. *East Sixth Street* says the letter in her pocket. *Glass winders. White paint. Cant miss it.* She hopes so. Because she needs to find it. Needs to close the door of her rented room, sit down on some awful lump of a mattress, and stifle this rising panic. Because what has she done? What nameless force has driven her to sever the lease on that small, comfortable house and – for *this*?

She presses on. Dogs bark. Cats slink between barbed-wire. Laundry snaps in the wind. A house rises above the rest. Not mud-brick. Not a tin-roofed heap of planks. Painted shutters, peaked triangular roof. A sign above the letter-slot:

Star Mansion
Madam Sadie Blair, Proprietor.
FIREARMS STRICTLY PROHIBITED

Guns? In a girls boarding house? But of course. Remember where you are: fresh off a stagecoach in Apache country. Yes, a stagecoach. Does that stir visions of adventure and excitement? Of sleek-muscled horses galloping over mesa and creekbed while Indians bear down, arrows drawn? Well, imagine this instead: a cramped wooden box jolting over ten miles of rock-strewn road, while busted springs prod the undersides of your thighs leaving bruises that will take days to yellow and fade, as you sit squashed between a bunch of nosy strangers who take your lack of male escort as a personal affront. *All alone, my dear? And in such wild country?*

So I'd lied. Told them my husband would be joining me in a few days' time. But speaking of Henry as if he were still alive was like striking my elbow on the corner of a table, and a vague oppression had settled over me after that. A forlorn melancholy that I could not shake.

I tripped up the steps and gave the brass knocker three brisk raps. Wind tore at my skirts, a gritty blast that made me screw up my eyes.

The door opened. 'We ain't hirin!'

Then it slammed shut and the bolt clanked back into place. The constriction in my chest tightened. Throat dry. I stared out across the high plateau country, creosote flats rolling on and on until rimrock reared up against a limitless blue. My fingers worried the brim of my hat. The sight of that stupid little bon-ton enraged me. Fool. Who buys such a hat? What a useless bit of frippery. It did nothing to protect my face from the sun. I closed my eyes against the grit and the wind and the stark expanse of land. Then I summoned all the stoicism of my youth. That strength I'd relied upon during the weeks after my father died, when I rapped on every door in town until

19

I'd found another book-keeping job. *This is no different,* I told myself bringing the knocker down hard. *No. Different. At. All.*

'I said we ain't hirin'!' came the gruff rebuke. 'Try Minnie Parsons. Word is she let a gal go few days back.'

I drew a deep breath. 'But I have already been hired!'

The door cracked open.

'I'm the new book-keeper.'

The thick-set man stood firm, until I could stand it no longer. Thrusting my rolled sunshade between his arm and the doorjamb, I slid into the vestibule. A pungent odour engulfed me. Furniture polish, hair oil, cigar smoke, stale perfume. I jabbed my hat onto a hook and began drawing off my gloves with a cool proprietary air. To my relief, he did not protest.

'Sadie Blair is expecting me,' I announced, voice far steadier than I felt, whereupon he stumped away down the hall leaving me alone. A gauzy half-light slanted into rooms furnished with plush-upholstered chairs, gilt-framed pictures, brass fittings, ormolu. Small tables of dark wood were all polished to a glossy shine. My spirits rose. I'd braced myself for something like Miss Stanton's Boarding House. That sad collection of worn, musty rooms where I'd lived after my father died. But this place looked pleasant. Rather elegant, even.

A tall woman burst from the shadows in a jangle of bracelets and keys. Pausing before a walnut cabinet, she ran a finger across the top and hollered, 'Jackson!'

The squat man with the bulldog face reappeared.

'Tell that damn houseboy to get down here and clean this.' She flicked a wrist at the offending cabinet, then flashed me a tight-lipped smile, wrinkles flaring. This was Sadie Blair, though she made no move to introduce herself.

'I'd planned to fix a room for you downstairs, but we have so little space on the ground floor once the evening entertainments get underway.' She draped a jewelled hand over my shoulder. 'Besides, you'll be more comfortable upstairs. Noise won't keep you awake. You'll be working the till nights in any case.'

A door slammed at the end of the hall and a man appeared. Not Jackson. Someone else. The force of his stride jangled the chandelier as he clumped towards us. He paused at the foot of the stairs and the tinkling glass stopped.

'So.' He hitched up his trousers, which dropped back to his hips the moment he let go. 'We got an agreement then, Miz Blair?'

'Yes.' Sadie forced the word through a thin smile.

The man ran a hand across his balding pate, revealing a sweat-stained armpit. A tarnished badge was pinned to his shirt. 'That cook a yours makes the best damn cup a coffee.'

'That's because it's not coffee,' Sadie fairly hissed. 'It's café au lait.'

The man's squinty gaze shifted to me, eyes roaming where they pleased.

I glared back.

Sadie hurried over and clasped my arm. 'Allow me to introduce…'

'Vera,' I supplied. 'Vera Palmer.'

'Yes. Yes, of course.' She waved a jewelled hand through the air. 'Vera will be assisting me in the *office.*'

The man hitched up his trousers. His stare felt like a crude appraisal, as if he were inspecting livestock.

'Deputy,' Sadie replied stiffly. 'She is our new *book-keeper.*'

'Ah,' he nodded. 'Should I tell Lyle he'll be gettin' your payments on time now?' A hearty laugh at his own joke.

'If you don't mind,' Sadie led him towards the door. 'My book-keeper and I have much to discuss.'

The man lifted his hat from the rack and took his leave. 'Miss.'

And at this one word, my face broke into a smile. For six years I had been M'am. Mrs Palmer. Henry Palmer's wife. The late professor's widow. *That poor gal. Husband spent time abroad, racketing around in the most uncivilised places. Years ago, yes. But illness can hang around! Wouldn't be surprised if he caught some rare tropical disease. They say she's had… difficulties. Pharmacist caught her pinching laudanum, went into a fit when old Leonard refused to sell her more.*

'Bastards!' cried Sadie Blair. 'Whole lot of 'em! Try getting a cop in here when some drunk tosses a chair through my window. Or an arrest when a john roughs up one of my girls. License fees *and* protection money? What next? Taxing my player piano?'

As she thundered on, her speech changed. She started dropping 'g's' and using 'ain't' and the angrier she got the more pronounced this tendency became. 'Nerve a that twerp! Criticizin me for sendin linens to China Mary, stead of some white-owned steam laundry charges twice as much. Sonofabitch. How dare he sit in my kitchen and tell me what colour my wash-tub mammy's gotta be!'

My gaze fell to a painting by the stair: a nude woman being chased by satyrs and goats. Skin impossibly smooth, nipples plump as strawberries. My eyes darted away, only to land on another, then another. Framefuls of bare breasts and naked legs, winking eyes and come-hither smiles… then it dawned on me. What should have been clear from the start – *Girls Boarding House seeks experienced book-keeper. Generous salary. Female preferred…* nobody ever prefers hiring a woman.

Should I claim I was trapped? That brute circumstance conspired to keep me under Sadie Blair's roof? The facts are there: widowed, almost out of money, a job with exceptional pay that includes room-and-board. Why not arrange them just so? Vera Palmer: motherless at twelve, orphaned at sixteen, widowed at twenty-three. Alone on the frontier. A five day rail-journey from the only life she has ever known. All true. But that is not the whole truth. There were plenty of shop-keepers who might have hired me to run their registers. Hotels where I could take reservations, hand out room-keys. But such a notion, if it ever crossed my mind, was swiftly overcome by another: I was going to have an adventure. The kind I'd longed for after marring Henry, a man who had courted me with tales of geological expeditions in exotic lands, but once married, could scarcely be persuaded to leave Connecticut. Besides, I'd been dreading my return to book-keeping. The cramp in the wrist, the ink-stained hands, the endless rows of numbers, my clumsiness with sums… this would spice up all that drudgery.

Surely there was a momentary shudder of distaste? A pang of moral compunction, coupled with nervous anxiety at the thought of what happened under Sadie Blair's roof each night. Honestly? I don't remember. I was young, still wobbly with grief. What I recall most vividly is the thrill of newfound freedom. My life was entirely my own. A quiver of excitement ran through me, a thrum of anticipation akin to the impulse that had driven me West in the first place. Now it was my turn for adventure. It was finally my turn.

The *Directrice* gives me the day off. A reward, she says. But her overly solicitous smile and pointed compliments on my *prudence* and *discrétion* are clear enough: she wants me out of the way. Tucked safely into bed where no one can ask about the village girl.

But what will happen when the morphine-haze gives way to the sharp outlines of her windowless room? To the sight of her wooden sabots tucked beneath a stool, dress laundered and tagged like any wounded soldier's uniform? What if she flails and screams? Resists treatment. Anything to keep her from returning to the *estaminet*. Because *Madame* knows. She knows about those nights when Estelle was left to close up. About the officer who used to linger, fingering his cigarette case, coolly waiting while she wiped down the bar and bolted the door.

Or perhaps the girl has no such fears. Perhaps we'll find her propped up in bed, flipping jauntily through a picture magazine. She may ask to borrow a cosmetic mirror, daub a touch of lipstick on her mouth. Flirt with the orderlies. Order me to wash her hair, then sulk when I refuse.

Poor Estelle. She has become a monstrous amalgam of the others: Evie, Contessa, Texas Lil. Gypsie, too. Yes, that is where the crass vitality comes from. It is a crime what I am doing – stealing from the past to invent a future. I must keep past and present apart. Restore clear outlines. Stick to the facts, Vera, string them together like beads.

Evie first. She entered without knocking, interrupting me as I stood on the deep-piled carpet of my new bedroom, trying to take it all in: the sleek walnut bed, finely pressed linens, washstand with porcelain basin. Chipped, yes, but still more elegant than Mother's pewter, or Henry's blue earthenware. I was fingering the tassled drapes and gazing down at the tin-roofed shacks clustered below. A gullied road wound between them to the edge of town then disappeared down the side of the mesa. Jagged mountains reared up against a never-ending sky. Great toothy slabs burnished to a rosy glow by the late afternoon sun. Granite? Henry would know. No. Would have—

Then came the squeak of a door-hinge, and I turned with a start.

'You the new'un? Didn't know there'd be a new gal. Sadie done said Dora Belle warn't gonna be replaced.' She stood twisting the sash of her robe between sallow fingers, nails bitten to the quick. 'Well, must be Tessy's out on the street. It were bound to happen, what with the trouble she's been causin' so recent. Gypsie'll treat you mean, but don't take it personal. Lil, too, I spect. Blame you for Tessy bein' gone an all. But she don't mean nothin' by it.'

A prickly heat crept up my neck. I had never spoken with a prostitute before. 'I'm not—' I fored a smile. 'I'm the new book-keeper.'

The girl looked at me with dull, staring eyes. There was a disconcerting blankness to her expression, a void behind the eyes that was not empty, but overfull. Like a page of characterless scribbling. 'You's an office gal?'

I nodded and introduced myself.

'Ohhh!' she clapped her hands then fell into an awkward curtsey. 'I'm Miss Evie. But you kin call me Evie. Evr'one else does. Most a the time.' She peered at the door, closed it, then lowered her voice. 'Is she out on the street?'

'Who?'

'Tessy, a course!'

A long moment passed. My blush was not fading.

'I done heard Deptee Barnes talkin' with Blair,' she whispered. 'He gone?'

I nodded.

Evie broke into an impish grin, cheeks dimpling. With her straw-coloured skin and the grey circles under her eyes, she looked like an overgrown child after a bad night's sleep.

'Not that I got anything to worry over. No, siree. No, M'am. I ain't the one to get into troubles. Evie's good as gold. Ain't no reason for me to gits rabbity over Deptee Barnes. Not like Tessy. She done acted up again last night. Threw a shoe at Billy Milgreen. Course he started it. Pourin' whisky on her and shoutin' he were gonna have him some Mexican flambay. That were a fancy way a sayin' somethin' nasty, I spect, cause Tessy near lost her mind. Smashin' bottles, yellin' a blue streak. Glass and whisky ever-where. Billy busted up a chair. Made such a racket.'

A prostitute. The thought snagged and held. I told myself to stop staring. After all I'd seen such women before. Hems dragging, faces powdered, they used to trawl the streets as I made my way home from the shipping office after dark. I'd never given them much thought. Just people whose work began when mine ended. But back then I was a young unmarried girl. Certain facts were still obscure to me. But not anymore. Now my mind swarmed with unbidden images. Of a stranger's hot breath. His looming face. Big open pores, hairs sprouting. Sweaty sheen of strange skin. Wet-lipped kisses, mouth tasting of what he'd eaten for dinner. How did they get over the fear?

The simple unpleasantness of most men?

If my expression betrayed me, Evie took no notice. Flitting about the room like a nervous songbird, she perched on the edge of the bed, paused, then leapt to her feet still chattering away. 'Sadie got steamin' angry. Yelled at the lot of us, though it warn't our faults. Just another a them johns what likes the rough stuff. Anyhow. Blair ain't gonna let Billy Milgreen back in, though after a good streak at the tables he throws money around like... well...' She gave a flat, slow-witted laugh. 'I cain't think a the 'spression just now, Miz Vera. But like something that spends a lot a money, that's sure.'

A shrill cry rose from the corridor and a russet-haired woman burst into the room. She had with a smooth willowy gait and wore a blue silk gown that rippled over her curves like water.

'Why, Gypsie!' warbled Evie. 'This here's the new gal. She ain't here to take Dora Belle's place or nothing. We was just chattin' bout all manner a things, warn't we?'

'Where are they?' snapped the auburn-haired girl.

Evie broke into a meek smile, dim eyes darting back to me. 'She ain't takin' Dora Belle's place or nothin'. Just an office gal. Ain't that right, Miz Vera?'

'My earbobs,' Gypsie's voice was harsh and low, almost manly. It did not fit the flowing waves of hair, the lithe grace of her body. 'Give them back now, you thieving little cunt.'

'I never stole nothing,' Evie cooed.

'Hell, you didn't.' Gypsie grabbed Evie, who let out a screechy squawk.

I was no stranger to rough ways. How many times had I tracked down my father among the ale houses and street-toughs, navigating block after block of gash peddlers and bindle stiffs? I'd seen dock-workers come to blows. Watched my father punch a creditor who'd come prowling round the shipyard bandying threats. But I'd never seen one woman strike another.

'Two bit twat,' hissed Gypsie, pinning Evie's arm behind her back. Evie whimpered and shot me a pleading look, but all I could do was stare.

The door slammed open and another girl stormed into the room. She was naked from the waist up, breasts juddering as she waved her fists in the air. 'I am sleeping you stupid cunts. Sleeping!' Then she dropped to the floor, sobbing. This, I would soon learn, was Texas Lil.

'Where are they?' demanded Gypsie.

'I ain't got 'em.' Evie wailed, throwing me a desperate glance. But I just stood there, paralysed by curiosity over what they might do next.

'What the devil's goin on in here?' cried Jackson as he marched into the room and flung the quarreling women apart.

'She done hurt me!' cried Evie.

Gypsie rose to her feet and gave her hair a haughty toss. There was something startling about her delicate features and ample curves: the sleek copper hair, her oval face. Gypsie was a beautiful woman. No, she used to be. Her face was too careworn now, eyes puffy, upper lip etched with lines. But with those high-cheekbones and auburn hair... there was a time when she might have had her pick of husbands.

A choked sob rose from Texas Lil, who lay curled at my feet wiping at her face with unwashed hands. I bent down, drawing a handkerchief from my pocket. But before I could slip it to her, she snatched it away. Bare skin puckered with cold, her arm hairs bristled like the downy ruff of some poorly feathered chick. I took a towel from the wash-stand and draped it over her. When my fingers brushed her skin, she flinched.

'Who'r you?' Her red-rimmed eyes narrowed.

'Yes,' chimed Gypsie. 'Who's this new quiff? And what the hell is Blair playing at giving her this room?' She swivelled round to face Jackson. 'Now Dora Belle's gone, it oughta be mine. I been here longest.'

'She ain't no whore,' sighed Jackson. 'Just Blair's office gal.

Now. One a you best tell me what this ruckus is about 'fore I knock it out of you.' Jackson glared at each of us in turn. Then, realising his mistake, his gaze scurried away from me.

Gypsie heaved an impatient sigh. 'Last night I put a pair of earbobs on my dresser. Now they're gone.'

Evie held out an arm tracked with nail-marks. 'Look what she done!'

'Search her room,' said Gypsie. 'You'll find 'em.'

Evie broke for the door, but Jackson was too quick. In one swift motion he'd caught her by the arm and plunged a knee between her legs, pinning her to the wall. Evie squealed and struggled to break free until Jackson slapped her on the cheek and she went limp. Then he thrust a hand into the pocket of her robe and tossed something at Gypsie.

'Looks like you could've found 'em yourself,' he said releasing Evie.

Gypsie bent over. Nightdress falling low, her breasts swung free. Pale cone-shaped tits. She paused and let them dangle there, nipples livid pink. Like a challenge or a dare. But to do what? My face went red, and she let loose a long voluptuous laugh. Then she swept her earbobs from the floor and straightened. 'Don't you look like the cat's dinner,' she flicked at my sleeve. 'What happened to your fashionable little frock?'

A stunned silence followed, and in my nervousness I laughed. It was meant to be a jolly, self-deprecating chuckle. A playful display of what a good sport the new gal could be. But what emerged was an anxious little titter that revealed me for the prim New England widow that, somehow, I had become.

'Next time,' drawled Jackson. 'Check the pockets fore you rough a gal up.'

'Ahhh yes,' crooned Gypsie. 'Of course. Beating up whores is your job.' And with that she flounced from the room, banging the door shut behind her. A door, I could not help noticing, that had no lock. My hand rose to the spot where I'd hidden my mining claim, fingers tracing its folds beneath the bodice of my dress. I would have to find a safe place for it. And my wages. Open a bank account, I promised myself. As soon as possible.

'Git gone,' Jackson prodded Lil with his workboot. 'Skedaddle.'

'You springing Tessy?'

'Might be.'

Lil's face brightened. Then she scrambled to her feet, naked from the waist up. I felt the heat of a blush creep back up my face and hated myself for it. I'd spent the past seven years refining my appearance, my carriage, my speech, my every gesture – even habit of thought – into what seemed proper to a professor's wife, only to find that, having worked so hard to smooth away all those rough edges, I now needed them back.

'Can I come too?' Lil pleaded.

'Not dressed like that, you can't.'

She looked down at her dingy drawers with torn hem, then gave a girlish whoop and raced out the door.

Jackson grabbed Evie by the wrist and shooed her out into the hall. 'Go on, git. And quit thieving. Next time I'll knock you for it.' He waited for her footsteps to die away and when at last he spoke his voice was low and gentle, apologetic even. 'Miz Blair wants you t'company me downtown.'

'Very well.' But I did not feel well. The room still vibrated with their presence. They raved, they slapped, they threatened, they wept… but what unsettled me most was my reaction: I was fascinated, awestruck. These women suppressed nothing. Every passing impulse was allowed to explode to the surface.

'Runabout's hitched and ready,' said Jackson. 'You'll deliver the money to the deputy-on-duty. Be Charlie Fisk most like. He'll hand Tessy over and we'll clear outta there before one a them reporters gets after you.'

The news calmed me. After my mother had died, my father would go on a drunken tear every few months. The first time I'd woken up to an empty house, it had thrown me. But it soon became routine: grab the roll of bills from the jar by the stove, walk down to the jail house, bring him home.

Here, then, was a familiar situation. A task I could handle.

'What's the bail set at?'

Jackson cleared his throat. 'Ain't bail money. An arrest gets listed in the papers. Sadie don't want that. Attracts the wrong kinda trade.' Then he fixed me with a long, penetrating stare. No arrest, no bail… I caught his meaning.

'Tessy may go after you,' Jackson warned. 'She been locked up since last night and it'll make her wild. Best be tough when she gets crazy. Blair's patience is about wore out. Firm hand is for Tessy's own good. Good for all of 'em, really. Keep 'em in line.'

We regarded one another across a length of carpet. His face had the deep-set lines of a sailor – forehead grooved, eyes in a perpetual squint, and on his left forearm were deep swirls of blue. On hot summer days at the shipyard, dockhands used to pull off their shirts to reveal thick arms and broad backs decorated with intricate designs as they hauled salt-soaked ropes and unloaded cargo holds. Only the men who had been on whaling ships had tattoos.

I pointed to his forearm. 'When were you in the South Seas?'

He flinched as if from a fire, then turned and walked towards the door. There was a heaviness to his gait. A slow roll as his weight shifted from one leg to the other that spoke to some old injury.

A steam-whistle tore through the silence and I jumped.

'Shift change at the mines.' He gave an apologetic shrug, as if he were the one responsible for startling me. 'You gits used to it.'

Pulling open the door he stood for a long moment on the threshold. Then he turned his head, slowly, like a giant tortoise and said, 'Hope you wasn't spectin' that hanky back.'

Chapter 3

Three weeks later I stood behind the till in Sadie Blair's barroom, stifling a yawn. I'd been on my feet for hours selling drinks, cigars, and brass checks – metal chips stamped with *Star Mansion* that johns would hand over to the girl of their choice. At the end of the week, each girl would bring her checks to the office in exchange for cash. This kept them from handling any money and allowed johns the illusion they weren't really paying for it.

I scanned the room. Men stood clustered around spittoons and brass ashtrays jawing about yesterday's cockfight, the declining price of silver, or whether a certain mine was pumping water at the rate it claimed. I wrapped a stack of bills in a dirty bar towel, then reached behind a row of bottles and dropped it into a slot that led to the safe. I'd been instructed to perform this task every hour, so that only a fraction of the night's take would be lost should an 'incident' transpire. Pressed for details, Blair had refused to elaborate except to assure me there would never be one: 'We cater to a steady trade. Hinchy types who know my rules and respect 'em. Your lawyers, your judges, your bankers and mining bosses. Few high stake gamblers, but no pikers or tinhorns. Just free-spenders who play by the rules, and if they don't, Jackson'll show 'em the door.'

So far, Sadie had been right. Every morning I would disappear into the office to balance the books, pay invoices, check deliveries, and file receipts. Afternoons I would emerge with a sore wrist and just enough energy to eat lunch before collapsing into bed. Often I napped until the supper-bell clanged. Then I would stumble downstairs to eat my evening meal while the whores bragged, bickered, gossiped, told lies, traded fashion tips, and ignored me entirely.

But I listened and I learned. I learned not to ask a whore her age, her real name, or anything about her past. And if, by some wild chance, she offered up such information, I knew not to believe a word. I learned that Little Casino (the clap) and Big Casino (syphilis) had nothing to do with gambling. I witnessed debates on how to check a john for disease, as the whores squabbled over the merits and shortcomings of various techniques – sparking the wrath of Madam Blair's cook, who made anyone who 'talked filth' answer to the back of Jackson's hand. I learned that Gypsie took on customers with 'exotic tastes' while the high-stakes gamblers preferred Contessa – which was why she'd landed in jail.

After a big streak at the tables Billy Milgreen had given her some emerald earrings, only to come back two weeks later demanding she hand them over. Contessa had refused and they'd fought, until Billy pinned her to the ground and forced them from her ears, whereupon Contessa chased him down the street half-clothed screaming obsceneties. She now swore never to let the filthy *ladro* in her bed again, but we all knew better. Refusing a john was a luxury none of them had.

I paid attention in the barroom, too. It wasn't hard to suss out the regulars and keep track of their preferences. Bourbon straight up, gin with water, or a snifter of brandy. Perhaps a cigar? I'd mastered the art of lighting one: hold the flame just so while he twirls it between his lips, taking care not to singe the wrapper. I tried to turn aside bawdy propositions without causing offense, but it was tricky. The bar itself was an effective barrier. But the moment I ventured out from behind it to use the bathroom or fetch Jackson, I became vulnerable to groping hands or bawdy whispers. If Madam Blair witnessed it, she chided the john ('we cater to gentlemen here, sir'), but once the novelty of my presence wore off, they tended to leave me alone. Most of my time was now spent feigning interest in the johns' dull-as-dishwater business talk. Hour upon hour of nodding and smiling and chiming in with the odd question while some lumber tycoon droned on about felling every tree in Wisconsin.

On this particular night, I'd had to endure a horsebreeder from Texas. It was a long lecture about brood mares and stud stallions and how you had to dig holes for a mare's feet then get two men to help a stallion mount while another one worked the horse's 'tool' into the mare's 'quim'. He seemed to get a perverse thrill out of uttering such words, hoping, perhaps, to provoke a blush or a squirm. But I'd just kept wiping down the bar. Now, hours later, he was still here for I could hear his voice booming away over in the side parlour.

My back ached. I shifted from one foot to another and stifled a yawn. The rush had peaked, although there were still plenty of men lingering over drinks and cigars. One of them looked vaguely familiar: tall, broad-shouldered, dark wavy hair. Young, though not what Blair would call a 'cherry cropper.' He had not purchased a brass check, but Gypsie was trying hard to persuade him, stroking his arm and flashing her *my-my-you-big-man* smile.

I bent to tallying the number of drinks served to each whore. They got a shot of rye every fifth round, but were allowed no more than two a night. In between, they drank cold tea brewed to look like whisky. Sadie was most particular about this. 'Drunks make lousy whores,' she'd said. 'And you can't hide their breath.'

Across the hall her player-piano cranked out one jaunty tune after the next. Bursts of laughter and conversation rose and fell over the music, broken occasionally by that horse-breeder's throaty guffaw. Still here. Still yammering away. Madam Blair strode into the room, taffeta sleeves shimmering in the lamplight. Every dress she wore was cut from the same pattern – tightly fitted bodice, high collar, slightly bustled skirt. The style, though a bit dated, flattered her full figure, though it took two houseboys yanking at the laces to cinch her into it.

'How we doing?'

I handed her the chart. Slash-marks indicated sales in three categories: drinks, cigars, girls. Most of her profits came from liquor, which surprised me until Blair pointed out that bottles of whisky don't need to be fed, housed, bathed, doctored, or bribed out of jail.

Sadie studied the chart and passed it back. Then she unlocked the till and glanced inside. I never knew what to expect from her. One moment she treated me as an equal, sharing jokes and confidences, only to turn brusque and dismissive the next. Pushing the drawer shut she stood upright and crossed her arms. 'Talked with Deputy Barnes today.'

So. News of what had happened down at the courthouse my first day on the job had finally reached her. Sadie's nails tapped idly against the bar. 'What's that new fella's name? One who collects the boodle on the protection now?'

'Charlie Fisk.'

She gave a brisk nod. 'Hear you gave him an earful.'

I stood twisting the key that hung from my wrist. She'd heard their version of events, but not mine. How Deputy Fisk had leered at me with hard wolfish eyes, insinuating that if certain 'favours' were forthcoming he'd be happy to hand over Blair's 'Mexican twat.' I wasn't about to follow him into some back room, so I'd handed over the envelope right there in the corridor for all to see.

I faced her, ready to explain. But a look passed over her eyes that gave me pause. Then she flashed me the hint of a smile, clapping her hand over mine. 'About time, I say! Shake those bastards up. Let 'em know we'll fight back. Bit of honest graft is one thing, but these frontier grifters – arresting one a my girls for disturbing the peace? And after raising license fees twice last year! They're strangling the goose that lays the golden egg. Want it both ways, these city hall boys. Protection money *and* fines! Well. I won't stand for it.' She pressed her lips together then went on. 'Course, Tessy was outta line. One more incident like that I'll have to let her go. She's popular with the johns. A self-starter. Won't balk at an older gent who needs special attention. Oh, a little trouble with the law does a house good out here. Keeps the frontier mystique alive. But an arrest?' She shook her head. 'This is a business I'm running. Not some charity house for wayward girls.'

But why am I dwelling on this? Enough. Wind the clock forward, thin out the crowd, send Blair off to bed after giving me permission to hand the key over to Jackson. *Go on up*, she tells me. But I do not. For some reason, I do not. Was it the thought of undressing in that dark empty room, then lying between cold sheets while the night's last round of johns moaned and coughed and pissed into chamber pots, every foot-shuffle reaching me through those thin clapboard walls?

Whatever the reason, on that particular night, I remained downstairs. Exhausted, still I lingered, watching Jackson fetch weapons from the lockbox and hand them over to their rightful owners as they departed. Soon the barroom was empty but for a few men in the far corner. After serving them a final round, Jackson returned with a drink left on his tray. He slid it towards me and said, 'Once it's outta the bottle, can't get it back in.' Then he took up a clean glass and poured one for himself. I wasn't sure which surprised me more: Jackson's light-hearted remark or his invitation to pinch Blair's liquor.

He tipped his glass back, then gestured at mine. 'Help you sleep.'

I lifted it to my lips and sipped, savoring the syrup sting on the tongue, the lazy heat flushing through me.

Jackson clamped a hand over my wrist and drew it down below the bar.

'Wouldn't want to appear unladylike,' I joked.

'Ain't that. Word gets round that Blair's cashier'll take a drink, folks might try something.'

'Like what?'

But my question went unanswered, for that is when you approached and spoke those very first words. And I jumped. Because I was holding a forbidden glass of bourbon when a stranger sidled up beside me. A man with a neatly trimmed goatee and wavy brown hair. The same man I'd thought looked familiar an hour before: tall, broad-shouldered, finely tailored shirt. You were not wearing a waistcoat. I remember that.

I kept my glass low, making sure you saw only my face. My cheeks were flushed from the heat of the barroom. My hair sagged against my neck in a loose brown puff, stray tendrils trailing down my cheeks. No doubt I flashed my usual smile, carefully calibrated to welcome regulars and set newcomers at ease, yet tinged with just enough chill to keep them from jollying me.

'At the courthouse,' you explained stroking the hair on your chin. 'Busy bribing Charlie Fisk, if memory serves.'

I shifted from one foot to another, wanting another sip of that drink but not daring.

'Relax,' you smiled. 'If Fisk thinks the graft they got running with the likes of Sadie Blair is a secret, well, the boy is even dumber than I thought.'

You spoke with a slight accent, one I could not place. And every so often your hand rose to smooth down a recalcitrant wave of hair. Jackson hovered around us, until you slipped him a coin and he took it. Another surprise. Jackson was meant to refuse all tips, lest it appear that the Blair's putter-down-of-brawls and keeper-of-the-lockbox was susceptible to bribery. But he pocketed yours and crossed the room.

You introduced yourself with a bow, an extravagant display of courtesy that made me blush. My thoughts flew to Henry. A man who had a talent for shirking social formalities without causing offense. A knack for knowing when to joke, when to stick to professional matters, when to broach the personal. Henry had a rare social instinct whose end was not to get into others' good graces, but to make those around him feel comfortable. Friends, strangers, maids, coachmen... they all felt at ease in his presence. And so, a confession: as I stood by your side that very first night and introduced myself, I ached for him.

'Do you know, Miss Palmer, this is the only place in town that serves real Kentucky rye.' The word came out 'raah', a long, drawn-out syllable that lingered between us. Was this, then, your reason for coming here? The bourbon alone? The question was too intimate, so I let it pass. 'Are you from Kentucky?'

You shook your head and smiled, a mischievous grin that dared me to keep guessing. To keep getting it wrong.

Did I smile? Sip my drink again? I cannot recall, but I know I said nothing.

'Old Jacks seems more bullish than usual tonight,' you observed. My gaze worked its way across the room to Jackson, who stood by the front-door looking hot and uncomfortable in the starched evening shirt Sadie insisted he wear.

'He's keeping an eye on you,' I joked.

'Or you.'

'Don't be silly. I work here.'

'Exactly,' you lowered your voice. 'Sadie's had some trouble in the past. Perhaps she suspects you of some misdeed.'

My unfinished drink remained inches from my hand, shoved back on the shelf beneath the bar. I lifted the glass and sipped, then flung you a bright smile.

'Sneaking bourbon. You raised an eyebrow in mock outrage, and I laughed. Not a polite womanly titter, but a real laugh. The kind that erupts when it is well past midnight in the barroom of a brothel and any pretense of delicate femininity would seem absurd.

'Oh, I don't think Sadie minds the odd tipple.' You swirled your drink, stroking your chin with your free hand. 'Skimming money. That's what old Jacks is on the look-out for.'

'Please,' I scoffed. 'If he thought I was pinching money, he'd be over here faster than Grant took Richmond.'

You drew a sharp breath. 'General Grant never took Richmond.'

The player-piano fell quiet. Your companions were gone. Barroom empty, I held that glass of bourbon openly now, pressing it to my breastbone between sips. My hands were grimy with other people's money. My feet were sore. And here was some stranger taking offence over a harmless quip.

'It's just an expression,' I sighed. 'Like whistling Dixie. If my mother suspected me of telling a lie she'd say, 'Vera, are you whistling Dixie?' And whenever my father caught me misbehaving, he'd shout, 'Stop that right now or I'll whomp you faster 'n Grant took Richmond.' Just expressions. That's all.'

You stared into your drink, face curdled with displeasure. Weighing your options. The impulse passed through you, didn't it? To plunk down your drink and walk out? But Blair's Raleigh Rye did not come cheap.

'Your folks abolitionists?'

'Were,' I replied. 'Before they died.'

The expression on your face was pinched and unhappy, and I thought again of Henry. How he would have deftly changed the subject, steering us all into calm conversational waters, and with that thought, all the old familiar sadness took root, lodging itself in the soft space between my ribs.

You must have noticed, because an expression of genuine concern came over your face and you asked if I was alright, for which I was grateful. And the thought that there was something gracious about a southern gentleman did cross my mind, but whether a man who frequented a brothel, even if only for its bourbon, could be considered a gentleman I did not know.

'I have upset you, Miss Palmer.' Your voice was calm and wonderfully soothing. Lower than before, softer. 'Please accept my sincere apologies.'

I tried to force a bright expression, but that tight fist of sorrow kept choking off my words. I could not speak without risking tears.

'This fella botherin' you?' Jackson strode across the room,

leveling you with a hard stare. Moments before I might have welcomed this turn of events.

'I'm afraid—' I cleared my throat and began again. 'I'm afraid that my ignorance of history has offended Mister Keane.'

'Not a whit, Miss Palmer. Not a whit.' You clapped Jackson on the shoulder. 'My good man, did General Grant ever take Richmond?'

A look passed over Jackson's face, and when he spoke his voice was hoarse and strangely quiet. 'Can't say I recall.' He looked down at his feet, toes of his scuffed workboots sticking out from sharp pressed cuffs. 'Union army got there in the end.'

'Ah. But General Grant wasn't *with* them.' Your voice rang out across the empty barroom in triumph. (At the time this meant nothing. But now I find myself wanting to expand this moment, make it accommodate all the resonance it has come to acquire.)

Footsteps sounded on the stair and Jackson hurried away. Faint noises floated in from the hall, as coats and hats were fetched and I cast about for something to say.

'What did you mean,' I ventured, 'about Sadie having trouble in the past?'

'Nothing certain.' You finished your drink and set the glass down on the bar. 'Just rumors.'

'Such as?'

'Where I come from, it's impolite to gossip about one's hostess while drinking her bourbon.'

'Where I come from, men don't pay their hostess cash for the privilege.'

A look of uncertainty crossed your face. Then you laughed. Eyes bright with surprise, you threw back your head and laughed. A loud, undignified laugh that burst forth with a lack of restraint that thrilled me, hinting at some unguessed quality. A vehemence that could not always be contained beneath that careful, decorous manner.

The front door opened and a gust of night air spilled into the room, stirring the haze of cigar smoke. I shivered – would I ever be able to talk to a man without thinking of Henry? Without physical pain?

You flashed a grin, as if you'd just told an extremely funny joke, then you asked me to dance.

I touched my throat, bare fingertips to skin. Gloves made counting money difficult, so I had ceased to wear them. Lack of gloves. This would be my excuse, for no doubt it was against house rules to dance with a potential customer. Blair had never said as much, but that didn't stop her reprimand ringing though me clear and sharp: *you're here to lift their money not distract 'em from my gals.*

I looked up to decline. But there were those grey eyes of yours smiling down. Mischievous grin playing at your lips, urging me on. It had been ages since anyone had asked me to dance. And how I wanted to.

So we did.

But not without difficulty. After ushering me across the hall, you dropped a coin into the slot of Blair's player-piano, but nothing happened. You tried the crank again. No response. Bought on the cheap, like so much else in that house where a veneer of elegance was meant to pass for the real thing. You shouted for Jackson, and, as he made his way across the room (I shall never forget this, nor forgive myself for it) I giggled. More from nerves and girlish excitement, but even so, the memory pains me. For it was the sight of him, stuffed into those starched evening clothes like a circus bear, that provoked my laugh. Dear old Jackson. The one who, in the end, would prove the most loyal and reliable of them all.

He fixed the problem, as always. Turning the crank three times, he gave the piano a swift kick and it shuddered to life.

You took up my bare hand and at the touch of your skin, my amusement died away. Instinctively my arms sought out Henry's shape. My torso swayed to his recollected rhythms, feet anticipating his movements, for although I had danced with plenty of other men, their step had never registered in my body. Never lingered.

But with you it was different. How my hand felt in yours, skin to skin. Top of my head grazing your shoulder, although it wasn't your height that felt strange. It was your brisk, assertive step. You danced like a man who knows well how to waltz, but does not dare surrender to the music. Those first few steps were awkward, but my feet soon awakened to the familiar three-beat and as you swirled me round Blair's side parlour my movements became fluid, almost natural, in your arms.

Then it ended.

With a laboured clank the scroll clicked back into place, and you stepped back and bowed. Do you know how I longed for another dance? How much I wanted to keep whirling round that tawdry parlour with its tasselled cushions and faded wallpaper and silly paintings of hunters and fauns and naked girls staring down at us from heavy gold frames?

But you did not ask. Escorting me to the front hall, you called for Jackson, who arrived promptly with your coat and hat. Lamps dim. House quiet. Lone maid clearing up ashtrays. The floaty warmth of the bourbon had drained away, leaving me with a dry tongue. I thanked you for the dance. Too shy to meet your eye, my gaze settled on your ears. Pink at the tips, and just a bit too big for your head.

I bid you a hasty farewell and ascended the stair. Should I have thought twice about this? Taken pains to avoid climbing the same stair the whores and the johns had used all night long? Would you have preferred me to retreat to the kitchen, step outside, and use the steps that ran up the back of the house? Truth be told, the notion never crossed my mind.

On the landing, a houseboy scurried by carrying a chamber pot that sloshed with urine. I let him pass then retreated to my room to wash and undress by the glow of the fire. My gaze fell to the boxy shadow of Henry's steamer trunk, thoughts flying to the folded piece of paper locked away inside, untouched since the day of my arrival. Working such long hours had left me little time for errands. I had managed to open a bank account in which to deposit my weekly earnings, but little else. No excuse. I must make time to seek advice on my mining claim. Tomorrow morning. Before turning to Blair's accounts, I would venture into town and find a law office. Yes. Tomorrow would be the day.

Chapter 4

The next morning Sadie's cook was bustling about the kitchen when I arrived. After wiping her hands dry, she poured me a cup of coffee. 'You up early.'

'Thought I might take a walk.'

'Colder 'n Hades this morning,' she shook her head and began ladling grits into a bowl. I did not care for grits, but knew better than to protest. Here in this corner of Star Mansion, Josie reigned supreme. She barked at the whores, dispatched brusque commands to Jackson, even tangled with Sadie Blair on occasion.

'There's a vacancy where I let rooms,' she declared, setting a bowl of grits down in front of me then swiveling back to the stove. 'Mister Clark runs a clean an' proper house. No vermin. Insect or otherwise.' She moved about the kitchen with the lithe grace of a dancer, stirring, chopping, rinsing. 'Shoulda seen what lodgings I had to tolerate when we first set foot in this place. Canvas tent not fit for a rat.'

'Why not board here?'

'Like some house slave?' she grumbled. 'I got my pride.'

Josie took the string from around her neck and unlocked the knife drawer. Then she withdrew a carving knife and swept the blade across a whetstone.

I sipped my coffee. 'Does working here make lodgings hard to find?'

'In this town? Folks don't care where the money comes from, long as they don't have to think too hard on it. Naw ain't that.'

Blowing at the steam rising from my bowl I did not see it coming. But next thing I knew, she was pinching my cheek. Hard. 'You never had folks do that. Rub they grimy fingers on your face then look see if the colour comes off. Well, Clark ain't

43

that kind. Sadie neither. This ain't no tea shop, believe me, I know. Say what you like, and there's plenty can be said, but Sadie... she never minded trustin' me with grocery money.' Josie sank the knife into a raw leg of lamb. 'Private house I worked at sent a scullery maid to carry the purse. Little white girl come trottin longside me, pay for everything and keep track a the change.' Josie dug the blade in deep and began sawing round a sickle-shaped bone. 'Say the word, I'll tell Clark.'

I scooped up some grits, recalling those dreary months at Stanton's Boarding House. The poorly lit rooms with scratched furniture and saggy cushions, the maid's hollow cough, the Landlady's nosy inquiries disguised as idle chatter.

'Jackson be willing t'walk you home nights. Worked with him back in St Louie fore the law run us outta town on some bull and nonsense. Dumb as a board that man may be, but he's a decent fella. Won't mind seein' you home safe.'

I nibbled at the grits and forced myself to swallow. It was like eating sand. 'How much for the room?'

'Three a week, no meals.'

Boarding at Star Mansion had its problems. Even if I used the back door, people saw me cross over from the wrong side of Sixth Street. Men stared, boys blushed, women hissed and yanked their children away. But living here also protected me. From prospectors on the make. From ageing widowers hunting for a spry young wife. 'I'll think about it,' I said at last.

Josie regarded me with a long, narrow stare. 'No, you won't.'

I gave a show of protest, but she held up a hand. 'I kin tell when a girl's mind is made. An' yours, Miz Vera, is made. You gonna keep on boardin' here an the reason ain't mine t' inquire after. But let me tell you this,' she shot a quick glance at the door, lowering her voice. 'Don't you take no sass from them whores. First sign a trouble, I gits Jackson on their tails fore they know what's hit 'em.' She set down her knife. 'Day we set foot in this sorry hole, I gave Sadie piece a my mind. Washed up here right after that big fire. Buildings burnt. Ever-one in

44

tents, sun hot as blazes. Hell itself, I done said. Like hell itself.'

I watched her clasp a large bone and yank until it cracked free with a wet snap. 'Them girls workin' the trade out here,' she tossed her head in disgust, 'they barely house-broken.'

And with that, Josie crossed the kitchen to fetch her trussing needle. It would be easy, in hindsight, to cast her words as a grave warning. But Josie did not traffic in such talk. Portentous declarations did not suit her any more than idle chatter did Jackson. This declaration was one of many she might make throughout the day. That I remember this remark in particular, well, perhaps something can be made of that. But in the moments that followed, as I bent over my grits, her words did not hang ominously in the air. Quite the opposite. A comfortable silence stretched between us as I finished my coffee and she neatened up the flaps on that leg of lamb.

When I stood and took up my empty dishes, Josie waved me away. 'Leave 'em.'

'It's no trouble.'

'What would Sadie say she sees you doin' my job?'

'Little chance of that. I've yet to see her out of bed before noon.'

'Oh, she up.' Josie carried my dishes to the sink. 'Grabs a cup coffee, counts last night's take, then she goes back t'bed.' It was said in a matter-of-fact way, but the implication was clear.

'I'm no thief,' I blurted.

'I know,' Josie smiled. 'I know.'

The day was windless and bright, air washed clean by last night's rain. Every breath brought a flinty tang of creosote and damp rock as I hurried past clapboard shacks and mud-brick walls toward the centre of town. Chinese women in bright silk dresses darted between horse-carts. Businessmen in sun-faded coats brushed by, their long rolling stride so different from the nimble, quick footed steps of men back East. Burros brayed, shop-keepers called out greetings, ore-carts clanked. Noise from the Faro tables poured into the streets, joining the rumble of cart-wheels and clinking tack, and I felt a surge of contentment as I plunged on through the crowd, buoyed by the clamour of this strange new world.

Despite its reputation Goose Flat did not seem any more lawless than your average waterfront. I'd witnessed no gun-fights, no Indian raids, no shoot-outs with cattle rustlers. I'd not even glimpsed a cow, although ranches were said to exist in the outskirts. The town was just a ramshackle settlement of miners, shop-keepers, Chinese merchants, Mexican labourers, and soldiers on leave from Fort Huachuca.

In two days' time, when an angry mob would force a jailer to hand over his keys then hang a prisoner without a whimper of protest, my opinion would change. But John Heath's lynching was yet to come. On that brisk, sun-washed morning as I passed beneath the telegraph pole from which his corpse – eyes blindfolded, ankles bound – would soon swing, the town's reputation for lawlessness struck me as the overblown fancy of a few eastern newspapers.

The courthouse hove into view. My destination was the shabby building across the street, where, after delivering Blair's bribe to Deputy Fisk, I had glimpsed a placard advertising legal services. But as I drew up alongside its long row of doors, my heart sank. *Attorney-at-law, Mining Claims, Insurance… Attorney-at-law Claim disputes, Personal Injury… Attorney-at-law Mining Claims, Land Disputes… Attorney-at-law, Surveys & Mining Claims.* How to choose? Whom to trust? People back in Connecticut had delivered stern warnings about the men who practiced law out here. Charlatans with forged degrees, corrupt judges who turned a blind eye, a territorial government where power lay in the hands of mining executives, land speculators—

'Miss Palmer?'

I looked up.

Will Keane stood before me, grey eyes alive with amusement.

How did I appear to him that morning? A coltish girl looking lost, or a woman who had danced a graceful waltz the night before?

'Allow me.' He extended an arm, and I let him guide me away from the crowded thoroughfare.

'What brings you to my door at such an early hour?'

'Your door?'

He tapped a placard on the wall. *Miller, Keane & Steinberg, Attorneys-at-law, Tracer documents, mining claims, surveying.*

'You're a lawyer?'

'To that accusation, I plead the Fifth.'

A look of confusion must have crossed my face.

'The Fifth Amendment, Miss Palmer. It grants every citizen in the land freedom from self-incrimination. The right, in other words, to remain silent.'

'Silence cannot save you, I'm afraid.' I tapped a finger against the nameplate. 'Not in the face of such condemning evidence.'

And he laughed. It was the same beguiling laugh that had burst forth the night before. A deep, full-throated rumble that shook his shoulders and softened his eyes. 'Condemned, am I? Harsh words. Yet since people persist in calling our offices here *Rotten Row*, I suppose I must plead guilty. Although not rotten to the core, just slightly overripe.'

'I shouldn't worry. Where I work gets called far worse.'

He grimaced, then forced a smile.

Miller, Keane, & Steinberg consisted of four narrow rooms strung together like a shot-gun shack. Will's office lay at the back. Bookcases lined the walls and the air held a sharp, unmistakable scent. Manure. It clung to everything in this town. Drapes, carpets, clothes. One tasted manure-dust in every breath. But Will Keane's office positively reeked of the stuff.

'In town three weeks and already in legal trouble?' Will closed the door behind him. 'I dare say, you move quickly Miss Palmer.'

I uttered a sharp protest, then noticed his moustache twitch. 'Mr Keane those whiskers of yours make it awfully hard to tell when you're joking.'

He gestured at a leather arm chair positioned before his desk and I sat down. 'What brings me here is a mining claim.'

'You and everyone else in this town.'

'Are you saying I lack originality?'

'Not at all. Only that mining claims are a somewhat popular pastime around here.' He leaned back in his chair. It gave a sharp creak. 'Where is your claim located?'

'I don't know.'

He shot forward. 'You didn't purchase it without a site inspection, did you?'

'No. I inherited it. From my husband.'

Will rested his hands on the desk. I remembered the feel of them from the night before. Strong fingers, calloused palms. Dry roughness of his touch. They were the hands of a man who spent his days wielding a pick-axe or hauling salt-soaked ropes across the deck of a ship. Not someone who worked behind a desk.

'Please accept my condolences. I had no idea you were...' he trailed off, considered, then began again. 'I did not know you were so recently bereaved, Miss Palmer. It is disrespectful to your late husband, going by *Miss Palmer* as you do.'

Another joke? Hard to tell, but the sharp lines on his forehead suggested not. I gave a small shrug and looked away. The courthouse clock began to chime. Waiting for it to cease, I stared at the book-lined walls. Packed with fat brown volumes. Gold numbers stamped to their spines. Henry's study had been filled with books of all shapes and sizes – scattered on chairs, stacked in teetering piles, splayed open on his roll-top desk. Pages tattered, spines cracked. Before moving west, I had spent an entire afternoon packing them into crates for a library clerk to collect. Now and then, things would fall from their pages. Scraps of paper scrawled with his airy Js and Ls, bits of string marking long-forgotten passages, brightly coloured leaves he used to pocket during walks through city parks or country woods. Each leaf pressed flat between the pages. Henry's books. The bell had ceased to toll. I could feel my hands fiddling with the gloves in my lap, fingers worrying their cloth-covered buttons.

'Mister Keane,' I said. 'Do you have any idea how it feels to be widowed at twenty-three? To be of marriageable age, yet already treated like an old maid?'

He bristled. 'How could I possibly know such a thing?'

I sank back into the armchair, feeling defeated and confused. The room was hot and stuffy, the flannel beneath my corset damp with sweat. I glanced over at the window.

'I'd open it,' he explained. 'But the stench is worse than the heat. We're backed up against the livery stables.'

I felt a constriction in my chest, pressure behind my eyes. I bit my lip and swore, softly. But Will heard it. No doubt he was surprised. Shocked, perhaps.

'Henry was…' I faltered, drew breath, and went on. 'My husband was not like most men. His geological expeditions took him to places many miles from civilization…' But this was hardly the point. I began again. 'Once, when we were returning from a dinner party, I criticised our hostess for pouring coffee into her saucer to cool. It was a judgment I had overheard from one of the other women, and because I was new to this circle of people, I adopted the opinion as my own. But upon hearing me repeat it, Henry took my hand and said that when one travels widely, one witnesses many different customs and begins to see that convention is nothing but a random code of behaviour. In this instance it would serve as an excuse not to invite Burt Fletcher's wife to dinner, instead of actually admitting what one didn't like about her. Then Henry asked what bothered me about Mrs Fletcher.'

'And?' Will prompted.

'She was boring.'

A smile played at his lips, amused though not at all sure he should be.

'So you see,' I unfolded the paper in my lap, 'Henry would not mind in the slightest. In fact, he thought customs surrounding widowhood particularly foolish. No dancing for a full year? Wearing nothing but black for six months, then grey, then beige? What purpose do such restrictions serve? Aside from lining the pockets of cloth-merchants and dress-makers. Henry thought it extraordinarily silly – especially your rather strident conventions in the South, which are rivalled only, he once said, by a widow's fate in certain parts of India.'

'What must she do?'

'Throw herself onto her husband's funeral pyre.'

'You don't really believe we're that extreme, south of the Mason-Dixon?'

I shrugged. 'Which is worse? To be consumed instantly by flames, or to have the life slowly drained from you by tedious conventions that make you feel like an old maid at twenty-three? Would you have me drag about town in black book-muslin, or some awful grey dress with gigot sleeves? Be honest.'

He thought about it, trying to decide, I suspect, between what he should say and what he actually felt.

I set the claim certificate down on his desk. 'Would you have me barred from the dance floor?'

'I don't believe I would.'

'I thought not.'

Fixing a pair of spectacles to the bridge of his nose, he took up the document. The expression on his face changed as he read, eyes narrowing in concentration, then widening. 'The name on this patent,' he tapped the paper. 'It's not yours.'

'Henry received it as payment. There was a letter to this

effect, which Mr Patterson – the lawyer who advised me back East – told me to keep. He said it was as important as the claim itself.'

'Who knows about this?'

'Mr Patterson, obviously. Henry's former colleagues. Their wives.'

'No one here in town?'

I shook my head.

Will removed his spectacles, slipping them into his breast-pocket. 'Not a word to Sadie Blair?'

'Why are you interrogating me?'

'To decide whether this job is worth taking. I work on a percentage basis. There's no percentage in a claim that's invalid due to an adverse filing.' Will rubbed the bridge of his nose and went on. 'Thomas Cox is the claimant listed here. Was he a friend of your husband's?'

'Colleague. No, former colleague. Years ago he became the official surveyor for the State of Indiana, but he took on independent jobs as well. You see, Tom was often short on money. Sometimes he would ask Henry for help with a survey or an appraisal, and I guess, at some point, he must've repaid Henry with this.' I waved at the certificate.

Will rubbed the hair on his chin, finger and thumb trailing down his goatee. 'I don't want to raise false hopes, but there is a chance this claim could be worth a good deal.'

'How much?'

'Can't be sure. It's dated well before the rush was on. That in itself is encouraging. But most promising is the claimant's name, this... this Thomas Cox.'

'Do you know him?'

'Only by reputation. But it's a mighty strong one. He's famous in these parts.'

Tom Cox? Famous? 'Are you sure we're talking about the same man?'

'Dates match exactly.'

'What dates?'

'We mustn't get carried away.' Will was busy scribbling on a scrap of paper. 'After all, you may not even own the mineral rights anymore. Cox filed this six years ago. The district has exploded since then. Still, I'll check with the county recorder, see if an adverse claim has been filed. Only thing that's kept certain areas from being staked is the Apache threat. But your claim looks to be south of town, so that won't be a factor. But an adverse filing...' he shook his head, still jotting down notes.

Mineral rights no longer mine? Mr Patterson had never mentioned this, and he'd marshalled every possible argument to dissuade me from coming west.

'Cox staked this claim before Cochise County was created,' Will went on. 'That means all relevant paperwork – locator documents, surveys, et cetera – would have been filed up in Tucson. County officials haven't transferred that stuff down yet. Could be what saves us.' He ran a hand across the top of his head, smoothing down that lock of hair that never quite stayed put. 'I'll be going up later this week. On a different matter. I'll drop by the County Recorder's Office, see what I find. In the meantime—'

A knock sounded at the door and a young boy poked his head into the room. His hair was combed back with a generous coating of pomade, accentuating a purple bloom of acne across his forehead. He looked about the same age as Texas Lil. Well. The age I guessed Lil to be.

'Excuse me,' he said. 'Mister Keane, court in ten minutes.'

Will stood abruptly and fumbled for his watch.

'Anything I can do, Sir?'

'No, Billy. Thank you.' Head bent, he began rifling through stacks of papers. 'Wait, Billy. Yes. Please fetch Miss Palmer's wrap and escort her home.'

Billy nodded and withdrew.

I tugged on my gloves. 'Thank you for your help.'

'A pleasure, Miss Palmer.' He looked up and smiled.

'You have some ink…' I touched my own forehead. He licked his thumb and rubbed.

'Other side… There.'

We shook hands and I made my way back through the string of small narrow rooms. Billy stood waiting with my wrap slung over his arm. Moments later Will swept past, walking stick and leather case in hand. 'Miss Palmer, it is best to keep a tight lip in this town.'

I nodded.

'I cannot emphasise this strongly enough,' he said, lifting his hat from its peg. 'Mention it to no one.'

Inside Star Mansion, the air was heavy with the smell of tired bodies, smoky carpets, and stale perfume. I paused at the bottom of the stair to catch my breath. I had walked too quickly in an effort to keep pace with Billy's gangly stride. Billy. How timid and awkward he'd become as we approached Sixth Street. To put him out of his misery I announced that I was not one of the whores. But this only made him more tongue-tied, until finally I insisted on walking the last block by myself and left the poor boy blushing on the sidewalk, too flustered to protest.

I gripped the banister and drew short rapid breaths, ribs straining against whalebone stays. Henry had always declared corsets unhealthy, yet whenever I wore one he could scarcely keep his hand from resting on the slope of my waist. Or stop his eyes from following the sharp curve of my breasts and hips. Our love-making had never been the terrible ordeal I'd once feared – imagination fed by whispered speculations at Stanton's Boarding House. Wondrous bliss? Agonising duty? On our wedding night I'd discovered it was neither. *That's it?* I'd thought, lying naked beside him. *That is what all the fuss is about?* I'd bled the first time and the second. But once the rasping ache subsided I began to lose myself in the slippery feel of flesh against flesh, moist flutter of lips against skin.

Mostly I enjoyed what came after. The warm comfort of our bodies twined together. And the transformation this strange act elicited in Henry. A man so composed by nature reduced to a quaking, vulnerable creature in my arms.

'There you are,' Madam Blair emerged from the office. 'You alright?'

I tightened my grip on the banister and risked a nod.

'Must be the air. It's thin. Not sure what that means, but it's what they all say out here. Ask me, it's all the damn dust flyin' around. Enough to choke a horse.'

My dizziness subsided and she came into focus. Not a hair out of place, waist tucked to sharp point above her bustled skirt. She looked tight and tidy as an envelope. 'What are you doing, racketing around town at such an early hour?'

'Walking.'

Sadie crossed her arms.

'It's become a habit since my husband died. The doctor recommended I get plenty of fresh air.'

'Well. Don't over-do it. This climate takes some getting used to.'

Sadie ran a jewelled hand down her skirt. Cut from bright red tulle the dress was not a terribly flattering colour, given her pale complexion and auburn hair. A rare misstep for Madam Blair, who relied on expensive clothes and a meticulous toilette to conceal her age and persuade men she was a beauty. Her success surprised me at first, but upon reflection it made sense. She knew how to convince men they wanted to buy a girl, smoke an expensive cigar, drink another bottle of wine… why not make them believe she was a looker, too?

'Mr King was particularly impressed with your performance last night.'

'My performance?'

She leaned against the wall, arms crossed below her breasts. 'Come now, you can't dance with Will Keane and think folks won't notice. And a waltz! Even a high class house like mine can't brag of such refinements. Back in St Louie I might have managed it. But not here.'

I could feel the sweaty flannel growing cold against my skin, as I wondered what my punishment would be. She fined the whores for minor infractions – returning downstairs after a trick looking 'unrefreshed' or using 'indelicate language' in the parlour. For major breeches of conduct, Jackson would knock them around. In the dim light of the hall, her expression was impossible to read. I braced myself for a severe dressing down. Or worse.

Sadie dropped her arms to her sides. 'Fact is, you've given me an idea. And a damn good one. If my gals could waltz, we'd be the only house in town with whores dancing like society ladies. Not even Blonde Marie could top that.' Her hand sought out the edge of a table, feeling for dust the houseboys might have missed. 'Bringing gals over from Paris! That flimflam artist. Courteezans, she calls em.' Madam Blair gave a dismissive snort. 'Use all the la-de-da words you like, but at the end of the day that's still just a bunch a French hurrs. Courteezans!' She flicked her fingers at the air. 'Well. What do you say?' Her tone was clipped, impatient.

'To what?'

'Teachin 'em a waltz!'

'I wouldn't know how.'

Madam Blair rolled her eyes. 'Just repeat what they told you at finishing school.'

I suppressed a smile, grateful for the relative dark. Nothing angered Blair more than amusement at her expense. Finishing school? Did such places really exist? Even the other faculty wives – raised in prosperous households full of music and books – even they were not educated abroad. Sadie could not possibly be so naïve. Perhaps she was aiming to flatter, the thought annoyed me. 'What makes you think I went to any school at all?'

'Been a madam long as I have you can size a gal up like that,' she snapped her fingers. 'Clever lady from back East, dresses in the latest fashions, dances a waltz…'

'If there was enough money to educate me abroad, do you think I'd—' but it was too late to take it back.

'Sell brass checks in a knockshop?'

An uncomfortable silence followed. From beyond the pantry-door came a clang of pots and pans, the faint sound of Josie humming. I had offended her. Not smart.

'Well. You seem to have caught the eye of Will Keane. A man of taste and respectability, although his refusal to take my girls upstairs drives me batty.' Madam Blair spoke in a soft, reconciling tone that unnerved me. 'What kind of education did you have?'

'I went to the city schoolhouse. Until my mother died. Then my father arranged for me to have lessons at home.'

Sadie's pursed-lip silence told me that she was jumping to the same inaccurate conclusion the faculty wives once did – envisioning some bright-eyed Continental tutor full of vigour and intellectual zeal. Not Old Man Connett, with his liver-spotted hands and flask of gin. A retired sea captain who owed my father money and repaid his debt by overseeing my conjugation of Latin verbs.

'It was my husband who taught me how to waltz,' I explained, scrunching up my shoulders to keep the damp flannel from touching my skin. 'I never had any musical training. That makes it harder.'

'I'll pay you.'

Ah, yes. Leave it to Madam Blair to interpret my hesitation as a ploy for more money. But my reluctance was real and it lingered. 'M'am, I—'

'Ah, ah,' she waggled her finger. 'Call me Sadie.'

I would force myself do this in the months to come, but it was an empty gesture, a display of intimacy to cover over the fact that none existed.

'Fess up. What you so itchy about?'

I met her eye and spoke fast. 'I don't think they'll be able to learn the steps.'

She drew a short sniff of a breath. 'Let me worry about that. Now. When I hire a new gal, first week – probationary. No house account, no personal effects in the boudoir. Not til I know she's a keeper. We'll do the same. Two weeks. Progress? Keep going. If not, call it quits. I'm the judge. Fair?'

Generous, even. Besides, a refusal might raise suspicions.

Sadie smoothed her skirts and gave a perfunctory nod, as if to say *I knew you'd come around*. Then she strode down the hall towards the kitchen, hollering for Josie to put the kettle on.

Chapter 5

A transport vehicle waits in the château's pebbled drive. Slipping into the backseat, we huddle under a wool throw the *Directrice* pressed on us during our hurried *adieux*. In those final moments she hovered about us in the *vestaire*, asking after our papers, my service kit – it has been loaded into the boot? Did I see the boy do it? And your sable cloak, Vera? *Vous n'avez rien oublié?* Then, after planting a delicate kiss on each cheek, she held my elbows in her rough hands and murmured, 'Je ne peut jamais vous remplacer.' Her warm farewell has left me plagued with doubts, but it is too late to turn back now.

A boy in a brown greatcoat is hurrying toward us. His drab-coloured uniform makes me wonder if our next posting is at a British-run unit, but there is no time to ask. Greeting us with a quick tip of his cap he slides behind the wheel, then the motor sputters to life and we are off.

Shattered trees flash past. Once a regal parade of poplars they are now mangled twists of wood, branches hacked off by soldiers who bivouacked here during the battle of the Marne. Scars from their cooking fires still mar the flagstones, and the *Directrice* never tired of remarking on the appalling condition of the place when she arrived: floors littered with straw, broken dishware, garbage piled high in fireplaces… how many times did I listen to her ramble on about the Marquise, holding my tongue all the while? Never confessing that I had been here before. Seen the château's parade of high-ceilinged rooms in all their pre-war splendour. Walked its chilly corridors on the arm of the Marquise herself, a dear friend of Louis' family.

We turn onto the main road. Rooks barb the barren branches, scattering at our approach like black confetti flung across a sullen sky. A stone farmhouse sits flush against the road. Intact except the façade, which has been stripped away like skin peeled back from a face. I avert my eyes the way one does when passing a *mutilé* on the street, aware of a tightness gripping my chest.

Years ago Louis and I quarreled on this very spot. It was our first trip to the French countryside, whose beauties Louis kept extolling as we ambled along in the full flush of summer. But these dull pastures and tidily furrowed fields did not impress me and I told him so. A grave mistake. How could I insult the land he had taken up arms to defend thirty years before? Did I not realise he had risked death, as a young cavalry officer, for this very soil? He'd dug his stick into the chalky earth and glared. Storming off in a huff he'd left me to find my own way back, which I did – unable to shake the image of him disappearing round the bend, jaunty stride sharpened by anger. Who was this irascible man lecturing me on what to think, how to feel? This stranger for whom I had uprooted my entire life?

We reunited at dinner, greeting one another with a stiff embrace, and nothing more was ever said of the incident. Back in Paris our lives resumed. The years rolled by. We traveled, as I had once longed to do with Henry, and Louis proved an admirable guide. He loved ushering me from one city to the next, drawing enjoyment from my enthusiasm for whatever opera house or museum we were visiting, and amidst those ancient streets and stunning boulevards, I thrived. Ceased to seek. Let go of the desert in a way that New Orleans had never allowed. Stopped longing for the exquisite elation stirred by those fat bright stars and endless skies, the brutal sun and violent storms. My life, in other words, became congenial. Why spare a thought, or a word, for that silly quarrel? We did not so much avoid the subject for eighteen years, we simply moved on. Learnt the trick of banishment. But glimpsing again that old stone farmhouse... these fields scored with crops beneath a fitful sky... I wonder.

Our driver slows as we enter the village, shattered walls

biting up through the mist. Tosh leans forward and asks him for a fag. He lights one, passes it back. She inquires after the sector where her brother is stationed. Her voice is cool and assertive, but a look of pained anxiety clouds her eyes.

'Arras, aye?'

She nods, exhaling loudly.

'Ach, nothing but the usual dust-up I expect.' Our driver grins. He has a freckle on his lower lip and were I far younger, I should long to kiss him. 'Took in a wee Belgian lass, aye?'

Tosh elbows me in the ribs, though she needn't. I have no desire to betray the *Directrice*, although I never saw any sense in trying to cover it up. Secrecy feeds curiosity and such things cannot be kept hidden long.

The motor grinds on. Past stubbled fields, scraps of battered hedgerow, dark clumps of woodland. River glinting between the trees. I catch a glimpse of myself in the side-mirror – grey wisps of hair, deeply creased brow, a tiny frown between the eyes. The face takes me by surprise. It looks far too old to be mine.

'Silent as the grave, the pair a you!' Our driver shoots a glance back at us. His eyes are sharp and clear and heart-breakingly blue.

I lean forward. 'What is it you wish to know?'

'Will the pur lass pull through?'

I give a brisk nod and Tosh changes the subject.

Yes. The girl will live. Which is why I'm here, lurching down this muddy road towards the rail depot. I had decided to refuse Tosh's offer. Then came the *Directrice*'s order for me to work the night-shift and care for Estelle.

The girl was awake when I entered, pale eyes burning from the sunken saucer of her face. I changed her dressings, bathed her wounds. Dr Rimbault examined her. Vitals strong. No sign of infection. Patting her head, he declared the prognosis good. *Tu as de la bonne chance, ma petite.* Then he left. Her oval face lay wan against the pillow, mousy hair clinging to her cheek.

Her wide eyes stared back. Vacant, morphined. But there was something more to this emptiness than drugs. And that blank stare of hers threw all my former speculations into doubt. The handsome officer with his freshly trimmed beard fell away, and in his place rose something far more brutal. A dry thrusting, elbow driven into throat, choked plea rasping out at me across the years... *One at a time, boys, please one at a time...*

Yes, the girl would recover. Return to Madame's *estaminet*. Pick flowers and sell them. In the wards, along the bye-roads. That pale visage ghosting into view without warning.

When Tosh asked for my decision, there wasn't one. Just a burning desire to flee that girl's blank stare forever. So here I am, rattling down a shell-torn road towards a train bound for Paris.

The depot seethes with men in uniform. Officers lean against sooty tile. *Poilus* crowd the benches playing cards, writing letters, reading newspapers. Others are blacking their boots. One sits, head bent over dirty fingers, sewing a button on his greatcoat. Pitiless *gendarmes* pace back and forth, inspecting papers. Beneath the giant clock a *fonctionaire* sits behind a table arrayed with gilded pens, ink pots, official stamps. I approach, dare to inquire. A long insouciant pause. Expensive cigarettes smolder in the ashtray. I stand my ground until he answers with a curt dismissive nod. As I suspected: troop movements, everything delayed.

Tosh and I repair to the restaurant. Short swords and belted pistols litter the chairs. A small black stove juts from one corner with tables gathered round. All full. We sit by a soot-streaked window looking out onto the tracks. Beyond the glass a work party stands huddled round an open fire.

A boy arrives, recites the menu, we order. Ham *à la gelée*. Eggs. *Frites*. *Deux cafés noirs*.

I draw a letter from my pocket and read through Camille's

questions about household management. These are followed by the inevitable litany of complaints about her friends – Annick never visists, Lisette has no time for anything but her war charity… the only surprise comes at the end: a postscript promising to meet our train. My heart sinks, then a wave of guilt. I ought to be grateful. *Ought.* How did it come to this? Obligations. Unspoken demands. Every kindness freighted with expectation. It makes sense for two women to live under one roof, stretching our meager coal rations. And yes, my *appartément* is far bigger. *Oui, bien sûr'* a great help to have a friend you can trust, so generous of Camille to look after things in my absence. And yet… why does every kindness feel like a debt accruing? One impossible to repay. Her son's death, as Camille never fails to remind me, is a loss I cannot comprehend. *Ma chérie,* to lose my only son! My only solace! All true. But why must our friendship become a balance sheet of sorrow, with my side perpetually in arrears?

I stare out the soot-smeared window across the empty *quai*, gaze settling on the woodsheds. Across one of the walls someone has scrawled *Q'Allah donne la victoire aux jeunes français.* A kind-hearted Zouave? One of the Sénégalais who have been defending this sector all winter? My thoughts fall to the men from Indo-China we treated last week, members of a labour batallion injured during a dangerous canal repair. With their sad skeptical eyes they'd put me in mind of Sadie Blair's houseboys.

'So,' I say at last. 'Our next posting. It is a British-run hospital?'

Tosh scoffs. 'Do you really think the War Office would authorise a woman to run a training hospital? I tried, of course. Through Father.'

The food arrives and we take up our forks. Through the clatter of dishes, spurred boots ring out against the stone floor. Cavalrymen. One pauses to light his pipe at the stove. His companions are scraping back chairs, draping their gold-trimmed coats across the backs.

'French, then?'

'It's complicated,' she sighs.

'Try me.'

'An independent unit.'

I narrow my gaze and fix her with a look.

'A former colleague in Philadelphia was kind enough to recommend me to senior staff in Camiers. We are to be under French military authority, but funded by the Americans.'

My hand floats to a spot where a pea-sized lump sits lodged against my rib. Scar tissue from an old injury. My fingers seek it out, instinctively rubbing.

'Why do you do that?'

'What?'

Tosh nods at my chest and I force myself to stop.

Outside, it has begun to rain. Fat constant drops plonk to the ground like coins. We finish our meal in silence.

'You don't have a lump there, do you?' Tosh arranges her knife and fork just so. 'On your breast?'

'No.' I squeeze my fingers, forcing my hands to remain in my lap.

'I don't believe you.'

An American unit. She has hidden this fact from me. Hidden it until there could be no turning back. Tosh said she wanted me because I spoke French. What use will that be among my boisterous, English-speaking compatriots? I gesture for the *patron*.

'Are you listening, Vera? I said it might need to be cut out.'

'Surgery?'

She nods. Now it is my turn to scoff.

'A lump on the breast is not something to take lightly.'

'I told you. It's not on my breast.'

'Well. I shall need to examine it.'

Another chuckle escapes me. Tosh swirls the remaining coffee in her cup. Watches it settle. 'I cannot imagine what you find so amusing.'

'That surgeons always seem to think you need surgery.'

The *patron* arrives. Sweeping up our coins he asks where we are going, then shakes his head. *Châlons, peut-être. Mais Paris?* He shakes his head again. He has an owlish face and jerky movements that put me in mind of a marionette. He has seen this before, he tells us. Many times. The troops get through, but the rest... he shrugs, hands upturned.

Tosh slumps back in her chair. I expected this from the start, but Tosh is angry. Once in Paris we must still get our paperwork in order. Entire afternoons will be frittered away in the *Ministère de la Guerre* as *petites fonctionnaires* rifle through forms and declare with implacable frowns *non* this is not what you need. The document needs a *visé* which only the *aide major* can issue. *Non*, I cannot *visé* it. Only the *aide major*. His office is upstairs, but he is not in today. Come back tomorrow. A futile cry of protest. Frown, shrug.

'By the time we get north,' Tosh grumbles, 'the offensive will be underway.'

'Cheer up. If we reach Châlons by nightfall, I can secure billets for us.'

A look of mild scorn crosses her face. As if my desire to sleep in a bed, instead of huddled under my army cloak on a bench in the depot, makes me morally suspect. 'Billets? Don't be silly. We don't have a *permis*.'

'My brother-in-law is *sous-préfet*. In Châlons.'

She shrugs, uncomprehending. Any Frenchman would grasp my meaning. Having a *beau-frère* who is *sous-préfet*... it is impossible to explain. How the complex hierarchies of French society rub and interweave and why a regional *fonctionaire* can, if sufficiently motivated, circumvent army procedure. So long as he does it quietly and without fanfare.

'Trust me,' I say at last.

Twelve hours later, we are mounting the stair of a half-timbered house in Châlons. It is the same every time I seek out Bérnard at the *Préfecture*. After receiving me in his matter-of-fact way, he invites me to dine at the *Haute Mère-Dieu*. An invitation always coupled with an apology for not being able to do more. By *en plus* Bérnard means that he regrets not being able to extend the hospitality of his own home, but his wife, Louis' sister, dislikes me and would make it very unpleasant. We have never spoken a word on the subject, Bérnard and I, and how we reached this understanding I cannot say, but I am glad for it because I enjoy his company. At least I usually do. Tonight's dinner was a strain. Tosh's French is not terribly good, and translating for people who do not know one another exhausts me.

At the top of the stair we find a small raftered room furnished with twin beds. After setting down the lamp Tosh flings her case down in the middle of the room and kicks off her shoes. A hurried toilette ensues. Bottles and jars get strewn over every surface, a soiled towel drops to the floor. Then she claps her hands with alarming vigour. 'Right. Let's examine that lump of yours.'

Too tired to argue, I remove my shift and lie back across the starchy coverlet. Tosh stands over me, kneading at my breasts. First one, then the other. I shiver and stare at the ceiling. It is a stiff little room. Empty of decoration, save for three little dolls tucked onto a shelf under the eaves.

'Have you ever given birth?' she asks.

'No.'

'Pregnant?'

I shake my head. 'Well, maybe. Once. I might have been.'

Her face hovers over mine, close enough to see the faint shadows cast by her long fine lashes. 'I intend to avoid it at all costs.'

Such an easy thing to say. To think. When one is young.

'More women must do as you have,' Tosh declares, pressing down on my rib. 'We must refuse the enslavement of motherhood in favour of higher ends.'

'They don't see it that way in France.'

Tosh frowns. 'There is no other way to see it.'

There is. But I am too tired to explain. Motherhood, Camille used to claim, is a Frenchwoman's military service, her *impôt du sang*. But I am not about to launch us down that path. All day Tosh has felt compelled to tease out my opinion on every possible topic: the French suffrage movement, Wilsonian neutrality, the Dreyfus Affair... hour upon hour of intense debate has wrung me dry.

'Seventh rib,' she announces. 'Near the sternocostal junction. Feels like a cyst. Or a build-up of scar tissue.'

'Can I get dressed now?'

'When did you first notice it?'

'Years ago,' I sigh. 'I injured myself. A few days later, there was a lump.'

'What sort of injury?"

A shiver runs though me. 'I'll die of pneumonia in a minute.'

'There's a bit of... I wouldn't call it discharge.' She kneads and squeezes my breast, forcing a tiny drop of fluid from the nipple. 'See?'

'Is that bad?'

She shakes her head, still massaging the hard knot of tissue. 'Just odd, given you've never lactated. How did you sustain the injury?'

'I knocked it against a saddlehorn.'

'Sorry?'

'A saddlehorn.'

She laughs. 'Since when do saddles have horns?'

'American ones do. Out West.'

'I thought you lived in New Orleans.'

'Before that, I lived on the frontier. For a time.'

Tosh crosses the room and washes her hands. 'Keep an eye on it,' she says, letting another soiled towel drop to the floor. 'If it gets any bigger, let me know. And stop touching it all the time.'

After extinguishing the lamp, Tosh undresses swiftly. Her clothes fall to the floor and stay there, heaped in shadowy mounds. I hear her eiderdown rustle and expect more talk, but Tosh is mercifully silent. After my arrival in France, Louis pressed me to have a child. I did not react well. Was that his real reason for wanting me to come here? To provide him with an heir? Why else would he beg me to move to Paris then carry on with his other liasons after my arrival? Do I regret not giving Louis the child he wanted? No, but it might have cost me his love, which is no small thing. Minutes pass, both of us lying motionless. Then comes the slow rise and fall of Tosh's breathing.

I take up the candlestick and step into the hall. The flame flickers in the draught then steadies. I pull my shift up over my head and knead my breast as Tosh did, working my fingers up from the base, squeezing hard towards the nipple. A tiny bead of moisture blooms from the tip. I touch it. Raise fingertip to tongue, expecting it to be sweet. Like nectar. But it is not. I examine the other. Pressing and squeezing I force another tiny droplet out. Watch it trickle down my finger. Clear and thin as seawater. Salty as a tear.

Chapter 6

Two weeks since my meeting with Will Keane and not a word since. I'd even dispatched a polite note. Still no reply. Blair's ledger book lay splayed before me, awaiting my tally of last night's liquor sales. I rubbed my aching temples and drew a piece of stationary from the drawer. The time for gently worded reminders had passed.

> *Dear Mr Keane,*
> *At our meeting on 19 February, you promised to apprise me of your findings in Tucson. I find this ~~unprofessional~~ silence un—*

Josie burst through the door, apron dark with coaldust. Jackson had been up on the roof all morning making repairs, so she'd had to fill the scuttle herself. A task that always soured her mood. Slapping the morning's receipts on the desk, she thundered. 'Dance lesson today? Tell 'em no food after. Supper at six. They hungry before, best eat breakfast. None a this nibble nibble, sip sip I seen Texas Lil do. Girl's not ate a proper meal in weeks.' Josie marched towards the door, plaited hair pinned above her neck. 'And don't let Blair catch you pinchin the house paper.'

Of course. How foolish to think I might be able to send a message without anyone noticing. Would she say something to Sadie? Last week I'd found the pair of them giggling like school girls while enjoying tea and cakes in the kitchen. Josie had always struck me as one to keep her distance, but nothing here was what it seemed. Or, to be more precise, what I had assumed it would be.

Goose Flat was not some wild frontier town, just a dusty

mesa scored with dung-laden streets and tin-roofed shacks. Blair's whores were not downtrodden victims, or at least they did not see themselves that way. To them, the degraded shameful lives were led by dancehall girls giving johns a dry rub for a quarter, or crib whores with oil-cloths on their beds because the roughnecks they serviced didn't take their boots off. Gypsie liked to brag about her 'kip work', sparking arguments at the supper table over who gave the best lay. Were they plotting to escape Star Mansion? Not that I could see. I kept the books. I knew how much they earned. And how much they borrowed against future earnings. Only Gypsie was in the black. Evie, Lil, and Contessa all owed Sadie money. Not much, but enough to see they had no plans to leave.

The clock in the hall struck one. Floorboards creaked, doors slammed. A shriek rose from the side parlour, followed by the flat slap of bare feet. That weekly ordeal known as 'waltzing lessons' was about to begin. I glanced at my unfinished note. Ink had dripped from the pen leaving a black blob in the margin. I tried to soak it up, but Sadie's blotter paper dissolved on contact. Thin ink, dull nibs, soft pencils… everything bought on the cheap. I tore the note to bits and flung them on the desk.

That afternoon's lesson was to be our last, though none of us knew it yet. Things began as usual. With tardiness and whining, bickering and dissent. Who spilled carbolic douche on the hall carpet? Fess up, or Jackson'll punish the lot of us! Lil blamed Gypsie, who claimed Evie had done it, but Evie saw Tessy sneak a dishrag from the kitchen and we all know who the clumsy one is after last week's broken chamber pot. Must have been some turd, Evie. *Eat your rhubarb, ya hurr*!

'Right!' I clapped my hands briskly. 'Let's get started!'

Nobody moved. Gypsie sat cross-legged, sectioning, combing, and rolling her hair. By the end of the lesson her head would be a snaky mass of curling cloths. She never rose to dance and I did not press her. Only Evie tried to learn. Enthusiastic and bouncy, she would leap to her feet and lurch through the steps with no sense of rhythm. But today, even Evie lacked interest. Perched on the edge of the couch, she sat massaging a thick white cream into her hands, taking great care not to soil her feather-trimmed sleeves as I droned on about the importance of counting time.

Evie yawned. Texas Lil whispered into Contessa's ear, while Gypsie remained hidden behind a coppery veil of hair. They recognised this whole exercise for what it was: yet another one of Blair's ploys to drum up business at their expense. Her last scheme had involved Jackson driving through town the week before Christmas, while the whores sat in the wagon singing carols. But the weather had been brisk and when the wagon got stuck in the mud, Jackson spent an hour freeing the wheel – if Lil's version of events was to be believed – while the whores stood outside in low-necked dresses, getting heckled by miners coming off the day shift. Gypsie fell to coughing, and Texas Lil spent three days in bed, delirious with fever. A doctor was summoned, accusations made. They lost money for missing work, and Contessa had levelled a stream of curses at Madam Blair, which, if uttered in English, would have gotten her tossed on the street. Or so Lil claimed.

'Okay!' I chirruped. 'Let's give it a try!' The player-piano burst into a jaunty run of chords as I soldiered through the steps. It was the same demonstration I gave every week, wheeling about the room, arms in the air, shouting *one two three, one two three, one two three*. It was stupid: trying to teach a waltz without partners to lead us through the steps. But Madam Blair had insisted. *One two three, one two three, jump up! Join in!*

Evie stood, then Lil. Arms out-stretched they clasped invisible partners and waited for the next song-scroll to click into place. When the music began Lil bumped into Evie, who steadied herself by grabbing Gypsie who then slapped Evie's feather-trimmed wrist and barked, 'Get this damn bird out of my face.'

'You're just jealous!' harrumphed Evie. 'Mister Francis gave me this wrapper. Comin' by 'gain on Sundee. Take me out walkin.'

'That ain't all he's taking,' grumbled Gypsie.

Evie ran a hand down her sleeve, smoothing the pale silk.

'He's gonna marry her,' blurted Texas Lil. 'Just like Jimmy McIntyre done married Dora Belle.'

Gypsie rolled her eyes. 'That man marries Evie, I'm President Grant.'

'El presidente,' said Contessa, 'is not Grant. We have Chester Arthur now.'

'We? What do you know about it, ya Mexican whore.'

The music ground on. Too fast, slightly off-key. Madam Blair never had that thing tuned. Or at least there was no evidence of it in the ledger books.

'You done said the same to Dora Belle,' Evie pouted. 'But it were the ring an' the parson and all. It's true, Miz Vera. Big fancy cereminy up in Preskit, then off to Colorado they went. Now Dora Belle's married to a rich and handsome man who loves her dear and true.'

'Guapo?' Contessa gave a husky laugh. 'Old Jimmy McIntyre?'

'Really, Evie.' Gypsie combed out a tendril of hair, smoothing it flat between her fingers. 'That masher had a gimp and an eye-patch.'

'Teensy prick, too,' giggled Texas Lil.

A slow, toothy smile spread across Gypsie's face. 'Scared the stiff right out of him, did you?'

Contessa laughed, which made Lil furious. She slapped Contessa on the arm and hurled a stream of curses at Gypsie, who responded by taking great care selecting the proper cloth for her next curl. Early on, I'd fought to keep them under control. But I was incapable of Josie's rough bluster, and treating them with aggression and hostility made them even less willing to learn. Better to cross my arms and wait. Let their dispute run its course.

'You don't know nothin'!' cried Texas Lil. 'I been swabbin' wicks since I was five. Cleanin 'em off fore Momma worked 'em over. Them johns'd pat me on the head an tip me a dollar. Nother if I stayed to watch. I seen more pricks 'n the lot a you and old MacIntyre's poke weren't no bigger 'n my thumb. Hard nor soft.'

Something must have showed on my face, for Gypsie gave a slow smile of delight. And then she pounced. 'Our talk too much for you, Miss Dance Teacher? Bet you're one a them likes that science talk. 'Tumescence' or 'coitus'. Or maybe 'Cunnilingus.' Yes. Let's talk about cunnilingus, Vera, is that your sort of—'

'Basta,' hissed Contessa.

'So what about his peter.' Evie gave her stringy hair a toss. 'Them's the nicer ones anyways. And he's no bastard neither. He done married Dora Belle.'

'What does that prove?' scowled Gypsie.

'That he loves her dear an' true an' forever!' Evie crossed her arms in triumph.

'You and your claptrap,' Gypsie jabbed at the air. 'Old McIntyre married Dora Belle because he needed help on that ranch a his. Fore the war he'd a bought himself a nigra. Now, he's got no choice but to find a wife. The man's no looker and he ain't got much money. But he's no fool either. Old MacIntyre knew that with his gimpy leg and his—'

'Teensy prick,' chimed Texas Lil.

'Most wives wouldn't find out about that til it was too damn late. But his gimpy leg and bad eye, well, that couldn't be hid. That old peckerwood, he knew the score. He knew he couldn't do better than some washed up old whore, so he fed Dora Belle a bunch of wine-and-roses bunkum, now she's scrubbin' floors and cookin' meals and cleanin' his chamber pot while he rolls on top a her t'unload his ashes any old time he please. And Dora Belle? She's not getting paid one red cent for it.'

Evie turned away in a huff, mousy hair tangled in the feathered collar of her gown. 'What do you know? Nothin' but a stupid parlour whore, is all.'

Gypsie shrugged. 'That's what a wife does, Evie. Works like a slave, gets fucked for free. Don't believe me? Ask Miss Dance Teacher.'

They all stared at me. Evie spoke first. 'Was you married?'

I nodded.

'It warn't like that, right Miz Vera?' She went on stroking her feather-trimmed sleeves. 'Not 'mong quality folk.'

'Quality folk!' scoffed Gypsie. 'You mean the kind what walks through that door every night? Fellas who come here to get their wicks dipped and complain about their wives not fucking 'em? That the 'quality folk' you mean? Women who spend their big railroad gent's money, live in his expensive house, then refuse him a good lay? Sounds like a whore to me, only not an honest one. They take their fee, but they don't put out.'

'Could it be,' I ventured, despising the high thin sound of my voice, 'that they are afraid of falling pregnant? The wives, I mean. Perhaps a doctor has advised them that a pregnancy would be... dangerous.'

'Yeah!' shouted Evie.

I hadn't meant to take sides. But didn't Gypsie just call me a frigid dishonest whore?

'Wife can fuck her husband without gettin' knocked up.' Gypsie heaved a weary sigh. 'There's ways, tricks of packing and douching. It ain't about babies for these prigs. They just think sex is filthy so they treat their husbands' needs like a bunch of revolting nonsense. Then their men come knockin on my door. Well, who can blame em?' She leveled me with a withering gaze. 'Hell ain't paved with good intentions, Miss

Dance Teacher. It's paved with bad marriages.'

The music ended. There was no sound but the whir of a song-scroll winding back on itself. They were all staring at me.

Texas Lil screwed up her eyes and said, 'Your old man beat you?'

'Shhh,' hissed Evie. 'Why else she run away?'

'My husband died,' I said. In the silence that followed I was seized by the urge to tell them how much I missed him. Let them know that not all men were like the ones who walked through Blair's door. That the world wasn't just dupes and rogues. Wouldn't that serve them better than waltzing lessons?

The doorbell chimed and we stood there, waiting for Jackson. It was his job to turn away off-hour callers. The bell rang again and Texas Lil leapt to her feet. Then she tripped across the room and flung open the door.

Billy stood on the front-stoop, clutching an envelope.

'Come in, my good sir!' Lil exclaimed. 'Why, I'll send for Josie to bring the tea things! Or would you prefer coffee? You know, my cook makes the best café au lait this side of the Mississippi. Not that dreadful idea of coffee they have in this town.' Contessa's full-throated laugh unfurled in one long naked burst, while Billy stood there like some tall weedy sapling rooted to the spot. Texas Lil seized his hand, neckline of her dressing gown dropping low to reveal a big red love-bite. 'My, what a big fine man you are! I'll bet you're a devil with a girl.'

Billy shot me a desperate glance as she pulled him inside. A gust of wind flattened the silk wrapper to Lil's body, and the pimples on Billy's forehead flushed to a deep purple. He opened his mouth to speak when his eye caught on something and he fell into silent puzzlement.

'Who let this boy in?' Madam Blair strode past and slammed the door.

Lil threw off Billy's arm as if she'd been scalded. Contessa's gaze settled on some distant spot along the far wall, while

Gypsie picked idly through her pile of curling cloths. Only Evie wore a suitably cowed expression as she raised a hand, ready to point at Texas Lil.

'I did.' My voice surprised me. 'I let him in.'

Madam Blair gave a start but recovered quickly, dropping into the chiding tone she used with the whores. 'Messenger boys are not allowed inside, Vera. Churchies give me hell for that kind a thing. You know the fine Deputy Barnes would slap on me, if this boy's momma decided to run me in?'

'My maw's dead,' said Billy.

'Lucky for me,' Sadie shot back. 'I catch you in here again, I'll have the law on your tail so fast you won't know what hit. Now hand over that message and skee-daddle.' She reached for the envelope, but Billy stepped away. 'Young man, you are threatening to have me shut down. Give me that message, or I'll have Jackson to toss you out.'

'I'm no messenger boy, M'am. I'm secretary to Mister Keane and he instructed me to deliver this note to Miss Palmer direct. I am not to place it in any hand but hers, and if she can't receive it, I'm to return with the note left undelivered. Mister Keane was most clear on that.'

Sadie tossed off a forced trill of a laugh. 'Well, you tell that boss a yours he'll have to defend me graah-tis if I get run up on corruption-of-youth charges. Town holies've got that new Sheriff ass-over-barrel these days.'

Billy handed me the note, then tipped his cap and left.

An anxious silence filled the room. The whores shifted about. Lil bit her lip as Jackson emerged from the back of the house, hammer in hand. Madam Blair strode across the floor and took it from him. Then she waved at Contessa. Evie slid to the far end of the couch, cowering against the pillows. Ostrich feathers hung about her wrists and neck in limp, stringy clumps.

I watched Jackson unfasten his cufflinks and roll up his sleeves. Then he stepped towards Contessa, clenching and unclenching his fists.

'No, no,' snapped Sadie. 'I want you to dance with her.' She thrust a slippered toe into Contessa's backside. 'Up, up, you little polecat. Show us this waltz of yours.'

Contessa stood. Barefoot with her dark hair unbrushed, she looked as if she'd just rolled out of bed. But her stance – loose-limbed, head cocked to one side – lent her an air of great composure as those dark eyes bore down on Jackson, flashing with defiance.

Jackson took a hesitant step forward and stared down at his muddy boots. He looked ill-at-ease amid the doily-laden tables and velvet upholstery.

'For God's sake,' I cried, 'he doesn't know a waltz from a polka. Besides, we're still firming up and the steps and—'

'Firming up the steps, are you?' Blair's mouth twisted into a smile. 'Where I come from, we have quite a different name for the kind of dance a girl does sitting down. In a chair. On a man's lap. But perhaps you society women like to use the word 'waltz'? Gives it a more dignified air.'

Society woman? Me? This was her stupid idea in the first place. For a long slow moment I simply faced her across the room. Then a soft ironic chuckle escaped my lips. Not what she expected.

For weeks she had been watching me. She'd noted my hesitation that first night behind the till, my disquiet at the whores' housetalk, and she believed she'd taken the full measure of me. But this laugh took her by surprise, and Madam Blair did not like surprises.

She compressed her lips, slapping Jackson's hammer against her palm. It made a flat ugly sound. Then she strode past, head held high, shoving the hammer at Jackson as she went. We heard a rattle of keys, followed by the low groan of a doorhinge. 'In my office, Miss Palmer.'

I did not move.

Texas Lil shot me a pleading look.

'Now.'

Anger swept through me, becoming more powerful with every step. I was angry at Madam Blair for treating me like one of her whores, angry at Jackson for failing to answer the door when Billy rang the bell, angry at Evie's stupid feathered gown and at Gypsie's fat white teeth. I was angry at Henry for dying and leaving me alone, but most of all I was angry at Will Keane for sending me a note at exactly the wrong time.

'Close the door.' Sadie stood with her back to me, fiddling with the lamp. The flame flared then shrank, casting a weak pool of amber light on the desk. When she turned, she drew herself up to her full height, powdered face glowering in the lamplight. 'Don't you ever contradict me like that again. I have a hard enough time keeping those sassy brats in line without my office gal gettin' lippy. Is that clear?'

Leave. Right now. Go upstairs and pack. Take the room at Clark's Josie offered you. Find another job. Keep accounts for a butcher, saddle-maker, saloon… anything. My hands were busy with something. Piece of paper. Fingers twisting it hard. Will's letter. Contents unknown. Steady, Vera. What if you need to pay for an assay, or a survey?

Blair's mouth was drawn into a hard, lipless line. 'Well?'

I squeezed the envelope and nodded.

She let loose a heavy sigh. 'The dance lessons are over. But you can't blame me for trying. Oh, how I try! I try to learn 'em a thing or two that might help down the road. Parlour whore's got about six years in a high class house, long as she lays off the booze and the drugs and keeps clear a moochers. But once a gal starts to lose her looks, she needs more than what's between her legs if she wants to avoid the cribs and the gash peddlers. Smart girl can figure her odds, but these frontier whores…' she shook her head. 'They got no sense at all.'

A lock of hair had slipped from her pinned twist, and she tucked it back into place. Sadie's hair was her best feature, and she treated it accordingly. Lavishing it with perfumed oils and expensive dyes. She lacked beauty, but worked hard at making the most of what she had.

'Why are you here?' She crossed her arms and stared at me.

'Because – by your own request.'

'Don't play dumb. You know what I mean. I'm here because I have to be. Incident at my last house got me run outta St Louie. Not permanent, mind you. Just a few years. But what does a gal like you want with this sorry-ass town?'

'A change,' I shrugged.

Her eyes narrowed.

'I could not stay. Not after what happened.'

Sadie raised an eyebrow, sensing – no, hoping – for some scandal to explain what had driven me to her door. Sent me flying into her charitable, rescuing arms like so many other helpless young girls. No, not like them. I was about to protest when her eye fell to the envelope in my hand. A moment's silence, I feared, might prompt her to ask me about it. So I just started talking. Fed her a tale about a dogged, unscrupulous suitor. Sam Brocklehurst, the stooped, pipe-smoking librarian who used to drop by for tea, became a lecherous man I was desperate to escape. His bumbling attentions were recast as aggressive, threatening. I kept it simple. Injected a bit of humour. Imitated his teeth clacking against his pipe, gave him a belly that sagged over his trousers. It occurs to me now that it was the sort of yarn the whores spun when asked how they'd ended up turning tricks. I doubt Blair believed a word.

Her smile said as much. It was the same forced grin she'd given Deputy Barnes my first day in town. Then, at the end of my little tale, she patted my hand. Her touch was cool and dry, and in the full glow of the lamplight, she appeared weary. Then her eye caught on something, and with two quick steps, she was at the door. Looking back across the shadows, she spoke in a brisk, diplomatic tone. 'Try not to waste my stationary, Vera. It does cost money.' Then, with a jingle of keys, she was gone. Once the clip, clip of her heeled shoes faded away, I tore open the envelope.

March 3, 1884
Miss Palmer,

Have received yr. correspondence. Please accept my sincerest apologies. Was invlvd. with several urgent matters; all required immediate attn. In future do not send messages via persons other than Billy. Very important. Will drop by SM soon to discuss yr situation further.

Most sincerely yours,
W. R. Keane, Esq.

I still have this note. Tucked away with all the others. Bound with a yellow hair-ribbon, they lie at the bottom of a drawer back in Paris. That first note of yours was curt and efficient and it made me furious. To be chided after weeks of neglect. Not to mention all the trouble it caused. And for what? Some little scribble that said nothing. Just a slap on the wrist and a demand that I wait longer.

I recall crumpling it into a ball and hurling it across the room. To retrieve it I'd shoved a crate of glassware aside. Then I'd taken the note upstairs, smoothed it out, and slipped it into Henry's old trunk. How vividly I recall all of this. And yet…

When Louis was sick that summer before the war, I'd had to move things to make space for his powders and tinctures. While drawing that packet of letters from my bed-side table, the yellow ribbon slipped its knot, spilling letters onto the carpet. I restacked them, in order, placing that note back in its proper place at the bottom of the pile. But before doing so, I stood stroking its folds with my thumb. Paper stiff and uncreased (I am certain) in my hands.

Chapter 7

The gun made me nervous. He'd offered no explanation, no mollifying word. Just slung a rifle across his lap then taken up the reins. It made sense. I'd lived in the territory long enough to know the risks: mountain lions, jumpy prospectors, horse thieves, smugglers up from Mexico on the lam. Still, no amount of logic could ease my jumpy dread as Will steered the two-horse team across town.

Storefronts jogged by. Russell's Cigars, McClellan's Liquor, Garvey's Dry Goods – each name linked with a column in Blair's ledger book. We crossed into Hoptown, passing chop shops, laundries, mahjong parlours, and hop joints. I watched old men shuffle ivory tiles across low tables, while stoop-backed boys hauled water-buckets on wooden yokes and a wheelbarrow ferrying a woman with tiny feet wobbled by. So. These were the 'evil slave-traders' Deputy Barnes liked to yammer on about. *Slant-eyes got a stagecoach hidden away over there. Drive it outta town each night packed fulla girls. Drugged and gagged. Load 'em onto a train bound for the coast then a slow boat to China. But we're onto 'em. We'll catch 'em at it.*

Whenever he went on like this, I would steal a glance at Sadie Blair. Watch her her face squeeze out a smile, teeth gritted at the back of it.

'Comfortable?' Will had to raise his voice over the creaking buckboard.

I nodded.

In truth, I was far from comfortable. Every pebble jarred the wheels, sending whalebone stays jabbing into my ribs. And I was hot. Flannels, stockings, garters, drawers, petticoats. My body felt like a tiny seed cocooned in cloth. But I refused to complain. It would have felt like a concession.

The road swung south, dropping down the side of the mesa into an undulant sea of grassland. Sharp peaks and blunt ridges rose against a cloudless sky, hemming the windswept distance. I tried to lose myself in this vision of broken escarpments and chalky hills, but my gaze kept sliding back to the gun, rifle grease blackening his trousers. How easily it rested there. As if it were of no more consequence than a walking stick or pair of gloves.

'You alright, Miss Palmer?'

'You've already inquired after my welfare once. Must I furnish you with constant updates?' My ribs ached, my skin pricked with sweat. But I wasn't about to say so.

All week my irritation at Will Keane had smouldered on. A slow burn of latent frustration that would flare whenever I remembered our argument. It had transpired on a very busy night at Star Mansion, when he'd dropped by to explain his findings. He seemed to resent having to conduct business while johns purchased brass checks. Yet the choice of venue was his, not mine. He'd explained that an affidavit attesting to the requisite on-site investment had been filed in Tucson, but no record of a patent application existed in the land office. A curious absence, he'd declared, because why should Cox go to all the trouble of filing an investment affidavit if he did not intend to seek a federal patent? All of this was delivered in a rush of legal jargon while I made change, sold checks, and sailed into breezy laughter whenever Jackson brushed past to toss weapons in the lock-box, or Sadie swooped down to ply Will with her 'hospitality.' But I understood enough: the paperwork in Tucson was inconclusive.

Perhaps the mineral assay had shown so little promise that Cox had decided the fees required to obtain a federal patent were not worth paying. Or perhaps Cox had bribed someone to 'misfile' the patent application in order to prevent an adverse claim. A common practice, Will had explained. If that were the case then my claim could be worth a great deal. And yet, Will had mused, why give someone a worthless locator document, rather than a proper patent?

It made sense to me: Tom Cox was just the sort of man who could spot a fault line miles away through a pair of field-glasses, but couldn't tell a bank draft from a railway ticket. A brilliant geologist renowned for bureaucratic cock-ups. But before I could say so, Madam Blair had descended on us in a flutter of taffeta and jewelled fingers, pressing Will to dance with Gypsie. He'd managed to get rid of Sadie by requesting a particular brand of cigar that was too expensive to store behind the bar.

'Sunday after church,' he'd said, 'is my first available opportunity.'

'For what?'

'To inspect the site. It's the only way to settle the question.'

'Fine. Collect me whenever you like.'

'Too dangerous. Apaches are still—'

'Do you take me for an idiot? Their strong-hold is twenty miles east; my claim is south of town. Apache threat! Not a single attack against a resident of Goose Flat has ever been verified.'

'The desert is no place for a lady.'

'Neither is this.'

He dropped his gaze and flushed. 'There is no need for you to endanger yourself, Miss Palmer.'

'I disagree. Given the lassitude with which you have treated my interests so far, how do I know you will report your findings to me in a timely manner? Perhaps I would like to confirm that you're the right man for the job.'

'Is that a threat, Miss Palmer?'

'No, it is a reminder.'

'Of what?'

'That it is you who work for me, Mister Keane.'

'Spoken like a true Yankee.'

'Carpet-bagger. Isn't that your meaning?'

He'd heaved an exasperated sigh, drained his bourbon, and left without so much as a glance in my direction. Nor did he bother waiting for his cigar. Blair then issued a stinging reminder that my job was to sell checks and make change, not drive 'gentlemen callers' away.

The rest of the week had passed in silence. Will sent no word of confirmation and I was too stubborn to seek any. Then, at a quarter past noon this morning, a pair of dun-coloured horses had drawn up alongside Star Mansion. Seduced by their sleek-muscled beauty, I'd failed to notice that these glorious steeds were hitched to an exposed, ramshackle buckboard.

But I noticed now. Juddering down a rutted track in the midday sun, corset stabbing me in swift stiletto thrusts, I gripped the edge of the seat to keep from sliding into him.

'Bit warm.' Will unscrewed the cap of a dented canteen and offered me a sip.

I declined, despite my thirst. How could I possibly avoid spilling water down my dress on this rough road?

Will drank deeply, wiping his mouth on his sleeve. I licked my lips, reconsidered, then held firm. Whatever surprises lay in store, a proper outhouse would not be among them.

The splintered wood of the buckboard creaked as we topped a rise, vast sweep of land spreading out below. Wavering grassland stretched on for miles, dimming to a distant haze against a serried fringe of mountains. I drew a breath, felt the dry air swell my chest. And in that moment something rippled through me. The same throb of excitement I'd felt my first day in the territory, a silken shiver stirred by this raw immensity of land.

I glanced over at Will, free arm tossed across the back of the seat, face tanned and lined in the way of all men who had lived in the territory for any length of time. He seemed not so much lost in thought as subsumed by the pleasure of the moment – the feel of the reins in his hand, the dry hiss of grass. His gaze wandered from the horizon to the horses, then came to rest on me, lips parted in a scarcely perceptible smile.

He let his free hand trail off the side of the wagon, fingers brushing bushy tops of grass. He broke off a piece and stuck it between his teeth. Then he leant back, and I caught a glimpse of the boy inside the man.

'I expect you used to drive your mother crazy.'

Will threw back his head and laughed. Then he fell quiet. His grey eyes caught my gaze and held it. 'You look quite fetching, Miss Palmer.'

A blush crept up my neck. So. My attire was the source of his amusement. No doubt the figure I cut in my pale muslin dress with straight-fitted sleeves was an entertaining one. But there had been good reason for wearing such a silly, impractical outfit. One I had to share.

'I should tell you,' I began, 'that this outing of ours has set a few tongues wagging.'

'Mmm?' He worked the straw lazily between his teeth.

'To keep the purpose of our errand a secret, I had to indulge in a slight fib.'

A puzzled look crossed his face.

'Sadie Blair and the… others. They think we're going on a picnic.'

Will toyed with the reins. 'Are you telling me that I shall have to feed you in order to make an honest woman out of you?' He smiled, flicking the bit of straw up and down between his lips. 'I think we can manage a meal before the day is out.'

I drew breath, considered, then fell silent. How to explain what had happened? Since the afternoon of the final waltz lesson, the whores had begun to take note of me. Conversing with me over supper. Seeking my opinion on hair-styles, hem-lengths. Evie felt perfectly free to saunter into my bedroom without knocking, while Texas Lil had fallen into the irksome habit of sliding into my bed whenever she felt blue. Kicking her out only provoked teary-eyed pleas, so I usually just rolled over and let her stay. Which only encouraged her visits.

But none of that troubled me. What worried me was their assumption that the note Billy had delivered was a love letter. *Love letter!* The very words (Evie's) made me cringe. It was all so juvenile. But I had played along. Relieved to have a pretext for our correspondence. But this fiction had quickly spun out of control. Last night I'd overheard Texas Lil gossiping with one of her regulars about us. Such tales would soon spread beyond the walls of Star Mansion.

'A few people seem to be under the mistaken impression that we are engaged in a romance.' I braced myself for an explosion of temper.

Will drew the piece of straw from his teeth, stared it for a moment, then tossed it aside. 'Why is it that women always seize upon the sentimental motive?'

It was a good question. Even Madam Blair had latched on to it with uncharacteristic enthusiasm, sauntering into the office at odd intervals to offer advice. They all seemed immune to any other possible reason for our relations.

'I don't know,' I said at last. 'What motive do men seize upon?'

'Money. Men look to see who stands to gain a profit.' He leant forward to free one of the reins from the handbrake, and his loose-fitting workshirt slipped down over his bare shoulder. I looked away, but not before glimpsing a faint splash of brown just below his clavicle. A birthmark.

'Miss Palmer, I have a bone to pick with you.' With a deft flip of the wrist he untwisted the reins and straightened, shirt falling back into place.

So. He *was* angry. 'I'm sorry. It's all very annoying. These silly assumptions. I know such rumours might affect your reputation, professionally I mean. I, too, am suffering consequences. Like this outfit.' I waved at my dusty white skirts. 'You see, Texas Lil burst into my room this morning and insisted I look my very best for our picnic. I tried to resist, but she grew sulky and I was afraid of making them all suspicious.

And now here I am, stuffed into this ridiculous, uncomfortable dress and—'

'I thought you were comfortable.'

'Do I look comfortable?'

'I don't know. That is why I asked.'

'I feel like a trussed turkey.'

'Well, you are the loveliest turkey I've ever seen.'

I looked away, irritated at myself for letting that remark slip.

'Miss Palmer, twice I've paid you a compliment, and both times you've responded most ungraciously.'

'You have been counting?'

'I suppose I have.' He tugged at the hair on his chin, then smoothed it between thumb and forefinger.

'Calling me the loveliest turkey you have ever seen is a compliment?'

'Most certainly.'

'I beg to differ.'

'You sound like a lawyer,' he parried.

'Is that a compliment, too?'

'Definitely not,' he laughed. 'But I did say you looked quite fetching. That, surely, cannot be disputed.'

I looked down at my lap. 'I assumed you were making sport of my outfit.'

'Why would I do that?'

'Because I look ridiculous. Who travels across the desert wearing pale muslin and white kid gloves? This will all be soiled beyond repair.'

'I find your appearance refreshing. It's been a long time since I've seen a young woman so exquisitely turned out.'

'That's three, I suppose.'

'Yes. And you continue to respond most ungraciously.' His southern accent lent the words a cloying sweetness. I sat in silence, unable to banish that glimpse of his birth-marked shoulder as we rattled past a lone wisp of creosote sprouting from the sun-baked earth. Wiry branches, ablaze with yellow flowers, wavered in the breeze.

Turning off the road, Will eased the horses down a wash that wound through a scrabbled expanse of scrub and rock. I watched a hawk circle and drift, riding swift currents of air.

'How would you prefer that I respond?'

'A simple *thank you* would suffice.'

'Very well, then. Thank you.'

'You're quite welcome.'

At the southern fork of Ajax Gulch, Will drew the horses to a halt. The wash had become a steep-sided ravine with bleached grey walls, leveling off into a rocky outcrop. Will pulled a cartridge belt from beneath the driver's box and strapped it around his waist.

'Wait here.' His tone was firm. 'If you hear shots, drive back to the road. Then wait for fifteen minutes. After that, head for town. Speak with no one. Stop for nothing. When you arrive, find Billy.'

Then he grabbed his rifle by the forestock and slid to the ground. His heels struck the soft limestone, stirring a puff of dust that settled on his boots like ash. I watched him advance down the wash keeping to the base of the ridge, until he curved round the ledge and out of sight.

The horses kept stamping and tossing at the reins. One of the mares turned her head and stared back at me, white limestone ridge reflected in her brown eye. Then she gave her tail an imperious swish and looked away. Never in my life had I held the reins of a horse, much less driven a cart-team. I'd been in town long enough to know Will's fears were justified. I'd heard all the stories. Ranchers getting stabbed by jumpy prospectors. Drunk soldiers wandering away from Fort Huachuca and dying of thirst, or that cavalry officer whose body was found when a wolf dragged it onto a nearby ranch. Last week, word went round that he was the victim of an Apache scout-turned-horse-thief who stole up on riders so silently they never heard a thing. Just woke up on the ground with a throbbing head, stranded in the desert without a mount. Back in town, such tales cast a glow of adventure on life in the territory. But out here… I gripped the reins hard, thoughts swarming.

The horses snorted and stamped, hooves scuffing at the powdery gravel. *Think, Vera.* The rebuke came to me not in my voice, but Henry's. Calm, ever practical. A scientist through and through. Do not imagine, observe. There, on the ground. Two scimitar scars in the soft white sand. Marks from Will's boot-heels. Follow them down the wash. What do you see? Nothing. No wheel-ruts, no stray horseshoes. No cairns. No axe-marks in the rocky ledge. Prospectors passing through here had kept right on going. Around that bend lay nothing but an arroyo-creased dip in the ridgeline, where Tom Cox had once staked a claim on a faulty hunch. The reins sagged, inert, from my hands. The horses had ceased to move.

Then it came. Pebbles rained down, clods of earth thudding onto the buckboard. I ducked. The horses whinnied and tossed their heads, but did not spook. Then silence. I did not look up. Face pressed to my thighs, I heard the crunch, crunch of footsteps in gravel. A metallic clink. Not a gun. A buckle. A belt being unclasped? I went rigid.

A hand touched my knee.

Blood roared in my ears.

'You may let go of the reins, Miss Palmer.'

Will stood beside me, shirt smeared with rifle oil. He had unharnessed the horses and now held them by lead ropes. 'I took a short-cut down the side of the ridge. Didn't count on setting off a landslide.'

I climbed down from the driver's box and followed him through the wash. Our feet stirred plumes of dust and I was glad of my gum-soled boots, having held firm on this point against Texas Lil's fierce protestations. The rifle clinked against Will's cartridge belt as we walked, horses trailing behind. Cactus and ocotillo jutted up from the rocky walls. A flood-tossed tree sat lodged in a crook of the ravine high above our heads, its black roots like a giant spider crawling across the sky.

A gully branched off to the left. We followed it up and around the back of the ridge until we stood high above the wash within sight of the buckboard. An abandoned camp lay scattered in the rocky hollow: discarded billy cups, charred stones of a fire-ring, a rusty tub with rainwater pooled at the bottom. Will led the horses to it and they drank, bridles clanging at the sides like the clap of a bell.

A ledge rose ten feet from the ground then broke off into nothing. I ran a finger along the silty limestone, trying to connect what lay before me with the squiggly-lined diagrams I'd pored over before moving West. Synclines, faults, glacial shelves… I wouldn't know a syncline if I banged my head on one. Or tripped over it. Was it a protrusion or a dip? Will stood so close I could smell his scent of collar starch and straw and, beneath that, a mild soapy sweetness. He pointed to a two-inch groove just above our heads. A second, identical cut ran vertically and a third sliced diagonally over both. Pick-axe marks, neatly carved, utterly straight. He trailed a listless finger through one and shook his head. 'Assayer's mark.'

So. We had our answer: Cox had not bothered to apply for a federal patent, because samples from the site had been assayed and found worthless. It made sense. Tom Cox was a gambler. In debt to loan sharks, forced out of his job at the college amid rumours about some chorus girl down in New York. No doubt when he gave Henry the locator document, he believed he was bestowing a valuable cache of silver on his friend. But this conviction was the misplaced optimism of a card shark, not the sober assessment of a geologist.

Will responded with no such resignation. He swore under his breath. Then he picked up a dented billy cup and whipped it at the ledge. It clattered to the ground.

'I am terribly sorry, Miss Palmer. To have come so far for

nothing.'

We are but an hour from town, I was about to say. Then I realised he meant my coming West in the first place. His booted toe kicked idly at the ground, stirring puffs of ashy dust. 'I wish the news were better. I wish I could tell you there was some hope.'

I was about to apologise for a job that had cost him a good bit of work, but would bring no commission. But his pained expression gave me pause. Someone in this strange new life of mine cared what happened to me. My head felt wispy and light, thoughts like smoke.

I stepped forward and felt a tug. My skirt. Caught on a scrap of barbed wire. Bending to unhook it I felt a wave of dizziness, then stumbled and fell. I scrambled to my feet, boots slipping in loose gravel. My hand stung, while the horizon kept bobbing up and down in a jaunty watery way. Like on a boat. Ribs pushing against my corset in quick short breaths that gave no air. Will's voice drifted towards me. I felt a soft pressure on my arm. His hand, forcing me to sit. His lips were moving but no sound reached me. Muffled. Every word wrapped in cotton.

'Smelling salts?' I managed to say, each syllable heavy as a stone. 'I've never fainted in my life.'

A hand shakes me gently by the shoulder. Hot whisper in my ear. Tosh's voice. 'Shhh, just a dream.' Her breath is sour with sleep. She tells me to think pleasant thoughts. Imagine walking through a rose garden. A rose garden? How quaint. This is a different Tosh. Unguarded, half-awake. Childlike, even. A rose garden…

No. My thoughts are far from such fertile, rain-washed ground. They cling to thorn and jagged rock. This dusty slope. Down which a young woman is being carried, unaware of the arms that bear her weight. Her pale skirts flutter in the breeze as he carries her back to the wagon, boots letting loose a shower of pebbles. A lead-rope wrapped around his hand. Because it is nothing for this man to lead a pair of horses while carrying her in his arms. Nothing at all.

He sets her down in the buckboard. Brow furrowed as he marvels at the spider-fine beauty of her lashes, lavender tint of her eyelids. In this moment does he fall in love with her? Or is that just a story he comes to tell in later days? A pretty thing to say as they lie beneath the shade of a cottonwood tree and he recalls the moment he first caught her up in his arms, bearing her body down that steep hill?

He covers her with a moth-eaten saddle blanket. The horses are hitched and ready. Will examines their harnesses, straightening straps, adjusting cinches. Dust coats the mare's sweat-sheened neck. He returns to the buckboard, to her. Lying on her back in the late afternoon light, eyes closed, unmoving. He paces. They must leave now if they are to make it back by dark.

He waits. Shadows deepening. Then she stirs. Smell of crushed hay and dusty heat heavy in her lungs. Cozy, warm. She would drowse on, but for the sharp sting in her hand. Her eyes open to rocky walls shearing across a thin ribbon of sky. She sits. Head reeling as she slides to the edge of the buckboard, splintered wood snagging at her skirt. One sleeve is torn at the cuff. Flecks of blood on the pale muslin. A stabbing pain behind her eyeballs.

'Easy, now.' He puts an arm around her shoulder, pressing a dented canteen to her lips.

She drinks. The water is warm and tastes of pennies. She has never felt such thirst.

He takes up her wrist, examining the scrape on her hand. His fingers are rough and dry, palps like leather. Pushing up her sleeve, he pours water from the canteen across her palm. It stings but she does not flinch. Thumb against the raised tendon of her wrist, he daubs a handkerchief on the scrape, wiping away water and blood. He tells her to put some iodine on it when she gets home. Home… her thoughts are heavy and strange. As if arriving from afar.

'Drink,' he whispers.

She lifts the canteen to her lips. Water dribbles down her chin onto the bodice of her dress, but she does not care. Reddish brown stains streak the pale muslin, the amber ribbon about her waist is twisted and askew. One by one, objects from her old life are falling away: cups Henry's lips touched, books whose pages he cut, dresses his hands unbuttoned and drew away from her shoulders. But she does not think of this now. Not yet. This thought arrives later, as she slides the soiled dress into her wardrobe. Right now, all that matters is to drink. To slake this thirst that aches more than the cut on her hand. Her very bones feel parched. She drains every drop and wipes her lips with her sleeve.

Then she slides from the buckboard. A short drop, but she stumbles. He grabs her arm and guides her to the driver's box, helps her up into the seat. Then he does something that is at once necessary and remarkably strange.

Climbing onto the buckboard, he slips in behind her and unbuttons the bodice of her dress. Then, with the able efficiency of a maid, he loosens her corset. Careful not to touch her bare skin as he refastens the ties, adjusting them just so. Fingers deft and impassive. Like a surgeon or a dress-maker.

Tosh speaks, voice hoarse and dreamy. 'How did you know?'

Her question confuses me. We are both lost in our own hazy netherworlds. I stare up at the ceiling, cross-beams laddering the shadows. The dolls are nothing but black shapes. But I can feel them there, perched on their narrow shelf staring down at us in the dark.

'Know what?' I say at last.

'That it was a bodged abortion.'

I reach for her hand, but end up grabbing a knee. 'Shhh, not now.'

A long silence ensues, broken by the faint rumble of the guns. A low consolatory murmur. Like surf pounding a distant shore.

Tosh rises from the edge of my bed. I hear the eiderdown rustle as she shifts and settles. A minute passes. Then another. Footsteps ring out across the cobbled yard, a military patrol enforcing curfew. Beyond the wind-dashed shutters trees shiver in the dark. Leafless and worn. Vehicles churn down the road, grinding past the looming bulk of the cathedral, crossing the bridge, speeding past the cemetery where Louis and his first wife lie buried side-by-side beneath a hard glitter of stars. I lie in bed and wait. For sleep. For daylight. For all the old voices to cease tumbling down through the dark.

My fingers rise to the lump on my rib. Should I have told Tosh? Described how it used to ebb and swell to my body's monthly rhythms, growing hard and sore in the days before I bled, then softening. Until last year when the bleeding stopped altogether and the nub of flesh ceased to wax and wane. No longer moon to my monthly tides, just a lump of tissue. Inert, tender. A bruise that feels better when pressed.

Chapter 8

We arrived at the field hospital ten days ago and every hour brings a fresh crisis. Not in the wards, but in my office. A wind-wracked tent where I battle the daily barrage of paperwork Tosh's surgical school has unleashed. Our CMO is French, the nurses British, and surgical trainees hail from the United States. Different allied authorities require different forms with different signatures at different times. Not to mention the rigorous inspections demanded of mobile surgical units. Every day another *inspécteur* arrives, demanding to sniff at the sterilisers or measure the distance between the wards and our *cabinets de toilette*.

'Vera!' Tosh bursts through the door and slaps a sheaf of papers on the desk. 'Cost of feeding personnel is listed in francs, additional funds are in guineas. That's the only confusing bit.'

I rifle through the yellow forms, ink smeary and hard to read. 'You might have kept them dry.'

'Pay no heed to bed-capacity. We can billet men in the village. Food and transport, that is what we need to calculate.' She gives a spirited wave, drops of rainwater flying from her sleeve. 'How many surgeons can we train with these funds? An estimate. That's all I require.'

Placing the damp forms on the old trestle table that serves as a desk, I grab one of our makeshift paperweights (small rocks, empty cartridge casings) and set it down on the pile.

Tosh groans. 'This cannot wait.'

'Yes. It can.' I take my coat from its peg. 'It is you who cannot wait.'

My shift in the surgical theatre begins in twenty minutes, which Tosh ought to know since she adjusted the schedule herself. When I remind her of this fact, she answers with a pleading look. Twenty minutes to myself. A rest, a walk, a cup of tea... but she expects me to cram another task into this precious sliver of time.

The door brushes open to reveal our matron-nurse. Part chaperone, part administrator Sister Hamilton handles leave requests, permission slips, and a thousand other duties meant to keep our contingent of British nurses healthy and safe. Or as safe as they can be five miles from the front. Sister Hamilton made an enemy of Tosh back in Camiers by complaining to our CO that a WSPU badge violated uniform regulations. I settle my face into an expression of affable neutrality and bid her good day.

She gives me a civil nod then taps at a poster on the wall announcing tonight's entertainment. 'My girls are prohibited to dance with officers in their own messes. The regulations are most explicit.'

Tosh throws up her hands, unleashing a fresh spatter of rain.

I clear my throat. 'I don't imagine there is any problem with the musical part of the evening?'

Her mouth tightens. 'In my experience, music in mixed company always leads to dancing.'

'Very well,' says Tosh lightly. 'I shall look to you to keep us all in line.'

'I'll not be in attendance.'

'How unfortunate. I'd hoped our entire unit would gather round the piano you so kindly procured for us.'

'Miss MacNeil,' she sniffs, casting a glance in my direction. 'We are not all as young and energetic as yourself.'

Tosh catches up my arm. 'Nurse Palmer will be there.'

Sister Hamilton regards me with a look that says *I took you for a more sensible sort*. And indeed I am. Sensible to a fault. Releasing myself from Tosh's grasp, I take up a pen. With several swift strokes I cross out 'dancing' and leave the rest untouched. Then I flash my most diplomatic smile, slip on my coat, and retreat into the lashing rain.

The wind has picked up, soughing across the darkening field. A strong gust buffets the tents, canvas snapping. Why must Tosh bait Sister Hamilton at every opportunity? Why does every slight become a battle that must be fought head-on? I hurry down the planked *trottoir*, taking care not to slip on the wet duckboards. Tent-ropes hum like ship's rigging in the wind, while the steady rumble of the guns grinds on. Like a thunderstorm that never arrives. Until it does. Or so we are told. HQ keep issuing warnings, which, so far, have come to nothing. Taube planes buzz overhead, dropping no bombs. Alarms sound, followed by the all-clear.

I duck into post-op, air heavy with ward-smells. Mud, idioform, soiled bandages. White-caped nurses float between the rows, cots arranged at odd angles to avoid water dripping in from the roof. A nurse brushes by to drop needles in the sterilising pan then glides back between the beds. I watch her adjust the pulley on a leg, bending her head down to speak softly to the patient. All cool competence and unruffled serenity. I fix myself a cup of tea and try not to think of what awaits.

My last shift was a disaster. *Hold the leg steady while the surgeon saws.* Simple enough. But it takes time to remove a leg, even one that is half rotten. And all the while you are breathing in that pond-scum stink of gangrenous flesh as the ding, ding of the chisel tingles up through your fingers until the leg comes off with a jerk and you stick it in the tub for the orderlies to take away. Except they don't. Because they are too busy subduing a man who is spitting blood and tearing at his field dressing, crying out for water he can't have because his stomach is shredded. So the leg stays planted there in the pus-soaked bandages. Knee bent, thigh covered in curly black hairs. You can't stop staring. At the calf-muscle with its intricate tattoo. Heel leathery and pink. Toes hard as pebbles. Everyone kept calling him *Apache* – slang for conscript, petty thief hauled off the streets of Paris to serve out his jail sentence in the army. But my eyes keep falling to the thick callused foot. Unaccustomed to shoes. A man just off the boat from Algeria, Senegal… then a blurry lightness and next thing I know I am flat on my back under a drawsheet. Five stitches in my chin.

Relieve me of all surgical duties, I said. Tosh refused. I insisted, pleaded. Confessed my appalling ignorance. Told her that the very sight of my dressings tray sends me into a panic. All those menacing twists of metal whose names refuse to stick. But to no avail. On the contrary: she doubled my shifts and aligned them with her own, placing me under her direct tutelage. As if my own personal short-comings might prove a blot on our entire sex. Should I have gone farther? Confided that assisting surgery puts me in mind of other things – things long buried that now clutch at me, demanding excavation. Said to her: for decades I have kept certain secrets even from myself, but when I breathe the steamy blood-stink of the sterilising vats and take up those cold metal instruments, they stir, become insistent. But that would mean speaking of Star Mansion. How to cast all of that into a shape someone else can grasp? Besides, Tosh can be an incorrigible gossip.

I clean my teacup and set it back on the draining board, then hurry to the scrub-room. Which is not a room, but a lean-to separated by a curtain that is not a curtain but an old horse-blanket. I roll up my sleeves. Grab a nailbrush, antiseptic. Snatch a glove from the ready-goop. I nearly cry out from the scalding. *Quel idiot.* No, you are not. Just unaccustomed to wearing gloves. In French hospitals only surgeons do, but the Americans… ah, the Americans. My compatriots have no shortage of supplies. I take up the tongs, shake out the hot water, then slide each hand inside.

Tosh stands across the ward amist a gaggle of students. I approach, gaze dropping to my tray. Knives, saws, chisels, bone hooks, needles… Why is she forcing this on me? Must we all be drafted into her Grand Plan for the Advancement of Women? My hand drifts up to press the ball of flesh on my rib, but I catch myself in time. Gloved hand left to float aimlessly.

Pale and strange.

Every patient is a stick man. A collection of body parts. This is a trick Tosh has taught me. A way to stay focused. Avert your eyes from the mud-spattered face, just focus on the wrist. Take his pulse. Wrist.

I tell Tosh.

'Five-hundred ccs and strychnine.'

A serum. I can do that. Funnel, syringe, needle.

Tosh is busy scraping away dead flesh. Grey spoonfuls slop into an enamel pan then comes a plink of shrapnel. An NCO is striding among the tables, bootheels striking the floor with quick sharp taps. He will sift through the chunks of tissue and examine any bullets, making sure they are not French. And if they are? Charge him with attempted desertion then a firing squad. All accompanied by reams of paperwork, no doubt. A nasty thought? Well, I seem to be in a nasty mood.

One of the trainees presses up close. He stands with a mild slouch, unopened notebook by his side. 'M'am?'

Tosh does not look up. 'Do I look like your mother?'

'No, M'am.'

'Then stop calling me that.'

'What should I call you?'

'Doctor MacNeil will do.'

I hand her the suturing needle. The boy shifts from one foot to the other. 'You gonna suture that up right tidy?' Raaht tahdy. His accent catches me off-guard and I fumble a spool of catgut. Tosh shakes the scissors at me and I take them in my gloved fingers, which are ghostly white. As if the hand belongs to someone else.

'You close it off all the way, pus gonna build up in there.' The boy's tone is deferential, but the way he stands – that slouch, the untouched notebook – betrays him. He points at the wound. 'Leave two small openings, set him to walkin' round post-op twice a day – force that pus right out.' Raaht out. Georgia? Tennesee?

'No fracture…' Tosh shrugs. 'Fine. Inform post-op.'

'Thank you, M'am,' he grins. Then he crosses his arms and leans back. 'Doctor MacNeil.'

Tosh fixes the final suture and looks up. To my surprise, she is smiling.

The days pass. We are drilled in air-raid protocol and ordered to carry morphine, hypodermic, and tourniquet in our aprons at all times. An attack fills the hospital and we fall to mad speculation. The offensive? It has begun? But the push fizzles and soon we are back to artillery fire and light raids. In the office any routine proves impossible. The moment I settle into a task, I am interrupted by another – a roof leaks, a drain clogs, a pipe ruptures.

For a book-keeper, such upheaval is rare. In civilian life no job is more predictable in its patterns. At the college bursary the busiest day of the week was always Friday, when salaries were paid and fees collected. At the cotton factorage it was Sunday as regional buyers flocked to the home office to deliver samples and report on crop production. At Star Mansion it was Monday. Always.

On Monday morning profits from the two busiest nights awaited calculation; the previous week's ledger had to be closed out, and petty cash needed to be reconciled. All amid a flurry of deliveries – wine, whisky, coal, ice, laundry – each arriving with its own scrap of paper that had to be filed away, yes, straight away, for we can't have essential documents like *Everhardy's Butcher Shop: Bacon 80¢* tossed willy nilly about the office now, can we?

Never mind that you are busy tabulating a lengthy debit column: broken glassware, ripped linens, china figurine that got knocked to the floor whose pieces now lie scattered on the desk. Locate the file, find the price list, search for ugliest-pug-faced-dog-ever-laid-eyes-on, copy down the figure (yes, that illegible scrawl in the margin), now add it to petty damages – quick, quick, for other matters require immediate attention. Like the provisions ledger. Last week's total does not reconcile, which means Josie has yet again neglected to hand over a receipt from the fish monger or green grocer or some supplier of exotic specialties that get laid out each night for the johns.

'Vera!' Sadie bursts into the office, gaze falling to the broken china dog. 'How much did I pay for that?'

'Fifty cents.'

A fib. I had no idea what the ghastly thing cost, but a low figure would soften her mood, which had been especially brittle of late. Contessa kept insisting that Blair's sometime lover, Anthony Mariano, had thrown her over, while Evie blamed the time-of-life change. I suspected money. Profits had dropped for two straight weeks, though she was hardly in the red.

Madam Blair stood drumming her nails against the clipboard. They made a quick sharp sound like rain on a tin roof. 'I have noticed a recent falling off in Will Keane's visits. Is it that you prefer him to stay clear of my girls?'

It was said as a joke, but it stung. I bit back a quip about a recent 'falling off' in Anthony Mariano's visits, too, as my finger traced a line from one column to another. The ragged sibilance of her shallow breathing filled the room. She was a great devotee of the tight corset, but these rapid exhalations made even her silence feel intrusive. I entered three more figures then, in a light breezy tone, asked if she could please tell Josie to hand over all the receipts from last week, as I had already wasted a good deal of time trying – and failing – to reconcile the provisions ledger.

'These came for you this morning.' She slapped two envelopes down on the desk, then marched off to find her cook.

I took up one and tore it open. A note from Gotthel's Millinery informing me that my hats were through being trimmed and could I please collect them before week's end, as the shop has limited space, yours sincerely, Virginia Gotthel.

Then came a post-script telling me how much I owed. Another receipt. Wonderful. I tossed it on the desk and rubbed my eyes. My mining claim, I now saw, had lent my days a deeper purpose. If cashing in on it had been a long shot from the start, well, it was something to aim for. But now…

I brought up a deep sigh and sat back. My days were nothing but paper-cuts and ink-stained hands. Sun hauling itself across the same featureless sky while I toiled away at Blair's books. And my nights? They were spent handling greasy bills with a smile plastered on my face and Blair's till-key dangling from my wrist, strap leaving a mark to be rubbed away later as I lay alone in bed listening to Lil's headboard beat against the far wall as she feigned little cries of pleasure, begging some john to hold back and show mercy because oh, oh, oh you are so much man! Or blocking my ears against the whip-slaps coming from Gypsie's room. The whores' vivid, off-duty talk had provided me with all manner of details. And as I lay in bed each night waiting for sleep, images would swarm through my head: the chubby-faced pay-master thrown, bare-assed, over Gypsie's knee taking his licks so he could perform. And that white-haired judge down from Prescott? The reason he always bought two brass checks? 'Blair says he gots to, wants t'fuck me while Gypsie sticks a whip up his ass.' Evie had paused after offering up this little tidbit, then added, 'The fat end. The handle.' As if that explained everything.

Will Keane had told me not to lose heart. During our journey back to town, he'd encouraged me to move my earnings out of Safford Hudson Bank into something more lucrative. Railroads, land deals, stock options… he'd promised to advise me, but several weeks had passed and I was still waiting. I stared at the torn envelope in my hand. Every note that crossed my desk raised the same dim hope. One that I nursed each night when I took up my place behind the till, secretly wondering if he might arrive. And it was this dashed little hope that Sadie's dart had struck. She was right. His visits had ceased altogether.

And I missed them. Time had passed swiftly when he stood beside me at the bar teasing, making wry comments, arguing. The moment things began to grow dull or predictable, Will would say or do the unexpected. Like loosening my corset. After six years of marriage, Henry had no idea how to perform such a feat. Yet here was an unmarried man, five years my junior, managing the task with calm dispatch – a man whose obsessive concern for propriety drove him to chide me for going by 'Miss Palmer' yet when it came to unbuttoning my dress, he'd not even asked permission.

Pushing back my chair, I noticed that the safe was unlocked. Empty, of course. Madam Blair always rose early, counted the previous night's take, scrawled the amount onto a scrap of paper, then spirited the cash away to some secret location in her bedroom. I bent to secure the door and heard noise coming from the barroom. Not unusual. The slot that led to the safe made it inevitable.

Voices. I stuck my head inside. Jackson was talking about the Bisbee Massacre Execution. A topic people had been bending my ear about ever since my arrival. The attempted robbery, the trial, the lynching of John Heath, the special gallows being erected behind the courthouse so all five convicts could be hanged at once, the formal invitations Sheriff Hatch had issued to families of the victims… how tiresome it all was. If one more john tried to engage me in a debate over whether the Sherriff ought to raise the wall behind the courthouse to keep gawkers from disrupting the proceedings, I was going to scream. Or so I liked to tell myself. But in fact, I knew I would smile and nod politely as I slipped his brass check across the bar, same as always. I was about to shut the door to the safe, but something in Jackson's tone gave me pause.

'Not in St Louie,' he said. 'Not even when times was tough.'

'Well. This ain't Missoura.'

'Don't I know it. But advertisin…' he faltered and trailed off.

'I told you. It's not advertising. That Purdy chap called it a 'feature'.'

'Who?'

'Lionel Purdy. One we helped outta that scrape with the gal over in Contention City. Remember? Well. He still owes me a favour. I had him put me in touch with a newspaperman down in Bisbee and on Purdy's say-so, this fella did a story.'

'What kinda story?'

'The kind that says...' there was a rustling of paper as Sadie's voice rose to a practiced lilt, like a third-rate actress reciting her lines. 'When business takes you north to the county seat, men desiring high class entertainment should look no further than Star Mansion, a tasteful palace of gentlemanly delights run by the charming Madam Sadie Blair, Queen of the Arizona Demimonde. Madam Blair has the distinction of reigning over the most opulently furnished parlour house on Sixth Street where beautiful women, fine wine, and sweet music reign supreme. Inside Star Mansion discretion and taste are the order of the day. Sports can rest easy as they sit back and enjoy old world hospitality in the company of the loveliest and most delightful young women in the territory. Men with sporting proclivities believe Sadie Blair's temple of joy to be the most refined parlour house west of the Mississippi.'

'Sounds like advertisin' to me,' Jackson grumbled.

'Don't be a knothead. You pay for advertising. This here's free! We're right in with the regular news. And it's about time, I say. Yes, siree. High time someone up and took note of all we've done for this raggedy-ass town. Remember what this place was like before we set up shop? Boil on the fat ass of nowhere, is what. Just cribs and cheap dancehall girls. Ugly tarts flashin' tit and husslin' johns into some basement room to get their joints copped. Well. Not any more. I'm bang up proud a this place, and I want folks to hear of us. Let 'em come see what real class is.'

There came a clink, clink of glasses being shelved.

'This newspaperman say we on'y take folks what kin name

a reference?' said Jackson. 'Fellas come recommended by a steady trick?'

Blair gave a long sigh. 'What's eating you?'

'How'm I gonna know who to turn away?'

'You got a bloodhound's nose for trouble. I'd trust you to sniff out the foxes from the sheep any day.'

I could scarcely believe what I was hearing. Madam Blair liked regular customers. Men whose preferences she knew and whose habits the whores could cater to without fuss. She preferred intimate gatherings of familiar faces to packs of unruly strangers. Crowds meant the whores had to turn tricks faster and hurry the johns along. 'We're not that kind of house,' she often sniffed. 'Exclusivity pays off in the long run.' Yet here she was planning to open her door to off-the-street trade.

'I'll get some fella in a uniform to stand outside,' Blair offered. 'Marshall or a deputy up from Bisbee who can point out the rotters.'

A long silence ensued. Jackson didn't like the sound of it and neither did I.

'Look,' she went on. 'Profits have been slipping ever since the mines hit water. Protection racket gets heavier all the time. I got the damn holy birds tryin to shut us down. Never mind it's us who keep their daughters safe!' Her voice dropped low and I strained to hear the rest, but all I caught was '...telegram from St Louie... head back... up stakes now gonna cost...'

I sat back on my heels and locked the safe. Jackson never argued with Madam Blair. He said little and enforced the rules. That was his way. I scrambled to my feet and fell to sorting all the papers into tidy piles. Neatness seemed to soothe Sadie. She never checked my work if the office looked ship-shape.

The other envelope lay before me, unopened. It was addressed in Mr Patterson's tight, angular hand. No doubt he was asking after my mining claim. He'd made no secret of his skepticism. One of many nay-sayers who had felt free to drop by for a little chat after learning of my decision to move

West. Henry's colleagues and their wives had all taken a turn, declaring it their duty to protect me from misguided notions. Their nosy queries veiled as concern, when their true purpose (I was convinced) was to sniff around and make sure I hadn't got my hands on more laudanum. They claimed to have my best interests at heart, and perhaps (the notion was hateful to me), they did.

I drew a deep breath and slit the envelope. Inside was a note from Mr Patterson, explaining that the enclosed letter had been found stuffed between the pages of a book I'd donated. The librarian had forwarded this letter to Mr Patterson, and he, in turn, was sending it on to me. He trusted I was well, gave warm assurances that he was at my service should I require it... *yours sincerely, A. Patterson, Esq.*

I let his note drop to the desk and held the envelope, stroking a finger across where it had been slit open. By Henry. With his ivory letter-opener. *72 Elm Street, New Haven, Connecticut.* Our old house. A vision of its white shutters and tiny scrap of lawn rose before me, and for a long moment I simply stood, vibrating with emotion. Then I withdrew the folded pages. Dated *16 December 1880* it was written in small, jerky handwriting that I did not recognise. I flipped ahead to the signature. *Yrs affably, Tom Cox.* My breath caught.

I read it rapidly, paused, then read it again.

Written from one geologist to another, it contained a lot of technical information – an estimate of the claim's depth of exhaustion, a long discussion of why Cox believed principles of mine valuation in this district were off target, a rant about the stupidity of mining engineers with their complicated formulas and elaborate assay plans, followed by a paragraph about clean-cut fissures and zones of brecciation – most of which I did not grasp. But I understood enough.

Clutching the letter to my chest, I hurried out the door and down the street, straight for Will Keane's office.

Chapter 9

'Absolutely not!' came Madam Blair's arch reply.

We were standing in the pantry, crammed between a sack of potatoes and the ice chest. From the kitchen came a clatter of supper dishes, Evie's insistent prattle, and Josie's faint humming as she scrubbed the stewpot.

'Execution's Friday. Men from all over the territory'll come to Goose Flat, and I aim to be of service to 'em.'

'But m'am, I—'

'Ah, ah,' she waggled her finger at me. 'Sadie.'

I swallowed, mouth pasty with the aftertaste of stewed rhubarb. Josie served it every few nights to prevent constipation, an 'occupational hazard' for the whores. I cleared my throat and began again. 'I have worked long hard hours for two months straight. I believe this has earned me some time away.'

'I said as much the day you arrived! When a gal's in her time-of-the-month, she takes three nights off and I told you to do the same. Three nights a month. All I ask is one week's notice. House rules, my dear, house rules. And leaving tomorrow,' she concluded, discharging her words like rifle-shot. 'Is. Not. One. Week. Notice.'

'But the letter just arrived this morning.'

'From your attorney. Back East. Requiring you to go to Tucson about your husband's will.' Each phrase was bitten off declaratively at the end, though the uplift in her voice implied these were questions. 'You can't manage this business here?'

I shook my head.

'Tucson! When we split off into Cochise County, idea was folks could avoid goin' all the way to kingdom come for every little thing. Now you're tellin' me you gotta git your hide up to Tucson to see these government grifters?' Her eyes narrowed with suspicion, but I knew what to say.

'The politicians seem to have made a mess of things. Some functions have yet to be transferred down.'

'Corruption and incompetence!' she exploded. 'Politicos and the courts all part of the swindle!'

A good part of this 'swindle' landed in her safe each night. The kitchen door swung open and Evie stepped into our midst.

'Get rid a those pink feathers!' Blair barked. 'You look like a cheap dancehall girl.'

Evie's mouth formed a tiny 'o' as Sadie shooed her back into the kitchen. 'I feel sorry for your plight, Vera. Dead husband's a hellava thing. Believe me, I know.' Her corset-strained breaths came in stale smelling puffs. 'Now. I happen to be in a generous mood tonight. You can have your days. Starting Saturday.' Blair made a move towards the door.

'Thank you,' I ventured. 'Very much. But I must leave tomorrow. Mr Patterson is waiting for me. Or he will be. He arrives – he arrives in Tucson tomorrow and we must complete this business before week's end.'

Madam Blair crossed her arms, breasts straining at the bodice of her dress. 'I don't take kindly to back-talk. Got no tolerance for it. Now I just made you a generous offer. Bent the rules. A thing I don't often do. Madam can't be playin' favorites.' She spoke with cool detachment, fingering her emerald necklace. 'Hotels in this town are booked solid. Come Friday, streets'll be packed with sports keyed so high only thing that can calm 'em is a slug of bourbon and a girl. I've seen this kinda thing before. War, executions... killing makes everyone rabbity. Your shop-keepers, your city hall boys... all of 'em need to let off steam and hell if they don't come here to do it. Ask Will Keane. Night we got word of the Massacre, he washed up on my doorstep... lordy, what it took to calm *his* nerve!'

My stomach clenched and dropped. I didn't care what Will had done on that night, or any other. Our romance was a fiction. But Blair believed it to be true, which meant she was trying to hurt me. Or bait me into lashing out. Three nights off and one week's notice? First I'd heard of that policy. As far as I knew we were closed Sunday, and that was it. There were no rules. Just Blair's whims, which translated into rules when it suited her. But a fight was what she wanted. I forced a bright smile. 'Just what *is* this Bisbee Massacre everyone's always running on about?'

Her face contracted in surprise. 'You don't know?'

I gave a small shrug.

'Terrible tragedy! Gang of thieves tried to rob a store just before Christmas. Packed to the gills with holiday shoppers. Hoodlums just walked in bold as brass and started shootin'. Killed a woman, three men, a child. Then they grabbed their spoils n' fled. Sherriff sent a posse after 'em, but one fella kept leadin' the others astray, til they turned on him and extracted a confession. Fella admitted to planning the robbery, then he led 'em to the gang's hideout.'

I adjusted my expression, adopting a look of grave interest.

'All five were tried and convicted, and now they're to be hanged. On Friday. As for the stupid mack who tried to hornswoggle the posse... John Heath got a life sentence, til that lynch mob took care a him.' Sadie drew a sharp breath through her nose. 'Ask me, his real crime was stupidity.'

I faked a little shiver of unease.

'Now, I despise a mob. But these murderers had their day in court. Every one of 'em. Tried and convicted, fair and square.'

'Oh.' I let my eyes go wide. 'Yes. Well. I can see why you want to be of service. Provide a little solace.' Sadie shot me a look so I toned it down. 'The moment my business is concluded, I'll catch the next stage. I'll make it back in time.'

Blair's lips smiled, but her eyes were frosty. 'I've no idea what this urgent trip is really about, Vera, and I don't aim to pry. I keep my nose clear of other people's business and expect them to so the same. You have three days coming to you, and you can take 'em. Starting *Saturday.*' And with that, she pushed open the door and strode into the kitchen.

I slumped back against a sack of potatoes. Why on earth had Will insisted I trot out that ridiculous fib? My idea was far better: dodge the question and let everyone assume my trip to Tucson was a romantic assignation. But no. Oh, no! Will could not countenance such a blot on my reputation!

Billy was due to arrive any minute with my ticket for tomorrow's stage, and now I would have to turn him away. My gaze fell to a metal tub. It contained a large ham that had been soaking for days. I poked at the greyish-pink slab, watching the tepid water slosh about. Two days. Who soaks a ham for that long? It was a larger joint than usual and twice as expensive. I'd filed the receipt yesterday. No doubt it would be laid out for the johns on Friday night. I stared at it, clenching and unclenching my fists. Why had I listened to Will Keane? Connecticut lawyer! Sadie hadn't believed a word. Next time I would do things my way. Will had no idea how to handle Sadie. I poked at the big slab of meat, saliva thick at the back of my throat. Then I leaned over the tub and spat.

In the kitchen Blair was performing her nightly inspections. Sniffing at skin, examining nails, ordering anyone who hadn't bathed to 'shake that dragass upstairs and wash.' When I entered she was busy plucking pink feathers from Evie's hair. 'Told you once, I've told you a thousand times, steer clear a feathers. This ain't a poultry farm.'

'Why you always lightin' in on me?'

Gypsie sniggered. 'Because the rest of us don't dress like two-bit twat.'

Evie leapt to her feet, brandishing a butter knife.

'Jesus,' breathed Gypsie.

'No blasplehmin' in my kitchen!' Josie spun round, hands dripping with suds. 'One more cuss' word an' that cathouse mouth a yours be washed out with soap.'

Blair clapped a hand over Evie's fist and lowered the knife

to the table. Evie stamped her foot, Gypsie hissed at her, Texas Lil tittered, and so it went. On and on and on. I stacked my supper plate in the sink and stepped outside. Behind the kitchen lay a dusty back-lot where a pair of half-wild dogs spent their days chained to a metal stake that Jackson had driven into the ground beneath the shade of a busted-up old wagon. At night, they roamed the lot to prevent johns from slipping out the back without paying. My appearance, as always, set off a frenzy of barking.

Mounting the stairs that scaled the back of the house, I gazed out over weathered hills tumbling on beneath a burnished slip of cloud. This was my only solace: to drink in the sight of wind-scoured peaks, sun-struck cloudbanks, gravel flats dashed with light. A chalky coolness wafted down from the hills, making the small hairs on my arms bristle as my thoughts slid back over the afternoon's events.

Tom Cox had, in fact, filed for a federal patent, but he'd neglected to pay the fee. Until this fee was paid, my claim was open to protest – which is why Will insisted we file in Tucson. The moment anyone in Cochise County laid eyes on paperwork bearing Cox's name, swarms of engineers would be scouring the site by lunchtime, any one of whom could see that the required annual improvements had not been made, which would give them legitimate grounds for protest. Then we'd be tied up in the courts for months, possibly years. Once a federal patent was issued in my name, however, the mineral rights would be mine. Incontestably. So Tucson it must be, Will insisted. He was convinced that Cox's letter, when shown to mining executives, would yield a generous offer. But I had doubts. Cox believed investors had relied too much on mathematical formulas, resulting in skewed valuations of certain sites. His letter argued that companies' over-reliance on statistical formulas had caused certain claims (like his) to be dismissed in the early days of the rush, while others were overvalued. There was more. Something about the district's high water table, modest claims with ore close to the surface…

My skepticism lingered. People do not take kindly to being told they are wrong, and in order to sell my claim, mining executives would have to accept that they'd been misguided in the past. This seemed unlikely. Night after night I overheard johns complain about the falling price of silver or the poor return they were getting from some investment in a local mine. All you had to do was listen to the talk in Blair's barroom to know that the pressure to continue issuing dividends to shareholders, even as water flooded the mineshafts, was making these companies take fewer risks, not more.

'Halloo!' Billy sauntered down the side-alley and the dogs burst into a fresh chorus of barking. He took the steps two at a time, my stage ticket in his outstretched hand. I made no move to take it, explaining that we had a change of plans.

'What was that?' he shouted over the barking dogs.

There was no peace. Squalling dogs, prying eyes, gossip-hungry ears… I beckoned for him to follow and continued up the steps. Then I swung open the door and cried, 'Clear the hall!'

Evie scuttled, half-dressed, into a bedroom. Houseboys darted by with piles of towels. Doors slammed, walls shuddered. Shouts rose from the commode for hot water. Billy hesitated, then trudged several paces behind as I led him down the carbolic-stained carpet toward my room. And there, curled in the middle of my bed, lay Texas Lil. Dressed in red velvet, hair unbrushed, legs bare. Filthy feet on my coverlet.

'Get out,' I snapped. Then, because Billy was there, 'Please.'

She did not move.

Billy stood hunched by the door, as if trying to fold himself out of sight.

'It hurts,' she whispered.

I glared at her soiled feet on my white coverlet. Warts on her bare soles. Gummy black dirt between her toes. I couldn't throw her out. Not in front of Billy. But her presence made a frank conversation impossible. I drew paper and ink from the night-stand. A raspy moan rose from the bed.

'She don't look good,' said Billy.

I mumbled some vague assent, but did not look up. No whore's crisis was going to get in my way. How wearying it all was. Lil's constant sniveling, the pouting and the tears. I'd shown her some compassion and where had it led? To an insatiable hunger for more. More consolatory words, more hand-holding, more sour-breathed weeping under the covers of my bed. How had I ended up living a life of lonely isolation, but without any privacy?

My pen scratched on as noise drifted in from the hall. Calls for houseboys to empty chamber pots, requests to borrow combs, a brisk scampering as the whores sought help with hairpins and buttons. I reread my note. Crossed a line, added a word, then blew the ink dry.

Lil's moaning had ceased, her bare legs poking out from rumpled skirts. Billy stood with eyes averted. I handed him the note, which he shoved in his pocket. He wore home-spun trousers, which were too short and his socks sagged. 'M'am, she's bleedin.' He swallowed hard, gesturing at his own midsection.

'She's just in her time of the month.' I gave a soft reassuring smile to cover over my irritation. Leave it to Texas Lil to turn cramps into high melodrama. I struck a match and lit the lamp. The flame flared and dimmed as I fussed with the wick.

A cry rose up from the corridor and Contessa burst into the room, shoving a small brown packet in my hands. 'She take these!'

Dr Samaritan's Gift for Females. A never fail cure for removing difficulties arising from Obstruction or Stoppage of Nature. Restores female system to perfect health by bringing on monthly period without distress. Do NOT take when pregnant, as miscarriage would be the result. No female who values health and happiness with married life should be without these pills! Remedies. I'd taken some once. As a young newlywed, haunted by visions of my mother lying grey and lifeless beside the rubbery corpse of a baby. Six weeks without bleeding and I'd panicked. Taken the omnibus to my old neighbourhood and found a druggist who'd never laid eyes on Henry and never would; he sent me away with a handful of pills and instructions for hot baths and foul tasting teas. It took three days. The bleeding was heavy with cramps like an iron band winching tighter and tighter. Painful, yes. But nothing a woman couldn't handle, if she bent her will to it. You just bear down and get through it.

Contessa sat on the edge of the bed, murmuring in Spanish and stroking Lil's pale gold hair. Lil began to convulse clutching at her bloody skirt and curling in on herself like a dead leaf. Contessa peeled Lil's fingers away. Blood smeared her palms, her fingertips, the counterpane. A dark stain spreading.

'Should I fetch doc Farley?' Billy's croaky voice.

Contessa shook her head. Taking a clean towel from the wash-stand she wiped Lil's blood from her hands. 'Go to Clark's Boarding House. Find a woman name of Josie May. Tell her bring her bag. Comprende?'

Billy nodded.

Contessa drew a coin from her pocket, but he backed away.

'Vete! The old perra see you, be hell to pay.'

Billy scuttled out the door and I suppressed the urge to shout: *Don't forget my note!* There's blood, yes. A girl spooned in on herself, shivering and pale. But other women have taken remedies. Bled. Endured pain. Alone, untended. Show a little grit, God damn it. A bit of pluck and gumption. I strode over to the window. Beyond the glass darkening shapes lay hulked against the sky. Tin-roofed shacks, far-off mountains. Everything fading to shadow.

Contessa went to fetch more towels, leaving me alone with Lil. She lay on the bed stunned and feverish, cheeks dewed with sweat. I forced myself to approach. To go through the motions: stroke her forehead, brush back lank strands of hair.

And when her parched lips broke into a smile, my antagonism drained away. So young. Just a girl.

'Read it.' Her hand nudged mine, and I saw that her fingers were curled round a crumpled piece of paper.

'Shhh,' I stroked her arm.

Lil grew agitated, shoving the balled-up paper at me. 'Read. It.'

I smoothed it open, casting an eye over the smeary scrawl. Barely legible. But I could make out enough. Enough to know that I would never read a word of it to Texas Lil.

'Please,' she wheezed.

Contessa returned. She set a stack of fresh towels on the wash-stand then grabbed the straight-backed chair from the corner and wedged it beneath the doorknob.

'Miz Vera,' pleaded Lil.

I folded the letter and shoved it into the pocket of my dress. 'Your mother says that she misses you. She hopes you are happy and in good health. She sends her love. She loves you very, very much.'

Lil gave a weak smile. 'I knowed so.'

'Tu madre?' Contessa shot me a worried look.

I drew a corner of the letter from my pocket and Contessa swore. Then she climbed onto the bed and started to unbutton Lil's dress. 'Aiúdame.'

I forced myself to take hold of the soggy fabric, to draw Lil's arms from the sleeves. But as I pulled the dress down over her hips, she began to buck and writhe sucking sharp breaths through gritted teeth. Contessa shoved me aside. Then she clasped Lil's ankles, swung her legs into the air, and yanked the dress off.

'Like changing a baby, no?' Contessa handed me the dress, sticky with blood. I bunched it up and went to wipe the blood from Lil's thighs when I saw it. A white stick jutting out between her legs. Pale and slick with blood. I froze, seized by an impulse to grab hold of it and pull. Yank it free like a splinter or a bee sting. A cry rose to my lips, but a hand clapped itself over my mouth and pressed. Then Contessa twisted my head away. I drew short sharp breaths through my nose, stink of Contessa's fingers thick in my nostrils. Medical douche, violet powder, Lil's blood.

'Shhhh,' she hissed marching me across the room to the window. My gaze tried to work its way out to the jagged peaks, but night had fallen. All I could see was my own face thrown back at me in the dark glass.

Josie arrived, canvas bag slung over her shoulder. She draped a towel over Lil's hips, but there was no covering over what I had seen. I squeezed my eyes shut against the vision but it was lodged inside me now. No fingers, no toes. Rubbery twig of bone jabbing out from her black tangle of hair.

I became aware of something sticky on my fingers. Lil's dress. It was still in my hand. Blood had dripped onto the floor, staining the carpet. I wrapped the sodden mess in a towel and placed it on the marble wash-stand, images rattling about in my head. Lil's warty foot. The blood-smeared thighs. Fingerless hand reaching out. Thin and terrifyingly smooth. Shouts rose up from the front-stoop. Deep-throated, rowdy. A harsh guffaw. A laugh of nerves, shot through with aggression. The parlour bell jingled, followed by Blair's falsetto trill 'Company, Ladies!'

A raucous cheer went up, and dread sludged through me. It was going to be one of those nights when a bunch of johns arrived together, already drunk. Some joker would haggle me for a discount, refusing to let up until Sadie intervened. Which always made her cross. Once upstairs they would pass out, too drunk to do what they had come for. A few would holler and swear and blame the whores. Or, as Gypsie put it, 'spend ages sawing away too soused to shoot.'

Josie snapped her bag shut.

'How far gone?' asked Contessa.

'Fifteen weeks…' Josie exhaled and shook her head. 'She

need cleanin' out.'

Another burst of laughter erupted from downstairs.

'Gentlemen Callers!' Blair hollered. 'Shake your asses, ladies!' Contessa cursed and darted towards the looking-glass, where she hurriedly smoothed down her hair, twisting and tucking in loose strands. Then she rushed to the door, pressing my hand as she went by. But there was no hiding the worry in her eyes.

Downstairs Sadie Blair was easy to spot amid the dark-suited men knocking back drinks and digging into the brandied paté. One pinched my rear as I pushed by and when I shot him a look he just laughed. Yes, one of those nights. I pulled Blair aside and upon hearing the news she hissed, 'Stupid cunts. It would be nice if once, just once, they showed some God damn sense.' Then she made for the kitchen, ordering me to follow.

Texas Lil lay strapped to the table. Old horse tack dug into her ankles as the improvised straps looped round the tablelegs and back up, forcing her legs apart. A piece of clothesline wrapped in flannel held down her arms, ropes tied off in some sailor's knot I half-recognised.

Blair tugged off her elbow gloves and clasped Lil's face in her hands. 'Sadie gonna take care a you, honey. Few days you'll be good as new. Good as new, darlin.'

A smile broke across Lil's face as Sadie stroked her forehead. Then she fed Lil a hooker of gin and told me to hand over the key to the till.

Josie took up a pair of tongs and began plucking instruments from a pot of boiling water. They clattered into a bowl that, hours before, had held our dinner of cooked crabmeat.

'I got no morphine.'

Blair made a little face.

'You listenin'?'

'Yes, Jo. Not a damn thing I can do about it.'

116

Josie gave a brisk nod, lips pressed shut.

'Not like last time, right Jo?' Blair lowered her voice. 'I don't want an inquest.'

'Oh, I ain't worried about no inquest. I'm worried about people takin the law into they own hands. I'm worried some john decides to use the back-stair, peeks through that winda...'

'Jackson has locked the side gate.'

'What about them young bucks in the parlour?' Josie shot back. 'One a them starts runnin' off at the mouth about your nigger cook abortin' a baby—'

'Pantry-door is locked.' Sadie's voice was calm, but firm. 'Nobody will get in, Jo, nobody. And if they do – they won't – but if they do, I've paid my protection fees. Hefty ones.'

'Momma...' groaned Lil. Then she reared back and bucked against the straps, as a long wild cry tore from her throat.

Sadie lunged at the table, stuffing a rolled up towel into her mouth. She bore down hard, veins on her sun-spotted hands bulging until Lil's thrashing subsided and Sadie fell to shushing and stroking the girl's cheek again.

'Be lots more a that,' muttered Josie.

'Just get her clean, Jo. I'll worry about the rest.' Then Blair shoved the towel into my hands and left.

Josie set her bag on the table and I searched for a sign that it was okay to speak my thoughts out loud. Acknowledge that I was fed up with Blair, too. It might have helped, saying it. Made me feel less alone. But Jo's face gave nothing away so I kept quiet, while she uncorked a small bottle and measured the dark liquid into a glass. Then she added water and stirred. I recognised the wood grain swirl. Recalled the medicine-sweet taste. Josie slid a hand beneath Lil's head and held the glass to her lips. A trickle of rust-coloured water dribbled onto Lil's camisole, turning it the colour of old paper, as she drank it down. Then Josie wrapped the pressure-cuff around her arm and pumped the bulb. The needle dipped and leapt.

'Why my momma leave?' Lil murmured. 'Why'n she take

me to Colarada?'

Josie breathed out hard through her nose. 'Listen here, child. Momma's gotta do what she gotta do. I got me two sons back in Missoura… ain't a day goes by I don't miss 'em somethin' fierce. But those boys gonna git educated, and this here's the on'y way I kin think to do it. Momma's gotta to do the right thing by her kids. Not the comfortable thing. And the right thing is usually the hard thing.'

Texas Lil's chin quavered, eyes clouding over. 'I don't 'spect Dora Belle aims t'send me to college.'

'Send yourself, child. Lord knows you got the money.'

Lil shook her head, weakly. 'I… cain't…even…read…' Then her eyelids fluttered and fell shut.

Josie tightened the straps and looked up. 'Keep her quiet.'

I twisted up the towel.

'Ready?'

I nodded, but when the first scream ripped free, I wasn't. Wasn't ready for the wet maw of her mouth. The yellow-brown teeth gnashing down, eyes wild with pain. Wasn't ready for the loopy twist in my gut on hearing those towel-muffled cries. Momma, momma, oh, help me, momma…

But I forced that towel down hard, until a thud-clink sounded in the bowl and Lil's body slackened. Then I took up the alcohol cloth and swabbed her burning forehead. Soon I got into a rhythm. Bearing down as Josie scraped and curetted, then her tongs would hit the bowl with a thuddy clack and I'd know it was okay to ease up. Moments later a clink of foreceps would alert me it was time and I'd twist the towel up and get ready. Then one time Josie gripped and struggled and I strained to hear the bowl-clank, but nothing came. A choking tightness gripped my chest and my face must have given me away, because Lil started to panic. She bucked and thrashed until her eyes rolled back and her body went slack and I shouted her name, yelled things that made no sense but seemed right and Josie didn't stop me. As if my voice could reach down to where she had gone and drag her back.

A wave of parlour noise burst into the kitchen. 'What the devil's going on in here?' Blair cried. 'You're meant to be quieting her, Vera, not raising a ruckus of your own.' She was pacing back and forth like a caged hen, wobbly from too much bourbon. 'Can you fix her up, Jo? I can't be haggling with the law again. A corpse, an inquest...'

'We doin' fine,' said Josie. A dull metallic clunk drew Madam Blair's eyes to the bowl. She winced and looked away.

'Go on,' said Josie.

Thankfully, she did.

The moment the pantry door shut, Josie leapt to her feet. She wrapped the pressure-cuff around Lil's arm and squeezed the bulb as the needle ticked round the numbers on Blair's diamond-studded watch and I stroked Lil's clammy forehead. And when a low moan broke from Lil's cracked lips, Josie crossed herself and stood. Shuffling back to the foot of the table, she took up her instruments again and I grabbed the blood-flecked towel. But Josie stayed my hand. The job was done. I sat back on the bench, heart thudding. My gaze strayed aross the room. Mouse trap in the corner, battered metal pots on the wall, Lil's rubbed-raw ankles and iodine stained thighs. Puddle of blood filmed over with a skein that came away in one piece when Josie's hand brushed it. Stuck to the side of her palm, it dangled there until she flung it off with a swift shake and it landed in a crinkly heap on the floor.

I bent and wiped it up.

'She's clean.' Josie announced. Then she wiped her hands on her apron and told me to check Lil's pulse.

For the rest of the night I did Josie's bidding. Tended the coal stove, boiled water, daubed lard on Lil's parched lips, prepared herbal pastes, applied gauze packs while beyond the pantry-door a muddy current of laughter and clinking glasses churned on deep into the night. Between tasks I would stand beside Texas Lil and stroke her arm, tracing out the same patterns I used to draw on Henry's back when he was sick. Those same lazy loops my mother once used to soothe me back to sleep all those long years ago. And when at last Jackson was summoned, he lifted her up as if she weighed no more than a bundle of twigs. And as he turned sideways to pass through the door, I saw Lil's hair swing out from the blankets and catch the moonlight. Then the back-door banged shut and I found myself seated alone at the empty table, shaking. The lamp burned low. Steam dribbled down the window in smeary trails, air rank with menstrual blood, spilled laudanum, Josie's sweat. Beyond the pantry door men were collecting their sticks and hats. Josie rubbed a hunk of lye soap over the sink until the water ran clear. Then she stuffed her blood-stained apron into a bag of dirty linens and sent me outside.

A half moon hung sharp and clear above the rimrock. A scythe of light, gleaming between a cleft in the hills. I stepped toward the rubble-pit, blood-soaked rags heavy in my hands. Josie had tipped the contents of the bowl out onto a piece of old flour sacking then knotted it up tight. Red spongy bits. Oily black chunks. And something pointy, like the tip of a willow branch, kept poking into my palm. At the far end of the lot, the dogs barked and strained against their chains.

Jackson had laid the fire. It was my job to light it, tend it, then once every scrap of this bundle was burnt to ash, douse the flames with water. 'Take care,' Jackson had warned. 'One stray spark, house'll go up like a tinderbox.'

But in my haste and exhaustion, I'd forgotten to fetch coals from the stove. So I set down the knotted cloth and went back inside. The smell of fresh brewed coffee filled the kitchen. Kettle steaming on the stovetop. Sink gleaming white. Platter of cold meats and cheese on the table. Just like any other night.

Contessa sat hollow-eyed before a slice of buttered bread. There were two red blotches on her neck and a scratch on her left cheek. I reached for a piece of cheese, then drew back. My fingers were smeared with blood.

Gypsie dragged into the room and poked Contessa. 'Jacks put Lil in your room. Stupid mack got so bottled, he passed out cold. Had to use Lil's bed for the next one.'

Contessa gave a weary nod, bread untouched. 'How is she?'

'Fever's down,' I said.

Gypsie popped a slice of cheese in her mouth. Chewed, swallowed. 'Going to Tucson, I hear?'

I looked down at my hands and kept on rinsing.

'Here tonight ole Willie boy was. Got all foul-tempered when he saw Sadie at the till.' Gypsie grabbed another slice of cheese, as I dried my hands and helped myself to a hunk of bread. Aware, for the first time in hours, of my own body. Its hunger and exhaustion.

Gypsie looked up from the meat platter and flashed me a grin. 'Let me be frank, Vera. Fella will tell you anything once his pants are down. A lot of it's lies, sure, but some of it's true. Fact is, I don't need a man to drop his pants to see which way his fancy runs. I seen the way Keane's eyes go all puppy-dog. What that man wants is plain as day. And you're a damned fool if you don't get him while the gettin's good.' Gypsie yanked the pearl-tipped comb from her hair and her auburn curls tumbled loose. 'If you're the marrying kind. Which, as I recall...' she smirked. 'You are.'

Contessa shot me a look of warning, but she needn't have. I knew enough not to be provoked. No cathouse ethics protected me. Contessa could smoke her opium-laced cigarettes without fear that Evie would snitch, and Evie could sneak out the window to meet her fancy man safe in the knowledge that Gypsie would never report her, despite the stolen ear-bobs. The stolen ear-bobs merited a reprisal, but telling Blair was strictly off-limits. The only betrayal worse than snitching to the madam was stealing another whore's steady-trick. But this unspoken code did not extend to me. Neither whore nor madam, I hovered on the margins where these unspoken rules did not apply. If I lashed out at Gypsie, she'd rat me out fast as a fingersnap.

In silence I shoveled coals into the tinderbox and slipped outside. Cold air shot through my lungs and I shivered at the sweet sharpness of it. Window-light spilled across the hard-baked ground, guiding me back to the rubble-pit. A lone howl rose from the hills and I glanced down at the blood-soaked bundle with its sharp tang of blood. Like bait. And with the dogs chained up, too. I'd been lucky. Drawn by the smell of blood coyotes could easily have slinked though the fence and gone after the dogs. Sadie had lost a dog that way last year. It's why the hens were in a raised coop and the reason Josie no longer kept a hog. Blair could not tolerate being wakened, yet again, by pig squeals and fresh slaughter.

I pitched hot coals into the rubble-pit. The wood was brittle and dry and the flames leapt to life, casting eerie shadows across the back-lot. I lifted my eyes to the black crest of hills and the starlit vault above. So vast and inaccessible I had to look away. Fix my eyes on familiar shapes. Jackson's shack, the stables, a disused outhouse, barbed wire strung between fenceposts. I drew Lil's letter from my pocket and glanced over it in the flickering half-light.

Dont dar come up here with a baby in tow.… Times is hard nuff with wintr stil bearin down an we kin bare feed two mouths, last week we had to pay a doctr becus my mouth swelt up so bad I culd not shut my teeth so the doctr burnt it with caustic then cut a pice off I kin shut my mouth now but its vry sor… Mr MacIntyre dont no about you an thats the way I aim to keep it so if you gets Ben Cooley to help rite anothr lettr, kwit callin me momma…when yr las fool lettr arrivd askin to com here an hav yr baby, luck for me Mr Macintyre was gon to town as he is rite now whil I strugl with a lamp & my poor skoolin to rite… On'y reeson is to tell you to gits rid a that baby kwik… havin a chil was the mos fool thing I ever don so gits yorself clean fore its to late… wont nobody hire a

hurr with a baby and Blair boot you sure as Sunday she finds
out you nocked up and to far gon to fix an you don want som
trick baby spoilin yr life
   – Dora Macintyre

I crumpled the paper into a ball and flung it into the rubble pit.
The fire leapt and snapped. The edges curled then dissolved
to black. Stoking the coals I stirred and blew until the embers
glowed and the fire threw off a fierce, steady heat that made
my eyes water. Then I lifted the blood-soaked bundle from the
ground and pitched it into the flames.

Chapter 10

This afternoon I have been granted a few hours *en repos*. Faith Hamilton gives a stern nod as she presses the necessary *permis* into my hand, but I am not about to protest. Grabbing my army-issue coat, I stride away from our sorry cluster of tents before some *inspecteur* arrives and orders us to relocate our toilets. Again.

A raw wind blows from the north. I walk with hands shoved deep into my coat-pockets, knuckles rubbing Camille's most recent letter. It contains the usual list of shortages (soap, oil, vegetables), a rant about the latest decree from the Food Minister (confectioners are prohibited from selling *marrons glacés*), followed by questions about household management labeled urgent (*cela presse!*), but are not. Yet the bulk of her letter is given over to recounting her most recent visit to a *clairvoyante* in Monmartre. Still no word from her son, killed at Verdun two years ago. But I am made privy to every last table-rap nonetheless. Told every detail of every message arriving from beyond the grave. Ah, well. Better than the usual litany of complaints about her friends, which always sets me to wondering what she tells them about me.

I sink my attention into every step. Soft earth underfoot. Smell of wet branches. Mud and leafrot. Stony fields lie naked beneath a low grey sky. I try to regard it all with Louis' affectionate eye, but the stark trees and brown clumps of earth defy me, and soon my thoughts drift back to Camille. Why does she insist that I participate in this folly? Whisking me off to a seance after meeting our train and now devoting most of her letter to another? Why can't she find solace by volunteering at some refugee charity like other war widows? Of course, it was her unconventionality that drew us together in the first place. Who else would fancy that little bistro tucked among the pawn shops on Rue Ste Geneviève? A place Louis dismissed with a wordless lift of his brow (*en mauvais gout, Vera*). Fine. I would go alone. Their *bavette au poivre* was divine. Then one evening I spied another woman dining *toute seule*. We struck up a conversation. Widowed two years before, she had kept her husband's pharmacy going after his death, but found the accounts a terrible burden. So I stepped in to help. Then, when Louis' heart began to go, Camille became my only solace. Her professional advice, yes, her powders and her tinctures. But I came to rely on her to take me out of myself. She would invite me to dine with her son and his friends, and we'd chat about politics far into the night. Pierre. After he was killed I tried to return the favour. But something went wrong. My attempts at consolation were clumsy, ill-advised. Never enough. Or so I was led to believe. Ah, *ma cherie*, but you have never had a child. You do not know a mother's suffering.

I pass into the village. Toppled walls, broken windows, a pile of fire-blackened rubble. Hurrying by the church before the *curé* can ply me for a donation, I spot one of our *camionettes* farther up the road. Red cross is just visible through a scruff of hedge. This morning we received a delivery from the American Base Hospital – gauze, gloves, syringes, morphine, coal. Obscene quantities of coal. I watched them shovel pile after pile of those precious glittering chunks into our storage bins and could not stop thinking of Camille. The very sight would make any ration-weary Parisian faint.

Perhaps the driver needs help. I approach.

What I find is Tosh. Locked in an embrace with some officer. I freeze, unable to look away. Tosh is standing on tiptoe, leaning into him. Pressed up against the supply-van, they bump foreheads, softly, then pull back, gazes locked. Tosh brushes a curl of sandy hair from his brow. A show of frank tenderness that makes my heart lurch.

Catching sight of me, she bounds over and grabs my wrist.

Which startles me. This avid display of girlishness. And no hint of embarrassment.

The officer stays slouched up against the van, hands driven into his pockets. 'Afternoon, M'am.'

Tosh ushers me over.

He doffs his cap. 'Blake Tyler.'

'This is Vera.' Tosh is beaming, hair a wild tangle of curls. 'Nurse Palmer.'

'You don't say,' he drawls. 'Why, there's a Lionel Palmer down in Chippewa County. Just across the river from my folks. Any relation to you, M'am?'

I shake my head, speechless. Why is he driving the school's *camionette*? Tosh could authorise it, of course. But petrol costs even more than coal. What if our American sponsors examine the expense reports? I wave at the muddied hem of her uniform. 'Were you planning to report back like that?'

A look clouds her face. As if I'd just slapped her. But what on earth is she thinking, carrying on like this in full view of the road?

'Have you considered the risk your behaviour carries for Tosh?' I turn to face him. 'Such indiscretions could get her dismissed. Not you, of course. You would suffer no...' *retentissement*. I grope for the word in English, but can't dredge it up. 'If Sister Hamilton were here, Tosh would be barred from service.'

'Oh, let the old prig have a look!' Tosh flings back.

I ignore this outburst, keeping my gaze fixed firmly on Blake Tyler. 'If you care about her, you'll be more prudent.'

'Yes M'am,' he nods, tipping his cap. But it is rote *politesse*, not contrition. That treacly southern courtesy doesn't fool me.

I watch him swing open the door of the motor-van with robust assurance. That blithe, unthinking confidence of young American men: I had almost forgotten it.

He catches up her hand and kisses the top of her head. Lips pressed to her hair, breathing in her scent. *To mock me* comes the thought, but no. The way he stands, eyes closed, lungs filling with her scent… this has nothing to do with me. I feel something shift and crack inside. Like an old house. Timbers swelling under a too warm winter sun.

Blake leaps into the driver's seat and motors away, waving out the open window. Tosh glares at me. Face florid. Then she turns and strides down the footpath. I follow. Squelch of muddy boots joining the chitter of birds. Overhead the clouds are breaking up, wind tearing them into scraps of white that tumble on high above the fields. Tosh snaps her head round. 'What are you doing?'

'I might ask you the same question.'

She spins on her heel and keeps walking. But I catch up, casting about for a way to explain the sort of fellow Blake Tyler is. Point out how his success with that knee patient made him puff up with pride. A response that struck me as callow, but revealing, for Blake Tyler is a particular breed of American male. One who has passed through life unscathed, his innocence still dangerously intact.

'Aren't you the least bit embarrassed?' she says evenly.

'Of what?'

'Spouting all that rubbish back there.'

'Tosh, you could be barred from service for the rest of the war.'

'Well, I don't give a toss!'

She does, but arguing will do no good. I choose my words carefully. 'Consider the consequences a dishonorable discharge would carry after the war.'

'After the war?' she gives a scornful laugh.

'Yes. Think of all the people who oppose women doctors. They'll use any excuse they can to deny women surgical posts.'

She stops walking and slips a hand inside the pocket of her greatcoat. A size too big, it flaps about her legs as she tries to light a cigarette. Soft scratch of a match as the flame sparks to life. She flashes me a knowing smile. 'This from someone who spent fifteen years as a kept-woman?'

I stare at the curve of her back hunched against the wind, whiffs of smoke torn away by the breeze. I want to grab her by the shoulders and push her into the mud. I bite down on my cheek. 'I was never anybody's kept-woman.'

Tosh's brown eyes flash with a defiant gleam. 'Come now, everyone knows about your wealthy cotton merchant.'

I squeeze my fingers. Feel the bones crush together. A kept-woman. She does not even know what that means. I resume walking, recognising in her rash words my own youthful fury, the urge to provoke that used to seize me if I suspected some crucial truth was being denied. Tosh ambles along beside me, flicking ash from her cigarette.

'Louis Dumont,' I say at last, 'was part owner of a cotton factorage where I once worked. When business brought him to New Orleans, yes, he shared my bed. But it was my bed, in my house. He did not set me up in lavish quarters like some retired whore, living off the fat of a john who wants a girl all to himself. That's what a kept-woman is, Tosh. Someone who owes her body to a man the same as any prostitute. Only she gets paid in furniture and jewellery instead of cash. Call me Dumont's mistress if you like; he had a wife back in Paris. But I was never anyone's kept-woman.'

We lapse into silence, and I can feel her anger drain away like the tick, tick of an engine cooling. Tosh flicks the fag-end from her fingers. The burning ember tumbles through the air, lands in the mud and fizzles out. 'They say you inherited a mint when he died.'

'They?'

She shoots me a sly smile, lips closed. Her teeth are crooked and faintly ash-coloured and she tries not to let them show. 'Well, go on then. Did he leave you his fortune or not?'

I fix my gaze on the curve of the towpath, follow its muddy crease along the brow of a hill. Light is draining from the fields, poplar trees etched black against the sky. Anything I say will be repeated. But gossip has already sacrificed accuracy for drama. Might as well set the record straight. So I nod. Yes, I inherited his fortune. 'Do you think that renders me a kept-woman after the fact?'

Tosh runs a hand through her curls, stiff from the salty air. 'Nobody cares about such petty moralities anymore.'

'Faith Hamilton does.'

I expect a laugh, but Tosh bristles. 'Old Haversham. Always poking that long nose of hers into everybody else's business.'

We pass the searchlight depot, crossing the bridge over the canal. The road dips into a patch of trees and just above the serried black of the pines, a lone star sparkles in the coming twilight. Venus. Not a star at all. I remark on this fact. That the night's first star is a planet.

'I know,' she replies.

Our feet make wet sucking sounds in the mud. Sticky clumps cling to our boots and every step is hard work. We must hurry. It is dangerous to be on the road after dark. And forbidden. A chink, chink of spades rises from beyond the hill where German prisoners are digging a bomb-shelter for us. Shouts of *Hier! Schisse!* ring out, followed by French guards calling for a sapper. We are close.

'This morning,' says Tosh, 'I received approval to outfit five surgical équipes for frontline aid-posts and casualty clearing stations.'

I congratulate her. For weeks she has been pushing to get our trainees front-line assignments, and to be honest, I did not think it possible. We tramp on, boots sucking at the earth. Scraps of fog drift through the dips and hollows of the wood.

'I was about to dash off a letter to Father to tell him of my triumph. But...' she trails off with a sigh. 'Now that it has actually come to pass, the prospect fills me with dread.'

It is the prospect of sending Blake Tyler to a frontline unit she dislikes, but I refrain from saying so. How long has this tryst been going on? What has she risked? What more is she

129

willing to jeopardise?

'You're sending them to aid posts and field hospitals, not over the top.'

'Do you know the death rate for medical officers at the front?'

I shake my head.

'Two hundred and three per one thousand.'

'Twenty three percent,' I mutter, more to myself than her.

'My,' says Tosh, 'don't you have the cold heart of an accountant.'

'Since when is accuracy cold-hearted?'

She makes no answer. The path widens, joining the main road. A motor clatters by, then another, and in the flare of passing head-lamps I glimpse her profile: high cheekbones, small nose, the shadow at the crease of her lips.

Tosh turns to meet my gaze. Her face wears same expression that settles over her in the surgical theatre. But her eyes shine with something else, sharp and mischevious. A dare. Because Tosh took me for a different sort. But I have proved to be nothing but a literal-minded accountant who quibbles over statistics and weighs the ethical intricacies of a dead lover's fortune.

Light is draining from the fields, tents nothing but black clumps huddled under a darkening sky. We turn down the drive. Tosh gives her belt a sharp tug. 'You *knew* that girl had a bodged abortion.'

I shiver and rub my hands. I can feel her staring at me, and under the unrelenting press of her gaze all those hours spent listening to her are cast in a different light. Her reminiscences were requests. She desired some return of intimacy, for me to answer her confidences with my own.

Her slender neck stretches up from her greatcoat, throat pale as milk. She is leveling me with a look of calm appraisal. As if I am a patient for whom she feels sympathy but whose body she must still slice open and repair. I do not want to be tiresome, nor feel this heart-lurch of things untold. But how to tell it? Where to even start?

Chapter 11

There is a smell to the desert after rain. Thick and sweet as incense it rises from the earth like smoke. Every cactus-leaf and treeroot, every thorn and scrap of sky stands rain-soaked and alive, exhaling this syrup sweet. You can get drunk off this heady fragrance. Lose yourself in its dewed perfume as you stand amid the bright wet shine, breathing.

That is one way to start. A truthful way, and rather pretty. But not honest. To be honest requires different words. Brutal, nastier ones. Because my journey to the low desert did not begin with rain. It began with darkness and with tears, as I lugged two over-stuffed satchels to the stage depot, alone and unaided. Drunken catcalls burst from the hazy saloons. I did not hate the men who uttered them. Nor did I begrudge anyone a good time. But I was fed up. With the whores and the johns. With sleepless nights spent nursing Texas Lil. But most of all I was fed up with Madam Blair. *Close just cause we're a gal short? Don't be a bohunk, Jackson! You start shuttin' down over every little thing, sends the wrong message. Whores get uppity. Hire a temporary gal. Hunt down that dancer goes by the name Baby Doll. Trim up her body hair, dunk her in a rosewater bath. She'll serve til Lil perks up.*

Never mind that 'Baby Doll' is a dope-addicted crook who tries to steal from the till every chance she gets until Jackson finally gives her the toss at ten o'clock. Is that what did it? How those nasty lowlifes managed to slip in past Jackson... *go on upstairs, second door on the left. Like gang-fucking them farm girls back in the war.*

I let my bags drop to the ground as tears of frustration and helpless rage rolled down my cheeks, gathering at the corners of my lips. Taste of hot salt. I scrabbled through my pockets and found a crumpled bar napkin, but its stink of smoke and spilled liquor made my stomach turn so I flung it to the ground and sniffed the snot back up. For two whole days I would be rid of this place. My breathing began to slow. The night was still, but for the soft thud of explosives. Stopes and cross-cuts ran beneath the streets, sending faint tremors through the planked sidewalk. Overhead a moonless sky swam with stars. Wiping my cheeks on my sleeve, I shouldered my bags and trudged on.

Daybreak found me packed into a Concord stage as it rumbled over parched gullies and rocky draws, putting mile upon mile between me and Star Mansion. But my thoughts would not snap free. They kept swerving back to what lay behind that door after Jackson had broken it down. Sticky white puddles on the coverlet. Bearded faces. Dropped trousers. A man holding his own wormy prick in his hand. Pleas breaking from her throat like a failed prayer. *One at a time, boys, please, one at a time...* hairy backside pumping up and down on the bed, then it rolled away to reveal Evie spread-eagled on the bed. Eye swollen, stockings torn. Spunk glistened on her thigh. Viscous thread of it strung across her cheek. Evie, not Lil. Evie. Evie was the one who lay there raving in a raw high voice, 'Gimme my brass checks! Make 'em pay, Jackson. Make 'em pay!'

What had possessed me to slide past Jackson's outstretched arm into the room? And why was my uppermost feeling, upon seeing Evie, relief? Relief that it was not Texas Lil splayed on those sticky sheets, because in all the confusion I'd forgotten Lil was recovering in my bedroom, hers having been given over for 'general use' since the houseboys couldn't change bedlinens fast enough. What the hell was Blair thinking? If the houseboys couldn't keep pace, neither could the whores. Temporary gal! Why did Sadie let Star Mansion become the sort of 'hook-shop' she always derided?

The stagecoach descended. The sun climbed. Buffalo robes

133

were stowed beneath seats. Ivory-handled fans emerged to flutter impotently before flushed faces. Forehead pressed to a dust-caked window, I sat and sweated and tried to find solace in something. Anything. Texas Lil. She was better. Able to sit up, eat solid food. Her fever was gone. No sign of infection. Josie had praised me. My nightly ministrations, she'd said, had saved Lil's life. But for what?

In Fairbank I treated myself to a dozen oysters, brought up fresh from Guaymas on the morning train. Each cool briny burst tasted of the sea and just when I'd managed to scrub it all from my mind, a familiar face bobbed through the crowd. My gaze skittered away, but too late.

'You the gal works the till at Blair's place.'

I dropped an oyster shell onto the heap by the porch and watched it land with a sharp slap.

'Ain't ya?'

I met his eye. 'No.'

He stood there, gaping.

'You must be thinking of someone else.'

In Tucson Will Keane was nowhere in sight. I watched my fellow travellers collect their bundles and disperse as the minutes ticked by. Women shuffled past with rolled carpets, babies, caged hens, sacks of grain. Men jostled by carrying dusty rucksacks or saddles heaved up on shoulders. So much for Gypsie's great insight into the hearts of men. Will Keane did not even hold me in high enough regard to arrive at the depot on time.

A cattleman in spurred boots rounded the corner and waved. I looked away, making my displeasure clear. Yet on he trotted, trying to catch my eye. Only when he bent to collect my bags did I realise it was Will Keane.

'Sorry to keep you waiting, Miss Palmer. I've had the devil of a time engaging a trap.'

'Trap' was a generous description. The vehicle that awaited us was a pig-cart hitched to a pair of sway-backed mules. Will tossed my luggage into the back and away we went, lumbering down the town's main thoroughfare at a pace no faster than a walk. Mud-brick houses stood flush against the street, windows like tiny unblinking eyes sunk into the folds of a chubby face. Every building was brown and slumped, except for a dry goods store whose walls were painted to resemble brick. Creosote twisted up through cracked pavement, rooftops lay smothered in thorny tangles of mesquite. Will and our driver chatted away in Spanish, which surprised me as much as his appearance. Grease-smeared trousers, a sun-browned face, shirt-tails flapping... he looked as shabby and untended as the town itself.

In the lobby of our hotel, sullen-faced men sat playing cards. Their attention swayed towards me, then drifted back to their game. Not one of them tipped his hat. An ill-mannered lapse? Or did they take me for the sort who did not merit such courtesy? The land-lady was busy serving a man who reeked of pig-slop, so we stood and waited our turn, watching her sort lazily through decks of cards, leaf tobacco, and nickel cigars until she chanced upon what the pig-farmer wanted. And all the while I could feel those bearded faces louring at me from the far corner.

Minutes later we were led down a dim corridor that smelled of mice and soggy tobacco plugs. The land-lady opened the door to a dark closet of a room, cobwebs strung between the legs of a saggy bed. I said nothing, certain Will would politely request more suitable quarters. But to my shock, he pressed a coin into her unwashed palm and she clumped away.

'I'll collect you at half past six,' he said brightly.

I was speechless. What had become of the gallant southern gentleman?

'People dine early here.'

'I do not intend to spend another moment in this filthy hotel, much less eat a meal here.'

Will hung his head like a boy who has tried hard to please, only to be met with scorn. 'And I had so wanted you to like it here,' he sighed.

'Well, you have an odd way of trying to secure my affection.' I ran a finger across the dusty night-table.

His face softened, grey eyes dimming in sympathy. But I did not want sympathy. I wanted him to know the exact measure of my suffering. To know what it had cost me to force that rolled towel over Lil's mouth while she'd bucked and sweated and bled. To hear the low animal howl that broke from her throat when she slammed a fist into the wall of the watercloset during her first bowel movement after the curretting. Let him sit beside Evie and breathe the hot stink of semen, chamber pots, spilled whisky, and horse-shit some john tracked in on his boots, while Jackson clears the house and Evie shakes so bad that her teeth clack against the spoon, spilling laudanum until you grip her jaw and press her head to your chest and then pour it down. And after: after. Once the house had been cleared. Except it hadn't. Because a pair of gap-toothed men were lying in wait, ready to set upon Texas Lil. But they don't. Nothing bad happens. Because you stop them. You do. You stop them.

'Did you see those men downstairs?' I said at last. 'Staring at me bold as brass, they were. Not to mention keeping their hats on!'

'What has become of the fearless young lady who regards etiquette as nothing but a collection of old-fashioned rituals?'

'She must have fallen by the wayside, as I dragged those,' I waved at my luggage, now flecked with straw from the pig-cart, 'to the depot *by myself*, because you insisted we travel separately. But you know what? That stupid lie about a lawyer from Connecticut is not drawing the wool over anyone's eyes. Least of all Sadie Blair.'

'Oh, to hell with Sadie Blair.'

'Yes. Well. We agree there at least.' And with that, I burst into tears. Eyes shut against the water-marked walls and the smeary window and the ceaseless sunshine pouring in through the plate-glass, I wept. Not quietly. Not daintily. But with great air-gulping sobs that no amount of shushing could halt. Will took me in his arms and stroked my back, but this only made me cry harder. Then, slowly, the fact of his nearness registered. I became aware of his shirt against my damp cheek, its smell of dust and cracked leather tinged with a mild soapy sweetness. My crying eased. I had forgot the gentle heat of another's touch, and for a long moment I gave myself over to its supple tug, until more conventional responses clicked into place and I stepped away. Will pressed a handkerchief into my hand, clasping my fingers until my breathing slowed. Then he let go.

From the street came a low-voiced murmur and a clomp, clomp of boots. Will stood in the middle of the small, dusty room stroking his chin. 'Friend of mine owns a ranch east of town,' he said at last. 'If we set out first thing, we could stay there.'

I shook my head, chest heaving with the clumsy aftershocks of grief.

'Miss Palmer, I'm afraid I shall have to ask you to tolerate this room for one night. After the territorial capital moved up to Prescott, most of the hotels here closed. This is the only respectable one left. Trust me. But if we ride out at dawn—'

'It won't work.'

A baffled expression crossed his face.

'I don't know how to ride a horse.'

We lapsed into silence. A hollow thump sounded form the hall, followed by the shrill laugh of a woman. I looked for a chair, found none, and sat down on the sagging mattress. 'I don't belong out here.'

'Don't say that.'

'It's true. I ought never to have come west.'

'Miss Palmer, I am glad you did.' A wry smile played at his lips. 'Still, you might have warned me about the state of your equestrian skills before taking the reins to my cart-team.'

A hazy shaft of light streamed through the plate-glass, dust motes swirling. I still held his handkerchief. I could feel my thumb rubbing the raised thread of his initials.

'You must learn to ride, Miss Palmer. If you are to live in the territory, you must know how to handle a horse.'

'Fine.' I lifted my eyes. 'When do we start?'

At first light I stood in a dusty corral watching a hollow-cheeked man tack up a grey mare. Al Montgomery took great pride in his corral, describing how he'd filled the chinks and secured the fence-posts in such hard ground. His shirt bore the sooty streaks of a blacksmith and as he walked his leather chaps flapped about his legs like sails luffing in the wind. 'Pandora's a steady mount,' he said, flipping up a stirrup to tighten the girthstrap. 'Older. Sure-footed. Docile, but she'll respond.'

I nodded, hands smoothing the skirt of my new dress. The previous evening Will had arrived at my door carrying a stack of boxes, each tied with a yellow ribbon. Inside were a lady's riding habit, leather gloves, a pair of wood-heeled boots and a wide-brimmed hat. He'd waited in the corridor while I tried everything on so we could return items that did not fit before the shop closed. But it was all just right, and I thought again of how he'd loosened my corset that day at the claimsite.

I regarded the mare warily. Her eyes were solemn and shy, and the tilt of her head lent her a demure, ingenuous look.

'Don't be nervous,' Will smiled.

'I'm too tired to be anything.' I paused to gather my courage then drew a deep breath and did as he'd instructed. Grabbing a hunk of the horse's mane, I hooked my left foot into the stirrup and swung up into the saddle.

Will was a patient and able teacher. He corrected mistakes gently, shouted encouragement, described what the horse felt. It was not difficult, and soon we were riding east on a dirt track, hats tugged low against the sun. After a time the road narrowed into a thin, whip-like trail and dipped down into a dry creek-bed. Saguaros grew in thick profusion along the bluffs, and I marvelled at their spongy-looking arms twisting up, up into the air.

The heat of the day began to build, and every so often Will would remind me to drink from a dented canteen tied to the pommel of my saddle. 'Smelling salts?' he'd declare in a high, falsetto trill. 'I've never fainted in my life!' Then we'd laugh and fall silent again. His attentions were a comfort. Someone cared whether I drank enough water.

We rode on, silent but for the soft clop of hooves and the leathery creak of our saddles. A pack-mule followed with our bags and Will kept circling back to urge the animal on. Lizards scampered over rocks, butterflies darted between wildflowers, and Pandora's gait lulled me into a hazy repose. Things were looking up. The night before, over a greasy supper at our hotel, I'd shared my doubts over the claim. He'd listened attentively, then dispelled every one. Apparently, Cox had staked a modest claim on a ledge that ran close to the surface. Then he had waited. Or, more accurately, he'd advised Henry to wait, explaining that the site would become more valuable once the big outfits hit water. 'This,' Will told me, 'is exactly what has happened.'

It was an impressive bit of gamesmanship, really. Seeing that the water table in the district was unusually high and realising that mining engineers had failed to account for this, Tom Cox had noted his opponent's weakness – mining companies' preference for numbers over geological observation – then played it for all it was worth. His wager was now about to pay off, and according to Will, I was to be the lucky winner.

Pandora plodded on, picking her way across a boulder-strewn creek-bed until we reached a place where dense tangles of mesquite choked the wash. Will dismounted and led his horse around. I was about to do the same when Pandora dropped her head and bucked her forelegs over, while I held fast to the saddle and drove my heels down hard until she landed with a soft thud on the other side, her hind-legs scrambling.

'You're ready for corrida,' Will cried, and I felt a rush of satisfaction. We rode on. The wash widened, mesquite trees thinned, and the sun climbed high into the cloudless blue. Will swung back, drawing his horse alongside mine. 'You are a pleasant riding partner, Miss Palmer.'

'Provided I do not fall from my horse in a faint.'

He laughed his full bright rumble of a laugh, then fell quiet. Will's jacket was lashed to the cantle of his saddle, and the sleeves of his work-shirt were rolled above the elbow, exposing his forearms to the sun. All morning he'd brimmed with exuberant ease. It was the same spirited serenity I'd witnessed during our trip to the claimsite. Everything he did thrummed with a keen sense of enjoyment, an untroubled lightness at being cut loose from his daily routine.

'I like your silence,' he said at last.

'You dislike conversation?'

'Idle chatter is what I abhor. One rides through open country to escape all that, don't you think?'

Yes, escape. Sadie Blair was not just an odd bird. When all went according to plan, she was regular as clockwork. But the slightest bump in the road threw her into a precarious panic, causing her to make dumb decisions. The whores suffered most. They would continue to bear the brunt of her careless choices and stinging whims. Disaster followed in this woman's wake. I saw that now. But what I failed to see was that such disasters could harm me. That, in fact, one already had.

Chapter 12

He had been a ranch-hand for Rafael Cruillo, he said, spreading an oil-cloth on the ground in the shade of a Cottonwood grove. Beyond the leafy treetops rocky slopes wavered in the midday glare. Will gestured for me to sit while he drew biscuits, cheese, hardtack, and tinned plums from our saddlebags.

Prying a lid with his screw-knife, Will spoke of the day he arrived at the Cruillo ranch. Smooth hands, barbered hair. No experience working stock. He'd marched right up to the main house and asked for the *haciendado*. Never thinking to present himself down at the stables. To the *gerente*. Will gave a rueful smile as he set the open tin on the ground between us.

Of course, Rafael had taken one look at his shiny, unspurred boots and laughed. What use did he have for a wet-behind-the-ears Easterner? City boy with no notion how to brand a calf or geld a horse. 'What I need, young man, is someone to get these government cabróns off my back. You Americanos sign a paper with the Spanish then tell me, no, this is not your land, Señor Cruillo. You must have this document. But before we can give it, you need this one, and this one, and another. Papelos! Documentos! We do not have enough trees in all of Sonora for this many papers.' So Will confessed to being a lawyer. One well acquainted with the territory's Surveyor General, Royal Johnson, for they had both studied law at Richmond.

Three weeks later Will presented Rafael with a title deed. In exchange he asked to be hired on as a cowhand. The *haciendado* was taken aback. What does a young man with an education want with ranch-work? Surely there was a job for him down at the Land Office. Or up in Prescott with the Territorial Governor? But Will was sick to death of riffling through books and papers all day. Of looking up precedents, slinging words in a courtroom, arguing cases before corrupt judges. The law was a game. Like chess or cards. He wanted real work. Work that made you collapse into bed at the end of the day with enough strength to pump blood and breathe and nothing more. Work that left no room for thought.

Rafael pressed him once more, but Will was adamant. So, shaking his head, Rafael had walked him down to the bunkhouse.

'First day,' Will went on, 'they made me doctor a calf. Juan roped it and pointed at a ragged hole on its left flank. It was packed tight with screw-worms. So I wrestled the calf to the ground, then poured this thick black gruel Juan had given me into the sore. The calf was squirming and kicking and squalling for its mother, but I somehow kept clear of its hooves and got the bottle corked back up and slid into my pocket without spilling any. But Juan was still hollering at me and poking the air with his finger. Well, I wasn't happy about it, but I didn't flinch. Just drew off a glove and stuck my finger in. The calf started bawling and by now the mother cow was bellowing, too. But I could feel more maggots wriggling away down at the very bottom. Then gobs of bloody maggots came oozing out, like ointment from a tube... that's when I lost it. All over the calf, my gloves. The other vaqueros laughed and one of the Texas boys said, 'Betcha he don't last a week.' But I kept twisting my finger in and out of that hole til it was clear. Then I stuffed it full of manure and let the calf go.' He put the canteen to his lips and took a long pull of water. 'Two seasons later that snickering Texan was gone and I was the corre in his place. He could never keep the brands straight.'

Will sat propped up on one elbow, legs kicked out, hat back. I had grown accustomed to his scruffy work-shirts and battered boots, the ever-present rifle. But this raw talk was something new. I glanced up from my plate and saw the way his eyes flicked back and forth beneath the brim of his hat. He was watching for my reaction.

'You'll have to do better than that,' I said, 'if you're trying to spoil my appetite and have the rest to yourself.' Then I fished a plum from the tin and popped it in my mouth.

A laugh burst from him, mingling with the silvery murmur of the leaves and the sedgegrass and as I chewed and swallowed that plum, a feeling washed over me like the cool pull of water.

'Why the manure?' I asked.

'Suffocate any maggots that might be left.'

The mule snorted and we glanced over. Its white-tipped ears flicked at the flies, thin tail snapping back and forth. The horses stood tethered to a nearby tree, ears pricked forward.

'Last night,' he began, 'you told me you never held out much hope for the mining claim. Which set me to wondering.' His finger flipped idly at the catch on his rifle. 'Why travel so far for a hopeless enterprise?'

I stared at the rocky bluffs scabbed with cactus and mesquite scrub, at the jags of granite cutting up into the sheer blue sky. How to explain the nameless confinement I'd felt? The way grief had begun to twist and harden me. Days passing in a dull grey haze, until that morning when I came across the mining claim. The moment my eyes lit on the words *Arizona Territory* something jolted loose. An impulse held me in its grip. The need to do something rash. To be bold, for once in my life, and just *go*.

I was about to speak when Will leapt to his feet, sighted the rifle, and fired. The horses balked and reared. Will swore and fired again. The mule brayed, a nasally screech that ricocheted off the canyon walls and I watched Will scramble up the runnelled soil, dust churning. Moments later he strode back down, holding a long skinny rabbit by the ears. Blood ran down his chaps, dribbling onto his boots. The rabbit's legs twitched and twitched again.

We rode on through the pulsing glare. Birds dipped. Shadows

shrank. Blood oozed from my saddlebag, smearing Pandora's flanks. Whiff of it in every breath until it dried in stiff black trails on her hide. A narrow track branched off the wash, carrying us to where the flatlands gave way to gently sloping peaks and there, nestled in the crook of the foothills, was the Cruillo Ranch. Tin-roofed shacks, stables, fenced corrals, paddocks, and a fair-sized hacienda lay tucked into a cleft between the hills.

Will called out in Spanish as we wound between the out-buildings. Two sheep-dogs circled and leapt, nipping at the horses' heels until a man with a bridle slung over his shoulder whistled them off. This was Esteban. Dark eyes shone beneath the brim of his hat as he greeted us in Spanish and grabbed our mule by the bit. Will swung down from his horse and the two men embraced, falling into an animated discussion during which Will pointed at Esteban's belted knife. Moments later the rabbit was lifted from my saddlebag and carried off.

I dismounted, legs juddery.

'You look like a drunkard,' Will teased.

'My legs feel drunk.'

'Wait until tomorrow.'

We led the animals into the paddock, where there was a constant hum of flies and the air was hazy with dust and bits of straw. Once the animals were watered and fed, Will slung my bag over his shoulder and we trudged up the path to the main house. As we knocked muck off our boots, Will explained that Rafael was in Sierra Bonita inspecting some short-horn steer. His wife Lupita spent winters in town so the children could attend school, and Rosalita, the cook, was off visiting her sister. 'Which means,' said Will, slipping a key into the lock, 'you'll have to eat my grub tonight.'

The heavy door swung open and we stepped into a cool dark room. The walls, plastered and white-washed, were bare but for a red-and-black patterned rug that hung above the fireplace. We passed through one low-ceilinged room after the next until we reached a small *récamara* with a narrow bed, rag-doll propped against the headboard. On the night-table sat a spirit lamp and box of matches. Will set my bags down and disappeared outside. I heard the squeal of a pump, followed by a clang of dipper and pail. Upon return he handed me a tumbler of water and ordered me to drain every drop. Then he bid me 'buena siesta' and promised to collect me in a few hours.

Left alone in the big empty house, I drifted back through the spare quiet rooms. No brass-fittings. No glossy patinas. No ormolu, or flounces, or gee-gaws. I ran a hand down the rough-hewn wood furniture, stood by the piano and plinked at the keys. Pressed my bare feet hard against the cool hard tile. The skin on my face felt tight with dried sweat, so I wandered back through the house to a door that opened out onto a square enclosure which was overhung by a bright patch of sky. In the corner was a well-pump. I drank straight from the dipper, running wet handfuls over my face, neck, and hair.

Inside, I yanked off my riding dress and self-lacing corset. Opening my satchel the smell of Star Mansion wafted out, but in the cool uncluttered silence of this room, it did not distress me. A light buoyant feeling came over me as I lay down on the narrow bed and thought back through the day. How it felt to sit astride a horse and ride like a man. The thrill that would quake through me sometimes as we crossed those vast uncharted miles. A delicious shiver I'd not felt since my first day in the territory. And it occurred to me that I had come west in the hope of something much more than a mining claim.

Hours later, Will led me down a winding path to the casita. Built on the spar of a steep-sided mesa, it overlooked a ravine where mesquite grew in choked black tangles along a dry wash. Brittle-brush and creosote fleeced the opposite hillside in silvery green, rimrock and limestone bluffs rising up against a limitless blue.

The casita had two rooms – kitchen and bedroom – but no connecting door. To move between rooms you had to step outside onto a covered ramada. The Cruillos had lived here while the main house was being built. Afterwards, the place had been given over to various uses – blacksmith shop, feed storage – until Will set out to make it habitable again.

'I was sick of that bunkhouse,' he explained. 'The snoring and the card-playing, and the Texans with their filthy talk. The extra hands Rafael hired on for calving season were always coming to blows. I asked if we year-rounders could bunk here. Juan, Tio the Indian, Miguel... but Rafael balked. Told me I was wasting my life, castrating steer and branding calves. He lit into me about the territory needing honest lawyers. Said if my father were alive he'd be appalled at the life I was living. Which was true. So he agreed to let me bunk here, but I had to promise to give up ranch-work the following season.' Will shook his head and grinned. 'The old fox.'

'Of course, I kicked up a fuss when the time came. Told Rafael I'd no license to practice in Arizona, no place to live while obtaining one. But he just laughed and told me to stay here. 'Mend the walls,' he'd joked, 'repair the roof.' So I did. Then, after learning to set explosives from a copper miner, I blasted out a well. After that I got carried away. Installed plate-glass windows, a bit of plumbing.'

I cast an eye over the ramada. Old traps, chains, coiled ropes, charred firetools. Spools of baling wire and bits of metal lay scattered across the low adobe wall, above which stretched an empty clothesline. In the far corner a small table was set with a red-checked cloth, tumblers, earthenware plates, and cutlery. I spied an open bottle of wine and poured myself a glass. It was the sort of thing I would never do in town. But out here, self-reliance seemed to be the order of the day. Fires had to be tended, water hauled, wood gathered, and to sit primly by, waiting to be served, felt wrong.

Taking a seat in one of the canvas-backed chairs, I watched

Will tend a fire that burned in a stone-lined pit. Beside it lay a pile of tangled black roots, still clumped with dirt. He tossed one onto the flames, then poked at it with an iron rod. He wore thick leather gloves. No hat. And his damp-combed hair had already begun to spring into untidy waves. Wiping a sooty hand on his trousers, he poured himself a glass of wine and sipped. His face puckered. 'Ugh. Why did you say nothing?'

'I assumed you knew.'

He flung the wine from his glass. 'How can you drink that?'

I shrugged and took another sip. It was a bit sour, but to sip tart wine while looking out over rocky buttes at sundown was a luxury. No Josie hollering at the whores. No Sadie Blair carping at Evie to shake her drag-ass upstairs and take a bath. Nothing but the snap of the fire, mingled with distant shouts and clangs floating up from the stables. Occasional bark of a dog.

Will emerged from the kitchen with a plate covered in blood-stained flour-sacking. Flies hovered, as he speared hunks of meat onto a rod which he then hung over the fire balanced between two forked sticks. Flames sizzled and leapt. Head bent against the smoke, Will turned the makeshift spit with one hand and poked a rod into the coals with the other. I had never seen a man cook before, but it made sense he would do it this way. Open flames, grease popping, eyes teary from smoke. But in the end, although the beans stuck to the pan and that rabbit was a bit tough, that meal was one of the best I have ever eaten. Or at least the most enjoyable.

As we dined, we talked. Will spoke of growing up during the war. Of having to hawk his mother's pies to Union troops to make ends meet after his father died of typhoid. How they'd buried him on a bluff high above the river with a view of Belle Isle prison, where you looked down onto the barrel staves marking graves of Union dead. He spoke of fleeing by his mother's side as fire raged through the city. Sky bright as day from the flames, as they passed soldiers in tattered grey uniforms dying by the road.

We talked of the Territory. How he'd come west to escape post-war corruption in the South, only to find corruption of a different sort out here. He bemoaned Arizona's lack of community, the transience of most settlers. People came here to make money, then spent their fortunes elsewhere. What the territory needed, he said, was for people to stay. And the mines, he shook his head, most of the profits went to shareholders back East.

A comfortable silence settled over us as we sat before our scraped-clean plates. The hills had gone a bruised, ashy grey and Will rose to light the lanterns. After clearing the dishes, he returned with two steaming mugs of coffee and a heavy wool blanket that he draped over my shoulders. It smelled of straw and wet horses and I welcomed its rough nap against my skin.

Will cupped the flame of a match and lit a cigarito. Then he sat down, legs out-stretched, boots crossed at the ankles. His mouth curved up slightly at the corners.

'Why are you looking at me that way?'

'What way?'

'As if you are laughing inwardly at some silly thing I have said or done. Like when I asked about those flat-breads.'

'Tortillas.' Smoke trailed from his lips as he gazed out across the darkening ravine. Shadows crept up the ridgeline like tidal waters on the hull of a ship. 'It pleases me to see you sitting here, on this porch, where I have passed many enjoyable evenings on my own.'

'To see me wrapped in an old saddle blanket with my hair tangled in knots?'

He nodded. 'Like Pocohantas.'

A warm lethargy settled over me and I said nothing. Sweet smelling smoke drifted over the ramada mingling with the cool air tumbling down off the mountains. Minutes passed. Full, abundant minutes in which we sipped hot coffee beneath the lanterns. Bats began to feed, dark shapes that jerked and wheeled through the twilight.

'Until today,' I said. 'I never thought the desert beautiful.'

'Where we live it isn't. Nothing but dust and scrub now that all the trees have been cut down to feed the ore crushers. But if you ride out toward the cienega, it gets nice again.'

'I hate it there.' I had not meant to give voice to my feelings, nor did I realise how intense my dislike for the place actually was. But hearing myself speak the words, I knew them to be true. Before today I had assumed the entire territory was rough and dirty, its settlers dissolute and mean. Some were. But Will wasn't. Nor were the Cruillos, I sensed. And the beauty of the low desert was a revelation to me. Wispy green Palo Verde trees, the emerald shimmer of Cottonwoods strung along a creekbed, sweet scent of creosote unleashed by the heat of the sun. All of it threw a harsh, unsparing light on that wretched boomtown. Life in the Territory could be lived against the backdrop of these hills. Inside the cool, uncluttered rooms of the Cruillo hacienda. All of which made the prospect of our return intolerable.

Will rose and strode out to the stone-lined firepit. Tossing the last twisted black roots onto the smoking embers, he stoked the flames back to life. On the ground sat a tinderbox. He would soon load hot coals inside and use them to light the fires they'd already laid in our bedrooms. A voice inside me cried out against this inevitability. Against the onset of night.

'Can't say I like the place much either.' Will slapped the fire-iron against the sole of his boot.

'Then why live there?'

He shrugged. 'Work.'

I watched his booted toe dig into the ground and flip a stray coal into the fire. His heavy-weave trousers were streaked with ash.

'We must leave at dawn,' he announced.

We had only just arrived and already he was planning our departure. But of course, he must. We were not here to ride horses, or eat meals cooked on an open fire. We were here to pay a fee on an outstanding patent application, then return to a mean-spirited town where I would resume keeping accounts for a brothel.

'Is something wrong, Miss Palmer?'

'I don't want to go back.'

'Nor do I, to be honest. But we both have obligations there, duties to perform.'

'Do not lecture me. Not tonight.'

He tugged at his beard. Deciding, perhaps, that no response was better than the wrong one. Then he sat down on the low adobe wall, elbows on his knees, chin in his hands. A look came over his face, the same one I had glimpsed the night before in that grubby hotel room.

'When you speak to me like that,' I explained, 'it is my lawyer talking to me, and I should much prefer to spend the rest of the evening in the company of the man who has cooked a fine supper on an open fire. The one who taught me to ride a horse and fed me those round flat-breads—what are they called again?'

'Tortillas.'

'Yes, tortillas and beans and sour wine. Do not say another word until he has returned and my stuffy old lawyer is gone.'

'Stuffy?'

'And tedious.'

He laughed. Throwing back his head he gave himself over to the ardent, full-throated rumble that shook his shoulders and lit his face. He sat toying with the stub of his cigarito. 'Most ladies would not take so kindly to being served a supper of burned tortillas and bad wine.'

'Who wants to be a lady? Whenever anyone talks of what a 'lady' does, or ought to do, it is always the most dull and dreary thing imaginable. Being a lady strikes me as a dreadful fate.'

For a long moment the only sound was the rattle of the lanterns in the wind, and when at last he spoke, his voice was almost a whisper. 'My mother always said that manners were the index of one's soul.'

'Do you believe that?'

'I believe we have a duty to treat others with respect and care, and quite often manners are those small courtesies we perform in order to show that respect to strangers. They form an essential part of civilised life, although as your late husband would doubtless point out, manners will vary from one corner of the world to another. That fact does not render these civilities unimportant, nor does it mean they are superficial niceties.'

'I never said they were. Nor would Henry have. The way I interact with my fellow travellers in a stagecoach is of the utmost importance. It is incumbent upon me to share a buffalo robe and not hoard it all to myself. But if I choose to go by 'Miss Palmer' or decide to wear colourful dresses after my husband's death, well, that is my own affair. Such matters affect no one but me.'

'I can think of quite a few people who would be horrified at such behaviour. Aren't you obliged to avoid inflicting paroxysms of anxiety on them? What if the shock of learning you were a widow were to prove fatal?'

I suspected him of being flippant and refused to be drawn. 'It's the difference between sharing a buffalo robe, which is genuine act of kindness, and acting a certain way only to soothe the sensibilities of my neighbours. Surely you can see that.'

Touching his fingertips together Will pressed the tops of his steepled hands to his lips and drew a breath. 'Miss Palmer, I have a confession to make.' His face had gone very grave. 'I did not ask you to travel separately because of the mining claim, or your reputation, or whatever pretext I fed you. I did not have sudden business in Tucson.'

The lanterns swayed in the wind, light trembling like water.

'I departed in haste, because I could not bear that circus of an execution. When I saw people erecting bleachers in the empty lot across the courthouse...' His face altered, voice growing more strident. 'It is bad enough for saloon-keepers to offer drink specials and the likes of Sadie Blair to turn a profit from the taking of men's lives. But when upstanding citizens erect bleachers and sell tickets...' he threw his hands in the air. 'I could not bear it. Miss Palmer, please accept my apology. I forced you to travel here without escort for my own selfish reasons.'

'Do you think those men ought not to have been put to death?'

He shook his head. 'Justice has been served. What I despise is people making a circus of it. As if putting a man to death were no different from a cock-fight or a horse race. Another chance to sell tickets and run whisky specials.'

The sordid events of that day came streaming back: the mayhem in the streets, a constant pop-pop-pop of celebratory gunfire, shouts of the crib whores, dogs bawling. A short man with thick lips, husband and father to two of the Massacre's victims, blubbering in Sadie's barroom. Evie's voice like cracked glass ricocheting through me... *one at a time, boys, please one at a time.*

'Consigning men to the gallows,' Will went on, 'should inspire something more than a rush to make a profit.'

'Such as?'

'A sober consideration of our laws. What we mean by 'justice.' When we declare one of our own guilty, we ought to ponder the limits we impose on ourselves and what we extract from those who breach them.' His voice had a strident, combative edge. 'Don't you see? Our Republic, to be worthy of that name, must be about something more than profit. And do you know who's to blame? Yankee industrialists. The North won the war and now we are all being trampled over by greedy profiteers. The South was fighting to save an agrarian way of life. We were defending our farms, trying to keep democracy from being pressed into the service of industry.' He drew breath then added, darkly, 'It was not about slavery.'

'I wonder if Josie would agree.'

'Who?'

'Blair's cook. Her mother was a slave.'

He slashed a hand through the air and turned away. It was hard to believe that a minute ago, his eyes had shone with laughter. The look on his face was still impassioned, but it was a dark, shadowy passion that set me on edge. How had an apology become a political distribe? A cold wind came slicing down off the mountains and set the lanterns rattling. It was a hollow, melancholy sound. I tucked the saddle blanket under my thighs and shivered.

Will clapped his hands together and cast about the ramada as if he'd lost something. Then he shoveled coals into a tinderbox, set it down, and took up two pails. 'Go on.' He waved at the path leading back to the hacienda. 'Or you won't beat the rain.'

But I was in no mood to comply. His sudden rancour had left a bitter aftertaste. Why spoil a lovely evening with such talk? I stared at the pails in his hands then out across the ravine. Night had fallen. No moon, no stars. Nothing but gritty wind and a gathering storm. How did he expect to haul water alone through the pitch dark? The genteel southerner was back, opting for gallantry over common sense. He'd gone from coolly rational lawyer to quarrelsome child to polite gentleman all in the space of a minute. I unhooked a lantern from the ridgepole and struck out towards the well. Will protested, but I kept on walking. The wind raged around us. Loose hair beat about my face in a swirling stinging mess, and I cursed myself for not tying it back. I held the lantern steady, shielding it from the wind with my body as Will worked the pump hard.

Buckets full we started back, one arm raised to protect my eyes from the kicked up dust. Then came a watery roar rolling over us from behind. We were soaked through in seconds. Water dripped from my hand into the lantern, flame guttering. My boots caught on rocks and roots, but I did not fall and just as the lantern went out we staggerd up the steps and set everything down – half-empty pails, the drenched lantern. Then Will led me inside. I stood by the grate shivering as he fumbled with tinderbox and tongs until he'd coaxed a fire to life. Then he leapt to his feet, tore open a drawer, and tossed dry clothes on the bed. He shouted something but his words were lost amid the deafening clatter of rain on the tin roof. Then he yanked the door open and left.

I trembled. Water ran from my clothes, puddling the floor. Fingers stiff with cold, I fumbled with buttons and ties until finally my dress fell to a sopping wet pile at my feet. Then I tugged off boots, stockings, underskirt, drawers – blundering at buttons and clasps until the last piece of cambric peeled away and I stood naked by the fire. My hair shed drops of rainwater, icy rivulets that kept trickling down my arms, waist, and back. The fire snapped and leapt. I closed my eyes and let my skin feed on the dim heat thrown off from the fire.

The door slammed against the wall. Blown open by the wind. I shivered, but did not stir. Unable to move away from the fire. But my hair kept shedding rainwater, icy droplets streaming down over my hips, torso, and thighs. Wind blasted into the room. My skin bristled. A convulsive shiver made me open my eyes. Will stood on the threshold. Towel in hand. Neither of us moved.

Rain drummed hard and fast against the tin roof drowning out every other sound. Hiss of rain that spattered down the chimney into the fire. The loud wet slap of water from the drain-pipe. Rattle of wind at the door. We heard none of it. I stepped forward to close the door. Took up his wrist and drew him in. Towel still clasped in his hand. I pressed my palm over his knuckles, fingers slotted between his, and guided the towel over my skin, brushing away the water. But my hair kept shedding more. Tiny streams of rainwater ran cold and clear down my torso, trickling over my arms, my hips. Dropping to one knee he swept the towel over my legs, my thighs. The fire drenched us with heat as the towel swept over me in long lazy loops, gentle brush of a knuckle, a bare thumb, then his palms full against the small of my back and the soft bristle of his beard on my thigh.

Moments later he caught me up in his arms and set me down on the bed. A pause as he wrenched the boots from his feet, flicker of uncertainty in his eyes until my hands slid beneath his shirt, sopping wet and smeared with soot, and he felt my fingers winding round to grip his back. Pulling him down and under.

Chapter 13

At first these eruptions of memory distressed me, but now I welcome them. At night, wakened by explosions or the *cloche d'alerte*, the task of giving them shape absorbs me. Broken sleep I tell myself. Broken sleep is to blame. No dark black line to mark one day off from the next. Night and day, past and present... they have all become one big tangle that I try to unknot. Straighten into a strand of words, until we reach a moment impossible to fix. When putting it into words would deaden it. Like pinning butterflies.

Much happened in those hours to come, but what can be said of them? What can be said of a man's body breaking like a wave over the naked torso of a woman, pausing to let the stillness breathe and then begin again? And afterwards? In the bright light of day? Upon waking to the boistrous clamour of birdsong and finding her still asleep beside him, does he lie still and savour the memory of what passed between them? The pale slope of her stomach gleaming in the firelight, skin spangled with rain... no. No, he does not.

Feeling the mantled heat of her body brush his skin, he rolls away. Lies on his back and stares up at the rafters. Which, to his relief, appear to be dry. His thoughts turn to their dilemma: the Agua Caliente swollen with water from last night's rain. Washes flooded. Snowfall in the mountains would prevent Rafael from crossing the pass. The ranch was cut off from town until the water dropped.

Three days, Will guessed, assuming no more rainfall. Of course, they could risk a different route. Ride south until the run-off thinned to tiny streams branching out across the cactus flats, then loop back and follow the rail-line into town. He'd done it once before, on a strong horse he had ridden hard many times. But who knew how those old Buckskins of

Montgomery's would perform. And what if the silty muck of the flatlands forced them to turn back? A full day would have been spent tiring the horses, to no avail. No. They would have to be patient. Practice what Rafael called 'the art of mañana.' The art of knowing when to sit tight and wait. For the heat of the day to ease, for a storm to pass, or for floodwaters to fall.

She shifted in bed beside him, wool blanket brushing his bare skin. How long had he been meaning to replace that threadbare top-sheet, which, torn in so many places, he'd finally just ripped into rags? Six months? A year? Of course, the Cheyenne blanket was wonderfully soft, and he rather liked how it held the heat close against to his skin. But had he known she would be here...

He squeezed his eyes shut against the thought. The situation required great care. No more blunders. To take ages to fetch a towel, then burst in on her like that... yet she had not flinched. She'd just stood there, gleaming in the firelight. Oval face, dense wet hair. Curl of shadow beneath her breasts. Years had passed since he had seen a woman's body, felt another's naked flesh pressed against his own. No excuse. Besides he had not missed it as much as he'd have thought. After New Orleans, it had become spoilt, suspect. Too complicated, dangerous. Life was simpler when lived alone, unburdened by another. Free from romantic entanglements with their brittle uncertainties and aching doubts. What a relief to be free from desire's frenzied undertow.

He pressed thumb and forefinger into his eye sockets, letting the colours bloom and dance. He recalled her slow turn towards the door, her body laved with tiny streams of rainwater. The frank openness of her expression came back to him. How she'd faced him cloaked in that vibrant sorrow of hers. A sadness that enveloped her like smoke. These are the facts, her expression seemed to say. The simple, undeniable facts.

A soft sound escaped her lips, like the coo of a dove. He opened his eyes. She lay dozing on her side, the pink whorl of her ear poking through dark tangles of hair. He noticed an ashy streak on her cheek. His fingers had been black with soot from the fire. He moistened his thumb, seized by a sudden urge to rouse her. Watch her eyes flicker open. Jade-green, still cloudy with dreams.

He pushed himself up, swinging his legs off the side of the bed. The cold morning air was a welcome shock. He gathered their wet clothes from the floor and resolved to apologise. It was not too late. He could still repair the damage. The very moment she awoke, he would make amends.

The door-latch released with a loud slap and he glanced back, but she did not stir. On she dozed, body coiled beneath the blanket. Curled in on herself like an animal in its lair. As if not quite safe. Yet her face bore the same beguiling candor as the night before. His gaze lingered on her bony nose, the thick arc of her eyebrow. Dark sweep of hair strung across the pillowslip. His heart quickened and he felt the old flip and tumble follwed by a hollow hungering need, as he stepped outside and shut the door.

The sun had topped the sharp rise of the ravine, but the air was still brisk. Shivering, Will slung their wet clothing over a rope strung between the ridge-poles. Then, sparing himself the trouble of pulling on boots and stumbling up to the outhouse, he stepped to the edge of the porch and relieved himself. Watching it froth and disappear into the ruddy soil, he could hear faint clangs drifting up from the stables and wondered what they were up to. Driving in fenceposts? Repairing tack?

He shook off the last drops, jigging his leg, and stared down the path that led to the stables. A day of ranch-work would snuff out whatever weakness had flared up in him last night. Leave his body with just enough energy to draw air into lungs and pump blood through veins, but nothing more. He beat back the urge to flee. March over to the corral and bury himself in some task. Anything. No, not anything. No negotiating with the Army over beef contracts, or travelling to the Land Office to perform some irksome bureaucratic errand. He wanted to haul mesquite, dehorn steers, burn grass in the middle pasture. Ride out to the range-fence and repair any flood damage. Find stock that had wandered too far in the storm, or guide bawling calves back to their mothers. Whatever Esteban needed done. Today. Now.

But what about tomorrow? And the day after that? There was a time when such a thought would never have occurred to him. When one long hard day of ranch-work would have been followed by another and another, until years had been spent rolling from a raw-hide hammock to pull on clothes still heavy with the fug of the day before, then stumbling uphill with six other heavy-eyed men to catch horses in the pasture and work until sundown. Such days had cured him, washing away the greasy residue of a dissolute life. But there were some confusions even ranch-work could not banish, and he suspected the woman who lay curled beneath the soft folds of his Cheyenne blanket was one of them.

The kettle whistled. He poured water over the coffee grounds, stretching the beans with parched corn. During the the final year of the war, shop-keepers in Richmond had cut their coffee with dried carrot peelings, sorghum, even sawdust. Who could blame them? Goods smuggled past Union picket ships did not come cheap. Will's mother had prided herself on being able to taste whatever they used and never missed an opportunity to take them to task for it. He'd been a boy of six at the time, and the memory of his mother chiding those men still made his cheeks burn.

He threw on his buckskin jacket, still damp from the night before, and strode down the path. He fetched eggs from the hen-house, milk from the dairy stable. Exchanged pleasantries with a Mexican boy repairing a snafflebit. Acrid smell of the hot metal wafting out from the smithy as he hurried toward the kitchen of the main house, where he helped himself to flour, butter, sugar, biscuits, raisins, cheese, tinned pears, a few sweetrolls. Then he made his way through the darkened rooms to the small *récamera* at the back. Her clothes hung from wooden pegs by the door. He took up her carpetbag and began stuffing it with drawers, underskirts, hose, a cropped corset. Then he tossed in her riding habit and gloves. They would ride up to Ribbon Falls, returning along the north slope of the ridge. He would show her the place where Mariposa and Mexican gold-poppy bloomed after a rainstorm. Tell her about the time he had tracked a calf that had strayed from its mother to this very spot, how Juan had roped it beneath a spar of granite just beyond the fenceline and they had led it home. Then they would seek out that rocky notch Tio the Indian had shown him. Where, after checking for snakes, you could sit high above the wash and look down at the water running cold and clear towards Mexico.

Then he paused. Yesterday had been a long day in the saddle. Her legs would ache, but she would never say so. Yet behind these stubborn displays of strength lurked a vulnerability that stirred a tender ferocity in him. Never had he felt this intense desire to succor and protect. It had formed no part of his love for Sophie. He scoffed the very thought. But even Alicia, in all her delicate Southern helplessness, had not stirred such an impulse.

Perhaps a picnic would be best. In the meadow where spring rains coaxed wild flowers into bloom. Or should they stroll out to where that lone Cottonwood grew near the old stone stocktank? He held a green tea-dress in his hands, paralysed by the same stifling impatience that used to come over him as a boy. When his mother would dress him in some uncomfortable outfit that never fit right because of the war and the fire and the family flour mill burnt to the ground. But still they would gather as they always had, labouring under the fragile pretense that nothing had changed – despite his older brother Samuel being killed at Bull Run and Uncle Robert with one arm lost to gangrene. After Sunday dinner his mother would still usher everyone into the drawing room and insist that Will play a tune. So he would slide onto the shiny piano bench and stare at his small hands emerging from the starchy cuffs, fingers hovering above the keys. Undecided. Agonising. For whatever song he chose would be greeted, every week, by the same lilting protest, 'Oh Darlin, not that that one. Play this.' Then his mother would da-dee the first few bars in her strong, clear contralto and he would play it. Why would she never say what she wanted to hear straight off? Why this infernal tit-tat game of ferreting it out?

He stuffed the green tea-dress into her bag. Then hairbrush, petticoats, lace collars… everything went in. Let her decide. He was through making decisions. It was scarcely nine o'clock and he had already been forced to make too many. Never mind that he had thrust this burden on himself (a fact that did not, most likely, occur to him).

Back at the casita he returned dishes to the cupboards. Scrubbed burned beans from the skillet. Hung pots onto hooks. Then he emptied rusty water from the drip-pans, examining a splotch of damp above the door-frame. That joint had always been faulty. He hauled water from the pump. Made hot cakes and put them in the warming oven. Then he weighed out the supplies he'd taken from the main house and recorded the amounts on a scrap of paper, even though he knew Rafael would never accept payment, yet still he weighed and scribbled until the only task that remained was to take her things into the bedroom so she would have dry clothes upon waking.

But she was already awake. Her desultory gaze swept across the room's plastered walls. Bare save for a narrow shelf that held a few books. The room's only window was a square of glass with a stiff little canvas curtain. Outside, water dripped from the eaves in a soft pick pock drop. The rain. It would prevent them from reaching town. He'd said so last night, just before she'd drifted off to sleep. The realisation arrived as in a dream, floating over her like a cloud. She trailed a hand over the curve of her hips, drawing it across the warm slope of her stomach. She remembered Miss Stanton taking her aside on her wedding day to inquire, in a curt matter-of-fact tone, whether Vera's mother had ever told her 'what to expect.' *Wifely duty* was the phrase Miss Stanton had used. She'd learnt with Henry that it could be something far more pleasant than a duty, but that it could be this... She drew a breath and let herself sink back into the warm lassitude of her own body. That such veiled mysteries existed was no suprise. She knew why men flocked to Star Mansion. But to experience it for herself... and to think that these secret shudders had been lying in wait all these years, locked away inside her, dormant and unperceived... little knots of heat waiting to be loosened and released in wave upon ripped wave – how could such a sensation have been denied her? And for so long?

She gazed through the plate-glass at a bright square of sky, framed by the slanted cut of the window. She studied the notches in the wood where the glass had been fitted. By his hands. Those rope-toughened palms, fingers dark with soot. She reached out and touched each item on the night-table – box of matches, candle, buffalo horn comb. After Henry's death, the sight of his possessions had scorched her. Stray pen-nibs, a letter opener, a single cuff-link unearthed beneath the bed would trigger hot bursts of pain. She had earned the right to luxuriate. To be a foolish girl.

The clang of pots on the stovetop ceased and Will's heavy tread sounded on the porch. Then came the click of the door-latch. Sunlight poured into the room. Her eyes struggled to adjust. He was facing away from her, busy placing something on the ground. She stretched out a hand and said his name. Voice still thick with sleep. She liked the feel of the word on her lips. The flavour of his name. Will.

A little frown creased his brow and the room went still.

She caught up his hand and pressed it to the warm hollow of her neck, burying his fingers under that dark canopy of hair. Sleep-heat rising from the bed, scent of last night still ripe within its folds. And as he breathed in the soot and the dust and felt her hair trail between his fingers, her hair still damp with rain, he said the only thing he could think to say, which was the truth. 'I had resolved to apologise, but I cannot.'

She stroked his hand.

'You see,' he went on, letting her pull him down into the bed. 'I do not regret a thing.'

'I'd be furious if you did.' She spoke in a hoarse whisper, breath sour with sleep and a mutinous innervoice cried out, dimly, that he ought to try harder and find a way to pass the next three days agreeably, companionably, to treat her with chaste respect... but the voice soon faded dead away as he closed his eyes and relaxed into her, breathing.

'What's for breakfast?' she whispered.

'Hot cakes. Eggs, if you like.'

'Coffee?'

He nodded.

'Mmm,' she groaned lightly and stretched, bare arm moving through sunlit air.

He left her to dress. Retreating to the kitchen he set the table with cutlery, plates, and what napkins he could improvise. He took hotcakes from the warming oven. Gathered butter, jam, a jug of milk. Poured molasses sugar into a chipped bowl. Stray bits of tack hung on the back of a chair. He cleared them away. Then he cast an eye over a pile of tools in the corner, wood-handles worn smooth by the grip of his hand. How could any trace of his former dissolute self have survived those years of ranch-work? What flaw in himself had rendered him incapable of retreating here and brewing up a pot of coffee while they waited for the storm to pass? Last night she had spoken of manners as acts undertaken out of respect for others. Not rote gestures performed in mere deference to convention, but instinct turned to civilised ends. Did something similar make last night different from New Orleans? How was one to know whether past mistakes had been vanquished, or if this was mere back-sliding?

Outside the hills lay bathed in light. He could hear the muffled shush of water rising up from the ravine, a river where yesterday there was nothing but a hollow cut of pebble and sand. She stepped into the sun-washed kitchen. Skirts wrinkled. Hair tousled and unbrushed. Her presence improbable as a star.

It is here that I lose the thread. No matter how many times I wind back through it all from your angle of vision, I cannot stay confined within your sights. For it is towards her, always, that my heart leaps. That girl in a pale green dress who trips towards you, laughing for no other reason than the simple excess of her own emotion. I cannot tear my eyes from her as she takes up your hand and kisses it, for passion has made her bold. Determined to unearth every precious scrap of bliss, to unveil every glorious secret that life has kept hidden from her and carry each one into the light. But here is what she does not know: some things are best left hidden and the future is one of them.

How grateful I am that she is ignorant of what's to come.

But do not dwell on that. Not yet. For now, they are still couched safe within these mud-brick walls. Locked in a warm embrace – her head to his chest, his lips pressed to hair – breathing one another's scent. They break away. Reluctant, lingering. Sun bathes the room in a honeyed light. She scrapes back a chair. He pours coffee. Steam rises from earthenware mugs. Tiny beads of moisture pearl the butter. Look at them, there, beyond the glass. Seated at a rough-hewn table, laughing at some long-forgotten joke.

Sunk deep in that fragile riot of the heart called love.

Chapter 14

Each night I slept by his side and prayed for rain. But the sky stayed clear. On the third day, Will returned from the creek to announce that the water had dropped. We could leave.

'Tomorrow,' he declared. 'Meantime, I must offer my services at the stables. Rafael will never accept money, but we must repay him.'

I tried to force a smile, but it died on my lips. I wanted one more day alone together. A morning spent riding our horses between arroyo-creased hills, then a picnic beneath some rocky outcrop watching sunlight play across a sparkling ribbon of water. Hours passed in meandering conversations, intimate revelations. Stories of his childhood. Richmond. The war. Family flour mill burnt to the ground. His broken engagement to a girl named Alicia. He could not explain it, he'd said, not to himself, not to her, not to me now. He simply awoke one morning and knew he could not marry her. I wanted another lazy afternoon of lying side-by-side as we waited for the heat of the day to pass. His voice washing over me as he talked of ranch-work, those incantatory words he used when speaking of horses *canelos, rocios, tordillos...*

Will sensed my disappointment and swept me up in a long embrace. Our lips met. Hands wet with dishwater I held him tight and felt the press of hipbone to thigh as his fingers gripped me hard round the waist and there was a moment when I thought he might lead me back to bed. But it passed and I let him go.

He strode down the path to the stables and when he disappeared from view, a juddery panic jolted through me. Some obscure distress born of a hungering need to keep him close at all times. I sought to banish it with activity, pitching myself into one mindless chore after the next. I heated water.

Scrubbed our bedsheet with a sallow chunk of lye and hung it out to dry. Dragged the tin washtub into the sun then hauled water from the pump to fill it. Cleared ash from the fireplace, swept the ramada. Piled all the old traps, chains, pails, and spools of wire into a corner, until there was nothing left to do but collapse in a rawhide chair and try to fill the arid hours until his return.

Sun blazed down from its high crest in the sky. Birds flitted and chirped. A rabbit skittered into a clump of soapweed, as I strained to hear the low murmur of water rushing through the ravine, but it had ebbed so much that no sound reached me. Just yesterday, we had scrambled down the slope and bathed in its icy flow. Will had plunged straight in while I stood waist-deep in the freezing rips, chest lunging for air. Later, on the flat rock where we'd shed our clothes, we lay like lizards soaking up the heat. Will had clasped my thigh. Planted a kiss in the warm crease between my shoulder blades. Then a press of lips. There, in the late afternoon. On a sun-warmed rock. It was like drowning, only I could breathe.

I sprang from the chair and let my feet carry me downhill. Past the stables, beyond the fenceline and into the foothills. I walked at a furious pace, thoughts reeling. Never had I felt so agitated, so elated and perplexed. Life with Henry had been a warm comfortable thing. There was a giddy excitement to our courtship, of course, a sparkle of anticipation before his visits. But his routine departures had never bred such agitation. I was unaccustomed to the fierce anxiety that now held me in its grip.

The trail continued its ascent and I climbed on. Distant mountains wavered in a silvery haze. The trail flattened out along the ridgeline. Nothing but shimmering rimrock lay before me. Thick clumps of thorny brush filled the canyon below. Up here, high on this sun-baked slope, there were few signs that the rainstorm had ever happened. I halted. Swept a lock of hair from my forehead and tucked it behind my ear. The top of my head was hot to the touch. Throat dry, mouth thick with thirst.

Stupid. No water, no sunshade. But of course, my folly ran far deeper. Will had made no promises. Given no sign. In fact, he had once broken an engagement to avoid the constraints of such a life. Why should this be any different? There was but one prize a woman could withhold to snare a man, and I had given it away. Freely, eagerly. Day after sun-soaked day, night after starry night. I was no different from Evie, believing every man who tossed her a few trinkets intended to marry her. Or Texas Lil with her fantasies of going to live with her mother up in Colorado. The one thing I might have held back in order to bind this man to me forever he already possessed. Had enjoyed over and over to his heart's content. And he would do so again tonight, for I did not have the strength to turn him away.

I began my descent, spying a precipice we had scaled that first morning after the storm. My gaze lingered on the red-graveled soil, thick with saguaros, prickly pear, cholla. Black remains of a dead agave plant lay baking in the sun. Ocotillo sprouted from the rocky bluffs, spindly branches wavering against the sky. I paused at the stone stocktank to wet my face, but the pooled rainwater had evaporated leaving nothing but a dark stain. The trail dipped down between two over-grazed pastures and carried me back to the Cruillo Ranch.

At the casita, I gulped down water. Ate strips of smoked pork, hard cheese, a few dried apple slices. Old magazines lay on a shelf in the kitchen. Tossed in among the almanacs and Sears Roebuck catalogs were a few books: *The Frugal American Housewife, Trapping Sonora: A Guide for Ranchers and Fur-traders, Childe's Book of Knots, The Bride of Lammermoor*. I picked one, then settled into a rawhide chair on the ramada and began to read. But details from the past few days kept streaming through me. Freckled pale of his skin. Feel of his shoulders in my palms like clasping hot stones. Forcing my attention back to the story, I tried to follow the adventures of Lucy and the Lord Keeper and *the savage herds of cattle which anciently roamed free in the Caledonian forests,* but my gaze just kept sliding over the words, until I could stand it no longer and slammed the spine of the book against my thigh.

The pages flopped open and a note fell out. Indigo blue ink. An elegant female hand.

Wednesday morning

Dear one,
Tonight is impossible. Come tomorrow eve'g. Eight o-clock.
Harry will let you in.

Adieu,
S

Sophie duBois. Her name had arisen several times over the past three days, but when pressed Will had been evasive. 'Let's not spoil a fine day with such talk,' or 'Just a faithless, immoral woman I once had the misfortune to know.' Then he'd kiss me softly on the lips.

I regarded the bold lettered note with its long-tailed 'y's and airy 'g's. *Harry will let you in. Eight o-clock.* They had been lovers. It had been there all along, known but not faced. In his silence about New Orleans, in the odd gaps between disclosures. His peevish discomfort when our conversation strayed to certain topics. Indeed, the passionate attentions he had lavished on me were indication enough. Such knowing ease in an unmarried man must come from somewhere. Or, more precisely, someone. *Tonight is impossible. Come tomorrow.* With what blithe indifference she put him off!

The planks of the ramada shuddered as Will sprang onto the porch. Sweeping me into his arms he pressed me up against the side of the casita and held me in a rough embrace, kissing my face and neck, his lips coarse with salt. Then he collapsed into a chair. 'I ain't the cattleman I used to be.'

I did not move, face tingling from the rub of his stubbled

cheek. Sophie's note was still clasped in my hand.

'I'd nearly forgotten what thankless work that is.' He held up his hands, palms blistered and raw. 'Once those heifers start calving, boys won't get a lick of sleep.'

I held out the note.

Will took it, glanced over it, then slumped forward in his chair. His head still bore the mark of his hat and I felt the urge to ruffle his sweaty hair and banish that weary look from his face with a soft caress. But I stood firm, refusing, for the first time in days, to succumb to impulse. 'It fell from a book I was reading.'

He pushed himself up, brow darkening. Then he crumpled the note in his fist and whipped it against the side of the cabin and set off down the path to the wash. I dug my fingernails into my palms, gouging them deep, and did not follow. Minutes later, splashes and whoops ricocheted off the rocky walls. Fine. If Will preferred to bathe in that icy trickle of water, *fine*. But I was not about to let all my hard work go to waste. I went inside and drew a towel from the cupboard. Then I walked round the casita to the bathing tub, stripped away my clothes, and lowered myself into the tepid water.

I scrubbed away the morning's sweat and chore-grime, tub clanging with every strike of an elbow or knee. *Come tomorrow eve'g. Eight o'clock.* Her words kept rattling through me. What did she look like? Sound like? What words did they whisper while lying together? I was seized by the most violent unhappiness, a swirling tempest of questions and visions and searing doubts. Every sharp-edged thought cutting me to the quick. How naïve and untutored I must seem to him! Enough. I dried myself and dressed. Watched the dirty bath-water drain out through the plug-hole and run into the castia's barren herb garden. I removed laundry from the wash-line. Folded and stacked each item. Stowed everything away in cupboards. I did not dare risk a moment's idleness, or my thoughts would roam back to Sophie. To all the terrible questions I was aching to have answered but could not bear to contemplate.

Inside my gaze fell to the bed. Was it all at an end? Would we lie here tonight, or would that sweet flurry and surge be denied me? And what sort of person had I become to be a slave to this need? Blankets. They had not been aired. I stripped them off and slung the heavy folds over my arm. Back outside I encountered a short, well-dressed man on the ramada. Hands on his hips, he stood peering out across the ravine.

'May I help you, Sir?'

'Why, if it isn't the missus herself.' He tipped his hat. 'Rafael Cruillo.'

'Pleased to meet you,' I answered him with a smile. 'Vera Palmer.'

This provoked a rich rollicking laugh. 'Old habits die hard, don't they, Mrs Keane?' Eyes alight, he winked and lowered his voice. 'I won't tell.'

'Patrón!' Will bounded up over the crest of the trail, hair wet and uncombed, shirt-tails flapping. The two men embraced, slapping one another on the back. They exchanged a few words in Spanish as Rafael pulled gingerly at a damp spot Will had left on his shirt. There was nothing careless or workaday about Rafael Cruillo's appearance. He wore a crisp yoked shirt and sharply creased trousers that came to a perfect point over a pair of scuffed riding boots.

'I hope you will join me for supper,' said Rafael, directing his words at both of us. '*Recién casados!* A celebration is in order.'

Will gave a sheepish laugh. *Recién casados?* I had no idea what that meant. But 'Mrs Keane'… that, I understood.

'See you this evening, my friend,' boomed Rafael. Then he turned to me and gave a polite nod. 'Until tonight, Mrs Keane.'

I did not trust my voice to hold steady, so I just smiled. It was the same warm regal smile I bestowed on Madam Blair's customers every night. Then I turned and carried the Cheyenne blanket, unaired, back inside. Will followed and when his eyes lit on my bags, neatly packed, in the corner – a result of this morning's overmastering drive to keep busy – his face fell.

His workshirt clung to damp patches on his chest, and his hands were raw with nicks and fresh rope-burns. I longed to catch up his hand in mine and tumble back across the bed, smothering this fresh hurt beneath the hard press of bodies. I forced myself to look beyond him, out through the half open door onto the ramada where Sophie's note still lay crumpled on the ground. *Tonight is impossible.*

'I hope you're not concerned,' Will said at last, 'what Rafael might think.'

'About what?' I flung the heavy blanket onto the bed in a heap and left it there. 'That you, his friend, have lied to him? I should think Rafael would be the person to consult on that matter.'

'I did not lie to him. I told Esteban and—'

'Don't split hairs. You lied to Esteban and Esteban repeated the falsehood. And while we are on the subject of lying, that silly fib about an East Coast lawyer was a terrible idea. We ought to have let Blair assume I was sneaking away for an illicit liaison. Which, as it happens, turns out to be the truth.'

'Don't say that.'

'Why not? Do you wish me to speak only those truths that are not unpleasant? You have an odd moral sense, Will Keane. You tell lies to your friends, but God forbid a man and a woman come together outside the sanctity of marriage. Or perhaps I ought to say, God forbid anyone should *know* that this has happened.'

Will gave a spiritless shrug. 'I have not explained myself terribly well.'

'Indeed.'

A fly droned in through the open door and bumped up against the plate-glass. Will ran a hand through his hair, stiff with sweat and dirt. Then in one swift motion he stripped off his soiled shirt and cast about for a clean one. My gaze caught on the sight of his bare chest, unable to break away from the freckled pale of his shoulder, birthmark by his collarbone. How dare he taunt me. It felt like cheating.

Will pulled a fresh shirt over his head, then took up my hand and led me outside. The book still lay where it had fallen, pages riffled by a breeze drifting down from the mountains. My gaze flitted between the cluttered ramada and the rocky hillside until it rose to the cloudless sky and settled there, sinking into the depthless blue.

'Do you still love her?' I asked.

A puzzled look crossed his face.

'Are you pledged to Sophie in some way?'

Then he laughed, not the warm bright laugh I'd come to love, but a gruff dismissive chortle. 'God, no.'

'Why did you not say so before?'

'I've said so now.' He gestured for me to sit, but I stood firm.

'I have a right to know how things stand.'

He drew breath, gazing out at the ravine as he spoke. 'You wonder at my silence, I expect. What conclusion to draw from it. Only this: that I am ashamed at taking another man's wife, though Edouard duBois was hardly a faithful husband. You're not likely to find a more avid whorehound in Sadie Blair's barroom. But that's no excuse. Nor, to be honest, is it the heart of the matter. I am ashamed to have given myself to such a faithless, immoral woman. There was no constancy in her attentions, no true affection. She liked toying with others and in my weakness I allowed her toy with me.' He turned to face me, eyes heavy and dim.

'Are you ashamed of me?' I asked.

'Of you? What on earth for?'

'Working at Blair's parlour house. For this,' I gestured towards the bedroom. 'For going by Miss Palmer and all that I do which seems to go against your notions of propriety.'

'I think working for the likes of Sadie Blair completely beneath you, of course. But ashamed?' He shook his head. 'Whatever gave you such a notion?'

'Your lie to Esteban. For a start.'

He flushed, drawing the back of his hand across his lips. His chin was bristly from days without shaving and the freckles on his face had grown dark, although the skin beneath his shirt was still pale as milk.

'I fear my Spanish is to blame,' he said at last. 'When talk moves away from horses… I told Esteban you were my *mujer*. I meant 'affianced' but *mujer* must mean betrothed…?' he shook his head. 'I meant to say that we were engaged to be married. It was not a lie. At least I did not think it so. When I left this morning I felt quite certain you would not refuse me. But now, I fear my confidence was misplaced. I ought not—' he slapped the ridgepole with the heel of his hand. 'I did not intend for it to go like this.'

'What did you intend?'

'Something finer. What I gave Alicia at the very least, a formal—'

'I don't want what you have given other women.'

'What *do* you desire?'

I lifted my hands, palms open towards the wide vault of blue that had sheltered us these last three days. I nodded at the casita whose walls had cradled us night after night. 'You. This.'

Will stepped across the ramada and drew me to him, and I stood pressed to his chest breathing his scent of horses and sweat and sun-heated straw. His heart a muffled thud against my ear. So close, his heart. Walled off by nothing but a thin hull of flesh and bone.

Then he drew back, holding me by the forearms. 'It's settled then?'

I nodded.

'We shall marry?'

'Yes,' I said. 'Yes.'

Chapter 15

When the alarm sounds I am ready. No, more than ready. I am eager to leave this cot where I have lain for hours, fretting helplessly over Camille. A letter reached me this morning: three overwrought pages about how the military authorities have lied to her: Pierre was not shot by a sniper, he was mortared and left bleeding in a shell-hole, because no stretcher bearer could reach him. Animals were better mothers! Never would a bear yield its cubs to such slaughter! If every mother in France had refused to hand over her sons, they would have been forced to sue for peace!

Where to even start? By reassuring her that Pierre's death was not her fault? Remind her that when the *tocsin* sounded and mobilisation notices went up all over Paris, he had to turn up with his *livret militaire* or face a firing squad. Besides, he felt it was his duty to defend France. Democracy and *liberté*, he believed, hung in the balance. And how does Camille even know this? From a comrade in arms? One of these damned seances? Is her source even reliable? But to question her facts would provoke such fury... no. Whatever I write is bound to fall short. Another failed attempt at consolation. *Tu ne comprends jamais, chérie, jamais...* Why, then? Why address these tear-stained pages to me? Here. In the *zone d'armée*. A two day rail journey from Paris. Even a pitch-perfect reply will never reach her. Not now, with the offensive about to begin.

So when the bell clangs I leap to my feet, grateful to be ripped from the snarl of my own thoughts. I scramble for boots, coat, gas-mask. Gas-mask. Falling to my knees, I forage under the bed. They are meant to be hung within easy reach, but I cannot stand those bulging eyes glowering down at me in the dark. My hand lights on the rubbery snout and I drag it out. After a quick check for morphine, hypodermic, and tourniquet, I am out the door and down the *trottoir*. Fields flicker with the flare of distant explosions, then fade back to shadow. Dark bird-shapes swarm overhead. Sky aglow. Munitions-wagons, motor-vans, horse-drawn vehicles, artillery and troops flow down the road. I glimpse a swish of hair and hurry to join a cluster of bob-tailed nurses tramping across the field to our dug-out.

Descent proves tricky. I step gingerly down the damp rungs, urged on by Faith Hamilton who waits below, grasping each girl by the arm so we do not slip. We are a disheveled, bleary-eyed bunch: boots yanked over pyjamas, dressing gowns flung atop night-shirts, short hair rumpled, long hair swept up into clips. The air is ripe with the smell of unwashed bodies, fear of pneumonia having kept us from risking a bath.

I cast about for a spot, engulfed by a swell of nervy chatter. *Them walls shook like the dickens t'other night when 'at shell exploded. Och aye. Narrow shave, that. Pull the privy sheet away from that there puddle, Kate. At's it. Lawks if them Hun prisoners ain't dug us a loo! Yus, but it's tiny. Tis indeed. Keep yer fannies over that there hole, guls, or this'l be one stinker of a pit. Aye, and yous cannay be doing a jobby down here, ken. What? Land sakes, what's that she's speakin? Let me tell yer summat, if nature calls—*

Three sharp hand-claps silence them, and after a quick head count, Sister Hamilton settles down on her rick-cloth and begins to knit. Weekly packets of yarn arrive from her parents' sheep-farm, and she transforms them into socks at a startling rate. She gives them to soldiers who arrive at the hospital with nothing but straw in their boots. Long legs bent to one side, she squints down at her stitches although she needn't. When we lose power in the ward, you can hear her needles clicking on in the dark. Her air of calm efficiency has soothing effect, as nurses fall to chatting, playing cards, and writing letters. A few curl up and close their eyes, army coats tucked in tight to keep out the damp. In the far corner I spot Tosh. All female staff were ordered to repair here. Tosh protested that she should take refuge under her cot, like the other doctors. But the *Médecin chef* would not hear of it.

I pick my way between cross-legged nurses and spread my mac beside Tosh. Water is seeping through the wall at our backs and the air smells faintly of animal dung. She is holding a necklace in her lap, worrying its beads between her fingers.

'The only danger is a direct hit,' I whisper, 'which is very unlikely.'

'I'm not afraid for myself.'

I nod.

Her gaze snaps up at me. 'Why do you dislike him?'

'Dr Tyler?'

Tosh rolls her eyes. 'No, Santa Claus.'

I laugh but Tosh gives me a hard stare. 'Stop playing dumb.'

My eyes fall to the gorgeous strand of jade beads in her lap. She rubs a thumb over each one then lifts the necklace to her cheek, pressing the cool stones to her skin.

'Did he give it to you?'

Tosh laughs. 'Blake doesn't have two shillings to rub together. It was a gift from Father. He gave it to me when I left for America. Mum made such an abominable rumpus, but Father... deep down I suspect he was proud. No one ever dreamt my eccentricities should lead to anything, much less a medical degree.'

I take up her hand and squeeze. Tosh flashes me a wan smile, but it is all in the lips. Her eyes remain dull and tired and I find myself longing for some plucky display. An irreverent joke. Or a fiery rant about her unfair treatment at the hands of the *Médecin chef*. 'You haven't answered my question.'

'I don't trust him. That's all.'

'Do you trust anyone?'

Good question. I'm not sure I know the answer. The earth trembles. A shudder runs through our legs shivering up our backs. The muffled pounding of the guns is eerie and all too faint. Nothing but the ghost of a sound, which unsettles me far more than the full-throttled roar we are accustomed to hearing. Having learnt to tell the screech and throb of enemy guns from the steady thrum of our own, I find myself straining to hear bursts of fire from our defense positions. Then, when nothing comes, a cold panic trickles through me.

'I keep thinking of Blake,' Tosh whispers, 'but it all feels so far away, even Blake, whom I saw just this afternoon in the village.'

My eyes bolt towards Faith Hamilton. I am about to make Tosh stop, when my thoughts slip to Camille and her letter and my tendency, always, to strike the wrong note.

A series of crashes sends dirt raining down. Lamps flicker, casting strange shadows across the chalky walls. Nobody cries out. Some grab at their macs, others lay a hand on those nearby. A few girls draw up their knees in a tight ball. Waiting til it ends so they can brush the dirt from their sleeves and laps and continue on as before. A look of anguish flits across Tosh's face, but she swiftly composes herself. We hear no clatter of metal and wood. The hospital is safe? Who knows. How much noise would a bunch of tents make?

I place a hand on Tosh's back, expecting her to shrug it off. But she does not. Mouth tight, she meets my gaze with an unblinking stare. Her long fine lashes cast smoky shadows under her eyes. A look of defiance and pain blended with a plea for me to understand, sympathise. So I try.

'Think of somewhere pleasant, a place you really love,' I whisper. 'Your granny's rose garden. Close your eyes and imagine you are there.'

She shakes her head and sighs. 'I wouldn't want to see Granny's rose garden now. Uncle Edward inherited the place, and no doubt Aunt Tillie has ripped it up and replaced it with clipped hedges and symmetrical plantings.' She wrinkles up her nose.

'Remember it the way it was before.'

She turns her avid eyes on me. 'Before Grandfather died?

Or before I found Mum kissing her lover in the orangerie?'

A shrill whistle sounds above us, followed by a blast. The walls shudder, more dirt sifts down like rough brown snow. I glance up at the earthen roof, which seems to be holding.

'Oh, I wish we were on-duty!' Tosh groans.

'Yus,' chimes Betsy, picking at her knee. 'Awful, this waiting.'

A murmur of assent. Then a girl with shorn-off hair snaps open a tin. 'Biscuit?' The tin gets passed from one pair of scrubbed-raw hands to the next, and I find myself listening to stories and jokes that I do not understand because I wasn't there – aware, for the first time, at just how much I have held myself back. I stare at these nameless girls with their lank, greasy hair and ruddy cheeks and wonder who they are and what has brought them to this dank hole. Duty? Maternal instinct? *Pitié*? No, that is what the War Office wants us to believe. What the girls themselves might even say, if asked. But that is just a ruse, a little trick they play on themselves to justify running away from poorly servanted homes where they must cook and clean and look after the little ones. The truth, I suspect, is that they are here out of a desire to count for something. The secret they keep even from themselves is that they saw a chance to flee their narrow, predictable lives and grabbed it.

The tin comes my way. I take a biscuit and thank the stubble-headed girl.

'S'awright,' she tugs at her wool cap. 'Ave another.'

I pass the tin to Tosh, but she declines. Rocking back and forth on her mac, she keeps rubbing the string of beads with nail-bitten fingers. She needs something to keep her mind occupied. To prevent her from imagining the worst. And before I know what I'm saying, I've offered to tell her a story.

Tosh looks up. I feel the attention of the room shift towards me. A few of the girls scrunch their macs closer, faces lit with surprise.

'It begins,' I say, 'on a narrow cart-track in the desert. At the end of it lies a hacienda, nestled at the base of some foothills with dusty mountains rising up behind. On the ramada is a young woman. Her dark hair hangs loose beneath her shoulders. A step ahead of her walks a man, sleeves rolled above the elbow, forearms dusky from the sun. He is leading her toward a path that winds between the stables. This path will carry them to a small cabin perched high above a sun-drenched ravine.'

A loud screech interrupts me, like a giant knife slicing through the sky. The earth shudders and quakes, showering us with dirt. Sister Hamilton keeps her needles going, her back ram-rod straight. One girl clutches her knees, rocking back and forth. Another twists a lock of unwashed hair between thumb and forefinger. I glance at Tosh. 'Go on,' she urges, brushing soil and pebbles from her lap.

And I shall. In a moment. For I am unsure how to proceed. Tempted, as I am, to make changes. To remain silent about Star Mansion and Sadie Blair. To strip the desert of its thorns, of its lonesomeness and its rain – no, never that, for without the rain, we might never have found one another. Or perhaps that is not so. Perhaps we had found each other from the first, and all that remained as we trod that narrow winding path toward the ranch-cottage, was for us to make our slow, circuitous way back home.

Chapter 16

Supper at the hacienda was simple but delicious. Sweet potatoes, *carne seca,* and *sopapillas* spread with honey. Will Keane sat across from me at the long pine table. Hair wet-combed he was dressed in the same jersey shirt he'd worn to collect me that very first day at the depot, and the sight of him suffused me with a quiet bliss.

We dined off porcelain plates with silver cutlery, napkins of pressed linen spread across our laps. Beeswax tapers rose from a silver *candelabro* and a fire blazed in the stone-lined hearth, casting a buttery glow over the timbered ceiling and white-washed walls. Rafael kept daubing sweat from his brow, but the fire's warmth did not seem to reach me and I spent much of the evening feeling chilled. Would I ever learn to dress properly for this climate? In the late afternoon heat of the casita's bedroom, I had settled on a light linen dress and thin shawl. A miscalculation. But, truth be told, my thoughts had not been focused on the task. Standing before a pile of folded dresses, my mind kept drifting back to that small *récamera* with a crucifix hung above the door. Will and I were engaged to be married, true. I was a widow, not some untutored young girl: also true. But the fact remained that we were not married, yet had been living as husband and wife under Rafael's very own roof. While I did not care what nameless strangers thought, the opinion of Rafael Cruillo, whom Will admired, meant a great deal. And so, as I'd struggled to pin up my hair before Will's cracked shaving mirror, I devoted little thought to my attire and far more to the question of how Rafael would treat me once he learnt the truth.

As it happened, I needn't have worried. Once Will had sheepishly explained the mix-up, Rafael threw me a quick wink then turned an expression of mock seriousness on Will and teased, 'Your Spanish is not what it once was, my friend.' Then he'd shaken his head with exaggerated despondency and made a remark in Spanish whereupon they'd both laughed. Rafael had then kissed my cheek and offered his heart-felt congratulations, expressing sincere regret that his wife and children were not present. Lupita, he continued, would be sorely disappointed to have missed this evening and he made me promise to return in good time. He went on to ask many questions, greeting my responses with an absorbed expression that seemed born of genuine interest, a desire to know this woman whom his dear friend was to wed. The conversation soon drifted to the subject of Rafael's family, the children, and then, after a few more glasses of wine, to politics.

'A territorial governor cannot tax.' Rafael smoothed his mustaches. 'He is nothing but a niñera. Responsibilities, but no real power. I pity the man.'

'Pity?' Will scoffed. 'Tritle's mine holdings are worth a fortune.'

'You accuse him of corruption?' Rafael rolled his eyes. 'You should see what those in power do in my country. This land beneath our feet was sold to Washington but for a song. As for Tritle…' Rafael eased back his chair, daubing his brow with a crisply folded handkerchief. 'You cannot believe how the Apache problem has improved. He saw that the only solution was the Army. In this, he was most correct. Inviting General Sherman to tour the territory and make a report, that was a very smart thing. Very clever. He knows Congress will listen to this man.'

Will frowned at his plate, fork poised. Then he lowered his hand and shot Rafael a severe look. 'Do not mention that man's name in my presence.'

'You refer to General Sherman?' Rafael flicked at the air. 'Do not presume to tell your host those things of which he can or cannot speak, William. And let us not forget, while we are on the subject of military conquests, the Venta de la Mesilla. During his lifetime my father witnessed the size of his native land cut in half – yes, cut in half – by the exploits of American generals. And, yes, the weakness of Mexican politicians. But if I were to become enraged every time someone mentioned Zachary Taylor or Winfield Scott... my life would be a misery indeed.'

Will gave a thoughtful nod. He greeted Rafael's views with an uncharacteristic openness, a deference I'd never seen him grant anyone before. And Rafael showed Will a great deal of affection. His manner was that of an elder brother toward a beloved, if somewhat wayward, younger sibling.

The serving bowls were passed round once more, and the talk shifted to workaday matters. The ranch. The town. Calving season. A water rights dispute. Throughout the meal Will cast furtive glances in my direction, his gaze catching mine in a way that made my pulse quicken.

Every so often Rafael would direct a remark my way, and I would respond with a smile or a polite word, then sink back into a luminous stupor. Content to let two old friends converse and laugh, while I basked in the warm conviviality of it all. The candles. The heat of the fire. Rafael's high spirits. His ability to soothe Will's most strident tendencies, while amplifying those traits I loved best. A gentle gust of feeling rippled over me. At the thought of a future that would hold more such dinners with this man who cared for Will like a son. A future where Will and I would never be parted, where we could sit across the table from one another in a warm, tranquil silence in which no words or actions were necessary, because just the sheer presence of the other was enough.

Rosalita entered to clear away the plates, and there followed a rapid exchange in Spanish while she loaded the serving tray. Then Will rose and accompanied her into the pantry. 'Provisions for your saddle-bags,' Rafael explained, leaning back in his chair. He brushed absently at his lapels before folding his hands in his lap as a comfortable silence fell between us.

The mention of our imminent departure had tarnished my mood. Tomorrow I would have to endure Madam Blair's anger over my tardy return, coupled with the news that I would soon be leaving her employ. A battle would ensue. On one front or another. Over wages, or remuneration, or some petty detail that hadn't even crossed my mind. I wilted at the very thought. Love had made me weak. Could I just depart without a word? I toyed with the idea, but it meant abandoning my belongings and relinquishing last week's pay, which, after all I'd endured, was far too galling a notion.

Rafael broke the silence. 'You are to be married at St Paul's, then?'

Will and I had not discussed the matter. Waking from our siesta amid the falling light with scarcely enough time to dress for supper, I'd had no opportunity to speak of my desire to marry straight away. Why wait for a church wedding? But I felt bashful confessing that such a consideration, one that Rafael would take to be of utmost importance, had gone undiscussed. So I simply nodded.

'This is your parish as well?' Rafael asked.

'It will become so.'

'You are of the Anglican faith?' His full round cheeks were flushed from the wine and the heat of the fire.

'I was baptised in the Catholic church, but my late husband was Methodist. I don't know what that makes me. A mixed breed, I suppose.'

'Once a member of the true faith, always a child of God.' The expression on his face was jovial, but the remark was not meant in jest. He was a man of sincere faith. Crucifix in each room; head bowed low as he uttered grace before the start of our meal.

Rosalita entered carrying three bowls, which she set down before us. It looked like rice pudding, but had a greyish tinge. As if ashes had been stirred into the pot. Will said something in Spanish that drew a laugh from the others.

'Algo más, Señor?'

Rafael shook his head. 'Buenas noches.'

'Buenas noches, Señor.'

'Gracias.'

Rosalita left and, following the example of the others, I added sugar. Then I stirred the pudding and nibbled. It had a flavour I could not identify. Sweet, but earthy.

'Atole,' Will offered. 'It's made from mesquite beans.'

'You have picked up Indian, my friend. In Sonora we call it pudín de mesquite.'

I sipped at my water to wash away the gritty texture. There was a mild smokiness that clung to the tongue. A tang of roots, but pleasingly sweet.

Rafael took up his spoon. 'Saw Montgomery's buckskins down at the stable. A stagecoach passes by once a day now. It follows the same road as old Ochoa's mule train.'

Will shrugged. 'I prefer my own mount.'

'Of course.' Rafael gave a deferential nod. 'But perhaps Vera' would like to arrive without feeling saddle-weary.'

A moment passed before I realised this comment was meant for me. 'A stagecoach is hardly refreshing.'

'No,' Rafael smiled. 'Lupita is of the same opinion. But with the children, it is a great help. I don't know how we managed before.'

Spoons clinked against bowls, the fire hissed and popped. A tin retablo of the Virgin hung above the mantel, and I found myself staring at her flat impassive face. She had almond-shaped eyes, a bright blue cloak, and a halo that was red as blood.

'How is the law treating you, my friend?'

'When people prefer street justice, lawyers become irrelevant. And I don't much like being irrelevant.'

'You speak of the lynching, no?'

'Among other things.'

'Don't tell me nobody seeks justice through the courts.' Rafael leant forward, hands folded on the table. 'They're clogged with cases over mining properties. Or so the newspapers inform me.'

'Oh, there's plenty of work. And I make a fair living. But at the end of the day, what have I accomplished?' Will paused, spoon poised above his bowl. 'Helped some enterprising individual file a suit with little basis in fact so that he can settle out of court? Don't give me that look. It's true. The big outfits are always willing to throw a few dollars at scoundrels who bring troublesome accusations, however false. Since the mines flooded, companies are so terrified of scaring off investors, they'll pay off some claim-jumper with a flimsy case just to keep his trap shut.' Will's tone was resigned, lethargic. 'I take my percentage and make a living. But it's not why I studied law.'

'And what, may I ask, were your reasons for that?'

Will tossed his napkin aside and pushed back his chair. 'I became a lawyer to defend people from the Yankee scoundrels who were preying on us after the war. Such an aim is hardly relevant out here.'

Rafael drew a silver cigarette case from his jacket pocket. Flipping open the lid he offered one to Will. 'Have you considered politics?'

Will scoffed. 'Only thing worse than New Orleans city politics is territorial politics.'

Rafael reached behind him and took up a pair of large handled tongs. Then he drew a coal from the fire and lit both cigaritos before tossing the coal back with a quick flip. They both puffed away in silence, filling the room with pungent smoke. A housecat crept in, slinking along the far wall towards the fire. It was skinny, ruddy-furred thing with only half a tail. The creature eyed me with suspicion, bitten-off tail flicking wildly, then it fled beneath the table.

'Lieutenant Pérez is selling up,' said Rafael, tapping at his cigarito. 'Some *ladrón* has convinced him that copper is the metal of the future, so he is transferring his assets to a mine in Bisbee.' Rafael rolled his eyes. 'There are times when a man believes what he needs to believe. And such times often involve appeasing one's wife.' He lavished me with a genial smile. 'María wants to return to Sonora, you see, so Pérez needs investments that require less oversight. Copper mines! Disparatado, is what I told him when he spoke to me of this plan. But one must keep one's wife happy in this life, my friend. María has never taken to living north of the border, not since all the changes.'

Will leant forward, gripping the arm of his chair. 'You buying?'

Rafael shook his head. 'What I need, my friend, is not more land. What I need is a better breed of cattle. A few more hard winters, losing stock at the rate we have…' he trailed off and glanced over at me in his easy amiable way. 'Cattle are not made for snow.'

'Still experimenting with those half-wild Mexican heifers?'

Rafael laughed. 'You know, there are still a few kicking around in the cañon. Every so often, one of those old cows will get herded back in with the others.' He tapped ash into a small earthenware dish then pushed it towards Will. Leaning back he drew on his cigarito, eyeing us both. 'I thought you might be interested.'

Will twisted in his chair.

'Good perennial springs. You could dam them, build canals. Grow hay, fruit trees, vegetables. You might even want to plant cotton. Governor's offering five-hundred dollars to the farmer who raises the most cotton from five acres.'

'Cotton?' Will scoffed. 'Why would Tritle encourage people to grow a crop like that?'

Rafael flashed me a barely perceptible wink. 'Turn the territory towards agriculture, and you no longer have to beg appropriations from Congress to catch cattle thieves.'

'You need water to grow cotton. A lot of water.'

'Haven't you heard? There is talk of damming the Salt.'

Will pushed back his bowl. 'Well, I'm no farmer.'

The remark roused me. Wasn't this the man who had praised the Confederacy for fighting to defend their cotton fields? But before I could think what to say, the conversation had moved on.

'It's a fair price, my friend.' Rafael regarded the tip of his cigarito. 'There's a stockade, corrals, stables, a bunkhouse with kitchen-shed for your vaqueros. A casita where the gerente lives. But no hacienda. Pérez prefers to remain in town and let Jacinto run the place.'

'Excuse me,' I leant forward. 'How much did you say?'

Rafael turned suddenly, as if he'd forgotten my presence, then repeated the figure.

I did some quick calculations. 'We could manage it.'

Will looked up with a start, then frowned. Rafael took up his cigarito and leant back in his char. His face remained neutral, but his dark eyes were smiling.

'I have close to half that in the bank, and if you are right about the value of my claim, selling it should secure the remainder.'

Will gave a slow nod, furrow between his eyes deepening. 'It might.'

A long silence ensued as Will descended into a state of perplexed abstraction, tapping ash from his cigarito with one hand and rubbing his chin with the other. Rafael looked on with an air of detached interest, flicker of amusement in his eyes. 'Shall I send word to Pérez? You could travel down to inspect the place next week.'

But Will just sat there, brooding. What was there to mull over? Here was our chance! A golden opportunity to escape that wretched town. We would not be starting out as homesteaders with nothing but a plot of unworked land. We'd be taking over an established operation. Yet here he was furrowing his brow and fretting. It was the money. And his stubborn pride. He resented the fact that he had not earned every penny himself.

Had I compounded his humiliation by outlining my plan in front of Rafael?

Sensing my distress, our host turned a benevolent smile on me. 'What do you think, Vera?'

I had many thoughts, but it did not seem prudent to voice them.

'About William's predicament,' Rafael persisted, mistaking my silence for confusion.

I drew a deep breath, lavishing them both with my most dazzling smile. 'I think that when a man wishes his life were otherwise, he should act to change it.'

Stubbing out his cigarito, Rafael gave a satisfied nod. Then he rose and pushed back his chair. Behind him the fire burned low, more ash than coals. Taking up the tongs he spread the burning embers which faintly pulsed.

I stood to gather the dishes, but Rafael stayed my hand. 'Rosalita will see to it in the morning.' Then he clapped Will on the shoulder. 'You have an early start, my friend, and I have been traveling far too long for a man my age. If you wish me to send word to Pérez, let me know in the morning.'

'Thank you for dinner,' I smiled. 'It was delightful.'

'A pleasure. One I hope to repeat soon, with my wife in attendance. Lupita would never forgive me for leaving her out twice.'

Will rose and the two men embraced. 'You needn't see us off tomorrow.'

Rafael waved in a way that gave us to know that such a notion was unthinkable. Then he bid us good-night.

After extinguishing the candles, Will linked his arm in mine and led me out onto the ramada. A half moon hung above the foothills, casting a silvery glow across the out-buildings and the paddocks and the cactus-studded hills, through which ran the long dusty road into town. It floated there before us like a wisp of smoke in the moonlight.

'You felt so far away,' he whispered, drawing me to him. 'All night I have longed to reach across the table and touch you.'

I let my head fall against his chest. A lone howl rose from the moonlit dark, echoing through the hills to be answered by another, and another until the dogs down at the stables erupted and a wailing chorus of yipping and hollering tore through the night. The coyotes soon ceased to howl, but the stable dogs barked on. At length Will spoke. 'Do you really desire this kind of life?'

'Yes.'

We walked, arm in arm, down the path as it wound behind the smoke-house. Breathing the scent of juniper smoke and animal fat mingling with the desert's night-time exhalations, we passed the gravestones of Rafael's father and mother along with a small white cross where, twenty years ago, Rafael and Lupita had buried a son. The path rose and dipped again. Will halted. Then he took up my hands and faced me. 'The first few years will be hard. We couldn't afford to keep on all the men Pérez has there now.' Will drew back, face shadowy in the moonlight. 'Make no mistake. It'll be a lot of work. You'll have to keep the books, the stud records. Do all the household chores. Pérez runs several operations. If one of his outfits falters, another can make up the difference. We won't have that luxury. It might be years before we could set aside enough money to build a hacienda. And we'd be isolated. Miles from the nearest neighbor. A ranch can be an awfully lonesome place, Vera.'

'I won't mind.'

Will touched his lips to my forehead. 'Remember those words when we're wintering in a two room dug-out with a dirt floor.'

We continued up the path to the casita as Will spoke of all that remained to be done. Inspect the place. Find a buyer for my claim. Sell some of his stock in Southern Pacific. It would take time. A month, he mused, perhaps longer. Meanwhile, we would continue on as before. He would need to extricate

189

himself from his law practice. I would need to give notice to Sadie Blair. A month, he declared, lighting the lanterns on the ramada. A month ought to be sufficient. He spoke as if all of this were obvious. An agreed upon fact.

'I'm not going back.' I lifted a serape from the back of a rawhide chair on the ramada, wrapped it around my shoulders, and faced him. 'She's likely to fire me on any account. I've been gone for days without sending word.'

Will gestured for me to sit. His actions were slow and deliberate, and his face bore the same troubled expression that had come over him at dinner. He drew a long breath, steepled fingers pressed to his lips. Then he drew them away and spoke. 'You heard what Rafael said about the bridge. Nothing has been able to travel south of St David. No stages, no mule trains. Blair will know this. If she does not, you can tell her.'

I released a long breath out. 'It makes little difference. You said yourself that working for Sadie Blair was beneath me. Well, I agree with you.'

'Vera.' There was a forced reasonableness to his tone, as if he were making a great effort to remain calm. 'I'm afraid you will have to return to Star Mansion for another month.'

I was incredulous. 'You cannot order me about as if I were your manservant.'

He sprang to his feet. 'Isn't a wife meant to obey her husband?'

'I'm not your wife yet.'

He began to pace, hands shoved deep in his trouser pockets. The stable dogs had ceased to bark, and the only sound was the sibilant hiss of the lanterns broken by the clump of Will's boots. The stillness set loose a terrible jangly feeling.

'I like what I propose as little as you do.' Will spun on his heel, rubbing his nicked-up hands as he spoke. 'But if we are to do this, we'll need every penny we can muster and we may still come up short. By remaining at Star Mansion, you pay no rent. You continue to earn a wage. Vera, please. Do not misunderstand me. I despise the thought of you continuing to live under Blair's roof. Why do you think I hesitated after Rafael told me of this opportunity?'

I made no answer.

'Why, Vera?'

'I – I can't say.'

'This opportunity, to purchase an outfit like Pérez's... it is a thing I never dreamed possible. Never dared hope. And to undertake such a life with you by my side...' he drew in a breath and let it go. 'But I hesitated when Rafael proposed it, because I knew it would mean prolonging your employment with Sadie Blair.'

Tipping my head to one side, I gave a shy smile. 'Then I shall live with you.'

He gave a start.

'In your rooms at the Oriental. For a time. Until the sale of my claim goes through and we can purchase the ranch.'

Will shook his head. 'We're not married, Vera.'

I smiled broadly, straining to catch his eye as his pacing brought him back towards me. 'That is why we shall be married tomorrow. By a judge in Tucson. Surely you know someone who might perform the ceremony.'

'We shall marry in a church.' His tone was stern. 'Our union must be blessed by God.'

'Alright,' I said evenly. 'Then in your church the day after we return.'

'That is not how things work.'

'What do you mean?'

He grew exasperated. 'It is Lent. We cannot marry during Lent. Besides, the bans must be announced over the course of three successive weeks. To proceed with such matters properly takes time.'

'Then we shan't do it properly.' I gave a small shrug.

He stopped pacing and drew up alongside my chair. I could have reached out and touched him, but for the reproach in his eyes. Beneath the wool serape my hands began to clench and unclench. I leapt to my feet and strode away from the ramada, halting before the firepit to let my gaze skim out across the desert unfolding in the smoky moonlight.

His arm circled my waist. Firmly, without a hint of doubt, he held me there, pressed up against him. His belt-buckle dug into the small of my back as he lifted a finger to the night sky and began naming constellations. He had done this the night before, then led me to bed. I felt a hot whisper in my ear. Then his lips ran down my neck, kissing me softly. Orion. Cassiopeia.

I forced myself to pull away. 'You have no idea what you are asking.'

He guided me back to the chair and I sat, although a small voice inside me cried out against this act of submission.

Will bent to secure the serape around my thighs. Then he knelt before me and clasped my hands. His voice was calm and forgiving, though what I'd done to require forgiveness I did not know.

'When I left New Orleans, I did precisely what you propose to do now. I fled a state of affairs I could no longer endure. I abandoned my law practice without warning or due preparation.'

I began to protest.

'Hear me out, please. I know that Sadie Blair is unworthy of you in every way. And if this were simply a matter of leaving her employ, I would not object. But there are financial considerations, Vera. Our desperate need for money, if we are to purchase the ranch without debt. Your plan for a swift marriage flatters me. Indeed, there is nothing I should like more than to have you as my wife tomorrow night.'

'Then for goodness sake, let's—'

'Our marriage is too important to be rushed, Vera. Don't you see how that would look? A hasty marriage enacted on the sly? After both of us have been away from town all this time? It would look very suspicious.'

'I don't care how it looks. I care only how it feels, and returning to Star Mansion feels intolerable.'

'Well, I care. I will not have people idly speculating about your character, or why we married secretly after a mutual, and lengthy, absence in Tucson. We must begin our life together on the firmest of foundations, Vera. We must not act heedlessly. We must take care. Be responsible. Even toward those, like Sadie Blair, who might not deserve such treatment. You are better than she is, Vera. Let your actions speak this truth.'

I waited for a long moment, picking at a loose thread on the serape. 'Does the prosecution rest his case?'

He pushed himself up and resumed pacing, back and forth across the sun-splintered planks. At the loss of his touch, I felt a stab of anxiety. I spoke softly, pleadingly. 'You do not understand what it is you ask me to do.'

He stood on the edge of the ramada, hands on his hips. For a long terrible moment, I sat gripped by the fear that he was about to walk off into the night and leave me to lie alone in that sheetless bed listening to the ghostly yip and howl of coyotes echo on through the dark.

Then he spoke. Standing outside the light cast by the lantern, his voice came to me from the shadowy edge of the ramada. His tone was not obstinate or angry. More than anything, he sounded tired. 'What I ask is simple, Vera. I ask that you to proceed with the dignity and strength of character I know you possess. That is what we deserve from one another. What our marriage deserves. We must not expose something so precious to idle speculation and lurid whisperings, because we lack the presence of mind to do things properly. We must both act with calm deliberation and propriety—'

'Propriety? I work in a brothel.'

The word seemed to startle him. His head dropped. 'Vera, I told you. We need the money.'

'Ah.'

He would not meet my eye, and I realised that this fact, this need for my money, shamed him.

'Okay,' my voice was almost a whisper. 'Then just say so.'

'I did say so.' His face bore a sulky expression that irritated me.

'Well, just say so and leave it at that. Don't fancy it up with all this nonsense about propriety.'

Return. To Star Mansion. For a month. I thought of Evie's torn stockings and swollen eye, her thighs shiny with semen as she struggled up from the bed trying to sound playful – to convince herself she was still in control... *one at a time, boys, I beg of you please, one at a time*. I thought of the man with his flaccid belly hanging over his shorts, his drunken stumble as he tried to pull up his trousers and flee at the same time, bumping into me as he passed – his stink of armpits and boiled cabbage. I thought of the drunk soldier from Fort Huachuca who had taken pot shots at the dogs. I thought of that bony limb and the blood-soaked bundle burned to ash in the backlot. Of Josie bent over Texas Lil with her tongs. And Lil's face, wet with tears for a mother who wanted only to be rid of her.

Will approached, and I let him take up my hands. He held them in his, stroking my knuckles with his fingers. The night air had thoroughly chilled me, and I longed for the warmth of the blankets. For the feel of his bare skin against mine.

'I know how hard it is,' he whispered.

And at that, Josie's words came back to me – about the right thing being the hard thing.

'I know,' he said again.

I shook my head. Words sticking in my throat. Because he did not know. Had no earthly idea. And his ignorance distressed me, for it marked out a chasm between us that could not be bridged.

Behind him stretched a black vault of sky, stars dimmed by the risen moon whose pale light spilled out across the desert, bathing the hills in a ghostly glow. The cactus and the boulders cast long shadows, smoky and indistinct. My hands, warm for the first time since we'd left the hacienda, still lay in his. Will stroked my knuckles. His palms were rough with sores already scabbing over, and on his thumb I could feel a patch of skin rubbed raw by a seam in his workgloves.

'I will do as you ask,' I said.

He lifted my chin with his thumb and kissed me. Lightly, chastely. No tongue to teeth, no hard crush of flesh. Just his lips softly grazing mine, mouth lingering there to draw in the breath my lungs released.

Then he stepped away.

Skin of my face tingling from the scratch of his beard, I watched him take the lantern from the ridgepole and let him lead me inside. Bedroom still warm from the heat of the day, we had no need of a fire. I undressed as Will repaired to the kitchen to prepare for our pre-dawn departure. Coffee ready to be brewed. Provisions for our saddle-bags stored in a tin box. Safe from mice and a ring-tailed cat that had been quite bold the previous evening.

Slipping into bed, I could hear the slap of cupboards closing just as I had on that very first morning. Drawing a hand across my torso, I banished all thoughts of tomorrow and replaced them with dreamy imaginings of what was to come. Moments from now. His body pressed to mine, embracing its entire length. Supple pressure of his lips, chafe of his beard on my thigh. The deep untroubled sleep that would follow.

I told myself to remember every detail, every touch. The memory of this night would sustain me through upcoming weeks. That is what I told myself, lying beneath the blankets as the blood thrummed warm and fast through my veins. Another month at Star Mansion was nothing in exchange for a lifetime of such nights. A small price to pay.

The lamp flared and sputtered. Then, with a final hiss, it went out, plunging the room into darkness. A tiny sliver of moonlight seeped around the edges of the curtain, etching out the barest sketch of objects in the room. Mantle, bookshelf, clothes-rack, luggage stacked in the corner.

The door opened and Will entered, shutting it quickly to keep out the cold. I could hear him step towards the bed, see his faint movements in the dark as he shed his clothes.

'Can't see a thing,' he muttered.

I lay still, soft nap of the blanket to my skin.

'You'll have to find me,' I said.

And he did.

Chapter 17

Emerging from the dug-out, we are ordered to pack our things and report to the mess-tent. A heavy mist lies over the fields. Ambulances line the road and German prisoners are yanking down tents. Hurrying to my quarters I pass a depression in the mud where the office once stood.

I toss my belongings into a kit-bag, which we are meant to believe will be reunited with us. I check that it is properly labeled, mentally bidding farewell to its contents, when I am seized by a sudden impulse. Unfastening the clasps I root through the clothing and toiletries until my hand lights on them. I draw out the packet and curse whatever silly impulse drove me to do such a damn fool thing. Why take Will Keane's letters from the relative safety of Paris and bring them here – only to leave them beneath a pile of socks, forgotten and unread?

Shouts reach me from beyond the canvas walls. Paralysed, I hold them in my hand. More shouts. They must start pulling it down. I unwrap the gas-mask pads we have been issued and force the waterproof wrappers around the letters. Then I unbutton my uniform, slip the entire packet beneath my undergarments, and head to the mess-tent.

After being fed a hot meal, we are issued steel helmets and directed to vehicles. Amid the flurry of activity I catch sight of Blake Tyler, hoisting himself up with a hearty wave. Tosh turns away, eyes puffy and red. Fighting through a press of orderlies, nurses, drivers, and doctors, I take her by the arm and lead her away to our *camion*. The driver instructs both of us to climb into the cab and ride with him and soon we are nudging into the line of vehicles crawling down the road. Pale and silent Tosh takes up my hand and presses it to her cheek.

Our *camion* grinds past fleeing civilians as they trudge

through the mist. Children wail, dogs bark, cowbells clang. They push carts laden with blankets, clothes, pots, hope chests, baby cradles, sacks of grain. Some have livestock in tow. At the sight of their travel-stained faces, a gathering dread creeps over me.

Tosh thinks I'm ready. Assuring me, time and again, that I've learnt everything a field nurse must know. But I have my doubts. What if her zeal for women to prove themselves under fire has blinded her to my short-comings?

Turning onto a sunken track, the car skids towards a steep birm. I grab the seat, bracing for impact. Then, at the last second, the car straightens and we continue on our rough juddery way. I glance at Tosh. Feeling my gaze, she turns and winks. The incident seems to have restored her.

'I'll not let you leave it at that,' she says.

I tug at my uniform, skin slippery with sweat from the waterproof wrappers. It was that damned séance. After meeting our train, Camille dragged me to her clairvoyant's *apartément* in Monmartre, where we all sat in a darkened salon that smelled of cat piss while listening to this woman drone on about this *revenant* and that *fantôme*. I was trying not to doze off when cries of *William, William* made me jump. Aware, all of a sudden, that the man beside me had begun to weep. A message from beyond the grave. From his dead son. William. The word became an irritant, an itch that had to be scratched. So I dug out the letters and brought them here where they have lain for weeks beneath a pile of folded uniforms, forgotten and unread. Camille's fault. Yes. Blame her. Your poor widowed friend taking care of your house back in Paris. Sure, why not.

'Your frontier adventure,' says Tosh, groping in her pocket for a fag. 'I must hear the rest.'

I keep my gaze fixed straight ahead. Discarded household goods litter the roadside. Broken carts, busted wheels, iron cooking pots, framed pictures, children's toys, a gramophone lie strewn amid shell casings from last night's bombardment.

'There is nothing more to tell,' I answer weakly.

She gives me a jocular shove then draws a pouch of tobacco from her greatcoat. 'Go on, then. We'll not be there for a while.'

True enough. Signposts have been moved or demolished; roads closed without warning. Key crossroads lie shelled beyond recognition. When not snarled in traffic, our *camion* keeps recrossing sections of road we have already traveled. My finger rises to the lump on my rib, but it is buried beneath the letters so my hand floats back down to my lap and settles there, fiddling with my gas-mask. At yesterday's drill I was hopeless. Fumbling with straps, struggling to force the tight rubber over my head, failing to secure it in time. These things were not designed to accommodate long abundant hair.

'Why are you in such a fidget?'

'I'm not.'

'Yes,' she jabs two fingers into my ribs. 'You are.' Her eyes widen with surprise. She gives the spot a sharp tap. 'Secret documents?'

A long moment passes. Then she faces me. 'You're not a spy are you?' But behind the joke, her tone is prickly. My silence lengthens and the quizzical lift to her brow gives way to something harder. My thoughts fly to Camille. Her letter, left behind. Unanswered. Not a moment's thought for it. Until now when it's too late. Perhaps, like so much else in life (surgery... love...), the art of friendship simply eludes me.

'Letters,' I offer. 'From Will Keane.'

Her face brightens. 'Recent ones?'

I stiffen. My tale of love in the desert is at an end. Or rather, it must stop there. With a man and a woman asleep in one another's arms, dreams broken by the lonesome wail of coyotes hunting in the hills.

Our driver halts to ask directions from a passing officer. Through the windscreen I watch an old woman struggle with a one-wheeled barrow piled high with bedding and cookware. A scrawny boy in knee-pants sits astride the heaped-up things, clinging to a rope. Just a boy and his *grand-mère*. He stares straight ahead, wide-eyed, knees thin and knobby. No shoes, socks full of holes.

'Well, are they?'

I meet her eye. 'Why must you press me on this?'

She shrugs. 'It would pass the time.'

'Just an idle entertainment to give us all a laugh?'

Tosh bristles and falls silent. The mist has begun to lift, but the air is still hazy with dust. A peculiar taste clings to the back of my throat, tang of plaster and pulverised stone. 'Why not tell me about your mother's lover? Let's pass the time that way.'

Tosh stubs the half-smoked cigarette out on her boot-heel and slips it into her breast pocket. 'Major Harold Gillingham. Third son to the Earl of Wyndham, whose country estate abutted my grandparents' home in Devonshire. After Sandhurst, Harold Gillingham went off to India. Years later, he returned to England and found my mother married with two children and alone for extended periods while Father was on assignment with the Foreign Office. During that time, Major Gillingham became a frequent visitor and that summer, while visiting my grandparents, I saw him kissing Mum. Rather passionately, I might add.' Tosh bites her lower lip and looks down at her hands. The skin on her knuckles is dry and cracked, cuticles split. Her thumb caresses a raised vein on the back of her wrist. When she resumes, her voice is firm and clear. 'With the outbreak of war, Major Gillingham was assigned to the staff of General Charles Townsend, who, after his failed mission to capture Baghdad, surrendered to the Turks. They have sat out the remainder of the war in Constantinople, enjoying a very comfortable captivity if the Major's letters to my mother are to be believed. I suspect she has taken up with someone else in the meantime, though I've no proof.' Tosh shoots me a grey-toothed smile. 'Now you.'

Last night in the dug-out was one thing, but I haven't the heart for such talk now. Still, the expression on Tosh's face wounds me. I shoot a hurried glance at our driver, who is busy cursing the condition of the road. Then I reach beneath my coat, unbutton my blouse, and draw out the letters. Tossing the crinkly packet into her lap. They will not tell her what she wants to know. How it ended. What went wrong. They do not explain why I am hurtling down this shell-torn road, instead of gazing at sun-baked hills with Will Keane by my side. But they will buy me time.

We emerge onto an empty road and our driver tears into action. Elbow against the horn to warn on-coming vehicles, he slams over shell-holes and ditches, flies through shallow puddles, slips through patches of mud. We bounce over something soft that bumps up against the under-carriage with a thud. A rotten stench wafts through the open window, swampy like the sour rot odour of gangrene. Only worse. My stomach grows queasy and I grip the upturned helmet in my lap.

Tosh jounces in the seat beside me, placidly thumbing through the letters Will penned in those heady weeks after our return from Tucson, while I served out my time at Star Mansion and Will travelled south to inspect Pérez's ranch. At the sight of Tosh's head bent over those blue sweeps of ink, something contracts inside me. What have I done? It will only whet her appetite for more.

We lumber up a steep hill, and as we top the rise my breath catches. Fields are riddled with shell-craters. Patches of woodland reduced to splinters of charred black stubble. Shrapnel and unexploded shells litter the ground.

Our driver is cursing, waving. The hospital should be here. That turn-off, suggests Tosh, a mile back? Our driver digs the gearshift into reverse. A loud click and the *camion* begins to swerve round, and that's when we glimpse them straggling over the rise. Filthy slings, bandaged heads. A few with rifles, most unarmed. A breeze kicks up, carrying the same sickly smell of the trash-pit behind the butcher-shop in Goose Flat.

A dispatch-bearer arrives. He leaps from his motor-bike and informs us that out unit has pulled up and retreated. Beyond the next hill is a *poste de secours* without a doctor. Our orders are to proceed, on foot, to this *poste*. All wounded are to be sent to the Advanced Dressing Station a mile down the road. Our driver is ordered to drive his ambulance to the village. Immediately.

'Village?' Our driver throws up his arms.

'À droit!' he shouts, motor-bike zipping away.

We unload our supplies and fill the *camion* with wounded men. One soldier's hand has been blown off. Tendons dangle from the stub on his wrist like stray wires. His face is white. Tosh tears off his good sleeve and ties it around the stump, then ushers him into the *camion*.

Moments later, we are tramping to the *poste de secours* laden with bandages, morphine, water, tetanus antitoxin. Simon, our orderly, carries a huge rucksack full of irrigating solution and demands to know why the ambulance has been sent back. Nobody knows. The stench grows more acute and I struggle not to gag. Rounding a corner we stumble onto a giant hole filled with shattered stretchers and jagged pieces of metal. The air stinks of burnt hair and cooked meat. Grilled chicken, to be precise. We walk on. Past a mangled door with a red cross on its side. Underneath a thin coat of white paint you can see the words *hommes 6, chevaux 4*. A direct hit.

There are bodies, but I am careful to avert my eyes. Gaze fixed on my boots as they strike the tamped down dust of the road. *Every patient is a stick-man. A collection of body-parts.* Head. Neck. Chest. Abdomen. Legs. Army of stick-men in my head, I walk on toward the brown clouds spraying up from the ground, sparing no thought for the fate of my precious letters.

A Red Cross flag hangs askew above the *poste*. We duck beneath it and descend into the hot fetid air. Sounds rise up from below. Groans, wheezes, coughs, cries for help, for mercy, for *monsieur le docteur, maman, Jesus, Dieu.* At the bottom, acetylene lamps cast a harsh white light over the earth-walled rooms, jammed with wounded men. Stretcher-bearers bump down the stair behind us, delivering more. A heated trestle stands in the middle, surrounded by soiled bandages, splints, blankets. The ripe metallic smell of a butcher shop mingles with the stench of open sewer. My throat convulses and I do not resist. Chewed-up food sprays onto my boots, spattering the hem of my uniform. Then a vague relief. Better to retch up breakfast than topple over in a faint and slice my chin.

A clammy hand grabs my wrist. I look down at a curly haired youth with a field dressing wound under his chin. Dried blood cakes his neck and uniform. Kneeling down, I unwind the filthy bandage. His chin waggles, floppy, too floppy. A sour panic churns through me. Stick-man. *Stick-man.* I bite the inside of my cheek, compose my face. *Head first. Head.* Tongue: swollen, purplish black. As if a dead fish were shoved in his mouth. He cannot not talk. Check the airway. Clear. I clean and rebandage his wound, administer tetanus antitoxin. Then I tell him to make his way up the stairs and start down the road to the village. I am shaking.

A man arrives by my side. His forearms are scabbed with blood. I search for a wound, then notice his medical insignia. He asks after *monsieur le docteur* and I point to Tosh. All by himself for hours, he says. Amputations piled up, he shakes his head, as if admitting failure. At this, I confess to my own inexperience, lift a trembling hand for him to see. He clasps it in his own and says that we are all just orderlies down here. Slap on a bandage and send them away. Bandage, splint, evacuate. Stretchers only for the *grands blessés.* Everyone else must walk. Save the ones you can. Tell the *brancardiers* to clear out the rest. Let the hopeless cases die above ground. With a view of the sky. There is no room for them in here.

With a shout, Tosh orders me to the heated trestle. A patient is thrashing against the straps, teeth clamped on a bayonet scabbard while Tosh lifts the artery and ties it in two places before she cuts. Haemostat. Done. I hold the leg tight. See that the blade reaches the membrane around the bone and brace myself. The patient moans. I hand Tosh the saw, eyes fixed on the leg. Nothing else. Artery, bone, tissue. He is bucking hard. Almost over, I shout, not looking at his face. Not daring, until the final stroke of the saw when he bites down hard on the scabbard and a tooth snaps off. The sallow chip falls to his chest. I stifle the impulse to pick it up and hand it back to him.

'Tie off the bleeders,' says Tosh. 'Nothing fancy. Flap over the stump.'

Blood spouts all over me.

'Tie them off!' shouts Tosh.

I lunge for the tourniquet and pull, press down hard. Everything slippery with blood. Something is wrong. Blood keeps pumping out. Too much. Haemostat. It is lying by my foot in the dirt. I grab it, wipe it on my apron, then clamp it back on. Seconds have passed. My heart pounds wildly. Tosh puts a hand on my back. I am drenched in sweat. 'Tie off the bleeders,' she says.

I do it. Sweat is dripping down my face, my arms. I turn away from the tressle. Men are moaning and bleeding everywhere. The stick-man is useless. I look for blood, slap gauze over it, then blunder on to the next. A stretcher-bearer calls me over to examine a man. A pale weathered face stares up. Grey stubble, skin weathered from years of sun and wind. A farmer. All day we have been seeing these *vieux pères*. I lift the blanket. Shrapnel has ripped into his thighs and pelvis, shredding the flesh, shattering bones. His mid-section is a pulpy mush studded with bone pieces. Skin clammy, pulse weak. He's in shock, beyond help.

I gesture toward the steps. The stretcher-bearers sigh. They have retrieved him under fire, carried him through a crowded trench, down those stairs… a wasted trip. The old man's lips are moving. I bend down. *Pardon.* My throat contracts, eyes burning. He says it again. *Pardon.* The *brancardiers* stagger off. I sniff back a gob of snot. Swallow it down. Then I wipe my eyes and move on.

Arm wound. Tetanus antitoxin. Bandage. Fingers puffy, purpling? Loosen the bandage, send him away. Next. A face with a frothy red bubble for lips. No shrapnel, no cuts. Wet gaggy sounds. Struggling to breathe. I slip a finger into the hot wet mouth and clear away broken teeth. I brush them from my hands and watch them fall to the floor where they lie in the dirt like bits of smashed seashell. How to keep the airway clear? I shove a wad of gauze between his gums and wave at the stair. *Évacuez.*

The hours pass in a blur of shredded body parts. More *vieux pères*, more young *poilus*. I keep my eyes from meeting theirs. It is simple this way. Terrible, but simple. The stink of excrement thickens. Explosions ring out, but the dug-out seems to be holding. We discover that the oxygen tank has a faulty valve, impossible to tell if it is fully closed. Difficult to open. Luckily, no gas cases arrive. Irrigating solution runs out. Then morphine. Water is in short supply. There is nothing to eat.

A runner arrives. We are ordered to pull back. Evacuate. Patients who can walk must push stretchers. Load men onto gun carriages, make-shift litters... Simon seems to be everywhere, bandaging wounded, lugging stretchers up the stair until only five patients remain. One has a crushed pelvis. Another has shrapnel embedded in his torso and thighs. Two lie immobilised with acute head wounds. A soldier with broken ribs can barely breathe. Propped against the wall, he has large ears and does not look a day over sixteen. They cannot be moved.

'I won't abandon them,' says Tosh.

'Devez partir,' Simon insists. Sweat drips from his forehead, trailing down his face.

The *poilu* with broken ribs gasps, squeezing out words between raw wheezes. 'Femmes…prisonnières…' An explosion drowns out the rest.

I grab a canvas bag and fill it with bandages, gauze, amputation knives, tetanus antitoxin, an empty canteen. The activity has steadied me. 'Come, we'll set up another aid-post.'

Tosh does not answer. The whomp of explosions is almost constant. In the brief pauses between blasts, the only sound is the wheeze of the boy with shattered ribs struggling to breathe.

'No soldier wants to be responsible for the capture of women,' I say. 'They would rather die.'

Tosh does not move. The urge to shake her, shove her, hit her – whatever it will take – is overwhelming. But Simon beats me to it. He grabs Tosh from behind and lifts her off the ground. Arms pinned to her sides, she flails at him, kicking wildly.

'Allez!' he shouts.

I hurry up the steps, boots slipping. I stumble and have to catch myself, hands landing in the awful muck. Wiping them on my apron, I scramble toward the mouth of the tunnel. Every step feels heavy, as if I am prying myself from the clutches of some giant beast. Behind me Tosh is shouting. For Simon to release her. That she outranks him. Threats to have him court-martialled. But Simon just hauls her up the steps like a sack of grain. I keep slipping and having to catch myself on the clay walls, which are sticky and cold to the touch. It is like crawling through a giant intestine – wet, slippery, clogged with half-digested food – and when I think I cannot manage another step, the cave spits us out into the trench.

Tosh's helmet falls from her head and lies upturned by the entrance. Simon kicks it at her, then flings a gas-mask out after, which lands at her feet. Chest heaving, he stands before the entrance. Simon is a brick-layer in civilian life. That is all I know of him – that and what he has done over the last few hours. Seeing him there, blocking the entrance to the *poste*, I realise that he intends to stay.

Soldiers rush past carrying rifles, bayonets fixed. They shout and wave at us. Évacuez! *Allez, allez!*

I touch Simon's blood-spattered arm and thank him. A lock of sandy hair sticks to his forehead, damp with sweat. I resist the urge to brush it back from his eyes. 'Á bientot,' I say, which sounds silly. 'Après la guerre.'

He nods.

'C'est promis?' My throat swells.

'Oui.' He cannot meet my eye.

A strange twanging rings out overhead. Like rocks plinging down on a heavy wire. 'Les mitrailleuse,' remarks Simon, ducking back into the *poste*.

I retrieve her helmet and shove it onto her head. Then I grab Tosh by the arm and we run, crouching low, gas masks swinging. A shell lands so close that it forces the air from my lungs. I stagger back, catch my breath, and move on. We stumble over shovels and pick-axes, boots slipping on rotten duckboards. Dense tangles of barbed wire coil over parapets. I train my attention on the rusty crimps. Twisted Ribbon? Telegraph Splice? S-barb, I decide. Definitely S-barb. What the railroads used to keep cattle off the tracks.

The trench takes a dog-leg turn and spills us into the road. The air has a dirty orange tinge, every breath sharp with fumes. Toppled gun-carriages and dead horses litter the roadside. Bodies, too. Fleeing soldiers stop to strip them of ration tins before continuing on. Puffs of dirty smoke float over the churned up fields. You can feel each explosion in the chest, a hard throb in the sternum.

We are running. Tongue dry, legs wobbly. Bag of supplies banging my hip. Throat fiery. Heart thudding. Hard. Too hard. Tosh keeps having to stop and wait. Explosions slacken. The sky is drained of colour, except for a raw glow in the west. Fields shadowy and indistinct. Soon it will be dark. Shouts rise up around us. Any redoubts? Who's covering our flank? Haven't heard any of our planes. Forget planes, what about a hot meal? *Il y a deux jours...* A complaint goes up about blisters. We have no ointment. Tosh pipes up: rub rifle grease on them. Heads turn. Her accent is so atrocious I wonder if they understand.

Bodies litter the roadside. Some are dead; others are unable to go on. The farther we go, the more there are. Bandages pale in the thickening dark. A burning shame rips through me.

'It was wrong to leave,' says Tosh. Her face is smeared with dried blood, a dull brown streaked lighter where sweat has rolled down her cheeks.

Faint shapes glow through the twilight: Tosh's eyes, shell-smoke wafting across the fields. A dark clump of trees rises in the distance. Shelter. The only evidence of it for miles. We hear a faint clang and scrape of shovels ring out across the field. Soldiers digging in.

The explosions have ceased. *Une pause* mutters someone. *Le dîner* cries another. *Oui, ils mangent.* Groans. Everyone is thinking of the food being brought up the line, of the Germans getting ready to tuck into a hot meal. A plane rumbles overhead with a loud, inconstant growl. Not one of ours. My throat constricts, heart racing. It is dark. Too dark for that plane to be a threat. Still, at the uneven throb of its engine I begin to shake.

'I'll not abandon my patients next time,' Tosh announces.

I lower my voice. 'These men are fighting to protect their womenfolk. For you to be captured... Or killed in their presence... it would—'

'Womenfolk! What kind of silly expression is that?'

'The sort Blake Tyler might use.'

I button up my coat, shivering beneath my sweaty uniform. Tosh has no coat. No blanket. The sight of her rubbing her arms against the cold angers me. How does she expect to care for others if she cannot look after herself? I shoved a blanket into this bag, but it's sure to be lousy. Perhaps a little chill will teach her a lesson

'Has it ever occurred to you that women possess certain

vulnerabilities that men do not?'

Tosh clucks and shakes her head. 'I took you for a different sort, Vera.'

I grab her arm. I do not shout. I speak in a low clear hiss, as I describe that night in Star Mansion. Old soldiers bragging about their exploits. Not on the battlefield, but in farmhouses and barns. The knowing leer in their eyes. *Gang-fucking them farm girls.* I'm about to tell her about the men clustered around Evie's bed – puddles of semen on the floor, the hairy-backed man pushing himself up with a grunt – when a flare floats down from the sky. It lands twenty yards away, casting a white glare over the entire road. Bright as lightening, but it does not blink out. It burns on and on.

Bullets tear into the road. Puffs of dust spurting up. Something warm and sticky spatters my face. I wipe it away. Soldiers are running, diving for cover in shallow ditches. Tosh drags me to an abandoned litter. We crawl beneath it and lie there. Dead body above, damp earth below. The flare fizzles out but the gunners know where we are. Shrapnel hisses through the air. A loud tearing sound. As if the sky were a giant piece of cloth being shredded to rags. Minutes pass. The ground judders. Nothing between us and the shell-bursts but a layer of canvas and a dead body. Something hot singes my neck. I brush it away. Damp and warm to the touch. Acrid smell of burnt hair. Panic jolts through me. But my skin is not cut. Burnt, but not cut. A realisation takes shape: hot shrapnel has ripped through the litter, tearing through the dead body. The blood is his. Not mine.

Explosions cease. A terrible whinnying rises from the road. The animal shrieks are fiendish and eerie and far more terrifying than the snarl of the German plane or the hiss of shrapnel. We hear the crack of gunfire, then silence. Boots beat against the earth. Shouts for help. Tosh has not moved. I can feel her heart hammering hard against my back.

'It's over,' I say.

She does not answer.

I shove the litter aside. The helmet rolls from her head, breeze ruffling her curls. She is lying on her side, hands to her throat. Blood trickles from her lips.

I throw myself on the ground and lift her hands away. A piece of shrapnel juts from her neck. Flesh burned where it entered.

I take her hands in mine, cold and slippery with blood. Her eyes are wide with fear. Half wild. A look of panic seizes her face. A convulsion of helplessness and terrible fear, of everything that is not Tosh. Looking straight into her eyes, I order her not to move. Somehow, my voice remains steady.

Neck wound. Clear the airway.

She coughs. A blood clot from her mouth lands on my chest. I am about to make a light-hearted joke, tease her for ruining my lovely military issue coat, when blood starts pouring from her mouth. A bright red stream pumping up and out. I hear a soft wet thunk as she struggles to breathe. She thrashes, grabbing at me, clawing at my arms, my clothes. Then she pushes me away, eyes bulging, rolling back. I reach for her. Clasp the metal, still warm, to draw it from her neck. She fights me. Is there something I don't know? A reason not to pull it out? No. She is drowning in her own blood. *Clear the airway.* I yank the shrapnel from her neck. She is still thrashing, unable to breathe. I roll her on her stomach, slap her back. She is clawing at the air, arms flapping, as if trying to swim. Her lips grey-blue, face ashen.

The blood pulsing from her mouth goes dark. Face black, she is no longer thrashing. I shove my fingers inside, press down on her tongue. Wet and hot. Feel for something that might be blocking the airway. Nothing. Empty. Her eyes open wide, as if in great surprise. Then her head falls forward, chin to chest. Her body goes limp in my arms. I clasp her to me. Hard. Blood still runs from her mouth, but slowly. Then in brief fits and starts, until it ceases altogether. And she is still.

Chapter 18

It was Friday evening and Star Mansion ought to have been buzzing with activity. Doors banging, whores shrieking for help with buttons and clasps, Blair performing her inspection of the 'boudoirs' while some poor houseboy struggled to keep pace with her demands. But even the kitchen was empty. Through the window I could see the long pine table wiped clean, benches piled up on top. No cold plate for after the house closed down. No coffee on the stovetop, ready to brew.

As I mounted the back-stair, Gracie barked and strained against her chain, but she was alone. Buster was gone, dead and buried. I steadied myself. Pushing open the door to my bedroom I was overcome with a stink of armpits and dirty feet, the faint whiff of Lil's soiled bandages. It was all still here. Embalmed in the carpets and the drapes, rank and unappeased.

I crossed the room and threw open the window. Hot air choked with dust swelled over me. For days I had given no thought to what had transpired here on the night of the execution. In this room. My room. After Evie's door had been broken down and the house had been closed and all that remained was for Jackson to tend to the injured dogs, their howls of pain driving me to seek refuge here – even though Texas Lil was still asleep in my bed. Drugged. Bandaged. Who cares. Just crawl in alongside her, draw the pillow over your head and squeeze. Anything to muffle the howls of Buster and Gracie.

A rap sounded at the door. Madam Blair? I did not move, gaze skimming out over the flat-roofed shacks and wire-fenced lots to the sharp line of the horizon. Another knock. I crossed the room and cracked open the door. Jackson was standing there, dressed in dirty coveralls. Where was his starched dress-shirt? And old Abe, Contessa's Friday night steady? He ought to be ringing the bell, ducking in and out before the other johns arrived as was his habit. And special privilege. Something was wrong. Had I allowed Blair's license to expire? Forgotten to drop the envelope at the courthouse before I left?

I waved him in and shut the door.

'Don't fret,' he said. 'Deputy Barnes sent word about a raid. Churchies been kickin' up a fuss. Noise complaints, mostly. Sheriff aims t' act on 'em. Let folks know he ain't deaf to their concerns.'

It took a moment for the news to sink in. House closed tonight. No standing behind the till for hours on end. No making change. A reprieve. And, yes, I *had* paid Blair's license fee. I recalled handing the money to the clerk at the court-house and walking away with a receipt – which had taken ages to procure amidst their flurry of preparations for the execution.

'Sadie done sent me.' He stared down at his boots. 'Wants to see you.'

I collapsed into the room's only chair, an uncomfortable straight-backed affair shoved into the corner. Jackson had not moved. I slapped at my skirt, sending puffs of dust rising from its folds. 'She planning to cut me loose?'

'Don't fret on that.'

'What should I fret on?'

Jackson said nothing, face slack with exhaustion.

'Oh, I'm not worried about losing my job.' I examined my hands, palms grey with limestone dust. 'In fact, getting fired would be just the thing. But it won't be that easy. Oh, no. Blair will want to keep me around. Balance the books, make change. Tear into me whenever she pleases.'

A smile tugged at his lips, and I realised that the noiseless bobbing of his head was laughter. Not cruel. Just amiable and helpless. The sort of laugh one convict offers another when they share the same cheerless prison cell. Jackson's freckled hands swayed by his sides, then he fell still, eyes resuming their sober squint. He looked tired. 'I done fixed a lock to your door.'

'Why not put locks on all the doors?'

He shook his head. 'Sadie don't want it.'

'Why not? It might save some trouble.'

'Apt to cause more than it saves.'

I saw his point.

'Keep track a this.' He placed a key on the dresser. 'Ain't no others.'

'Blair must have one.'

Jackson gave a long slow nod. 'Funny thing. Few a the teeth look to be filed down a bit. Be hard to catch and roll that bolt back.'

Now it was my turn to laugh, which I did, rising from the chair and slipping the key into my pocket. The sun had dropped below the mountains, drawing a thin veil of shadow over the room. I stepped to the open window, letting my gaze settle on the lonely rugged slopes to the east. Those sheer granite slabs said to shelter renegade Apaches, Chiricahua warriors who'd fled the reservations and not been caught. No settlers ever ventured into those mountains. Not even for timber. My eyes fell to the streets below lined with tin-roofed cribs. You could see the whores who worked in them, slouched in crooked doorways, wearing thin shifts and some parlour whore's discarded slippers. Soon their shrill cries would start drifting up through the twilight.

I turned, expecting to find Jackson gone. But he had not moved. 'It were on me what happened,' he said.

I shook my head, flinching from what he might say.

'It were on me, Vera.'

I drew a shallow breath. Unable to keep it all at bay. How, that night, I had ducked behind the Chinese screen, same as any other night, and shed my clothes. Cast about for my dressing-gown. Then emerged to find dark shapes stooped over the bed. Two men. Drawing the blankets off Texas Lil. She lay motionless. Sunk in a drug-induced slumber. One

213

spread her legs, tugging away the blood-soaked poultice and letting it drop to the carpet. I froze, stifling a cry. Get Jackson. A shadowy hand was pushing up Lil's nightdress. Stroking her bare breast. Blood hammered in my head. So loud they must hear it. They must. I could not move. Did not dare. Not even to duck back behind this screen. Creaky floorboards would betray me. And still, through it all, came the awful bawling of the dogs.

I'd fled the first chance I got, bursting into the corridor as a shot rang out. Gun-shot. I screamed, but nobody had fired at me, or at Lil. It was Jackson. Outside. Putting Buster out of his misery. Moments later he was beside me, shirt smeared with rifle-grease and dog's blood. By then, it was over. Save for Gracie whimpering in the back-lot and Buster dead on the ground beside her, needing buried. It was over.

I lowered my voice. 'You told her not to do it. I heard you warn her, but she didn't listen.'

'Sadie told me…' Jackson trailed off, shoulders stooped with a heaviness that resembled grief. 'She knows what happened weren't right.'

'Well, anyone with an ounce of sense ought to have seen that staying open for business that night was stupid. Dangerous and stupid.'

He shook his head. It was a slow, grave gesture. 'Ain't how I see it.'

The last thing I wanted to hear was how he saw it. This, I now realised, was what I had been dreading most – having all those slumbering details stirred awake and then being forced to hear other people's thoughts on the matter. I had no desire to sound those murky depths.

'Keepin gals safe is on me,' he said. 'Y'all are mine to protect. You, Tessy, Miz Blair, even Jo.'

I saw my chance and turned him away with a laugh. 'Can't imagine Josie needs much help, judging from the way she wields that kitchen knife.'

'I guess you're right,' he gave a long slow nod. 'Trouble come Jo's way, she be faster n' a longshoreman with his chiv.'

We faced one another across the gloom, shouts from the crib whores growing louder in the gathering dark. Jackson seemed to think shouldering all the blame was noble. But I thought it foolish, which irked and confused me because Jackson was no fool.

'Please.' I forced a smile. 'Let us say no more on the subject.'

The sound of a slow-drawn breath reached me, as if he were about to start up again, and I held up a hand.

He turned, shoulders stooped, and made for the door.

'Alright, then,' came his words across the lampless dark. 'Alright.'

Downstairs I hesitated before Sadie Blair's door. Will had made me promise to inform her straight away, but what business did he have extracting such a vow? He had no idea how to handle Sadie Blair. Drawing a deep breath, I lifted my hand and knocked.

'Ah,' she crowed. 'Come in.'

The door caught on a fat rug and I had to shove it hard. Discarded crinolines lay heaped on the floor. Dodging them, I banged into her marble-topped dressing table, setting off a mad rattle of gee-gaws and glass bottles. Every surface was littered with expensive-looking objects: silver-handled brushes, tortoise-shell combs, store-bought lotions, face-creams, powders... all flung carelessly about. A man's waist-coat lay draped over a chair. Silk-lined, without a hint of wear. Anthony Mariano. Loan shark. Fastidious dresser. So, he was back in Blair's bed. Or had been. As to whether he would return, and how many days had passed since his visit... I would have to tread carefully.

'Sit down, my dear. Make yourself comfortable.' She gave a listless wave at an upholstered chair draped with garters and stockings, which I shifted onto her unmade bed. Handling

Madam Blair's undergarments unnerved me almost as much as her appearance. She wore a silk dressing gown under which her uncorseted breasts lurched and swung whenever she moved. Her hair, stiff from its weekly dose of red-brown dye, hung loose below her shoulders. I'd never seen her looking so undone.

'Drink?' she offered, leaning back on her chaise lounge.

'No. Thank you.'

She poured me one anyway. 'Damn fine brandy. Napoleon Bonaparte's favorite, if you believe that old coot Judge Wallace, which I'm not sure I do.' She set the decanter back down on the table. 'Still. Stuff's a darn sight better than that cheapjack you and Jackson pinch. Oh, don't look so surprised. Just cause I let a few things slide, doesn't mean I don't know about 'em. Tessy's hopped-up cigarettes, Gypsie's clit bumping with that girl works for Blonde Marie, you and Jacks knockin' back a belt of rye before bed. Good madam knows every damn thing goes on under her roof. Smart ones know when to look the other way. You ride your girls too hard, grind 'em down on small stuff...' She took a long slow swallow and let her head fall back against the chair. 'Whore needs to have pride in herself. Feel she's got something t'offer a man. All the brass fittings and velvet drapes – sure, it's for the johns. Part of the fantasy. But it's for us, too. Give a gal fine surroundings, you give her confidence. Big soft bed, fancy furniture, dab of scent behind the ear lets a gal know she's high class. You want to charge top dollar, you need whores who feel, right here—' she pressed a jewelled hand to her chest, 'they're worth every penny. That's why I don't ever cheat 'em. Plenty a madams do. It's easy enough, but it's bad for business. Tells a gal she ain't worth what she's taking.'

My gaze roamed over the rumpled disorder of the room. I'd never been inside and found it plush, uncongenial, and cramped. Which was odd, given her habit of referring to it in the plural: *I'll see you in my rooms, please... I'm off to my rooms for some shut-eye... I'll take breakfast in my rooms, Josie...* So. These were her *rooms*: a thin-walled box with a window that gave onto a dingy side-alley, packed with over-sized furniture that jutted out at odd angles. An obstacle course of sharp corners and elbow-bruising shelves.

'I never ask my gals to do anything I haven't done myself. Or wouldn't have done, back in the day. But mistakes get made, Vera. They do. No use wallowing in the mud. Brush off your tail and move on.' Madam Blair gestured at the brandy she'd poured for me. 'Go on, then. Or do you only drink cheap rye?'

'Would you prefer we pinch the expensive stuff?'

'No, dear.' She lifted the drink to her lips. 'We need to save that for Mister Keane.' Then she drank deeply and let her hand drop to the arm of the chair, fingers clasped around the empty glass. 'Haven't seen ole Willie Keane in a while. Not since you ran off to Tucson last week.'

So, this is how it would be. No thundering salvos or torrents of abuse. Just a steady trickle of furtive innuendo. And yet, this little dart of hers was oddly welcome. A barbed exchange, at least, was familiar territory.

'Business with a lawyer, I believe?' She said it with relish, flashing me a wry smile. 'Over your husband's will?'

It was a stupid lie. Stupid then, and no less stupid now.

'Connecticut to Tucson…' she mused. 'Long way to travel. You must be rather special to this Mister…'

'Patterson.'

She gave a long slow nod, fingertip circling the rim of her glass. 'Keane know about this fella?'

'It was Mister Keane who advised me to go.'

'Really?' She sat forward. Her rings went clink, clink, clink against the side of the glass. 'See, I always took Keane for the jealous kind. Protective. Possessive to a fault. That's why he won't tup whores. See, at heart, a whoring man's a sharing man, but Keane… he wants a woman all to himself. Needs to possess her to enjoy her. Keep her like a prized thoroughbred in his stable. Oh, I recognise his kind. Yes I do. Handsome as the devil, but lacks confidence. Had a husband who was the same way.' She waved at a gilt-framed photograph. Then, seized by a sudden impulse, she lifted it and shoved it in my lap. It was a formal portrait of a young man with a thin moustache and blonde hair, parted and combed flat down along the sides of his long thin head. He wore a collar and bow-tie, and although everything about his appearance was youthful, there was something world-weary in the droop of his eyelids, the soft resignation of that mouth.

'Killed himself,' she announced in the same minced, business-like tone she used when discussing the night's take or informing me of a delivery. 'Found him swinging from a rafter in the shed. No note. But I didn't need one. He'd just come off a bad streak at the tables. Worst ever. Bindle growin' thinner by the week, but the extent of his losses, well, he'd kept that from me. Wasn't til a friend of his showed up late one night that I learned the full story. Now this friend was a bit of a lush. Used to drop by and play cards with Sonny some nights, always pinching our darkie maid on the rump after he'd had a few. But I trusted him far enough to know he was tellin' me the truth. Sonny had borrowed money to cover his losses, then tried to win it back. Fella told me the men Sonny owed were some nasty characters. Said they'd try to shake me down for it if I didn't skeedaddle. He saved my life, I expect. Packed me a bag, shoved some money in my hand, and shipped me downriver. Got off in St Louie with...' she trailed off and sipped her drink. 'Funny. I barely remember that boat ride.'

I'd no notion how to respond. I let a long moment pass to let all her strange talk leak away then asked after Evie.

Blair shrugged. 'No more chowder-brained than usual.'

'Texas Lil?'

'Worked last night. Pale as a fishbelly, but the johns didn't seem to mind. Turned five tricks. Went a bit hysterical at the end of the night. Nothing a bromide couldn't fix.' Blair gave a busty groan and closed her eyes, hair falling forward against her unpowdered cheek. Stripped of powder and lip rouge, her face lacked its imperial, mask-like quality. Made her appear softer, less impregnable. And old. Her eyes snapped open. 'Why the hell did Lil wait so damn long to get cleaned out?'

I said nothing, assuming the question was rhetorical.

'Well?'

I shrugged.

'She talks to you. Confides.' Sadie rolled her eyes. 'Hell, take a guess."

I temporised, but Blair would not be diverted. So, in my most speculative tone, I suggested that perhaps Lil wanted a baby.

'Pah!' Sadie gave a limp-wristed wave. 'Shows you never had one. Baby's the ruin of a good whore. Makes you all moral and high feelin' inside. Next thing you know you're sewing buttonholes for a measly wage, determined to raise up your son like some respectable woman you got no notion how to be. Up nights holdin' that hot little body, all shivery with fever and coughing, and you too poor to pay for a doctor. All that saintly livin' and for what? Baby that goes an dies on you.' Her face was fixed in a frown, wrinkles puckering her chin. Her eyes had shed their hard vivid glare and for a long, terrible moment she looked as if she might cry. But she recovered herself. 'Okay, Vera. Let's say you're right. Say that fool girl wanted a baby. Lord knows, some women do. Lil knows the rules. No trick babies. Not under my roof. Moment a gal gets knocked up and too far gone, she's on the street.' Sadie shot me a penetrating look. 'Well?'

'Maybe she planned to go live somewhere else.'

'These gals ain't got a somewhere else!' Blair thundered. 'That's why they're here.' Her eyes narrowed. 'You ain't talking about that low down mother a hers?'

I shrugged.

'Dora Belle,' she muttered, scowling. 'Lil tell you that?'

'You told me to take a guess!'

'Well, shows you never met the woman.' Blair harrumphed and knocked back her drink. 'Dora Belle ain't the grand-motherly kind.'

A staccato tapping filled the silence as she drummed her nails. Then she stopped and fell to twisting all her rings so the jewels faced out. 'Back in St Louie I had a few solid girls. Pretty ones who didn't drink or have some pimp to keep in high style. Professionals. But these frontier whores are all touched in the head. Cept Gypsie. She could make something of herself if she set her mind to it. At first I thought Contessa might, but that temper of hers... and the gambling. Hop smoking don't help either.' Sadie set her glass down on the table and heaved a weary sigh. The crease in her brow deepened, and for a terrible moment it looked as if she might be keeping back tears. Then her face sharpened and out of sheer relief I blurted out an apology for my late return.

'Floods knocked out the bridge,' I explained.

'Though not,' she reproached, 'the telegraph wires.'

'I sent word.'

'Not til yesterday.' She poured herself another drink. 'Feared you mighta lost heart and upped sticks, after what happened.'

'I considered it.'

'Running off with Patterson?'

'God, no.'

She flashed me a controlled, tight-lipped smile. 'Another lawyer, perhaps?'

I flushed and looked away.

Mouth turned down at the corners, she was glowering at my untouched drink. A mistake, I now saw. My refusal had forced her to drink alone. I took up the glass.

'Atta girl.' Sadie clinked her drink to mine. 'You handled things just right, by the way. Did just what I tell my girls to do if a john gets rough. Buy time. Then holler like hell and wait for Jackson.'

I stiffened.

'Bastards,' she grumbled. 'Buncha grubby rabble-rousers.'

Whose presence here, I wanted to add, was her fault entirely. Instead, I took a sip of brandy and changed the subject. 'What's this about a raid tonight?'

Blair flapped a hand, as if pooh-poohing the imaginings of a small child. 'Holy birds runnin' on about Sodom and Gomorrah. Cops and the higher-ups wringing their hands like a buncha pissant cowards. Truth is, Sheriff and his kind... they love the churchies. All this hollerin' about God and the corruption of the town's menfolk fills their pockets. Raises protection costs and keeps the graft sweet.'

This sent her off on another flight of fancy, as she prattled on about her time on the frontier being temporary. Bending my ear about her parlour house back in St Louis with its brass-fittings and high ceilings, its prestigious location on Lucas Street. Edge of a good neighborhood. Fashionable. Not shoved away in some tawdry red-light district. But I was only half-listening, waiting for a pause that might allow me to break away. Here I was, still wearing my dusty travel dress, and Madam Blair was running on about marble fireplaces.

'Well, what do you say, Vera?'

'I'm sorry?'

She threw up her hands. 'To taking over the business! To buying this place when I up stakes and head back to Missoura. You're salting away a tidy sum in that bank account, though you're madder than a march hare trusting your hard-earned cash to a bank.' She wagged her finger at me. 'Those places are run by the same dupes who walk through my door every night. Bust my tail for every gold coin I can get off 'em and there you go givin' it back!'

After the thieving I'd witnessed my first day in the house, I wasn't so sure. But I said nothing.

'Rubies, diamonds, emeralds.' Sadie lifted her hand from the arm of the chair and waved her jewelled fingers at me. 'That's where smart women put their money. Stones you can pawn for quick cash. Real estate ain't bad either. Madam I knew back in St Louie bought up a few lots outside town and made a fair profit. You put your money into this house, Vera, you won't regret it.'

So that was the reason for this little *tête-à-tête*.

'The johns like us. Town's growing. Railroad be coming through any day. And they'll be pullin' silver from these hills for a coon's age.'

Tom Cox didn't think so, but I kept that to myself.

'Running a bangshop's not a bad way to make a living. There's worse, believe me.'

I gave a noncommittal mumble, and just as she started to press me, Jackson rapped at the door. My luggage was being delivered. Did I want to inspect my bags before he sent the boy away? Why, yes. Yes, I did!

I set down my drink and escaped into the hall. Finding everything in order I thanked the boy and tipped him. And there, slipped beneath the handle of my carpet bag, was an envelope. *To Vera*. Penned in Will's bold, unwavering hand.

'Think about it,' said Sadie, emerging from her *rooms* in her crumpled robe, hair undone. A lamp burned on the table between us, giving off a sibilant hiss. 'Consider it a fall-back plan,' she persisted, eyes falling to the note in my hand. 'Should things with ole Willie Keane bust apart.'

Jackson hefted my bags onto his shoulder and I followed him up the stair, desperate to tear open Will's letter and devour its contents. But Jackson plodded on, one creaky step at a time.

'Think it over,' Madam Blair called after me.

'Yes,' I lied. 'I will.'

Chapter 19

I awoke with a start to find myself in the whores' dayroom. A converted store-room where they retreated while the houseboys cleaned their boudoirs. Afternoons, they'd loll about on stacks of old mattresses, flip through picture magazines, quarrel, brag, try out new hairstyles. Oily light smeared the papered window, objects in the room reduced to shadowy lumps. Shot mattresses. Old postcards pinned to timber walls. Throw pillows embroidered with flirty little sayings. *Daisies won't tell... Oh, Dearie I give you great pleasure!* Brushes, hair-switches. Bottles of scent. Jar of white liquid powder Evie had used to paint over her bruised face after her 'unfortunate accident.' Blair's phrase. As if she'd fallen from a horse, or slipped on a patch of ice.

I lifted my cheek from an itchy pillow. Contessa was asleep on a bare slab of mattress. Face shiny, blanket bunched between her legs. She'd come here after work to smoke, though there was no evidence of it. She'd exhale into a rolled up towel then pop the end-nub into her mouth and swallow. I'd seen her do it the night of Lil's abortion.

Texas Lil. She was the reason I was here. I recalled storming down the hall in the middle of the night to escape her loud, ragged snores. What use was that stupid lock? Lil just banged on the door until I opened up. Tonight I would not even bother locking the damn thing. Last week's fire at Ida Crowley's place had set me to thinking. Maybe locking myself inside wasn't such a good idea. It certainly wasn't conducive to a good night's sleep. Better just to let Lil just slide into bed alongside me the way she used to.

I slipped into the hall and saw Jackson lying on a pallet outside Gypsie's door. Some john was sleeping off a bender. It happened all the time, despite Blair's 'no all night tricks' policy.

Jackson would try to rouse the fellow, fail, then have to spend the night on a make-shift bed to guard against theft or damage. He cracked an eye, squinting up at me as I tip-toed around a heap of stained linens. A capsized whisky bottle lay by the door to my room.

Texas Lil was still sprawled across my bed, bare breasts splashed out to the side. Snot-clogged breaths rattled out from her chest. How could she be so careless? With her body, her life. I wanted to shake her awake and scold her for making no effort whatsoever to avoid the sad, inevitable fate that drew closer every day. Crib whore. Streetwalker. Cheap dance hall girl. But the sight of those downy tufts of hair under her arms put me in mind of baby chicks and little ducks and all manner of cuddly vulnerable creatures, rekindling the compassion that had gotten me into this damn mess in the first place.

Not a day went by without Lil weeping over my imminent departure, sobbing that I was the 'on'y one what loved her now Momma up and left.' She kept begging me to stay. Or she'd just cry and reminisce about her life back in El Paso at Alice Abbot's brothel where she'd been born, living in her momma's boudoir until Alice had turned Dora Belle out on suspicion of rolling a john. 'She never done it,' Lil claimed. 'That john were just mad cause Momma wouldn't let him pop me. I done heard her tell that filthy liar 'No fuckin' til a gal's fourteen! An my Lilly here's on'y ten. She kin use her mouth on you. But no more 'n at.'

Then Lil would get all misty-eyed and run on about how her momma never even let her stroke a john's balls while he was screwing, like some of the other mothers with trick-babies did. One time she told stories about their flight across New Mexico. After Dora Belle found she'd been frozen out of all the high class houses in El Paso, they'd hopped freight trains – copping brake-men and cargo-loaders in exchange for food. 'But Momma never let any of 'em get in my pants. There was one fella asked if he could suck my cunt and she said yes for ten dollars and it felt real nice. But nothing happened cause I was too young. That's how I know my Momma loves me.'

Some nights, I would lie awake and convince myself that we could bring her with us. Texas Lil could work for us on the ranch. As a kitchen-maid, perhaps, in exchange for room and board. Then I would drift off to sleep having resolved to talk to Will first thing in the morning, but upon waking sanity would always reassert itself. Lil had never done a lick of housework. She'd been waited on by houseboys and knockshop maids since birth. Her very first memory was of prancing around the parlour of a brothel in El Paso in a white frilly dress while everyone fussed over her. Besides, deep down, I recoiled at the prospect. I wanted my life with Will to be fresh and untarnished, free from all the mess and bother of Star Mansion. What was wrong with that? Fastening the last button on my riding dress, I grabbed my hat and stole out.

This morning I was to accompany Will on his daily ride. Before sun-up, he'd saddle Lacey and ride out to the rangeland west of town. The prospect of being alone with him ought to have heartened me, but exhaustion and over-work had worn me down to a dull nub, and as I stepped onto the wide dirt street, I found myself wishing I were back in bed.

Night was fading. But the town still lay sunk in shadow, everything lifeless and pale. At Fifth Street miners in sou-westers and oilskins poured from shaft-elevators. Dripping wet, they might have been taken for sailors but for the pick-axes and drilling rods that swung from blackened hands. They fell into a watchful silence at my approach. The whole town was on edge. Tensions had risen to a fever-pitch over the last few days, as union leaders were fighting a pay-cut and vowing to strike, while mining companies claimed the declining price of silver, combined with uncertain monetary policies in Washington, left them with no choice but to slash wages. All of which had made my claim impossible to sell. Will felt the situation would eventually right itself, but in the meantime we were short of

225

Pérez's asking price. Will had met my suggestion of a bank loan with a firm refusal, muttering something about the banks being heavily invested in the mines and a high risk of repossession.

Then Colonel Pérez made us a generous offer. His *gerente* had been arrested for corralling other people's horses and clipping their manes. It was not the first time he'd been caught stealing hair for his *bosalillos*. The man had been warned. Owners of neighboring ranches were angry and it was causing bad blood. This *gerente* had to go. Did Will want the job? If so, we could pay down the rest of what we owed by managing the ranch for three years. After that, it would be ours. The details were in the papers Will had drawn up and would carry down to Bisbee tomorrow. The deal was back on. Why, then, did I feel so low?

I turned south at the lumber yard, stacks of cut-timber pale with alkali dust. More miners just off the night-shift swept past, and beyond their wary stares I caught sight of Will. He was standing at the hitchbar by the livery stable, just where he'd said. He kissed me chastely on the cheek then gestured at a wall-eyed horse whose name, Will told me, was Apollo. I unhitched the rangy creature and mounted. Then we rode side-by-side down the broad street, empty but for a mule team hauling ore from the mines.

Crossing Third Street we wound between chopshops, laundries, mahjong parlours, and opium dens. Thick sweet smoke drifted over us, mitigating the stench of manure and cookfires. Old men sat bent over low tables, shuffling ivory tiles. Shop-walls were stacked with tea, canned fish, firecrackers, and burlap sacks stamped RICE. Then came a rambling labyrinth of lath-and-plaster shacks, flophouses, cribs, abandoned buildings. Roofless dwellings had been plundered and stripped, weeds sprouting up through caved-in porches. Knee-high grass, old trash-heaps, mesquite thickets. Where, exactly, was the great fortune amassed from the white slave trade being spent? I resolved to put the question to Deputy Barnes next time he showed up at Star Mansion, angling for a freebie.

Sighting the edge of the mesa, Will's horse gave a spry leap and broke into a trot, while my old grullo just kept poking along behind, his halting gait like a cradle set on uneven floorboards. Will reined his horse and drew up alongside me. 'Why the long face?'

I shrugged.

'Are you having second thoughts?' His tone was gentle, touched with worry. 'About the ranch purchase?'

I shook my head. The heaviness I felt arose from exhaustion, a bone-deep tiredness that no amount of sleep could cure. Everything about Star Mansion was sharp-edged and mean. No matter how hard I tried, I could not clap a shutter down against the endless stream of sordid details I was forced to confront. Lil's depressing childhood, Gypsie's snotty comments, Blair's unsought advice… the stuff just kept chiseling away at me.

Will reached out and swept a gloved hand across my thigh, and at this show of tenderness I said, 'I do not want you to leave tomorrow.'

'I'll write. I always do.'

Yes, he did. Long marvellous letters, full of unrestrained avowals, prosaic details about work, ruminations about the past, his hopes for the future. The last one had mentioned Alicia, his erstwhile fiancée. A pretty quiet girl whose brother was killed at Cold Harbor three months after Will's eldest brother, Samuel, had died of wounds. This shared loss had drawn them together in a bond of sorrow Will mistook for love. He felt no remorse at having broken their engagement, his letter went on to say, only regret at having hurt her. But Will's mother had raged at him, issuing threats. Ordered him to apologise, recant, do the honorable thing and marry the girl. So Will had fled to New Orleans, landing a job as legal counsel for a cotton factorage. That was seven years ago. Not a word from his mother since.

Will's letters were my lifeline, rife with forthright confessions and marked by an unfettered honesty that, of late, our seemed to lack. In those letters, I encountered the man who had held me in his gaze the night of the rainstorm. The one who bathed in cold clear streams of rainwater and made love to me when the impulse seized him. On hot stones beside a flooded creek, under the fat shade of cottonwood trees, on a bed beneath a roof of tin and beargrass thatch. And I was in sore need of such reminders, for since our return to town, this man had been eclipsed by a deferential suitor. Will never dropped by Star Mansion anymore, nor was I ever invited to his rooms at the Oriental. All we did was stroll the streets or sip tea in the lobby of some hotel. Activities suitable to a chaste, conventional courtship – something Will seemed to think I wanted, or ought to have.

To be fair, our interactions over the last three weeks had been dominated by the ranch-purchase. Every conversation was consumed by financial questions, logistical obstacles, a constant weighing of possibilities. Most of the time I managed to convince myself that this change was an inevitable result of being forced, all too swiftly, into the dull business of living. Still, his reserve dispirited me. Every Sunday he would wait for me on the respectable side of Allen Street, and upon glimpsing him, my heart would soar – only to plummet swiftly earthward when he greeted me with a cordial smile. His constraint seemed to rise from some unexamined notion of propriety which he felt obliged to follow when back in town, a compulsive deference to convention that had taken such deep root he could not even see it. But complaint was impossible. For he was always solicitous and kind, lavishing me with polite compliments and tender reverence. Yet I did not want to be revered. I wanted to feel free to press my palm to his cheek or plant a kiss on his lips if the urge seized me.

We rode out from under the shadow of the mesa and at the first touch of the sun, my fatigue began to dissipate. The road was nothing but a whip-twist of hard packed dirt that wound through the gravel flats, until it crested a gentle swell of land and miles of unbroken range unfurled before us.

'Penny for your thoughts,' said Will.

'I thought you abhorred idle chatter.'

'Talk needn't be idle.' He caught at the brim of his hat and tugged it down.

For a long moment I said nothing. His constraint during the preceding weeks had fostered in me a corresponding instinct to hold back. But out here, this impulse was overrun by another – a desire for candour awakened by the sight of every ridge and rocky draw laid bare beneath a shadowless sky.

'There is something,' I began. 'A question I have hesitated to ask for fear of upsetting you.'

'We must not be ruled by fear.' His tone was mild, and I knew that the remark was not meant as a rebuke.

'I wish to ask about Sophie.'

He frowned at the pommel of his saddle.

'I would not speak of it, but for something in your last letter. You wrote of her in such a way as to—' I broke off but having begun, retreat was impossible. 'You wrote that you had dishonoured yourself. But you made no explanation. Forgive me for being dull-witted, but I don't understand.'

The only sound was the leathery creak of the saddles, the dry clop of hooves on a hard-trampled road. Apollo swerved his head to crop at a long swale of grass, but I checked him, tightening the rein while he tossed his head and played with the bit. 'You are not dull,' Will said at last. 'Whatever dullness you perceive in yourself is a testament to your own upright nature.'

He sat staring at the parched bluffs to the west as we rode on through the wild radiance of day-break. Will's rifle clinked against some bit of metal. Wind riffled the grass, my skirts. When at last he spoke, he looked straight out across the high desert as if addressing the horizon.

'I met Sophie while doing legal work for her husband. She was always at the house when I arrived, greeting me after I was shown through to the parlour where we would sit and chat politely until Edouard emerged from his study. I thought nothing of this. One afternoon I received an urgent summons from Monsieur DuBois but, upon arrival, I found him absent. Sophie met me in the parlour, as usual, but she was smiling in a strange way. She then confessed to forging the note and when I rose to leave, she broke into peals of laughter. Then she placed a hand on my wrist and whispered, 'Haven't you ever had a lover?'

'After that I would go whenever she sent for me. Drop everything the moment a *billet doux* arrived. I became ruled by her whims. She could go weeks without sending word. Or I might be summoned twice in one day. Other times I would fly to her door only to be turned away. That summer was a torment. She repaired to Grand Isle, leaving me alone for six long weeks in the humid oppression of the city.

'I was nothing but an artless boy, but my inexperience seemed to charm her. At first. For several months our liaison amused her. But her affection ran no deeper. Whenever I spoke of serious matters, or tried to share what was in my heart, she would turn me away with a laugh or grow bored. Then, at the end of that long solitary summer, she did not summon me. I knew she was back in town. I tried to force myself to be patient. But I could not. I became frantic, enraged, suspicious… until I could stand it no longer. One afternoon I waited down the street from her house and it was as I'd feared. At three o'clock, the very hour she used to send for me, a carriage rolled up and a man stepped out. Wordly, distinguished, elegantly dressed… he carried a silver-tipped walking stick and wore an expensive frockcoat. I watched him walk down the garden path and climb the back-steps to where Harry would be waiting to let him in. I was wild with fury, and before I knew what I was doing I'd dashed down the street, pushed past Harry and run up the stairs to her bedroom, where I accused her of being a faithless whore and at this—' He winced. Then he thumbed his hat and went on. 'At this she burst out laughing and informed me I was a terrible bore. Then she told Harry to throw me out.'

I made no response. Starting out across the shoreless expanse of grass, I sensed that the slightest word from me would cause him to lose courage, so I simply listened. His words skimmed over me, almost refusing to settle. But as I fixed my eyes on the far-off hills, now leached of colour, the story began to sink in.

Weeks drifted by in a fog of jealousy, humiliation, rage, and thwarted desire. Then, early one morning, a note arrived summoning him as before. To Will's great shame he raced to her door, ready to sweep her into his arms and forget everything. But Sophie met him in the parlour. Face puffy, eyes red. She had not slept, was in desperate straits, needed his help. Edouard had been caught out in a real estate deal. Some fellow had run off with a bundle of cash and the investors were vicious, mercenary Yanks who were going to bring criminal charges. She and Edouard stood to lose everything. Everything! There was no reasoning with these Northerners, these carpet-baggers with nothing but greed in their hearts. A judge had already been assigned to the case. Would Will have a word with him? She had it on good authority he was susceptible to persuasion. The claimants were Yankee speculators, trying to make a quick buck off a war hero and a duBois, at that. The judge was a war veteran himself and did not take kindly to such people. But he was touchy about who approached him. If the go-between was to his liking... Will knew Judge Theriaux socially, did he not? They belonged to the same club...

Will had tried to dissuade her, begging her to let him defend her husband free of charge. If Edouard were innocent, the case would be won on its own merits and his name cleared. But Sophie met the suggestion with scorn. If Will's 'commonplace proprieties' were going to get in the way, she'd ask someone else. *Commonplace proprieties*. So. It was this she despised in him.

'To my eternal shame, I agreed. But on one condition.'

The horses jolted on and I had to strain to catch his words. 'I demanded that Sophie renounce her new lover during the time it took me get the job done. She gave her word, and I believe she kept it. After all, it was a small price to pay to safeguard her husband's name, his fortune…' he frowned. 'But she made her contempt for me clear. And when Judge Theriaux threw out the case, she flung me aside as well.'

Will sat looking off across the country, hair on his chin coppery in the low morning light. 'I sacrificed my honour for her, and for what? She made a fool of me. A laughing stock.'

I did not know what to say. His revelations had made me bashful, which was strange given all that I'd heard and seen at Star Mansion. Will sensed my discomfort and gave my arm a reassuring squeeze. A sensation akin to a sigh washed through me. I smiled up at him then returned my gaze to the road, which unfurled over miles of open rangeland until it disappeared into the hills. 'Let's keep on going,' I burst out.

'To where?'

'The ocean. All the way to the ocean.'

Will gave a soft chuckle.

'I'm serious.' I pointed to the mountains that lay across the river on the opposite side of the valley. 'I want to know what's beyond that rise. And the next one, and the next.'

'I've been through some of it.' Will shifted the rifle that hung by his side, and I imagined him urging Lacey across the river, then dismounting on the opposite side to tighten the girthstrap and pour water from his boots before leading the mare up through the sedge grass and the willows and back onto the trail. Rider and horse dripping wet under a hard dazzle of sky.

'What's on the other side?'

He shrugged. 'Not much.'

'Come on, tell me.'

'Town of Charleston. Whetstone Mountains. A ranch or two.' He looked askance at me, shine of amusement in his half-hidden eyes.

'Then the ocean, right?'

He laughed. 'We'd need to hop a train for that.'

'No trains. Just this road.' Our eyes met in a flirtatious gaze that heartened and urged me on. 'Well?'

'After we've come up out of the valley and crossed Whetstones?'

I nodded.

He let out a long breath and rubbed his bristly chin. 'Then we become very, very thirsty.'

And we both laughed. A bright rich sound that rang out in the clear morning air before being swallowed up by land and sky, and when our eyes met I saw that he felt as I did – enchanted by the feel of being plunged into this bright arid sea. It was just the sort of moment I'd longed for, and it dispelled the disquiet that had crept over me.

At the base of the foothills a narrow cattle-path broke away from the road, and Will reined his horse down the thin ribbon of trail. I steered Apollo in behind Lacey, following Will to the bottom of a shallow draw that opened out into a clearing that held the charred remains of a one-room house. No doors, roof gone. Walls scorched to a black so deep that it glittered in the sun.

Will swung down and led Lacey beneath the shade of a walnut tree. He bent to pass a length of rope through a stake already driven into the ground, then looped another rope through Apollo's headstall and tied it off. Then he grabbed his rifle by the forestock and said, 'Follow me.'

We crossed the clearing side-by-side, and as I watched him count off the paces to the charred house, I found myself unable to suppress a smile. This was how I liked him best – deerhide gloves shoved into his hip pocket, shirt smeared with rifle grease, wholly at ease in this sun-struck land.

He placed a rusty pail on the empty windowledge then trotted back to the edge of the clearing. Balancing the rifle in his palms, he said, 'This is a lever-action, repeating rifle.

Breech-loading, chambered for a 44 caliber cartridge.' He levered it open and started removing the shells. 'Some people prefer the Centennial, but I like this better. It's light, reliable, easy to handle on horseback, and it takes the same ammunition as my revolver.' He set the rifle down, drew a box of shells from his pocket, and held it up to a cartridge from the rifle. 'You don't even need to remember what caliber. Just carry a spare shell in your pocket then match it.' He tapped at the picture on the box. My gaze caught on the words written beneath and I pointed at them. *Winchester Repeating Arms Company, New Haven, Connecticut*. 'Fancy that. My hometown.'

'Don't remind me.' Will tapped at the hammer with his thumb. 'Bullet that killed my brother was probably made in your hometown.' It was said without rancour, but a momentary hush fell between us as he weighed the shells in his hand. Then he reloaded the rifle, raised it and fired.

Apollo jerked up his head and looked warily about, rolling a wide eye skyward. Lacey whinnied, but did not stir. Will fired again and the rusty pail clattered to the ground. At that, Apollo shied and skittered. Will retrieved the pail and placed it back on the empty windowframe. Then he trotted back and held out the rifle. I stepped away.

'You must learn to shoot, Vera.'

'Why? What will I be shooting?'

'Rabbits, quail...' he shrugged. 'There will be times when I'll be away from the ranch for days, even weeks, at a time. You must know how to handle a gun.'

I took hold of it. Trigger rubbed shiny from use. Stock worn smooth. I balanced the rifle in my hands. It was not as heavy as I'd expected.

He tapped at a metal bit, flipping it back and forth. 'When it's like this, it won't fire.' He pointed the gun across the clearing and pulled the trigger. 'See? Locked.'

Then he flipped it back and shifted in behind me. Wedging the rifle-stock into the crook of my shoulder, he issued

234

instructions on how to brace against the recoil. My pulse quickened at the feel of his arms as he showed me how to level and sight. How to aim, give lead on a moving target. Then he stepped back and told me to fire.

I glanced back at the horses, stake-ropes stretched taut as they grazed on a swale of gramma grass.

'They're behind us,' Will laughed. 'You can't possibly hit them.'

The rifle felt heavy and awkard against my shoulder. I hesitated, struggling to remember all he'd said. About the kick-back, the smoke, the heat of the barrel… until in the end I just squeezed up my face and pulled the trigger. The rifle slammed into my shoulder and a bullet tore through the wall well wide of the mark.

'Try again.'

I aimed and pulled the trigger, hitting wide on the opposite side.

'Spread your feet apart. Like this.'

I fired and missed again. Riflesmoke mingled with the smell of burnt hair. I raised my free hand to tuck a stray wisp behind my ear, but the moment I raised the rifle, the hair fell forward again. I heaved an impatient sigh.

'Here.' Will swept up the loose strands and tucked them firmly into my hat, fingertips brushing the tender skin behind my ear. Then he stepped back and told me to try again. After that I would have to reload. My stomach growled with hunger. My legs ached. I lifted the rifle and fired. Crack, slam. The pail went zinging from the windowledge and clattered to the ground. Will let out a great whoop and ran towards the house.

The dented pail lay on the dirt floor. Will retrieved it and tapped at a hole in its side. Then he caught me round the waist, eyes shining with a fervour I had not glimpsed in weeks as he swung me round to face him. Gripping the rifle in both hands, he used it to draw me to him and pressed his lips to mine. I closed my eyes to the hard crush of his mouth. Tasted the cool bone of his teeth. Warm gunmetal driven into my spine as he jerked me up against him. Once, twice. Forestock grinding into my back until we slid to our knees and fell to the painstaking business of unlacing and unclasping and wrestling off boots until enough skin was bared to tumble across the dirt-floor and make love between the fireblackened walls.

After he cried out and fell still, I lay beneath him, breathing. Awareness crept back one sensation at a time: hard ground, stingy patch of skin at the base of my spine, sound of a horse urinating beyond the walls. Will shoved himself up and stared down at me. Then he brushed the hair from my face and gave me a warm, affectionate kiss. But a shadowy flicker passed over his eyes that gave me pause. The expression on his face had faded, then not quite brightened.

'Penny for your thoughts,' I whispered.

He trailed a finger down my neck and kept going, down between the unbuttoned bodice of my dress. I lifted my lips to his and kissed him full on the mouth, but he broke away.

I put a fingertip to his frown. 'Why the long face?'

'There is something I'd like to ask,' Will rolled away and began pulling on his trousers. 'About your late husband. May I?'

A sigh broke from me. 'You may do to me as you like. Is that not clear?' I gave an impatient wave at my tumbled skirts and unbuttoned bodice. Then I set to work forcing tiny buttons through stiff unyielding slits.

'Please. Don't be offended.'

'What offends me is to be treated like some fragile debutante.'

He retrieved his rifle and set it upright in the corner. Then he crossed back over the dirt floor and sat down, placing a hand on my knee. 'I would like to have children one day.'

I smiled up at him. 'As many as you like.' How easily it fell from my lips, the same assurance I used to offer Henry.

'I have been wondering, lately, over... you and your late husband – you never bore any children.' He glanced up at the

236

patch of sky that hung above the roofless walls then back at me. 'Do you understand?'

I nodded and looked down, thoughts drifting away to all that had gone unsaid with Henry. The details of my mother's death. My terror of childbirth. That furtive trip on the omnibus to my old neighborhood to purchase those black pills. The gripping pains and the hot baths and the water threaded with blood. It had been a mistake not to share my fears with Henry. One I would not make again.

'You are worried that I might not be able to bear children. Well, you needn't fear. I once fell pregnant, but I was just a young girl. Happy for the first time in my life. Terrified I would die during childbirth like my mother. But I am older now. And far wiser. I would never do anything like that that again.'

He drew back, recoiling from my touch. And in that moment I saw that there were things a woman could never tell a man. Things a husband, no matter how beloved, could not ever understand. I swallowed hard, mouth dry.

'What I did,' I faltered, then began again. 'What I did was to let fear get the better of me. But, as you have so wisely said, we must not be ruled by fear.' I placed a reassuring hand on his arm. 'I was pregnant once, you see, but I miscarried. The doctor said it was because I was so afraid. He explained that fear can make a woman nervous and unwell and that my nerves had caused me to miscarry. He examined me and said there was no physical reason I could not bear many children. In future, he said, I mustn't be so afraid. He instructed me to conquer my fears and assured me that once I did this, all would be well. But then Henry fell ill and...' I sensed a lingering suspicion and forced myself to meet his gaze. 'I am no longer afraid.' My eyes burned with conviction. It was true. With Will by my side, I feared nothing.

Clasping his hands in mine, I drew them to my lips. Kissed the pale flesh of each wrist. One by one. That tender spot where the skin is thinnest, soft throb of blood pulsing through veins beneath. We lay back and began again. There on that dirt floor among the mouse droppings and the candlestubs and the spent shell casings. Will's leather chaps, stiff against the back of my head. Feather-scratch of his beard, tongue to teeth, every scrap of breath forced from my lungs as he reared up above me, torso blocking out the sky.

Chapter 20

My last morning at Star Mansion dragged on into the afternoon as Madam Blair heaped on task after task, punctuating every request with peevish remarks disguised as compliments. 'What a bang-up job you've done, pointless to train a new gal with our return to St Louie bearing down so fast.' Forlorn head-shake. 'Gotta unload this place first. Furniture, whores, the whole shee-bang,' followed by a corset-shortened sigh. Then, as I was leaving the office, she issued one final command: 'Quit that bedroom faster'n a turpentined cat. I'll be turning it into a Turkish themed boudoir for tonight's entertainments.'

'Of course,' I replied. But as I climbed the stair, her comment set me to worrying. Will's return from Bisbee was to have transpired three days ago, yet I had received no word. Had he gotten me a room at the Cosmopolitan Hotel as we'd discussed, or did he expect me to wait out some unforeseen delay at Star Mansion? The prospect was intolerable. Another night of selling johns brass checks then hoping they don't choose Evie, face heavily made-up, walk still gimpy? Another supper choked down while having to endure Gypsie's mockery? (Upon hearing my reasons for not marrying Will straight away – a sacred bond, the firmest of foundations – she'd burst into a toothy guffaw: 'I took you for a sensible girl, but you're pie-eyed as they come. Fallin' for that shill talk.' And she'd never let up since.)

I shoved at my bedroom door. The warped wood resisted until I bumped it open with my hip. Silk pillows and tassled draperies lay piled in the corner beside paintings of exotically dressed Arabs surrounded by coffee-skinned women. I stood motionless before Henry's steamer trunk – half packed, lid open – and saw a pair of nail scissors left in full view. Careless.

After Evie's 'incident' Blair had asked if I had any. I'd lied, then been very careful to keep them hidden. Madam Blair was so afraid of 'sharps' in the boudoirs that she snipped the whores' toe-nails and trimmed their pubic hair herself. Every Friday. But why should my nail scissors be spirited away to some inconvenient location to be locked up with Jackson's razors?

I swept them under a pile of clothes, fighting to steer my thoughts clear of why they were out in the first place. Loud whumps had wakened me in the middle of the night, and upon investigating, I'd found Evie kneeling on her bed ramming her head into the wall. There were red scratches on her arms, legs, stomach. Clumps of dull brown hair strewn about. Jackson was summoned and after he'd calmed her with a dose of laudanum, he instructed me to clip her nails short. I'd done it, struggling to keep my eyes from her face, which was gripped by a wild look. Then, as the drug did its work, the look drained away and she relapsed into blank bewilderment.

No. I would not spend another night under this roof. I flung more clothing into my case, then took up my bottles and jars and plinked them in after. Jackson would transport my things to the Cosmopolitan Hotel an hour from now, as arranged, and I would wait there for word from Will. I emptied dresser drawers, rooting through what remained of Dora Belle's left-behind possessions to see if anything might suit. Bottle of scent? I chucked it into my case. Why hadn't I heard anything? Another unforeseen delay?

I tore down my dresses and tossed them into the trunk, until the wardrobe was empty but for a bundle of letters. I withdrew them and rifled through the pile, until I lit on Will's most recent missive. I scoured every sentence for some sign of trouble, some hint of what might have caused him to fall silent. But there was nothing. His instructions were most explicit: after drawing up the final papers with Pérez, he would send a telegram. I would then take my savings out of Safford Hudson Bank and deliver them to Billy, who would place them in a locked vault where they would remain until Pérez arrived to sign the papers and receive our payment. Two days, Will had said, three at most. A full week had now passed. Although Blair had been happy to keep me toiling away here as long as possible, this afternoon's remark about the Turkish themed boudoir made it clear that she was becoming impatient with my ever-changing departure date. The message was clear: unless I was here for the duration, it was time to skedaddle.

Cries rose up from the street. Angry shouts, loud clangs. I glanced out the window. Dust boiled up from the road. Glints of metal shone through the brown haze, and it took me a moment to make out the drilling rods and pick-axes being swung and cracked into cooking pots, metal lids, lanterns. There came a loud shattering of glass as men in leather brogans swarmed past, shouting. What if some voilence had befallen Will?

Billy. He would know something.

I bolted down the stairs and into the street where the sun beat down on the men and the horses and the hard-packed earth, as I shoved my way through the jostle of knee-high boots and mine-wet brogans. Their smell of sour sweat and mule dung pressed in on me, and in the years to come I would often wonder whether this stink of miners sweat clinging to my clothes influenced what happened next. But at the time, my thoughts were for Will Keane alone. Shoving my way clear of the angry throng, I held fast to the hope that this mob was the reason for Will's silence. His savings were bound up in the mines. Once news of the strike reached the exchange back East, stocks would plummet. Perhaps he had failed to sell his shares in time, and could find no way to break the bad news? I turned south towards the courthouse where a spooked mule had broken loose, dragging its reins through the street. Its unholy bray pierced the clamour like lightening in a storm.

A cluster of dark-suited men were milling around Billy's desk.

When I entered, they turned sober gazes on me and fell silent. Billy looked up from his typewriter with a spooked expression that reignited all my former fears. Then he waved me back, and I felt myself crumple inwardly. Will was fine.

Crossing into his office, I was hit by the usual sharp smell of livery stables, leather-dust, drying ink. Yet something was different, a shift in atmosphere that I could not name. Will stood at the window, hands deep in his trouser-pockets. His shirt-sleeves were clasped firmly at the wrist, not rolled to the elbow as was his usual habit, and at the sight of him a feathery lightness riffled over me. In anticipation of his touch. Our imminent embrace.

But when he turned, a dark look clouded his brow. His face was pale and haggard, and the tired stoop of his shoulders moved me almost to tears. Things were worse than I'd imagined.

'Darling, you look exhausted.' I stepped forward, gloved hand outstretched. 'Have you slept?'

He stared down at his shoes, dull with street-dust. A soft clap of hoofbeats resounded through the wall, followed by the clang of a horse's foreleg against a trough.

'Will,' I pressed him, gently. 'Tell me what has happened.'

At length he spoke, voice neutral and distant. 'I think you know.'

'Trust me when I say that I do not.' The air between us was hazy with dust motes. I advanced towards him, hand outstretched. 'Whatever has happened, do not fret. We can make a modest start. Even if your share is gone, my portion is in cash, not stocks. And there is more where that has come from. Blair still owes me for—'

'Oh, I am sure she does.'

My hand fell to my side. 'What are you implying?'

'From the beginning,' he went on, 'I have observed a certain elasticity in your ethics, a moral compass whose magnetic north is not, shall we say, as constant as one might like.'

'What on earth…'

'A woman who works for the likes of Sadie Blair,' he proclaimed in that rich-timbred drawl he usually reserved for judges hailing from the South, 'one who elects to live under the same roof as a bunch of prostitutes when perfectly suitable accommodation exists throughout the town, this is not the sort of woman a man ordinarily selects to be the mother of his children.'

I began to tremble.

'More to the point, Miss Palmer, these are not traits I wish the mother of my own children to possess.' He stared into the middle distance as if some imaginary jury were ranged along the far wall. 'I am partially to blame. I did not fully consider the moral hazards to which you would inevitably be exposed living under Blair's roof, the corrupting influence such an atmosphere would have on a young woman.' He paused to draw breath, pressing his palms to the surface of his desk. Then he withdrew a pile of papers from a drawer and placed them before me. My letters.

The pious absurdity of this gesture appalled me. How dare he treat me as if I were some schoolgirl he'd been courting with flowers and penny candies! I looked beyond him, taking in the sun-faded baize on his desk, the tattered ink blotter, all the tidy piles of papers and books. Then I saw it. The difference. The subtle change I had sensed upon entering. The worn carpet had been cleared. His desk tidied. The table by the door held no carelessly tossed walking sticks, no stray books. Every dull brown volume had been returned to its proper shelf, every paper was filed and stacked. And this meticulousness extended to his own appearance. His hair had been combed carefully into place, every tousled wave subdued by a layer of pomade, and a hard imperviousness had come over him, distorting his face into a remote and unrecognisable mask.

Something was terribly wrong. And it was up to me to fix it, a task that required great care. Say nothing rash. Do not provoke him. I took a turn about the room, pausing by the grimed window. Beyond the glass flies swarmed while horses shifted and stamped beneath the corral's shaded overhang, and arced above it all was a shimmering blaze of sky. The same vast and cloudless vault that had sheltered us at the Cruillo Ranch. I used this thought to steady myself, clinging fast to all that had passed between us during those sun-soaked days. Taking a seat in the leather armchair, I recalled the avid avowals of his recent letters (*your consoling presence, your cool and steady hand against my arm...*). The stale heat of the room was suffocating. I opened my fan and waved it before my face with an air of great patience. 'I am not leaving without a full and satisfactory explanation.'

'I have given it.'

'No. What you have given me are excuses, half-truths.'

'Are you calling me a liar?'

'Of course not.' I drew a deep breath. 'But no man of honour would consider what you have said sufficient grounds in light of—'

'How dare you speak to me of honour.'

'And how dare you offer up facts that you have known since the day we met and expect me to accept them as a reason for this – this change. From the very first, you knew that I lived under Sadie Blair's roof, sold brass checks to her customers, lived off her wages. Since the moment you sought me out and asked me to dance – yes, *you* came to *me* – and you kept coming. Night after night you came to me and did such things that no honourable man can do and walk away from. And not once did any of these troublesome facts give you pause. Not once did they prevent you from taking your pleasure when it suited you, not when we were in Tucson, not when—' my voice broke but I steadied it and went on. 'What is the true cause of these sudden misgivings?'

He held up a hand, face curdled with displeasure and pain, and this brief glimpse of feeling beneath his obstinate exterior gave me hope. Perhaps exhaustion and overwork were to blame. 'Will, darling, what has happened? Never did the prospect of a child… you never gave voice to such a worry before. Not the slightest hint. Not even last week, when we spoke of—' I paused, voice soft as a caress. 'Such matters.'

'I have said my piece.'

'Please,' I breathed, note of supplication in my voice that I loathed but could not quell. 'Do not insult me with these platitudes.'

'Insult you? Insult *you*! It is I who have been insulted.' He thrust a finger into his own chest. 'Humiliated. Made a laughing-stock. Word is all over Bisbee that Sadie Blair's book-keeper – my future wife! – can be had for a price.'

I rose from the chair and stole slowly towards him. Every movement calm and deliberate, as if to avoid startling some wild creature whose broken wing could be mended, if only the poor thing would let me come close enough. 'Gossip and ugly speculation,' I said evenly, 'the slanderous remarks of a stranger have caused you to doubt me.' He turned away, and for a moment I faltered, but with a quick-drawn breath I carried on. 'Consider the degree to which you, too, are open to wrong-headed assumptions. Think what would anyone who saw you leaving Star Mansion would assume you had been doing there. And they would be wrong. We are both equally faultless in our actions under Blair's roof. Why do such ugly falsehoods bother you? Why, all of a sudden—'

'What bothers me,' he broke out, 'is to walk into a bar and hear lurid tales of debauchery involving my future wife. What humiliates me is to hear a pair of filthy slag-shovellers bragging that they saw the prim and proper cunt who works the till for Sadie Blair naked as a jaybird. And to hear that this woman – the woman who was to be the mother of my children – offered herself to these bastards for a price!'

I felt a hot, scrabbling panic and made no answer.

'It is true, Vera?'

'No, it is not.'

His face clouded over. Then he turned away, hands thrust into his trouser-pockets. When at length he spoke there was distain in every word. 'Then how is it that one of those damned powder monkeys knew of the mole on your back? Knew just where it was and—' Grabbing me by the elbow he jabbed his thumb into the soft spot above my hip and hissed, '*just above that prim and proper ass, one look at that ass makes you ready to fuck, that ass with a mole right up there, one look and you're ready to fuck her.*' Then he twisted his thumb, hard, digging it deep into my flesh until I wriggled free and crashed into the bookcase. A leather-bound volume fell to the floor with a thud.

Effort spent, Will collapsed into an arm-chair and buried his head in his hands. 'God, what a fool I looked!' he broke out, 'defending your honour to a bunch of grubby slag-shovellers. Christ, I nearly challenged the drunken sot to a duel.'

'It's not too late.'

'You know I abhor frontier justice.' He tossed off this reply without thinking, but the moment my words penetrated his self-pitying gloom, he levelled me with a hard stare. 'Are you really urging me to such a foolhardy course of action? A duel? Do you want me dead?'

Maybe I did. Better dead than alive but not mine. Alive but refusing me. The grief of death, at least, had the advantage of being familiar.

'I am urging you to do whatever it takes to resolve this situa—'

'Damn it, Vera. It can't *be* resolved. Some quiff-hunter brags about seeing you naked, and when I challenge him, the lecher offers me proof positive of his claim. Incontrovertible proof! Evidence that would stand up in any court in the land. And to make matters worse, you have the nerve to stand here and deny it.'

'Evidence? You speak of evidence. Do I get a chance to defend myself?'

He shrugged and collapsed back into the chair.

'Two men barged into my room one night. The night of the Bisbee Massacre execution, as a matter of fact. An unhappy event which you fled, but which the rest of us were not so lucky to escape. At the end of a terrible, terrible night – one of the worst I have ever passed – a night when Jackson had to go outside to wrest a pistol from some idiot putting slugs into our dogs. Yes, Will, they were shooting the guard dogs. Not to mention what happened to Evie – a horror for which I have no words to describe – and amid this mayhem, two drunken bastards snuck into my room and hid. Unbeknownst to me. They snuck into my room and lay in wait. They watched me undress and then they went after me. I fought back, screaming. But before Jackson could reach my room, one of them had laid a hand on me. Both of them saw me naked. Can I help this? I was lucky they went no further, that they were so drunk, that Jackson was so quick. I was lucky not to have been beaten, violated, shamed. And now these bastards spout lies in saloons and beer halls – lies about me offering myself to them. Well of course, they do! They are scoundrels, Will. And you stand here believing their word over mine.'

He endured my speech with an air of weary forbearance, like a man resigned to hearing out his wife's grievances over a difficult servant or surly shop-keeper. And when he spoke, his voice was strained with sorrow. 'An entire bar full of drunken micks was laughing at me, Vera. I would never have expected it from the likes of you. Of all the women… ' He gave his head a forlorn shake. 'Not from you.'

Vera. Not Miss Palmer. *Vera*. I felt a faint surge of hope. 'I am sorry for what you have endured, but I have done nothing wrong.'

'Did you not offer yourself to them for a price?' he thundered. 'To both men at once at a bargain rate?'

I met his eye. 'No, I did not.'

He made no reply.

I swallowed hard, voice raw in my throat. 'Have you ceased to love me?'

He looked up distractedly. 'I have ceased to comprehend you.' All trace of sorrow drained from his face and he unleashed a wretched laugh. 'This betrayal cannot be undone.'

I stood in mute shock. Taken aback by the news that there were, in fact, things in this life that could not be undone. Birth and death, surely, were the only truly irreversible events. I felt a sour churning in my gut, and a realisation began to take shape – an understanding that, in fact, some spark of youth had survived Henry's death, a tiny shard of that irrepressible faith in self and in love and in one's ability to make a mark on the world that the young possess. But it would not survive this.

Will lifted the letters from his desk and extended them to me. The sight of his sun-darkened hands triggered a fresh burst of pain. The only power left to me was resistance, and I seized upon it. Feigning that I would take up the letters, I stepped forward and at the very moment he let go, I drew my hand back and let the packet fall to the floor.

'I would appreciate the return of my own,' he said evenly, face petrifying into a remote implacable mask. His composure set me shaking. How I despised his brutal self-command, his need to force me into following into some rote formula of leave-taking.

Lifting my letters from the floor, I flung them at his head. But in my fury they missed their mark and they fell with a flop to the carpet where they lay at his feet like a dead bird.

Then I gathered my gloves and walked out.

Chapter 21

Contessa found me, curled up with a pipe in the back room of some Chinese grocery. Swept-dirt floor, thin yellow pallets, lone candleflame to light one's way to the door. Stink of outhouse wafting in, or did someone soil himself?

Her reedy voice arrived first, drifting down through the feathery soft. *O María, Madre Mía, O Consuelo del mortal, Aparadme y guiadme, A la patria celestial...* Gentle swell of light pulsing through me as her voice rasped out its *oracion*. Then a man's strong arms. Rough nap of a workshirt. Not his. Not his, yet familiar. This scent of axle grease, mules, black tobacco. Jackson. His tattooed arms carrying me away, then dumping me into Josie's washtub out in the moonstruck yard. Clothes and all. To kill the bed bugs or the scabies or whatever vermin teemed in that grimy mattress.

Hours later I awoke with a terrible thirst. Glass of tepid water on the night-stand, taste of chalky stone. Beyond the flat glass was a fiery sky. Dusk or dawn?

The room was just as I had left it. Carpet bag half-packed. Clothes piled by Henry's steamer trunk, lid open. My gaze slid along the scratched and faded leather. Scars from journeys to distant lands. Places I had once dreamt he might take me. Henry. In recent weeks he had been consigned to some remote, unvisited hinterland. No, worse. He had been judged and found wanting.

Will Keane's letter still lay on the floor, pages scattered where they had fallen from my hand. I leapt from bed. Gathering them up, I tossed it all into the trunk and banged the lid shut. A satisfying slam. But his words were still inside me, ringing out like some mutinous cry of pain and outrage impossible to silence. I glimpsed a small dark shape lying clumped in the corner. I approached on tip-toe, expecting a mouse. But it was only a tassle. Lone remnant of the silks and cushions for Blair's Turkish-themed boudoir that had been whisked away. By Jackson, no doubt. To let me know, wordlessly, that I could stay on. And at the sight of those bare floorboards, I wept. Sobs that shook me with such force I feared I might break in two, until my grief had spent itself and I saw that light had suffused the room. Colour of tarnished brass. Clatter of hacks and wagons came filtering up from the street. Clang of pots downstairs. Morning. I forced myself to dress. To descend the stair and take up Blair's ledger book. Numb to everything but the scratch of a pen, the dry page beneath my fingers.

Houseboys arrived to clean cigar-trays, empty spittoons, rub out wet glass stains, and roll back carpets. Their high youthful voices reached me through the thin board walls, as Josie brought coffee and a slice of buttered toast. Setting the food on the desk, she told me Blair was laid up with a headache. This news was delivered in that warm, matter-of-fact way she had of being kind without inviting intimacy. I wanted to thank her. But when I saw that her face bore the same expression it had on the night of the abortion, when she'd cupped Lil's face in her hands and told her to be strong, I felt my throat tighten and did not dare speak.

'Be thankful for small mercies,' she said at last.

I nodded, eyes cast down at a fresh sheaf of paper demanding its proper dose of leaden figures. Then with staunch, dry-eyed discipline, I complied.

At supper the whores bickered over the spoils from Blair's Turkish-themed boudoir, while I pushed catfish and stewed rhubarb around my plate. Nobody acknowledged my presence, which was a relief. My misfortune, I decided, would be treated the same way as Evie's 'accident' or Lil's aborted child. Like a disfiguring scar one took great pains never to stare at. But no,

Gypsie was just waiting for the right moment, because as soon as Josie slipped outside, Gypsie shot me a look and said, 'Sweet Willie done the skip on you, eh?'

I felt my face tighten.

'You had that man by the short hair,' she clucked. 'Shoulda done like I said and landed him quick, stead a lollygagging fore tying the knot.'

I kept on chewing, food like ashes in my mouth. Then she flashed me a grin, and at the sight of those hard square teeth something long imprisoned broke free and the next thing I knew I was on my feet brandishing a fork. She flinched as I made a few false thrusts at her smooth, powdered face, exulting in the way she ducked and recoiled. Then she twisted her lips and spat, hitting me square in the chest. At that, I brought the fork down hard on her bare arm. A thrill rippled through me at the feel of those metal tines breaking skin, a soft resistance before the doughy flesh yielded. She cried out and swung a fist at me, but I spun away in time.

I let go of the fork, but it stayed stuck in her arm. Evie gave a pinched cry, but Gypsie just yanked the thing free and hurled it at me. I ducked and heard it clatter to the floor as Texas Lil roared with laughter. Then I stacked my plate in the sink and walked out.

That night, I performed each transaction with ruthless focus. Making change, wrapping up bills, totting up sales. The hours dragged by as men drank, spat, talked, went upstairs. Mine bosses chewed cigar-ends and jawed on about the strike. I knew I should listen. Try to suss out when I might be able to sell my claim and get the hell out of Goose Flat. But I found myself indifferent. Where would I go? What would I do? Doubts whirled, questions spun. And beneath it all smouldered a faint unacknowledged hope: if Will Keane had a change of heart, I wanted him to know where to find me. I tried reasoning with myself. Played back all the wretched things he had said. Poked and salted the wounds he had inflicted. But it was no use.

Reason was no match for the memory of his hands on my hips, that feather-scratch of beard against thigh. A heart-felt apology over that eruption of madness in his office would suffice. *Just a momentary fit of jealousy, I panicked. But I find that I cannot now stay away, what a mistake I made.* These were the fantasies that flared up when I lay in bed each night, unable to sleep.

A paunchy man approached with Gypsie on his arm. Skirts tumbled, hair tousled from a long night's work, she clung to him gamely and fed him the usual housetalk, 'Ohh, hurry up, handsome! Quick! I haven't had any all night.'

The man fumbled through his pockets, giving his cigar a brisk chomp.

'Big strong man,' she breathed. 'Quick! Take me upstairs!'

I slid a brass check across the bar, and as he lunged for it, the tip of his cigar grazed her shoulder. Gypsie leapt back, making it out to be a coy flirtatious gambol, but she never cried out, never stopped smiling gamely even as the burning cigar-tip touched her bare skin. She just plucked the cigar from his lips then, without missing a beat, shoved it at me. Spitty end first. 'Be a doll and take care of this, Vera.'

I snarled inwardly, but took it. Soggy with some stranger's spit. Because what choice did I have, with Madam Blair just a few feet away? Gypsie gave a triumphant smirk, then clasped the man's small hairy hand and led him away, fishing ice from an abandoned drink and pressing it to her shoulder as she went.

Every so often I stole glances at Madam Blair, searching for some sign that she knew of my scuffle with Gypsie. But the dull squint of her eyes and the cringing tilt of her head revealed only that she was still in the grip of a headache. Once Blair found out, what would my punishment be? Would she have Jackson knock me around, or cut me loose altogether? I tried to whip up some interest in the question, to manufacture a little inward drama to divert myself, but lacked the energy.

The night wore on. Johns collected their hats and sticks. Firearms were holstered, cigars stubbed out, drinks emptied.

Madam Blair retired early. Jackson slid me a particularly hefty belt of bourbon, and when at last I stumbled upstairs to bed I lay amazed. The day had passed. Somehow I had managed to march myself across its colourless expanse of hours and reached the end.

I lay between the sheets, watching the curtain billow in the breeze as cries of *dollar a doee, fifty a feelie, hey handsome, c'umere pretty baby* drifted up from the cribs. How I longed to flush every trace of feeling from my heart. Corral every barbed and useless memory into some distant outpost of self then chop it off. His red-brown beard and blue-grey eyes. The way his steepled fingers pressed to his forehead or lips when he paused to gather his thoughts. The curl of muscle on his shoulder that I used to trace with my tongue, taste of soot and rain. How he had once taken my bare feet in his hands, knelt before me by the stove to rub the chill away—

I wrenched my thoughts back to the present. To the sound of Lil snivelling in the hall. A dogfight breaking out in the street below, their snarls mingling with shouts and deep-voiced curses, raucous songs, laughter, celebratory gunshots. Since the strike had begun, soldiers were posted in town to guard the mines and at night they flocked to the cribs, blowing their pay on whisky and dollar whores. I slid from bed and stared down at the bare lath shacks, lamplit windows burning sallow stains into the dark. I lifted my gaze to the ridgebacked summits, tarry black and ragged under a night sky, and struggled to locate some stir of feeling – some sense that what might happen to me mattered. But I could not.

I rose early the next morning and set to work, holding fast to the hard clarity of numbers. A strange stillness had fallen over the town now that the mines had gone quiet. There were no knock-off whistles, no explosions in the shafts to set off faint tinklings of lamps, glassware, or bottles.

At noon Madam Blair flustered into the office to check deliveries and take stock of her whisky stores. 'Well, honey, seems life's come up snake eyes for you again. When that happens, you gotta just keep rollin' the dice. Trouble comes like a run a bad cards, gal's gotta dust herself off and get right back in the game.'

There was no venom in her words, but they still stung.

'Got word from the higher-ups that I can take back my house on Lucas Street,' she prattled on. 'Be high tailin' it to St Louie before summer's out, which means I'm dead set on finding a buyer. Vera, I'm sure we could come to some arrangement. You got grit, gumption, a good head on your shoulders. Fact is, you'd make a damn fine Madam if you could just harden yourself against those chowder-brained whores. Maybe this business with Keane'll do the trick. Good Madam needs a bit of steel in her spine.'

My pen scratched on.

Sadie huffed air from her mouth in noisy puffs as she mussed about in the safe. Then she rose to her feet and slapped some coins on the desk. 'You'll find it's a bit short. I'm fining you for misbehaviour. No gal of mine gets seen smokin' hop at a gow parlour. I got a reputation to maintain. Then there's that silliness with Gypsie. Lord knows what came over you.' Sadie lifted her chin, eyes narrowing. 'If you were a whore, I'd have Jackson knock you around.'

'Go ahead.' I tossed the pen aside and looked up. 'I'd rather take my licks and have the money.'

Sadie raised an eyebrow and said nothing. Her mood had spun on a dime, and I was tired of it. One moment she was all wise words and business-talk, the next she was docking my pay and threatening me with Jackson. The lamp guttered then went steady, flame sucking at the coal-oil.

'I meant what I said,' she sniffed. 'About the offer.'

'So did I. Give me the back of Jackson's hand and pay me what I'm owed.' I'd seen him cuff a girl. He never closed his fist, just slapped her face hard from side to side with his palm and the back of his hand. Sure, it hurt. But it was over in a flash and left no mark. And I wanted my money.

'I'll give you a fair price.' She slapped dust from her hands. 'But you won't bite, will you?'

'It is unlikely.'

'Think you're better than me. Better than all of us.'

'No, I don't.' I sighed and took up my pen. Anger took too much effort. 'Nor does anybody else, for that matter.' And with that, my eyes burned with tears.

Sadie reached out to pat my hand, but the gesture contained more condescension than comfort. *Oh, little Vera* that quick dry tap of hers seemed to say, *there are worse things in life than a broken heart…* I braced myself for one of her lectures. Some version of I-told-you-so, Keane's the possessive kind. Or, *shoulda got yourself knocked up. That's what I tell my gals who get set up as kept-women. Get pregnant, right away. Baby's a thing you can hold over 'em.* But she said nothing. And by the time I had composed myself sufficiently to offer some mollifying word, she was gone. I stared at the coins and found that I no longer cared. Wiping my eyes, I pocketed the money and returned to work.

And so it went. Mornings were a flurry to tallying profits and expenditures, while evenings were given over to making change and counting coins. Each task was a tiny upright on which to lean. But afternoons… afternoons were a torment. The solitude, the idleness. The sweltering heat as the midday sun beat down on the shingled roof. Impossible to sleep. Hours spent hauling myself over the same tractless waste of remorse and recrimination, indulging fantasies of reconciliation and revenge. Then, repulsed by my passivity, I would seize on a course of action. A written appeal, angry recriminations flung at him in the street, a visit to his hotel to plead forgiveness. But a conflicting impulse would always rise up and rebel, hurling me back into yet another forced march across the same barren terrain, operations that yielded nothing but a fitful trembling to repossess, at any price, that which had been lost.

After days of these ceaseless rigours I no longer craved happiness, or love, or even contentment. Only release. Just a few hours of unbroken sleep in place of these futile forays through the irrevocable. After Henry's death a few drops of opium in water had done the trick, so one night when Blair retired early and it fell to me to administer Evie's nightly dose of laudanum, on impulse, I pocketed the bottle. Then, to my utter surprise, Blair never noticed it was gone. So the following day I locked the office door and climbed the stair with a light step. The whores were lolling about in the day-room. Josie was out doing the day's shopping, while Sadie made her weekly social rounds – a quick word with Big Minnie about the assault outside Pasquale Nigro's saloon, tea laced with rum at Ida Crowley's as they indulged in a long gossip about the new dancehall down the street, or exchanged a few scathing words about Blonde Marie's *filles de joie*, as her new sign read.

I measured out a dose, swirling it in a glass of water. Then I downed it in one smooth swallow and lay across the bed, waiting for the warm drift of narcotic slumber. Cocoon of drift and dream snuffing out all that useless contemplation, and it did. For a time. Until I awoke shivering in a cold bath, teeth clacking, reek of vomit in my hair, chunks of it floating in the water as Contessa slapped my face, reproaching me in Spanish. *Bad shellfish at a Chinese chop house*, she kept saying. She drilled this story into me, insisting that if Blair knew the truth she'd toss me into the territorial asylum like she'd done to some whore who'd tried to kill herself last spring. Before I could protest that Blair had no legal authority to do such a thing, my stomach convulsed. Nothing came up. After houseboys had changed my bedding and cleaned the carpet, I was ordered back to bed. I lay beneath the blankets, watching Jackson remove the lock from my door while Contessa stood over him with a grave face.

'It was an accident,' I protested, but Jackson kept twirling that screwdriver, catching the screws as they fell. 'Sleep,' I added. 'That's all I wanted.' But Jackson pocketed the bolt and the screws and the metal plate. Then he stepped into the hall and closed the door, leaving a hole where the lock had been.

Contessa clasped the high-backed chair and dragged it across the room. Every boudoir had such a chair. It was where the whores were told to hang a john's shirt, trousers, and jacket. Then afterwards, they would help each customer into his tidy, uncreased clothing with a cheerful smile. These were the small courtesies, Sadie believed, that elevated Star Mansion above the other knockshops in town. 'Remember,' she would trill. 'Screwing is just one of the services we offer.'

Why were these details leeching into my thoughts? Perhaps Will was right. Perhaps living under Blair's roof had corrupted me, like that old well next to the Contention Mine whose water was now undrinkable. Did my in-depth knowledge of the flesh trade make me an unfit wife and mother? *Flesh trade.* Sadie Blair's phrase.

Contessa sat down by the bed and lay a deep-veined hand on mine. Her uncombed hair looked like wildfire in the wind, and her mouth had that slightly withered look that Sadie's had, upper lip wrinkly and thin, shrinking into her teeth. My thoughts fell to a story Lil had told me, about Contessa being given over to a mission when she was twelve, because her father could no longer feed them all. Long hours of floor-scrubbing meted out as penance, for what sins aside from poverty she did not know. Until she'd run off with one of the harvest stiffs, handsome enough, young. She'd known the price of going with him. Prepared herself by imagining the stink of chaw and coal oil and unwashed clothes pressing down while he slammed away like the nasty old rooster on the farm who used to peck and hiss and ride the hens until their asses were rubbed raw. Just pale pimpled flesh, no feathers. Yes, she knew the price she would pay for hopping on that horse and riding north towards the border. Never suspecting that he would pimp her off to any *vaquero* who could flash a few pesos. Stand with his back facing while they went at her right by the side of the road. In an ash-pit, behind a tree. On the swept-dirt floor of some shack at the edge of a village. I knew never to believe a word of such tales, but as my hand lay beneath hers, I perceived some terrible loss imprisoned deep within her and wondered if it all might be true.

'If I were trying to kill myself,' I said, 'I'd have locked the door.'

'Then why you spit up? Why I hear you choking?'

I sighed. Because my body refused to cooperate? Because this tincture was stronger than what I had been given back East? Because I had eaten so little in the past few days? Because this was the way my luck ran?

'Try or no try, Blair ship you off to that asylum she think you take the deep six. She done it to Peek-a-Boo.'

'Who?'

'Peek-a-Boo Penny.'

The name sounded familiar. My stomach gave a churning lurch, but the nausea passed. Yes. I had once come across a piece of paper bearing that name. A receipt from the Territorial Asylum, signed by Jackson. The paper had been stuffed into a folder labeled *Broken furniture, misc damages*.

Contessa took up my hand, eyes bearing down on me black as polished marble. 'Keane,' Contessa knocked at her chest. 'In here, he is a coward.'

She took my chin between her thumb and forefinger and forced me to look at her. Her eyes, those dark obsidian whorls, locking onto mine. 'Hold your held high. Once he feel you stop loving him, maybe he think again. Have some… regret.'

I nodded, but without much conviction.

'Venga. Take pride in your hair, your clothes.' Contessa gripped my wrist. Her eyes flashed with the intelligence I had always sensed in her. 'Look your best every night. Show him you are not what those pendejos say.'

'Then what?'

She shrugged. 'This, I cannot say.'

I stared at the fly-spotted walls, at the sunlight slashing through a gap in the curtains.

'We all of us try to help. We say poor Vera has been wronged. Is innocent saint.'

I wiped my eyes with the sheet.

'The johns, they ask us. What happen to Vera? We tell them Keane is a fool. We cling to them when we say it, beg them to talk sense to him.'

'Thank you,' I whispered.

'De nada,' she shooed at the air. 'Men like this kind of talk. It make them feel... less bad. So what I am in bed with a perra. So what! I am not a bad man. Not like those bastardos from Bisbee! Those dogs who ruin poor innocent Vera!' She gave a crooked smile. 'Sí, sí, johns love this talk.'

I heaved a listless sigh. 'I don't think I can live without him.'

Contessa drew a breath through her nose, nostrils flaring. Then she slapped me, hard, on the face. Too stunned to speak, I simply stared. At the creases of shadow beneath her eyes, at the tiny wrinkles hatching her upper lip. My cheek burned.

She leant over and kissed my forehead. Moments later she was pulling clothes from the wardrobe. Dresses, jackets, gloves, garters... soon all manner of tulle, lace, worsteds, pads, pins, and veils lay spread across the floor. She assembled things into suitable outfits, casting some pieces aside, praising others. She offered to do my hair each night and urged a few strategic purchases. Ivory combs. A pearl necklace. Fake, she winked. Much cheaper that way. And all the while she spoke of dignity and pride. *La dignidad, el respeto. El respeto, la dignidad.* Saying the words again and again, as if they were some kind of magic spell.

And so, I allowed myself to be drafted into Contessa's plan.

An operation whose ultimate aim remained obscure, but whose tactics seemed sensible enough. Shelve this dress (too drab). Avoid this bodice (too much décolletage). Wear soft, neutral colours. No red. It was a relief to have a set objective. To fill each afternoon with choosing an outfit, selecting a hairstyle, taking a perfumed bath. These small vanities gave me a purpose. A week passed and I felt better. Believed myself fully recovered. Until a single turn of events proved otherwise.

It happened on a routine Friday night. Rooms packed with men smoking cigars and drinking whisky, Jackson confiscating firearms and turning away 'undesirables' while Madam Blair buzzed about like an overbearing hostess, plying the regulars with drinks, cigars, and girls. She'd drop a genial word here, an encouraging smile there, then bestow a careful touch on the sleeve of a newcomer, followed by a well-timed laugh to set the jumpy ones at ease as the whores sauntered from parlour to bedroom and back. Powdered and perfumed, always ready for the next trick.

Old Abe, Contessa's Friday night steady, had come and gone hours ago, stealing glances at me while knocking back his bourbon. It was the kind of look I'd been getting all week. Inquisitive, furtive. The look of someone trying to make up his own mind about Star Mansion's notorious book-keeper. Sometimes, over the course of an evening, a john's expression would soften, and I would know that the whores had said something to him upstairs. My predicament, it seemed, had become a source of light entertainment. A welcome distraction from the town's economic woes, which grew worse every day. Mining companies had offered a wage compromise, but the unions had balked. Shareholders then accused union leaders of being corrupt grafters, enriching themselves at everyone else's expense. The president of the union fought back by declaring that he feared violence if companies refused to meet miners' demands. Sheriff Hatch had taken this as a threat and responded by swearing in fifty new deputies. And all the while the price of silver continued to fall, and what was the 'hard money' crowd in Washington doing about it? Not a God damn thing.

Such was the talk in Blair's barroom, where my travails seemed to provide a refreshing distraction from all the money being lost. Far more pleasant to debate the whys and wherefores of Will Keane's cancelled nuptials, or speculate about what really happened the night of the Bisbee Massacre. And, to Madam Blair's delight, men came to Star Mansion to study the object of these rumours and decide for themselves.

On this particular night I had outdone myself, wearing a dress of watered silk with modestly cut bodice, three-quarter length sleeves, and princess drapery trimmed with Egyptian lace. It was to have been my wedding dress, but I refused to let this bother me, although I had let this fact slip in front of Texas Lil who then fell into a fit of sentimental weeping while stroking its slippery folds. She then told everyone else – which meant that the whores would be offering up this melodramatic tidbit to any john who would listen, giving them one more reason to stare as they knocked back their last drink of the night.

Fine. Let them. If that's what it took for people to see that I had been wronged. That Will Keane was a fool. And tonight this was the conclusion being drawn. I could tell from the way men were looking at me, eyes full of commiseration and pity. Faces of the older ones grave with paternal concern. Younger ones unable to check their furtive glances. Even Gypsie's customers seemed persuaded. One of her regulars, a bald heavy-set man in a houndstooth coat, had stared at me long and hard, then looked away shaking his head.

As the evening wound to a close, I gazed out over what remained of the night's 'entertainments'. Wet glass stains, crushed cushions, cigar-stumps, half-empty drinks. Scraps of bread and smoked ham littered platters on the buffet table. Only a few laggards remained, jawing over who ran the best poker game in town. Soon the parlour lamps would be extinguished and Star Mansion's doors locked for the night – and not a moment too soon. My nerves were frayed from calculating change, tallying sales, and trying to avoid doing anything that might provoke Madam Blair. Despite a hefty take Sadie had been cantankerous all night. She'd lit into a houseboy for tripping over a carpet and fined Texas Lil for swearing within earshot of a john. If she turned on me, I did not think I could endure it stoically. Anthony Mariano, I suspected, was the reason for her foul mood. He had not dropped by for days.

A crash sounded in the foyer. Walking sticks clacked to the ground. A man swore, then swore again. Blair issued her customary reprimand, 'In this house we cater to gentlemen. Kindly reserve that sort of talk for the saloon, Mister Keane.'

The men in the corner fell silent as Will walked into the room. Face flushed, gait unsteady. He wore a yoked linen shirt, sleeves rolled above the elbow. I gripped the shelf beneath the till, casting about for a task to occupy my hands. Dirty glasses. Stray bar napkins. Anything.

'Drink,' Will snapped his fingers.

Jackson stepped forward. 'Bar's closed, Keane.'

'Closed? Hang on, old fella.' Will clapped Jackson on the shoulder. 'Ain't ya heard? This here's the Wild West!'

'Certainly is,' trilled Sadie as she bore across the room. 'Rye whisky, Mister Keane?'

'Thank you, M'am. Don't mind if I do. Best rye in the West is what I always say.' He shot a look at Jackson. 'In the *Wild* West.'

Madam Blair's face shone with petty excitement as she poured out a whisky and handed him the glass. Then Will swayed across the room to join the men over by the window. Bursts of laughter rose at his approach. A flurry of hand-clasps. Hearty back-slaps. I tried to keep my gaze averted, but could not stop myself from stealing glances at the movement of his shoulders beneath that rumpled shirt, at the curve of his sun-darkened neck. And his ears. This was the detail of his appearance that my mind's eye never sketched correctly, the one thing that always took me by surprise after a long absence.

My face must have betrayed me, for Madam Blair shot me a withering look as she banged the cash drawer shut. 'Toughen up, Vera. Who told you being a woman was easy?' Then she struck across the room and disappeared into the hall.

I bent to lock the till. Key. Latch. Turn. Click. Every move slow and deliberate in a vain attempt to divert my thoughts from Will whose presence sparked little jolts of panic and excitement, for the sight of him sent a warm rush of feeling through my veins.

I rose to find him standing before me. He set his glass on the bar with exaggerated care then pressed both hands against the dark wood, fingers spread. My eyes bolted away. Contessa and Texas Lil were standing in the doorway. Hair tousled, dresses creased. Lil stared, mouth agape, while Contessa shot me a stern look.

Will slapped down some money. 'Take what you need, Miss Palmer.' He waved at the pile of crumpled bills. 'Gonna have me a gal tonight.'

A tremour passed through me.

Jackson appeared by his side and placed a hand on his shoulder. 'Go on home an' git some shut eye, Keane.'

'Now, wait just a dog-gone minute!' Sadie Blair descended in a flap of crinolines and creaky stays. 'If Mister Keane fancies a girl, then a girl he can have.'

A stir of excitement passed through the room. A man in the corner cleared his throat. Others swirled drinks or shifted in their seats. Nobody rose to leave, and I felt wave of disgust for these men with their stinky cigars and their sweaty faces. How dare they all just sit there, greedily devouring this spectacle.

'Vera,' reproached Sadie.

I plucked bills off the bar. Legs weak, heart hammering. Then I pressed a brass check into Will Keane's palm, touching his callused palps with my bare fingers. I stared at the pale underside of his wrist, where a dark flat scar ran up his forearm. A burn from installing the roof on Rafael's casita. In one careless moment he'd slipped and caught himself with his forearm, hot metal singeing his skin. Smell of burnt hair and seared flesh full in his nostrils, like when you brand a calf, he'd said.

Blair gave two sharp claps, and the whores dutifully lined up by the buffet table, which now held nothing but a ravaged ham and discarded shrimp tails. Texas Lil stood fidgeting with her skirts, while Evie looked worn-down and confused in a dress the colour of sallow butter. Contessa scowled and muttered something that provoked Madam Blair to give her a swift poke in the backside.

'Fine strong man like him,' Gypsie crooned. 'I reckon he can hold his liquor.' Then she gave her hair a lavish shake. Her fine blonde lashes blinked rapidly, as if their seductive flutter were entirely beyond her control.

'That one,' declared Will, swaying as if he were on a boat. Then he waved in my direction.

I felt a rush of satisfaction.

Madam Blair gave a nervous laugh. 'Come now, Mister Keane. Letting guests lay the help never improves a house.'

'That's not what I hear.' He wheeled round sharply. 'Word on the street is she likes a real bang-out hog wallow of a night. Word on the street is—'

Contessa broke into a torrent of angry Spanish.

'Ah, ah,' Blair made a slap, slap gesture with her hand. A signal for Jackson to knock her around after the johns had left.

Will harrumphed and looked down at his feet, swaying. 'I'm just saying what I hear. Telling Miss Sadie that I don't necessarily agree with her… former claims.'

'Go on home, Keane,' said Jackson. 'Fore I throw you out.'

Sadie waved Jackson back, fixing Will with a starchy smile. 'We cater to gentlemen, Mister Keane. And I'm sure you are one.' Then she snapped her fingers and Gypsie sauntered over with a well-practiced swishing of hips. Wide smile spread across her powdered face, she was all teeth and rouged lips. The blood beat hard in my temples, thoughts blurring to a high-pitched whine.

'Well now, Lil' lady.' Will gave Gypsie an affectionate pat on the rear. 'You come on home with me, now. Snuggle up in my bed and keep me warm.'

A look of displeasure crossed Sadie's face, but she forced a smile. 'This is a not a livery stable, Mister Keane. You'll take your pleasure under my roof.'

Gypsie draped a long willowy arm around his shoulders, and at the sight of her copper hair falling across his shirt, I tore the till-key from my wrist and strode out from behind the bar. A swell of anticipation rippled through the room, and Madam Blair shot me a testy look. But with 'guests' watching, she had little choice but to stand by helplessly, lips twisted into a smile. I slid past and plucked the brass check from Will Keane's hand.

'Trick stealer,' Gypsie hissed, pinching me on the arm. At this, Sadie Blair let out a brisk staccato laugh and I knew that she would not stop me.

Will wrapped his arm around my waist, and I felt all the old vibrations quiver and thrum to life.

'Pearl of the house,' said Sadie, gesturing toward the stair. 'You've got the pearl of the house tonight, Mister Keane.'

Chapter 22

Will flopped across my bed and fell into a deep unmoving slumber. Jackson made several attempts to rouse him before informing Madam Blair 'ain't no use' whereupon she kicked up a fuss about 'house rules' and 'no all night tricks' even though some john was always sleeping off a drunk in one of the boudoirs and Sadie knew it. Yet here she was, railing on about 'damn highbinders who try n' pull the wool over everyone's eyes with their big la-de-dah words. Well, it don't fool me! You keep a hawk's eye on this fella, Jackson. Keane's a shiftless peckerwood same as the rest of em.' But her words did not touch me. I was aware only of Will Keane's presence in my room, my bed.

Loud ragged snores shuddered from his chest, but his face was open and at peace. Gone was the aloof, implacable stranger who had greeted me in his office ten days ago. Gone, too, was the juvenile drunk who had caused me such mortification downstairs. I flung my arm over his side and let my fingers fill the valleys between his ribs. I thumbed the bone thickened by scar tissue from the time a cutting horse had thrown him and the rib had cracked like a green twig. Lucky, Juan had said. Lucky that rib had not snapped and punctured a lung. I stroked the soft fine hairs on his chest, pressing my palm to his breastbone. And there, lodged at the very core, beat the smooth-muscled drum of his heart.

My mind jangled with thoughts, possibilities, doubts. Vivid eruptions of memory. Nights at the *casita*. Stirred from sleep by a hand gripping my knee, rolling me over. Air cool between my legs then one long thrust to slide me into wakefulness in that pitch-dark room, blind to everything but this wild jerking at the depths until he tumbles off and I am left panting on the damp sheet like some wild animal ambushed in the dark.

I must have him came the thought, breaking free from the clogged up churn in my head. I calculated my time of the month, counting back to the belts and the napkins and the blood-stained drawers. Eleven days. Which ruined everything. Not safe. Then, fast on the heels of that thought, came another. *Gal gets set up as a kept-woman, I tell her to get knocked up. Right away. Baby's a thing you can hold over a man.*

I slid a hand between his legs, but he was soft and flaccid as a glove. Which fairly settled the question. Noise drifted up from the parlour – glasses being cleared, cigar trays emptied, carpets swept back into place. Beyond the open window fireworks fizzed and cracked. I tried to sleep. But Will's nearness made me restless and alert. My leg wound up over his torso until I found myself straddling his hip, jut of the bone spreading the folds as I rocked back and forth. A bump sounded outside my door. Jackson arranging his pallet. My unlocked door. I brushed the thought aside, narrowing my attention to the slip, slip between my legs and the knot of heat balling up inside until it burst apart and I flopped down over his body, face wedged in the crook of his armpit breathing the oniony stink, but not caring as I brought myself around again and again until nothing but a dull worthless throb could be had and I rolled off and wiped away the wet with my hand. Then I pressed my hand to his back, sticky as glue, as my fingers went tak, tak, tak with every touch until my own clear sap had dried there.

Drawing the sheet up over us, I lay still. Mind empty but for the hiss and pop of fireworks, acrid scent of explosive powder wafting into the room. Shouts of the crib whores. Shattering glass. Distant bleat of a goat, followed by some john hollering that he'd been robbed.

I awoke to the faint scent of vomit. Will sat slumped in the high-backed chair, gripping his head. On the wash-stand was a glass of viscous yellow liquid. Jackson offered the same crazy concoction to all the johns who woke up here after a bender. Swore it cured the after-effects of drink.

I reached for the wrapper that hung from my bedpost. It was a ratty old thing with a hole in one elbow. Contessa would not approve, came the thought, as I slid my arms into the worn-out sleeves. But I was sick of orchestrating every detail, calculating my every move. No more tactical maneuvering. No grand strategy. I would just take things as they came.

Crossing the room I heaved open the window. Sixth Street had gone quiet, though the red lanterns burned on through the pallid light. Dogs nosed through trash-heaps as a few stragglers dragged through alleyways littered with bottles, ripped clothes, husks of fireworks, shell casings, a crushed hat. A lone cat came slinking between the cribs then darted out of view.

I turned to face him. Dressed in a dust-smeared shirt and wrinkled drawers, he looked shame-faced and woozy. I lifted Jackson's cure-all from the wash-stand and sniffed it. 'What's in this anyway?'

Will groaned, hand pressed to his forehead.

I took up the jug by the washbasin and offered him a glass of water.

'Don't dare.'

I drank it down myself. His lips parted as if to speak, but he said nothing.

'What?'

He shook his head, wincing.

'You're laughing at me.' My voice was light and carefree, almost teasing.

'I am definitely not laughing. Hurts too much.'

'What is it? Tell me.'

He toyed with a loose thread on his shirt. 'Seeing you drink that glass of water just put me in mind of…' he winced and gripped his head. 'God damn. Feels like I've been chewed and spat.'

I placed a hand on his neck without thinking. His body

tensed against my touch, and the guarded look on his face pained me more than any harsh words ever could. The silence dragged on, until at last he spoke. 'What happened last night?'

'You tried to buy Gypsie.'

He groaned and slumped back in the chair.

'But you settled for me instead.' I took the brass check from my bed-stead and flipped it at him, watching the coin tumble and fall to the carpet by his feet.

'And then?' He made a quick survey of the room, searching for clues. He really did not remember.

'Then nothing,' I said at last.

His face softened with relief, which hurt and enraged me.

'Not that you didn't try,' I burst out. 'You hollered and cursed. Said you'd paid good money for me and damned well better get what you came for. But you were far too drunk.' I paused, savouring every false delicious word. 'Jackson was worried, but I knew you would not strike me.'

He straightened. 'I would never strike a woman. Not even Sophie saw the back of my hand.'

'That may be, but you were hardly a gentleman.' His mention of Sophie had fueled my baser instincts. 'You swore a mean streak up and down. Flung all manner of insults at me. It was quite a performance.'

'Forgive me,' he muttered.

I felt no remorse for my lies. 'What was that?'

'Forgive me, Vera.'

My gaze fell to the floor, where it lit on the brass check and stayed there. So much easier than looking at his face. I cleared my throat. 'Perhaps we could, each of us, see our way clear to forgiving one another.'

He gave a weary nod and all my former hopes took flight. In spite of everything he had said and done. Love had made me stupid. No, not love. Raw animal need. A desire over which I had no control, no say. I approached and knelt at his side, burying my head in his lap. A dry billow of heat came drifting

269

in through the open window, bringing with it the smell of trashfires and livestock. Will stroked my hair and whispered, 'I am ever so tired.'

I rose and led him back to bed. Then I gave my hair a few quick strokes and exchanged my tired old wrapper for a sleeveless night-dress. Cut from fine muslin and trimmed with silvery-green ribbon and touchon lace, it was part of a bridal set. The only pre-nuptial indulgence I'd allowed myself. I regarded my image in the glass. Face a bit too thin. Pale after so many nights of broken sleep. Ink-stains on my right hand that no amount of lye soap could scrub away. Yet my eyes were avid and bright, bare arms shapely and unblemished, and the way my hair cascaded down over the white muslin was handsome enough. I crossed the room, which was brightening with the break of day. Outside, sunlight shot across the creosote flats, striking the sheet-metal roofs of the cribs with a hard diamond glare.

Will was already fast asleep. My body wound around his, sinking into the familiar curves and hollows. An embrace that felt like yesterday. That felt like home.

A fat dull buzz woke me from sleep. Then came a tickle on my lips. A fly. I leapt from bed, grabbing the swatter. Nothing bothered me more. Not the heat, not the noise from the cribs, not the nightly stink of spilled liquor, tired bodies, and slop water – nothing was worse than being wakened by flies. I smashed one on the wash-stand, three on the walls. Then I yanked the window shut and realised I was naked. Which was not unusual. Since the onset of summer, my body seemed to have fallen into the habit of peeling off nightdresses while I slept.

I glanced at Will. He sat in the high-backed chair, drawing on his socks. I allowed myself the pleasure of watching his hands clasp the hem of a trouser-leg and draw it down, then brush at dust streaks on the dark cloth. I set down the fly-swatter and went to him, aglow with the frank tenderness that had passed between us in sleep. How he had placed a hand on the inside of my thigh, letting it rest there as we dozed.

I stepped towards him and waited, ready to be drawn up into his arms. But when his attention did not stray from the task of adjusting his braces, a cold uncertainty stole over me. When at last he lifted his eyes, they were sober and unfeeling. 'What are those stains on the walls?'

'Dead flies.'

His face contracted, gaze lingering on the oily-black smears a moment longer. Although he said nothing, his silence was rebuke enough. A sharp retort rose to my lips – something about having remained in this filth at his insistence – but I bit it back. And this need for self-censure, coming so swiftly on the heels of our heartfelt exchange before falling asleep, landed like a blow. How wearying it all was. These wild extremes of emotion, hopes raised then dashed.

The room was hot, as the morning sun beat down on the tarred roof behind the board ceiling. My skin felt itchy and tight with dried sweat. Drawing a damp cloth from the washbasin, I passed it over my arms and legs letting the whispery coolness wash over me. I could feel his eyes on me, staring. Good. Let him look. I squeezed the cloth, releasing long trails of water, then turned to face him as the cool rivulets rolled over my bare skin and dropped onto the carpet. A flicker of warm feeling passed over his face – some trace of desire or affection that could not be snuffed out. Then his eyes slid away and the expression on his face darkened. When he spoke his voice was even and resolute, 'Get dressed.'

My hand reached for the soap. Clasped it. Rubbed the sallow cake against the cloth. But it was like watching a stranger, as if my entire body had become a shell into which I poured rote, mechanical acts.

'Get dressed,' he said again.

I wheeled round to face him. 'Is this what you call

forgiveness?'

He made no answer, bending to pull on his boots.

'Well, you ought to have a nice long chat with Father Peabody about what that word means.'

'Get dressed, Vera.'

I dipped another cloth into the basin and pressed it to me. Felt the water trickle down my arms, neck, chest. My nipples tightened and went hard. I met his eye, daring him to look away.

Will's jaw twitched, and the planes of his face went rigid. Then he leapt to his feet and tore open a drawer and started hurling clothes at me. Drawers, nightgowns, hose, wrappers, and crinolines hit me and gathered in a pile at my feet. Others missed their mark and lay ranged about me in a skewed half-moon, like the prelude to some bizarre tribal ritual. But I stood firm, recoiling from any gesture that bore the slightest hint of submission.

A knock sounded at the door.

I did not budge. Another knock and a command to open up. Jackson. I threw on my nightdress and jerked open the door.

'You alright?' Jackson stood in the threshold, heavy eyed and unshaven.

I nodded, forcing a smile. Jackson leveled Will with a hard, glowering stare. It was the look he reserved for Sadie's worst customers, the ones who busted up furniture, or tried to bugger a houseboy. 'Keep it down, Keane.' Then he bent towards me and lowered his voice. 'Sadie's got one a her headaches.'

I thanked him and closed the door. Angry that Jackson's arrival had forced me to dress. To capitulate. I spun around, not caring what showed on my face. 'Stop behaving like an unruly john.'

A wool stocking still hung from his hand. Will let it drop and shook his head. 'Forgive me.'

'I do. We, each of us, forgave the other. Before bed. You said you forgave me and—'

'I never said that.'

Words failed me. There was no way to explain what I knew. That love does not speak in words, but in every breath and gesture, every glance and unspoken tremor. That its signs cannot be read, but are writ large nonetheless – seared into the tough-muscled tissues of the heart.

I stared at his disheveled workshirt and dust-streaked trousers. At the rumpled waistcoat. He had come to me like this. Like *this*. No collar. No cravat. Just a yoked workshirt smeared with grime. He'd come straight from the gaming tables in clothes that stank of the streets and the saloons. He had come to me stumbling drunk, he had – but it was no use. I still wanted him, loved him.

'This is not a courtroom,' I managed to say. 'We are not testifying under oath, or – delivering some – giving a testimony—'

'*Deposition* is the word you are looking for.'

'Stop it.'

'You may not realise it's the word you're looking for, but it is.' His tone was calm and didactic, and this professorial air enraged me.

'You forgave me, Will Keane. You stood on that very spot and forgave me.'

He ran a hand through his hair, leaving it mussed. 'I assented to what you said, because after my behaviour last night, an apology was certainy owed. It was not insincere. But I fear that certain implications… that a degree of misunderstanding may have – for God's sake, why are things always such a damned muddle with you?'

'I might ask the same of you.'

He marched across the room and threw open the window. I saw him lift the washbasin and realised he was about to hurl the dirty water onto the street. Except it was not the street that lay below, but Sadie's front stoop. I tripped across the room and stayed his hand. Dumping wash-water out the window

273

was strictly prohibited. Madam Blair thought it low class and bad for her image.

'Please.' My hand rested on Will's wrist, just below the burn scar. 'You'll get me a fierce scolding. Or worse.'

Washbasin poised before the open window, he looked down at my hand, eyes blazing with something I could not read and for a long moment I thought he might turn and dump the dirty water on me. Because it was something to do. And his face betrayed a ferocious, overwhelming need to act.

But in the end he simply stepped away and set the washbasin back down. Instinctively, I scrambled to anticipate what he might do or say next, but found myself unable to muster the strength for another weary round of conjecture.

'I came here last night to deliver a message.' His voice was crisp and coolly rational. 'To warn you that Safford Hudson has engaged in unwise speculations.'

The hard bright light of day poured into the over-heated room. Drapes needed to be drawn, but the effort was beyond me. How tired I was. So bone-crushingly tired.

He paused to draw a handkerchief from his pocket, but came away empty handed. When I made no move to supply him one, he drew a soiled sleeve across his brow. 'The Tucson branch of Safford Hudson is about to fail. When it does, the one here in town will go down with it.'

He seemed to expect a response, but I simply bent to the task of picking clothes off the floor.

'When this happens, you will lose every cent you have deposited there.'

I straightened and faced him, a pair of drawers hooked on my finger.

'There is still time. I do not expect it to fold until next week. Tuesday at the earliest. But you should act swiftly. Today, to be safe. Because once the strike keeps dragging on into next week and people begin to realise—'

'Drag on? They are close to an agreement. The owner of

Contention Consolidated said so. Last night. I overheard him telling Gary Bidwell this whole mess would be wrapped up by Monday.'

Will shook his head. 'Unions are going to balk.'

I began to protest, but he held up a hand. 'I have it on good authority. This strike could drag on for weeks, and when it becomes known how deeply Safford Hudson is invested in the mines, when certain facts that I know but cannot share with you... when these are disclosed, the bottom is going to fall out of the bank. Trust me on this, Vera. If you believe nothing else I have ever said to you, please believe this.'

I nodded distractedly, words plinking down on me in a cold, steady drip. *If you believe nothing else I have ever said to you...* I stared at the pair of drawers still hanging from my finger.

'You must do exactly as I say,' Will went on. 'Withdraw your money today. Quickly, calmly, and above all *quietly*. You must never breathe a word of this conversation to anyone. Never mention my name in conjunction with what you are about to do.'

I found myself staring out the window. At the faded walls and wrung laundry. At the half ruined roofs and the cart-ruts grooving the mesa until they tumbled down off the edge and led out across the high plains desert to where the sun-glazed hills rose up to meet the sky.

'Do you understand?'

'Perfectly. If anyone suspects that a lawyer who works for Safford Hudson warned his fiancée of the impending collapse...' My predicament began to register. 'Sorry. I meant 'former' fiancée.'

A slight grimace passed over his face. He stood wringing his hands, palm passing over knuckles again and again. They made a soft dry sound.

'Vera,' he said at last. 'I cannot marry you.'

From downstairs came the shrill cry of Sadie's washer-woman. One of China Mary's girls, here to collect last night's linens. Will's hands had not stopped moving, one passing over the other. Those large beautiful hands.

I clasped my night-dress tight and wished him gone.

'I thought I might be able to see past it all,' he continued in that soft timbred cadence I had grown to love. 'But upon waking... I kept seeing their faces. That pair of filthy slag-shovelers leering at me. Their words—' his face curdled. 'They would always be there, Vera. Coming between us. The knowledge that here, right before Tucson, you were... in this room. Right here, before you came to me those men had – the knowledge that they had been here before me, in this room, where there was—'

'What? What was there?' My tone was cold and exact. 'You know nothing. You assume that you know. But you do not.'

'I know that I have endured one too many humiliations in my life and I haven't the strength for another.'

What did that mean? Alicia? Sophie? His mother? That business with the judge, or was he alluding to some event of which I was wholly ignorant? He was all hard eyes and cryptic assertions and to press for an explanation felt intolerable. Anything I might say would sound like a plea. For atonement. Reconciliation. None of which I wanted anymore. I wanted only to be spared the pain of his nearness.

My gaze wandered to the window, as Will rambled on about honour and the mother of his children, and a woman who becomes a mother, moral rectitude, judgement. His words flowed over me. Reputation, shame, humiliation... abstract empty words. But on he droned... children, a mother's reputation... and as he talked I was struck anew by the sound of his voice. Its cool neutrality. Which no longer wounded me, but arrived like any other fact floating in. Mingling with the wooden creak of wheels in the street, the slap of a horsewhip, the smell of cisterns and privies rising up from the cribs. Sight of a bush-wacker slogging at his ragged mules.

He fell silent and began to cast about in search of something.

'Your hat is downstairs,' I offered.

'Thank you,' he said.

Then came the steady strike of wood-pegged heels and he was gone.

Chapter 23

An hour later I stepped into a shadeless blaze of midday. Around me heads drooped, legs shuffled, dogs slept, horses flagged. In the distance, mountains lay hammered flat by the glare. My stomach tightened. Such a heavy meal in this heat had been unwise, but Josie's breakfasts were not to be resisted. Crossing Sixth Street I felt a wistful twinge. I would miss her cooking. The rich dark coffee, eggs cooked in pork dripping, river fish fried to a golden crisp.

'Dirty whore,' someone hissed and I glanced up to find a dumpy, sun-bonneted woman clomping by. Women, every time. Always women who marched through the Red Light District castigating the whores, railing against sin. Never once had a man shot me dirty looks, or hurled insults upon spotting me on the wrong side of Sixth Street. Was this podgy woman's life so dull that she had energy to waste on the likes of me? Silly fool of a girl who had failed to hold on to the man she loved.

I shuffled through a hot press of bodies. Shouts in English and Spanish flew back and forth, as shop-keepers kept stepping out of their establishments to glance about warily. A butcher in a blood-smeared apron was shuttering his windows, which ought to have been a sign. But I was too busy adjusting my linen wrap to conceal the bag slung over my shoulder. No need for anyone to notice a telltale bulge when I left the bank. No need, as Sadie would say, to risk 'an incident'.

Rounding the corner I halted before a throng of miners. Angry cries tore from their lungs, until they fell to coughing and then bent at the waist, hawking up grey spit. The smell of chewed-up stone and mine-drip still rose from their leather brogans, though no miner had been down a stope for days. A crowd rushed up from behind waving fists, drilling rods, wooden handles, bits of machinery, and this surge of sweaty backs and greasy hatbrims carried me to the edge of the raised sidewalk, where I grabbed a wooden upright and hung on. The street was jammed with stalled carts, blocked by a line of soldiers that extended the full width of the street. Farther down, more soldiers stretched from Woodhead's Grocery to Ritchie Hall. I watched a few miners try to pass, only to be shoved back by rifles held crosswise. Strange. There were no mines on Fifth Street, nothing to guard. Trouble at one of the saloons? Whatever the case, my access to the bank was blocked.

I felt a hard shove at my back, followed by the metal press of a gunbelt and a forearm sawing through. I let go of the ridgepole and dropped down into the street among the mules and stalled carts, horsewhips rising high like ships' rigging. Then I strode back the way I'd come, formulating a plan as I swatted flies and dodged livestock. On Sixth Street, just beyond McAllister's General Store, you could enter a disused alley then thread your way between outhouses and trashheaps to a vacant lot where, after passing through an abandoned flophouse, you emerged directly onto Fifth Street. Right beside the bank. Access lay within the Red Light District, so few people knew of it. But Texas Lil had showed me this route on our way to the milliner one day. Whores used it to pass into the respectable part of town unseen.

I pressed on through swarms of delivery boys, tradesmen, saloon keepers, gamblers, Faro dealers, laundresses... all flocking to Fifth Street. I gripped my wrap to keep it from slipping, empty bag still pressed to my side. Every breath was a sharp rasp of dry heat, like cinders at the back of the throat. At the corner I saw McAllister and his son standing before their shuttered storefront, arms crossed. At my approach, he gave a curt nod and touched the brim of his hat. His son, a fat-cheeked youth with downy scraps of a beard, flushed and looked down at his feet.

Several months ago, the boy had arrived at Star Mansion

only to be shipped straight out the back, with Blair threatening to tell his daddy if he ever darkened our doorstep again. Old Man McAllister gave Sadie discounts on bulk purchases and she was not about to let 'some young buck wantin to get his cherry cropped' jeopardise that arrangement.

'Seen anything?' shouted McAllister, working a lump of tobacco against his cheek.

I told him about the soldiers on Fifth Street.

'Figures,' he grunted. 'Protect the bank and leave us ordinary folk to fend for oursels.'

Something must have shown on my face.

'Ain't you heard? Tucson branch gone belly up. Word hit the picket lines, started a rush on the bank. Clerks just bolted the doors.' McAllister rocked back on his heels and spat and I felt something inside me tighten, then unravel.

'Any troops headed this way?' asked the boy.

McAllister adjusted his hat. 'Son, on'y thing headed this way be looters once them miners see the bank can't pay out.' He thrust his chest forward, paunch filling out the girth of his apron. 'Could be worse. Could be I had money with them crooks.'

The crack of a rifleshot tore through the din of the crowd and McAllister gave a grave nod. 'Grab that pistol by the register, Son.'

The boy ducked inside.

'You all right, Miz Palmer?'

I nodded, voices in my head rising to a crescendo while McAllister cursed the unions and the sheriff and the damn federals who wouldn't do a thing to protect his property if a riot broke out. But his words barely reached me. The air crackled with heat. It quivered up from the dusty earth, reverberating off the sun-beaten walls and the weatherboard fences in a sibilant throb.

The boy emerged from the shop and handed his father the pistol. McAllister checked the chamber and shoved the muzzle beneath his apron string. Then he crossed his arms and squinted out from beneath his tipped-back hat. I bid them good day, affecting a careless stroll towards Star Mansion. Then I broke into a trot and doubled back between the cribs, taunts from the whores raining down as I tripped by. *Get outta here, rich bitch... Ssss, parlour house cunt... hasta la vista, puta... go on home an' suck yer madam's tit.* A baby in a tattered dress sat beneath the shade of a canvas tarp, slapping a deflated ball with dimpled hands while several feet away a stray dog licked shit-smears from a slop-pot.

I ducked down the alley and kept going. Past the ugly backsides of buildings with their trash-heaps and half-dried cesspools, black-scabbed cactus and trees shaved down to sickly nubs. The bank lay just ahead. White-washed to throw off the sun, the paint had long since blistered and peeled away, leaving nothing but a flaky skein. I'd given no thought to what I would do once I got there. Something would come to me. I halted at the abandoned flophouse. The door hung from a single hinge. After checking for scorpions I clasped the splintered wood, pushed, and stepped inside. Shouts rang out from Fifth Street. A deep-voiced command issued from the front room, followed by the tramp of boots.

Soldiers were entering the flophouse from the other side.

I slid into a narrow space behind the sagging door and swept up my skirts. Mouth pasty with thirst. The boot-clomps and shouts grew louder. Then came the unmistakable pop of gunfire. Quick little bursts. Like fireworks, only softer. Screams and angry cries rose from Fifth Street. More loud-voiced commands rang out. Face pressed to the parched wood, I did not wonder if anyone had been hurt. No flicker of compassion for innocent bystanders who might have been shot or wounded passed through me. My money. The urgent need to rescue it snuffed out all else.

Urine-stained walls pressed at my back. Some officer was barking commands – sweep this, secure that. A door slammed open and the walls shook. Floorboards rang with heavy-booted steps. More rifle-clicks, clack of an ammunition belt. Through cracks in the splintered wood, I could see shadowy shapes in the unlit room. One was busy removing the oiled paper from the window. Two more looked on, rifles poised. I stepped out from behind the door, determined not to be found cowering in a corner. Or shot by mistake.

'M'am?' said a high, boyish voice.

'How the devil'd you git in here?' barked another.

I considered bolting right past them, or better yet, just sauntering on by as if I had every right. They wouldn't dare fire on a woman, would they? Then the oiled paper came away from the window and light poured into the room. My eyes struggled to adjust. I glimpsed an ashy hive. Flaccid egg-sacs clung to the wall beside me, and the floor was riddled with holes. Roughsawed planks had been peeled back and carted away. Desiccated egg-sacs littered the place. What had hatched from them? I imagined my foot breaking through the rotted floorboards to be set upon by stingers and fangs and retreated outside.

A blonde haired man in a smart, tight-fitting uniform strode over. He wore a pistol holstered to his belt and his cap sat at a jaunty, roguish angle. 'M'am, I'm going to need you to clear on out and go home.'

'Not without my money.'

The officer brought his hands to his hips. His belt-buckle was polished to a vigorous shine and shot the sun's rays back at me in a hard brassy gleam.

'I came for my money. And I won't leave until I have it.'

The officer breathed out through his nose. Something in the stoop of his shoulders, the way he averted eyes from me when he spoke, told me McAllister had been right. My money was gone.

'Go on home,' he said at last. 'Your husband'll be worried sick.'

'My husband's dead.'

Staring down at his smart field boots he said, 'Well. I'm sorry for it, M'am.'

I gave my sunshade a defiant twirl. Having discerned a hint of compassion, I intended to exploit it. 'Now, Officer. You look like a kindly young man. Why don't you just turn that gun of yours round the other way and help us hard-working citizens retrieve our money? Then we can all go on home, safe and happy.'

'M'am, this unit's got a job to do.' He tugged at his tobacco stained-beard. 'An evacuation operation's about to commence and things are looking to get pretty rough.'

'Do you know whose money is in that bank? People like you and me, Officer. Hard-working people who have scrimped and saved. And do you know what those bastards did with our hard earned money? They speculated, gambled and lost. When their job, their *job* was to keep it safe.' I was waving my hands like a crazy-woman, hollering things that could get Will Keane in trouble. About the mines and the banks and the crooked politicians who would cover over their tracks while the rest of us ate dirt.

'M'am, this is the last time I'm gonna ask you nice and polite. For your own safety. You must vacate the premises.'

'Or what?' I gave a caustic laugh. 'You'll shoot me?'

He looked over my head and made a sign. In an instant, my hands were forced behind my back and something hard and knobby was shoved into my spine – a knee? the butt of a rifle? Two soldiers were dragging me away, their smell of armpits and tobacco and unwashed socks pressing in on me, stirring up memories of those men skunky with mule-sweat and tanglefoot whisky who'd gone after me that awful night.

I threw my head back to breathe, squinting at the pallid shimmer of the sky, as I drew air in through my mouth. I stumbled forward, driven by their rough shoves. My vision began to fuzz at the edges.

'Water.' I heard myself say. The word sounded clattery, like a pebble knocking about in my skull.

'Keep goin, M'am.'

My legs felt juddery and everything seemed to drift farther and farther away, as if I were staring down a long corridor of of blue sky.

I came to on a shaded bench. Hard metal shoved at my lips. Wet. An army canteen. My throat choked and gagged, then gulped the water down. My hands clasped the canteen and held on. Shouts were rising from the far end of the block and moments later troops rounded the corner and swarmed past. The soldiers flung a second canteen at my feet and raced to join them. A few harried civilians were caught up in the melee. One of the fellows looked familiar: balding pate, spectacles askew. Instinctively I averted my gaze with that slow, practiced slip of the eyes I had honed to perfection. Then I realised: this chap was not a john; he was a clerk at Safford Hudson. A fellow to whom I used to hand over weekly deposits was now running inside a protective ring of soldiers. Evacuation operation. That's what the officer had said. An Apache scout dressed in buckskin leggings and a faded infantry coat brought up the rear. Steps silent as the grave, he crossed the dusty lot without once glancing over. But I could feel him taking note of me, absorbing the fact of my presence as he slipped after the rest.

Moments later, miners surged into the back-lot. Had anyone come this way? Did those dirty rotten crooks pass by here? I bent, head reeling, and lifted the canteen the soldiers had tossed at my feet. Then I unscrewed the cap and drank. 'Have you seen 'em?' I shook my head. What would attacking a few lowly clerks solve? It would be akin to holding me responsible for Sadie Blair's watered-down liquor. I tipped my head back, drinking down the last drops and by the time I was through they were gone. Head aching, I gazed out at the foothills scarred with hoisting works and head-frames. Sun blanched the cart-tracks a lurid white. Everything stood motionless.

Ridges where ore-carts had once crept continuously now lay naked and forlorn. There were no mule-trains ferrying ore from the mines, no horse-teams pulling carts laden with men and equipment up the dusty slopes. Just a throbbing haze of light.

All my money was gone.

This fresh predicament drove all my former woes to dash and scatter, and there was grim satisfaction in that. My left sleeve, pressed to a wooden barrel, felt damp. I lifted the lid of the barrel and saw dark ripples bounce and rebound. Dipping a hand inside, I drew it over my face, across my hair. Then, with a furtive glance towards the boarding house kitchen to which it undoubtedly belonged, I dipped each canteen into the barrel until it was full, screwing the caps on tight. Then, slinging the straps over my shoulder, I began walking. Over woodpiles, through gaps in fences, under barbed-wire, between buildings, through vacant lots. Canteens going clink, slosh with every step. Lack of money had befallen me before. Here, I told myself, was a familiar, straight-forward dilemma.

I kept walking. Past the Dry Goods store that sold Sadie Blair her awful, watered-down ink. Past the brewery with its wall of empty casks reeking of stale beer and wood-damp. I crossed the alley where Curly Bill Brocious had shot a frontier Marshal four years ago, thoughts winding back to the day Madam Blair had sent me to see Mr McClelland about a whisky order, and he'd regaled me with details about the murder while searching for our invoice. His talk had bewildered me. What shop-keeper brags about a man being killed half a block from his store? But Joe McClelland's view was not uncommon. Residents of Goose Flat took a curious pride in the town's lawless past, even as they hastened to assure newcomers that the whole Wyatt Earp business had been blown out of proportion by Eastern newspapers, as if simply living here made each one of us a courageous son-of-a-gun.

Crossing Toughnut Street I wound my way between miners

cabins and unfenced yards. Clothes-lines sagged between the half-ruined roofs, crude pathworks of timber and tarpaper. The air smelled of hog-slop and dumped coffee grounds. A dog barked from beyond a fence. Smoke threaded up from cookfires.

At the edge of town, I unscrewed the cap from a canteen and drank. The water had already grown warm. Around me heat boiled up from the rocks and I tried to find solace in these blistering surfaces. As if the sheer force of the sun might burn away my troubles and leave me stripped clean as the deer bones that littered the wash. At the bottom of the mesa the trail flattened. My arm ached from holding the sunshade, and my eyes throbbed against the dusty glare. Hiking up my skirts I dropped my drawers and urinated. Ahead of me lay a blasted expanse of loose gravel. Every tree had been felled to feed to the smelters, every sprig of green flattened by the roll of cart-wheels and mule-trains, every inch of land axed or mined or churned to bits by explosives. I stared at the road-scarred slopes, at the deep grooves carved by run-off from the winter rains. Ashy limestone dust lay caked in the creases. Like the face of an ageing, over-powdered whore.

The sun pulsed and throbbed. Smell of mule piss rose from the churned up road. A few agave plants clung to the weathered hills, like sea urchins stranded at lowtide. Up, up I went until the hill crested and the road wound on along the ridgeline. An iron penstock still held an inch of water. I dipped a handkerchief into the stagnant pool, draping the wet cloth over my neck. There was a canvas tarpaulin stretched between poles, and the ground was littered with dung, fire-rings, soot-blackened pans, discarded tobacco plugs. With the onset of today's unrest, the soldiers who had been guarding the mines had been called into town and their camps now lay abandoned.

Seeking shelter, I stepped inside a headframe and felt cool air ripple over me. Machinery lay scattered about. Bent drilling rods. A broken hand-pump. Timbers from a busted ore cart.

I stood in the sunless silence, breathing the tang of explosive clay, sun-baked wood, and damp oilskins. My skirts billowed with the air that rose up from the chilly depths of the mine. A wood platform hung two feet above the gaping hole, held in place by giant chains looped through a huge winch that loomed in the dark heights overhead. Shaft-elevator. To lower the men then raise them up after hours of setting explosives, shovelling slag, fixing ceiling cribs, and hacking ore from bedrock.

I sat down, savouring the cool air that washed over my face and neck. I imagined dropping down into the mine day after day. Worming through the dark stopes by candlelight and carbide-lamp. Chill of wet rock on my hands, in my lungs. Pitter-pat of mine drip. And always the danger of a cave-in. I thought of the men who had drowned when they'd first struck water last year. Trapped behind a rock-fall, stope filling too fast to get them out. I thought of the shift-boss who always came to Star Mansion and wondered if he worked at this outfit. Or the pay-master with long white sideburns, the one who took Lil upstairs every fortnight. Had those men lost money in the crash. Or had someone warned them, too?

I was penniless. Except for the brass check Will Keane had given me the night before. That, at least, was safe. I'd buried it in a jar of handcream before going to the bank. Exchanged for cash, that brass check would yield enough money to buy a ticket on the next stagecoach out of town. And then? Then, after a night in some dingy boarding house, I would be broke. Stranded in Benson. Or Fairbank. Or some other railroad town. With no job and no prospects. Which was exactly how women ended up working for the likes of Madam Blair.

There was no choice. I would have to continue to live and work at Star Mansion. Keep bearing up under the lash of Blair's petty antagonisms. *Toughen up, Vera.* There would be plenty more where that came from. Yet Sadie Blair's antagonism could be endured. What I could no longer tolerate was Will Keane. Whenever he sauntered into Blair's barroom for a glass of bourbon, I would be forced to bear the sight of those callused hands, to endure the fiery unhappiness that tore through me at the sound of his laugh. Or worse. What if, one day, I were to catch sight of him in the company of a well-dressed young woman? Round the corner on my way to the courthouse to pay Blair's license fee and glimpse him offering his hands, basket-like, to help boost her into the saddle?

I leapt to my feet. Kicked a dented helmet. It skidded into the mineshaft and I waited for the loud satisfying crash when it hit bottom. But even this was denied me. A soft plash rose from the murky depths. Of course. Now that the pumps had ceased to operate, the shafts were flooded. I kicked more objects into the giant hole – discarded food tins, a busted drilling rod, broken coffee pannikin, empty explosive case. Then it struck me. The utter simplicity of my dilemma. Lack of money. Unlike my love for Will Keane, this problem could be solved.

Chapter 24

Scrambling downhill in the dark with wads of cash strapped to my chest, rattlers were the least of my problems. It was night. The air was cool. No snake would have the energy to strike, or want to waste precious venom on me. Yet every hiss of dead grass, every mesquite pod rattling in the wind set my pulse racing, and I kept pausing to search for flat speckled heads nesting in their beds of coils.

The night was crisp and clear with a half-moon slumped on its side. The wash at the foot of the mesa glowed as if carved by the plash of light, instead of the tumbled rush of rainwater. Halfway down, my toe caught a rock and I stumbled but did not fall. Pausing to catch my breath, I fingered the stacks of bills wrapped against my chest. They had not slipped.

Things could not have gone more smoothly. From sliding bundles of cash into the pockets of my dress, to the laudanum drops I had slipped Texas Lil to keep her out of my bed, to the fib about coyotes sniffing round the back-lot so that Jackson would put Gracie in the stables for the night – nothing had gone wrong.

Assuring everyone that my money was safe – every cent withdrawn from the bank before the crash – had gone well. Enduring the onslaught of innuendo while Blair exchanged my brass check for cash had not been difficult. After visiting the general store, I had worried about smuggling my strange purchases (length of cotton cloth, a boy's riding habit, pair of shears) into the house. But nobody noticed.

The hardest part had been waiting. For Sunday to come and go. For day to give way to night, for the doors of Star Mansion to open and the money to start rolling in, always wondering if *this* would be the night when Anthony Mariano would drop by to provide the necessary distraction. Four agonizing days had passed before he finally strode into the barroom with his customary swagger. Still, I had to wait for their flirtation to begin and for Sadie to whisk him off to bed. Then, even after I had done the deed, the wait was not over. The johns had to leave, the houseboys had to finish gathering and sorting linens, the rush of water from the flush-toilet had to cease. And when at last the final window had been shuttered and Jackson's heavy-footed stomp could be heard on the back porch as he retired to his quarters, still, I had waited. Only after a solid twenty minutes did I dare ease myself from bed, fix the money to my torso, wrap my breasts flat, and steal out the back-door and away.

At the edge of town, I had exchanged my faded print-dress for the boy's riding habit. If questioned, I would reply 'Boquillas Ranch' in an accent like Contessa's. My skin had darkened in the sun, and with my hat pulled low, I could pass for a light-skinned *vaquero*. Except for the chaps. I'd done my best to scuff them, but a real vaquero's chaps would be black with the smoke of branding fires and stiff with dried blood. But I could hardly slaughter one of Josie's chickens for the purpose.

I halted at the wash. Instinctively, my hand rose to brush back stray wisps of hair. Then I remembered. Lifting my hat I ran a palm over the stiff bristly shock. This had been the only difficult part. When the time had come to shear it off, my resolve had faltered. But I did it. Catching the hair in a bowl, I'd tied it in a thick sweep and draped it over clothes stuffed beneath the blanket. The ruse might buy me an hour. Madam Blair would holler at Jackson to get my lazy ass out of bed, but he would leave me a bit longer. Then, twenty minutes later, he would check again. Until, concerned that I had not moved, he would cross the floor and discover my deceit.

Blair would go straight to the safe. But detection would take time, for I had not lifted the entire night's take. Only what I needed. The remaining cash would have to be counted, while the whores were roused from bed and ordered to tot up their checks. Only when this total was compared with the cash in the safe and found wanting could Sheriff Hatch be notified. By then I would be long gone. Out of Cochise County and beyond his jurisdiction. And what federal agent was going to give a damn about a few dollars pinched from a brothel? Well, more than a few dollars.

I continued down the wash, picking my way between loose rocks and fallen branches. Something moved in the scrub-brush. I froze, heart racing. A creature loped into the wash, moving with a graceful stealth that dogs did not possess. Thin and scruffy with a bony slope to its back, it halted and stared straight at me. Its gaze yellow-eyed, quizzical. Then, with a flick of its tail, the animal slid up through the brittle brush and faded back into the shadows.

I trod on, faint murmur of the night's revels drifting down from the town. A pile of boulders had tumbled into the wash and I scrambled around them, marveling at my freedom of movement. No bending to gather skirts. No worrying over torn hems. Both hands were free and the thick leather allowed me to stride straight through the brittle-bush and cat-claw. I forced myself to slow down. The cloth that bound my breasts trapped my chest at mid-breath, giving me the same airless feeling as a corset.

I took a sip from one of the army canteens in my saddle-bag. Filled days ago and stashed in my wardrobe until the time was right, the water left a stale metallic film on my tongue. I sipped again then screwed the cap on tight. A stiff breeze sent a shiver through the mesquite trees, branches scraping and creaking in the wind. I stowed the canteen, aware of another sound. Sharp, unmistakable. Crunch, shuffle, crunch. Boots. But the rhythm was strange, slightly off. Hooves as well as boots. A man leading a horse. Getting closer.

I cast about for a place to hide. Nothing but scrub and small boulders. I considered running, but my breathing was too constricted. No choice but to sit down and arrange myself into what (I hoped) looked like a drunken slump against a rock. I hitched up my jacket to reveal the pistol. If this fellow wanted to roll me, fine. There was a thin wad of greasy bills shoved in the side-pocket of my saddle-bag. No more than a man would expect to find on a drunk *vaquero*, but enough to keep a thief from looking for more. Hat pulled low, I feigned sleep. My heart beat too fast, chest straining against the cloth.

The footsteps drew closer. A dog yelped. Then came the sound of scrabbling paws. A snout nudged my hat off, then a cool wet nose brushed my face. My eyes snapped open. Gracie. Several feet away Jackson stood holding the lead rope to Sadie's mule. 'You steal that hogleg from the strongbox?'

I scrambled to my feet.

Jackson nodded at the pistol in my belt. 'Think I wouldn't notice?'

No, I figured he would. I'd felt certain this gun that had been left behind in the lockbox, unclaimed for weeks, would not go missing without Jackson noticing. Which is why I'd had my excuse ready. A speech about wanting to protect myself after what happened on the night of the execution. It was a believable pretext, one that might even sway him to bend Sadie's rule prohibiting weapons. Most likely not. But the fib seemed worth a try. To my surprise, Jackson had never mentioned it. So I'd just hung on to the gun, marvelling at my good fortune. Big mistake.

Jackson rocked back and forth on his heels. 'When you has to discipline a gal, you gits to know her some. If they crumple up under your hand. Or maybe they try little tricks, thinkin they can screw or flirt they way out. Others… well, they hold straight and proud, daring you to come right back at 'em. Goadin you on almost.' He paused. Behind him stretched the shadowy dip and swell of the foothills. Hoisting works crouched along the ridgeline in a hulking black mass. 'I always wondered how you'd take your licks.'

'That a threat?'

Jackson tipped his head back, as if pondering the question. Caught in the lustre of moonlight, his face, grooved and weather-beaten in the way of all seafaring men, bore a wounded expression. In some mysterious way, what I had done hurt him.

I bent to collect my saddle-bag. It held very little. Hunk of bread, wedge of cheese, my ink-print of Henry, Will's letters. Everything else had been left behind. 'You running me in?'

He kicked at the dirt, thick powerful body stooped with some nameless sorrow. His sleeves were rolled high above the elbow, and at the sight of those tattooed forearms emerging from his starched evening shirt, a soggy mournful feeling rose within me. Like homesickness or regret. So far, I'd kept my thoughts from settling on how my theft would affect the others. Madam Blair would lash out at the whores, as always, but she would come down hardest on Jackson. He would not lose his job. Sadie relied on him too much. But she would ride him hard for what I had done. Blame him for failing to notice and stop me. For a time. Until some fresh outrage came along to distract her.

Gracie whimpered, nudging at Jackson's legs. He bent to comfort the dog.

'Coyote,' I offered. 'One crossed my path on the way here.'

He nodded, giving Gracie's haunch a firm pat. 'Spect she caught the scent.'

Then he pushed up to his feet and clumped towards me, hand outstretched.

I backed away.

'That hogleg ain't much good without these.' In his palm lay a fistful of cartridges.

I levered the pistol open. Empty. Except, when I'd lifted it from the lockbox five days ago, it had been loaded. I'd checked the chamber before hiding it under my mattress. Jackson's handiwork. But why sneak into my room, remove bullets from a pistol, then chase me down in the middle of the night to give them back? What was he playing at? I slid the cartridges into the chamber and levered it shut.

High above us icy shards of starlight pricked through the velvet dark. As though the night were riddled with holes. I shivered and rubbed my arms.

'Cold?'

I nodded.

Jackson pulled an old blanket from the mule's saddlebag and handed it to me. It smelled of stables and wet dogs, and beneath that, the faintest trace of the parlour house. Tired bodies, stale breath, faded perfume. Draping it over my shoulders, I clasped the ends firmly to my chest, hand lodged between the hidden bundles of cash.

'Want to buy Pecos?' He gestured at Blair's mule, cropping at a tuft of dry grass. 'Sadie told me to sell her, but she's too old to work a mule train. Got some life left in her, though. Enough to get you far as Fairbank, tho' I'd keep to the wash. Follow the gulch down to the river. Them bluffs'll give you shade once the sun's up.' He tugged the mule up, stroking her under the jaw. 'Bought her off Ray Burgess a few years back. Nothing fancy, I told him, just an animal to pull Sadie's runabout. She's lost some a her toughness, but the old gal'd be some use on a ranch or a farm. Blair ain't laid eyes on Pecos in days. She'd be none the wiser if I sell to you. Long as I hand over the cash.'

It was too strange. Jackson following me down the wash with a handful of bullets and Blair's old mule? Stalwart, predictable Jackson? After I'd run off with half the night's take? He didn't know that, but the man was no idiot. And what was all this patter about Ray Burgess? Was he trying to delay me?

The mule was nosing at the wiry shrubs along the wash. Flowering yucca stalks poked up at the sky, white petals catching the moonlight in a pale, ghostly bouquet.

'You got a fair chance with Pecos,' he said in a low voice. Eyes downcast, lips twisted with sorrow. 'Better'n fair. What with the strike on. But you go stealin' a horse, they'll run you down for sure.' His face bore an ardent mournful expression I was too young to understand. Unable to see beyond my own misery, I failed to perceive the guilt that still preyed on him.

'Where you aimin' to get?' he asked. Then he held up a hand and shook his head.

'Nogales,' I lied, catching his eye.

He gave a slow solemn nod, then threw me a look that carried a promise. To remain silent. This would reinforce everyone's assumption that I had fled to Mexico, leading Madam Blair and everyone else astray. I considered telling him about the receipt for a stage ticket to Nogales I'd tossed into the wastebin of my room, but decided against it. Better to let Sadie discover that misleading bit of evidence herself.

I did not dare look at Jackson, but kept my gaze fixed on the sky beyond. His kindness was too much to bear. Then, fast on the heels of that thought, came another: Sadie's loyal strongman, standing here in a dress-shirt and thick-laced workboots, trying to sell me Blair's old mule? Doubt seized me. No. I did not trust it.

The pistol was heavy. It pulled at the tendons in my wrist. I remembered the powerful kick of the rifle when Will had taught me how to shoot. The bruise on my collarbone. The deafening burst of the rapport. How it echoed off the walls of the ravine. The heady rush when I'd hit my mark.

'You can't walk,' he said.

The moon hung above the serried edge of the mountains, fringing the ragged summits in a silvery glow.

'Just, please—' I holstered the pistol. 'Just leave me alone.'

Then I spun on my heel and ran.

I had planned to wait out the rest of the night in the wash. But not anymore. What if Jackson tried to come after me? It was all just too much. Scrambling uphill I found myself headed back towards town. Fine. Passing the next few hours indoors might be best. The night was cooler than I'd expected. What if I couldn't keep warm, or if my body heat were to attract snakes?

I navigated by the looming shadow of the courthouse, its bell-tower hulking up through the dark. After scavenging some empty explosive crates from a mine's scrap-heap, I stacked them into a high step. Then, with the help of a twisted old tree, I managed to scale the wall and drop down into the livery stable. I crossed the empty corral. The horses were locked away in their stalls, but I wasn't there to steal a horse. Unlike pinching money from a brothel, horse stealing was a serious crime. Jackson was right about that.

I stood in the dusty enclosure, picking tree-thorns from my rawhide gloves. Then I knelt by the window and gave a quick hard punch with my gloved fist. Nothing. I took up the pistol and brought it down hard. The glass shattered. After clearing away the shards, I draped Jackson's blanket over the empty frame and tossed my hat and saddle bag inside. Then I shimmied over the window-frame, and landed, arms outstretched, on the floor of Will Keane's office.

In the pallid light of the moon, I could make out the shadowy outline of his desk. Papers, ivory pen-knife, length of rope, some books. A table by the door held his walking sticks, a wide-brimmed hat. Cool air poured through the busted window, carrying a faint whiff of raw desert. Chalky hills, gravel washes, undulant grassland. That heady scent of heat being released from aching roots and silty soil. I drew a hunk bread from my saddle-bag. Took a bite, chewed. But my stomach was in knots so I wrapped the oilcloth back around and slipped it away for later.

Then I rifled through every drawer of his desk until my hand brushed the cool muzzle of his revolver. I withdrew the gun, emptied the chamber, and stuffed it into my saddlebag. A strip of moonlight fell across the carpet. I paced its entire length, stumbling over a stray book. In some ways, this next bit was the riskiest part. I had no idea how Will Keane would react. I would reveal nothing about the theft, but he knew of my lost savings. Only a fool would fail to suspect.

I collapsed into the leather armchair, beyond caring. Let him grow quarrelsome. Or treat me with indifference, smothering every spark of feeling in cold formality. Better yet, regale me with a lecture on the sin of stealing. Yes. Rancour might even help. Perhaps one more searing burst of severity and disapproval would cauterise this festering sore.

I sat with the pistol in my lap and waited.

Chapter 25

I awoke to the click of a latch-key. The room was suffused with grainy light. Beyond the shattered window the corral lay sunk in an ashy gloom, everything the colour of smoke. Will crossed the threshold with a quick sure step. He wore knee-breeches, riding boots, and a cambric workshirt, and for a long moment I did not move or speak, but simply watched him close the door and place a freshly pressed shirt on the table with his sticks and hat. Looking up, he gave a start.

I rose from the chair, pistol aimed at his chest.

'Vera?'

I said nothing.

'My God, it is you.' His voice swelled with feeling, a tender-hearted warmth that took me by surprise. 'What have you done to your hair?'

I gripped the gun harder, taking pains to steady myself under the warm confusion of his gaze. I had not anticipated the effect it would have, seeing him dressed like the scruffy cattleman who had met me at the stage-depot in Tucson all those weeks ago. I pressed back the feeling and waved at his desk. 'Sit down.'

He did.

I shoved a piece of paper at him, then brought both hands back to the gun.

'That a pistol you have there?' A smile twitched at the corner of his lips, which only compounded my confusion. 'Myself, I prefer a revolver. Colt Cloverleaf would be a nice choice for you. Elegant, lightweight, easy to load.'

I waved at the blank page. 'You're going to write a letter."

He took up a pen, eyes brimming with amusement. Like a child delighting in the unexpected. 'And to whom shall I address this letter?"

'It's to be a letter of introduction, praising my skills as a book-keeper and recommending my services. Direct it to one of your former business associates. In New Orleans.'

His face darkened. 'Why on earth do you want to go there?'

'Want?' I unleashed a scornful laugh. The sound shocked me; its bitter ring was the very echo of Sadie Blair. 'This ceased to be about what I *want* some time ago. I need a job. I must go to a place where someone will be inclined to hire me. Any old place will do, so long as I have a letter of introduction to someone who can take me on right away, the moment I arrive. Otherwise, I shall end up like the women at Blair's place.'

'Don't say that.'

I shook the gun at him. 'You are hardly in a position to tell me what to say.'

He gave a docile nod and bent his head to the task, pausing only to dip his pen in the inkpot. My eyes followed the smooth motion of his hand, callused fingers drawing the pen-point deftly across the page. My hand began to shake.

'Pistol a bit heavy for you?'

'No.'

He signed his name and sat back, waiting for the ink to dry. 'There's no need to point a gun at me.'

I made no answer, wrists aching under the weight of the gun.

He reached for an envelope and I watched his hands fold the letter and slide the paper inside. Then he took up his pen and addressed it in the same heart-breaking sweeps of blue. 'Take this to the Cotton Exchange and give it to Mister Lebrun. He knows all the shipping firms, factorages. Buyers, too. But first, you have a bit of explaining to do.' Will rose, hands raised in an exaggerated display of acquiescence. Then he reached over, armpit grazing the muzzle of the gun, and ruffled my cropped hair. 'Why?' he whispered. 'Why, oh, why did you do this?' His hand slid down to the spot at the back of my neck. Here he paused, hand resting gently against bare skin. I gripped the pistol hard, struggling against a hot rush of feeling.

His fingers trailed down the side of my neck, tracing my jawbone, my chin, then gliding down my throat until his palm reached my breastbone. His hand stopped there, lodged in the valley of bone between my breasts. He pressed at the cloth that bound and flattened them.

He waggled his thumb. 'This the money?'

I broke away, taking three swift strides across the room. Glass crunched under my boots. Beyond the busted window a lone star hung in the brightening sky, a shimmering thorn lodged in the lilac glow before dawn. I did not have time for this nonsense. His emotional caprice. These brutal extremities of feeling. Raising the pistol I swung round and faced him. 'By God, you will help me. If it is the last thing you do on this earth, you will help me escape.'

He lifted the envelope from his desk and held it out. 'There's no need to aim that pistol at me.'

'Maybe not,' I snatched the letter from his hand. 'But I want to.'

Hands clasped below his belt, he looked like a chastened choirboy. But he recovered quickly. Gesturing at the leather armchair, he adopted a calm solicitous air, as if I were just another client here on routine business. 'Tell me what you have done, so I can help you.'

I stuffed the envelope into the pocket of my buckskin jacket and brought my hand back to the gun. 'How do I know you won't turn me in?'

'Attorney client privilege. As your lawyer, I am obliged to keep whatever you say to myself.'

'You've taken an oath to this effect?'

'Nothing so formal. But it is my professional duty, sworn or not.'

I let my elbows fall, resting them against my torso. 'You're telling me it's your duty to help a thief escape?'

'I'm telling you that, as your lawyer, I am obliged to keep whatever you reveal to me in the strictest confidence. As for helping you leave town unhindered...' He trailed off and fell silent.

'Tell me.' I approached, stepping over the broken glass. 'Tell me why.'

'Because if any harm were to befall you, I could not live with myself.'

'Spare me the gentlemanly pap. You know how much I hate it.' I drew closer. Close enough to watch the confused sensations flit across his face. 'I want the real reason.'

He did not raise his eyes.

I placed the muzzle of the gun against his heart. 'Because you love me, right?'

He nodded.

'Say it,' I whispered.

His face was weary and unshorn, and when he spoke his voice was strained with feeling. 'Of course I do.' Then he turned away and I could not see what was in his eyes.

I lowered the gun.

Will waved at it. 'Been locked the entire time.'

'I know. I did not want to shoot you by accident.'

He gave a weak smile. 'Much obliged.' Then he stroked his chin and checked his watch. 'I'm afraid we haven't much time.'

I outlined my plan but when I reached the part about riding Lacey to Fairbank and leaving her at the livery stable, Will shook his head. 'Take Billy's grullo. He's short enough for you to mount unassisted, and you won't have to worry about him throwing a shoe. No danger of becoming the target for a horse thief either. Go on.'

I resumed, only to have him cut me short again.

'You cannot hop a freight train.'

'Of course I can. Texas Lil traveled all the way from El Paso riding freight cars.' She also turned tricks in exchange for food, but I kept that part to myself.

'It is far too dangerous. Please, promise me you'll buy a ticket on a passenger train.' He gave his head a vigorous shake, as if trying to free himself from the grip of some terrible vision. 'That disguise will get you out of the territory undetected. Fifteen miles east of Benson you're in Pima County, those boys won't lift a finger to help Sherriff Hatch. Not with all the bad blood since we broke off into a separate county. As for Hatch, he can't afford to waste men on the likes of you. Not after last week's street clashes. He needs every deputy here in town. Even if he wanted to send out a posse, he can't.'

'I figured as much. But he'll do whatever he can to placate Sadie Blair. Like telegraphing the station-master in Benson, who will put every station in the territory on alert.'

A lone fly buzzed through the glassless window, circling our heads. Sounds rose form the corral. Horses nickering, tack clinking. Sun-up. The chalky grey shadows in the room had given way to a sallow light. I grabbed my saddlebag. 'We don't have time to argue over this.' I strode across the room and pulled open the door, bracing myself for the usual onslaught of arguments and pretexts, all his chivalrous instincts rising up in revolt.

But to my surprise he gave a brisk nod and began issuing sensible instructions on how we would proceed. Then he opened a drawer and pulled out a sheaf of papers. 'You need to sign these. That is, if you want me to sell your claim once the strike ends.' Will mistook my confusion for doubt. 'I will not defraud you, Vera. Whatever else you may think of me, trust my professional integrity. I will forward the money to you through Lebrun. But the sale will take time.'

I glanced them over and signed. Confident he would not cheat me. He was too guilty. Like the johns who came knocking at Blair's front-door after busting up a chair or shattering a vase the night before. Sheepish and apologetic, eager to pay for the damage. Madam Blair called them 'high-binders with a morning-after conscience.' Well, Will Keane had a 'morning after conscience' alright.

He crossed the room, lifting his wide-brimmed hat from the table as he went by, and I followed him down the dim passage then out onto the street. While he lingered to lock the door I strode away towards the edge of town, passing its sun-scarred walls for the last time.

Day broke across the desert in a tidal rush of light, bathing the dusty streets in a golden haze. Slipping between the miners' cabins, I darted past fenced-in lots with rutting pigs and baying dogs, past chained up goats and paintless walls stacked high with mesquite grubbed from the sun-baked earth. I scrambled down the side of the mesa, boots slipping and scrabbling in the loose graveled soil. Deep tints of gold, amber and rose flushed the rocky hillsides, every cleft and dip brought into sharp relief by the low lying sun. Soon this suffusion of light would give way to a hard, obliterating glare. But for now the land lay washed in a lavish ruddy glow.

There was time to reflect, but I did not. I did not ponder the realisation that had begun to take shape: that his passion for me was real, but had become so fused with past hurts, confusions, and humiliations that no amount of time or forgiveness or penance on my part could return us to that clear bright space we used to inhabit where we talked and laughed and made love freely, without shame or hesitation. Something deep within him was twisted and hard and no matter what I did it would never unkink. Indeed, anything I did seemed to make it worse.

Such thoughts would goad and haunt me in the months to come. But now I simply walked, senses sharpened. A fragrant wind drifted down from the hills and as I passed over the sunlit land, I felt a kind of peace settle over me. No, not peace. What I felt, with every breath of creosote and sun-warmed stone, was a cessation. I ceased to worry, to calculate. Since the bank's collapse, every action had been plotted in advance, every move gauged against a host of possible outcomes. Facial expressions were carefully calibrated, seemingly casual remarks designed to allay suspicion. Now I simply put one foot in front of the other, following the rocky wash towards the spot where Will had agreed to meet me with Billy's grullo.

At the stocktank I sat down in the shade of a boulder. Air brushed the nape of my neck, exposed for the first time to the dry kiss of the wind. I sipped the hard limestone water in my canteen – water drawn from the Huachuca Mountains through an iron pipe that lay baking in the desert day after blistering day. Then I chewed my stale bread and sweaty cheese while gazing up at the blazing rimrock. Every surface gilded with fire.

I drank more water, tasting that twenty-one mile pipe in every sip, and into this quiet solitude stole a secret hope. The kind that only a desert morning with its sudden rush of light can nourish. A belief that the lacerations of the past few weeks would heal and leave no scar. That the speed of the train would wipe me clean and in a few days' time I would emerge from the juddery comfort of that iron womb, smooth and unblemished as a child.

Footsteps sounded in the gravel. I tugged my hatbrim low and touched my pistol.

'What's in your grub-sack?' called Will.

'Afraid I've eaten it all.' I scrambled to my feet as Will tossed me a small canvas bag cinched with a drawstring. Inside were tinned plums, a buttered roll, some hardtack. His breakfast. Eaten each day on his morning ride.

I thanked him and stuffed it into my bag.

Will dismounted and led Lacey to the stocktank. An ugly, dun-coloured grullo followed on a lead-rope. And at the sight of that low-backed rock horse, a lump rose in my throat. But I swallowed it down, stroking the old gelding under the throat.

Then, clasping the reins and a clump of his scraggly mane, I swung myself into the saddle and we set off towards Masons Camp. Birds chittered and darted through the brush as we rode west with the sun at our backs. A long silence stretched between us. In spite of all that had happened, and against every expectation, it was a relief to have him with me, easing a burden that I had been carrying for days. Long solitary days of planning, making choices, weighing outcomes, and most burdensome of all, maintaining secrecy. A secret, I now knew, was a terrible affliction. Nothing had oppressed me more than keeping my plans hidden from Contessa and Texas Lil, then absconding without a proper farewell. I had left them each a small gift, belongings I had been forced to leave behind. Even Gypsie got a tortoiseshell haircomb, although that was more of a bribe than a heartfelt expression of feeling. Yet somehow all the gifts now felt like bribes, crass attempts to atone for my deceit by tossing them a few trinkets.

As the day warmed, Will began to issue reminders. Go to the livery stable by the depot where the proprietor speaks only a few words of Spanish. His name is Larrieu. Say only the words 'una semana' and 'gracias' then hand over the exact amount for a week's feed. If you have to wait for a train, do it down by the river and pretend to fish. No one will pester a man while he's fishing. 'And whatever you do,' he concluded, 'keep that pistol sheathed. You can barely hold it steady. You pull that trigger, God knows what you'll hit. But one thing's for certain, you'll spook your horse and they'll come after you faster than a fly—' he broke off and shook his head. 'Sorry, I forgot myself.'

'Faster than a fly on shit?' I offered.

'Something like that.'

'I've heard worse.'

He tugged at the brim of his hat and fell quiet.

'On the waterfront,' I explained, unable to refrain from pressing the point home. 'Blair's customers treated me just fine, most of the time. And if she hadn't opened her doors to off-the-street trade that night, I'd be able to say they did so all the time. Well, no worse than the drifters and the longshoremen who used to hang around my father's shipyard.'

Will shifted the reins from one hand to another and said

nothing. Our silence was no longer comfortable but I did not care. It was a relief to speak freely.

Lifting my eyes from the trail I glimpsed five antlered heads bobbing and dipping through the tall grass. Antelope. I pointed them out, but Will did not even reach for his rifle. He just sat there, motionless, hands resting on the pommel of his saddle. There was a spiritless sag to his shoulders.

The sun climbed, and I could feel those wads of cash growing slippery against my skin. We rode into the shade of a high bluff, passing an abandoned wikiup. Its grass walls were shredded and the door was just a dark empty maw with scraps of old animal hide jagging down like rotted teeth. Apollo plodded on, but Lacey whinnied and shied as Will tried to soothe her. We searched the trail for rattlers and animal scat. Scanned the ridges for mountain lion, but found nothing. Will booted her on, but she kept tossing her mane and whinnying until we were well past that skeleton of a house, spooked by the ghost of some animal memory of which we knew nothing. Riding out from under the shadow of the bluff, she quieted.

'Was Jackson your accomplice?' Will said at last.

I turned the question aside with a laugh.

'Gave you his pistol.' He gestured at my saddle bag.

'Don't be silly. Some john left it in Blair's lockbox weeks ago.'

'That's a navy pistol, Vera.'

We exchanged a wary look.

Will touched the brim of his hat and went on. 'Back in New Orleans, all the old salts used to carry them.'

'Stop, will you? This thing was in the lockbox for weeks.'

Will shook his head. 'Only an ex-Navy man would have a pistol like that. Those things are useless out here. Heavy, hard to load, jams easily…'

Then it dawned on me. Madam Blair did not allow Jackson to carry a firearm. But after the night of the execution, he must have decided that he needed one. So he'd stashed his old navy pistol in the lockbox where Sadie would never know, pretending some john had left it behind. I bit my lip.

'Did you steal Jackson's piece?'

'I may have.'

He gave a low whistle. 'Lifting a man's firearm… that's no small thing. I can't see Jackson coming after you for Blair's sake. His loyalty won't extend that far. But if he has reasons of his own to chase you down?' he turned to face me, eyes scrunched up against the sun.

'He won't.'

Will thumbed his hat. 'I expect you're right.'

In the middle distance grassland gave way to pockets of tilled soil. Bright green squares scored into tidy rows, these were the fields where Chinese farmers grew all the vegetables sold in town. Whenever anyone made a fuss over 'all them Chinks takin over' within earshot of Josie, she'd tut-tut and say, 'You drive them folk out, won't be a vegetable from here to San Francisco. On'y ones what grow and sell anything green are the Chiney.' We turned the horses out onto open range.

'But whatever happens,' Will went on, 'don't steal a horse. You do that—'

'I know, I know. They'll be after me faster than Grant took Richmond.'

He nodded, hat pulled too low to see his eyes. Then he laughed. A hearty convulsive laugh that shook his shoulders and clutched at my heart. And with that, we topped a rise and caught our first glimpse of silvery green leaves shimmering in the sun. Cottonwood trees. The cienega.

The horses broke into a trot. Lacey pulled away and Apollo struggled to keep pace. My too big hat juggled about my head until it flew off entirely, swinging from its rawhide strap and slapping against my back as the grullo's short, muscular legs pounded on. With every hoof-strike that green froth of leaves came into sharper focus until I could see the boughs dip and sway in the breeze. I expect that I am the only person in the history of this sad beautiful world to cross a desert and despair at the sight of water.

The ground softened and the trail disappeared into a stretch of moist earth pocked with animal-prints. Cattle, antelope, coyote, javalina. The horses slowed, winding their way past the pale trunks of cottonwoods, through sedgegrass and reeds until we reached the spot where water bubbled up to the surface. Dismounting I caught my leg and pitched forward, slamming into the saddlehorn. It did not hurt, but days later the bruise would surprise me. The fact of it – that even through all those layers of cloth, this knock to the bone could turn flesh black-and-blue.

Watching for snakes I led Apollo to the spring and let him drink. I counted to six as Will had taught me, then tugged his muzzle from the water and drew the old grullo away. Stroking his warm damp neck, I unlooped the bridlereins and hitched him to a nearby tree. Cottonwood tufts blanketed the damp ground. The air winked and shimmered with them as the trees shed their soft milky seeds and the breeze carried them gently down. Like snow against a clear blue sky.

Will stood in the leafy shade, boot-heels digging into soft earth, as I drew up alongside and handed back his revolver. He took it from me without a word, sliding the muzzle under his belt. Then he plucked at the straps of my army canteens, gently lifting each one from my shoulders and carrying them to where water bubbled up from the ground. Cottonwood saplings bent in the breeze, leaves a shimmery silver in the low slant of the sun, as he filled and screwed the caps back on. I took them, cool and wet, from his hands. A senseless havoc coursed through me as I slid the straps over my head, adjusting the one on my right side so that it did not clink against the pistol. The shaded air of the cienega was cool and damp and I shivered.

'What you are about to do is dangerous,' he said. 'And unwise. Though I don't expect being horsewhipped down Main Street by Sadie Blair would be much fun either.' It was a joke, but neither of us laughed. 'No man in his right mind would permit you to travel on like this, unaccompanied. But as my mother would be quick to point out, a proper gentleman I am not.'

We stood amid the drift of cottonwood seeds, a vast silence bearing down on us. Interminable as the sky. One of the horses began to urinate, the other snorted and stamped. Their hooves made soft sucking sounds in the mud.

Will took up my hand and pressed it. And at this, my composure broke. Burying my face in his chest I clasped his sun-faded shirt and breathed in the sweat and the straw and the soap-washed cotton. Then he took me in his arms and our lips met in a hard, unyielding kiss. A crush of bones beneath skin, his breath sweet as water.

'Come with me,' I murmured, voice drowsy. 'To Mexico. We can follow the river south across the border...' I drew back, trailed a finger down his unshorn cheek. 'We'd be there by night-fall.'

'I know,' he whispered. 'I've done it.'

I recognised the quickening gleam in his eye. And at the sight of his face alight with the whir of assessment and calculation, I felt the dim flicker of some unsuspected hope.

'Thirty-three miles,' he said. 'But it's Cochise Country all the way.'

Gripping his shirt I pulled him against me, full and hard. Our belt-buckles clinked, butt of his revolver digging into my stomach. I touched his rough cheek, ran my fingers through the wavy brown hair, coarse and stiff with sweat, as all the old vibrations thrummed to life.

He raised a hand to stroke my hair and when his fingers touched the stiff bristly shock, he flinched and drew back in surprise. At that, all the light went out of his eyes and his hand fell to my shoulder in an apologetic caress.

I turned away. Before me stretched a heavily tracked strip of ground that led through sedges and saplings out onto the old

Spanish trail. There was nothing left to say.

I strode across the soft mud and prepared to leave. Removing my buckskin jacket I was hit by a sudden wave of exhaustion. A fatigue so debilitating my ability to move, or even breathe, seemed miraculous. I watched my hands roll up the jacket, tie it down behind the cantle of my saddle, then stroke Apollo's flank as he shivered against the flies.

Will approached, weary but unbowed, as I checked Apollo's girth-strap, tightening it a notch. Then Will unhitched him for me. A helplessness in every gesture. As if the bodies performing these acts were somehow separate from the hearts that leapt and reared within. As if some terrible storm were rolling over us to force this wretched sundering. Some violence from without. When always, at every turn, it was us.

'Where's your jacket?' he asked.

I gestured at it, rolled up and lashed behind the saddle.

'You should wear it.'

I shook my head, unable to speak.

'Your skin,' he touched the bare nape of his own neck. 'The collar of your jacket will protect it. From the sun.' He flipped up his own to show me.

I nodded, not daring to risk anything more. My eyes rested on a patch of air in the middle distance, but I saw nothing, absorbed nothing. When I made no move to untie the jacket, Will did so himself. Then he held it up for me to slip my arms through, and as I did, a terrible heaviness sludged through me. Then I took up the reins again. Standing beside him I drank in every detail of his weathered face, the tender ferocity of his gaze. White tufts of cottonwood seed kept drifting down, flecking his hair, his jacket. I plucked one from his beard and he flashed a grin. But the smile was spiritless and weary.

He reached behind me and lifted up my hat, which still hung from its rawhide strap around my neck. He brought it down onto my head, tenderly. It promptly flopped down over my eyes. He raised it up, tucking a folded handkerchief into the space between the back of my head and the hat.

'Old cowboy trick,' he winked. Then he wove his fingers together as he had done that first morning in Al Montgomery's corral and boosted me up into the saddle. There was no need, for I could mount Apollo without help and something about this, the superfluousness of the gesture, made it even harder.

I swung my leg over and hooked into the stirrups. My rib had begun to throb, a dull ache where it had bumped the saddlehorn. I could not bear to look at him.

'I told Lebrun to let me know you have arrived.' He laid a hand on my arm. 'His telegram should read: *secretary safely arrived*. Nothing more. It's in the letter, but remind him. You must not contact me, nor anyone else in town. It's too risky. I shall be in touch when the claim is sold. You have my word.'

I nodded.

Apollo shifted and tossed his scraggly mane, bridle jingling. My gaze fell to Will's hand, still resting on my arm, but the sight was too much to bear and my eyes bolted away, falling on the spot where the trail rose up from the cienega towards a hard pale sky.

I dug my heels into Apollo and broke away.

The old grullo stepped briskly over the well-trod earth, carrying me away from the cienega. Away from the spot where Will Keane stood amidst the downy drift of spring, as the soft suck of hooves in the mud gave way to the crunch of dry leaves before fading into silence as the trail opened out onto empty desert and I crossed that final stretch of grassland, motionless and dry under the heartless blue.

Chapter 26

Of the retreat I remember little. No, that is not true. Scraps remain. Lodged in me like thorns, or shards of glass. Shells falling. Taste of sulphur and chalk. Abandoned sentry-boxes, unmarked cross-roads. Dead pack mules. Supply-wagon shredded to bits, mangled ration tins strewn across the road. Taste of cinders, explosive powder. Wrists aching. Wrestling a litter down flat packed earth. Bandages scavenged from the dead to lash the body down. Dead officer's face unshaven, skin grey, waxy feel to his arms as you peel uniform away, fingers shaking so bad it's hard to undo the buttons. Find his pistol, shove it into supply bag. Field boots? Too big. Tramp on.

A creature darts into the road whinnying and snorting, dragging an empty hitch. A soft whispering. Not in French or English or any language at all, just a low murmur of sound as you sidle up alongside to take up the reins. Foot hooked into stirrup. Jumping once, twice, three times. The mare lurches and rears, but once mounted she is soon curbed. Ride on down the road past boarded shop-fronts. Crunch of glass underfoot. Haze of pulverised stone. Sausages and preserves pulled from empty kitchens. Rifle grease smeared on horse's flanks, improvised hitch rubbing them raw. Cowslips and daisies blooming in fields. Little stone bridges. Keep tucking hair under helmet. Cuffs covering hands. Skin red and scabbed from scratching. Itch constant and unrelieved. Delirium, aching bones. Shins too sore to stand.

Then everything goes white. No sound but the quiet murmur of the sea. Death has come. The thought drifts and settles over me, like sinking into a warm bath. No itch, no stench. Just a bright blaze of acetylene lamps. A face appears. Beaky nose, grey hair pulled taut. No, someone else. Give me

Tosh, or Louis. Eyes close. Open to a different slant of light. My body feels heavy, like a giant anchor tethering me to breath.

Faith Hamilton is telling me a story. About a woman on a runaway cavalry horse. Gun-carriage dragging behind. Dead body lashed to it. Rotting. A macabre sight, this woman. Dressed in some lousy officer's uniform, dark hair whipped and tangled by the wind. Like a savage. Tearing between the tents on horseback, horse and rider racing west toward the sea. I shake my head. Not me. I am not guilty of upsetting her patients, of causing disorder in the wards.

A stranger arrives. He speaks of *trench fever*, s*hell shock*, *morphine*, *dehydration*. Then he marks some papers and hands them to a girl in a VAD uniform. She smiles, fetches a glass of water. I am told to drink. Everyone speaks English. Not me. No words pass my lips. Why bother? I like the murmury silence of my little corner of the world, where I lie partitioned from the officers by red screens – the same ones that get placed around the beds of those who are dying. But my condition is not fatal. I am simply in possession of body parts that require isolation and privacy. My affliction, commonly described as 'womanhood' – and here the thought breaks off, for it is not really mine, but hers. Tosh's wry humor, her sardonic point-of-view. Yes. How outraged Tosh would be. No. Would have been.

The days pass. Air-raids slacken. I sleep less. Eat solid food. Endure the strident ring of the ward's gramophone. Between songs, there is talk. I learn that the German offensive has been halted outside Amiens. That Paris is being shelled by a long-range gun. American troops were seen marching up the road to Camiers. The Germans have been repulsed before reaching the channel ports. We have not lost the war. From the ailments discussed and the relative verve of patients' voices, I surmise that I am in the light medical ward at a British Base Hospital near Boulogne. A nurse informs me that Sister Hamilton has kept me here to convalesce over the objections of the CMO, who relented only when it became clear that nothing else could be done. Under the command of the French Army, I cannot be shipped to England, and in my condition there is no way to get me back to Paris.

But I hardly mind. How lovely it is to be cared for! To be bathed, watered, fed. Given books to read. The dressing on my neck gets changed twice a day. Competent hands like the touch of a lover, smell of lint, castor oil, and piric acid filling my lungs. Beyond the screens officers banter and play cards. Share cigarettes, tell racy jokes, and talk of home. Every few days the voices change. Then, one day, a different voice reaches me. Brash and cheerful, with lazy drawn-out vowels. A cheer that is a bit self-satisfied, a bit too shiny for British officers who have seen four years of war and will soon be sent back up the line. A nurse peeks round the screens to make sure I am awake, dressed. Ready to receive a visitor.

'M'am?' Blake Tyler ambles into view, cap in hand. His other arm is in a sling. Cheeks ruddy. The skin of his neck and face is freshly shaven, pale from where a beard used to be. He taps at his sling, tamped-down sound of a plaster cast beneath.

'Fractured tibia,' he shrugs. 'Few more weeks, it'll be healed up right tidy.' Raat tah-dy. He stands so close I can smell his shaving cream. 'Thank you for bringin' her away, M'am. So she might have a proper Christian burial.' The word *burial* sticks in his throat, but he swallows hard and goes on. 'I reckon you were with her. At the end.' He shakes his head and when he resumes his voice is low but firm, as if, having settled on what he means to say, he will not be deterred. 'Now I know how ugly death can be, M'am. And I'm not just talking bout this war. There's things a country doctor comes across in the back of beyond, things I seen done with guns and knives fore this war ever became my problem. Or my country's problem.' He paces down the length of the bed in his slow ambling way, shoulders scrunched to accommodate himself to the narrow space, good arm pressed to his side. 'They say you don't talk, or won't. Now I'm not partial to leanin on a woman, and I ain't gonna press you on a thing you got no heart for, but if I was to ask...' he made his way back from the foot of the bed in three swift strides, fidgeting with a seam on his cap. 'I just thought... maybe you could tell me if she said anything. A last word?'

His face is watchful, waiting. Not humble, but patient. Hopeful, even. As if I might actually tell him. About the blood pouring from her mouth. Wet thunk of her last breath. Neck swollen. Lips blue. Chest pumping and heaving against mine as she fought for air.

His fingers have ceased worrying his cap, and my eye falls to his good hand, resting by the bed. Not idle, just still. A motionlessness that is full of graceful poise. As if waiting, calmly, to be called into action. It is a beautiful hand. Long-fingered, slim, strong. A hand to wield sterile knives, to slice open flesh and repair the damage beneath then stitch the skin back together just so. A hand that can elicit vibrant, strangely syncopated songs from a piano – those jaunty rollicking tunes that used to roll through our rain-dashed tents whenever he had a free afternoon.

I shake my head. No last word. Nothing.

Blake falls silent as he absorbs this news, while I stare down at my legs. Two lumps beneath the blanket. Shins still sore. Aching from yesterday's turn through the grounds. From beyond the screen comes the clink of dishware. A hearty, sardonic cheer from the newly arrived who unleash the usual quips about no more bully beef. My thoughts drift to lunch. Tired mutton with over-cooked vegetables? Beef stew and potatoes? Blake is talking again. About Tosh's injuries, what he has heard.

'Some nights I lie awake, and I can't help wondering if I'd a been there... I don't mean to lay blame. No, M'am. But there's things only a doctor can do. Something quick and simple that other folks just can't. Incision to relive pressure. Tracheotomy...'

The word hooks my attention. I once saw Tosh perform one. Watched her plunge a blade into a patient's neck. Heard the sharp crunch as it broke bone, then a hiss as of air rushing in. He died three days later from wounds that went septic, breathing softly through that hole until the very end.

Tracheotomy? No. I remember the shrapnel jutting from her neck. It cut through an artery. I force myself to look up. At his face. I shake my head again. To impress this fact upon him. But the hard bright shine of his eyes deflects my gaze. He cannot accept this. Not out of stubborn pride, or gross vanity. Just a simple inability to conceive of his own helplessness.

He lifts his injured arm and flashes me a smile. Face wayward and forlorn but still full of life, and all at once I see what Tosh loved in him. The vigour and unswerving faith. His passionate belief in himself and their shared profession. In the God-like miracles a doctor can perform. Confronted for the last time with his unalloyed self-assurance, the slow lilt of his speech, the sandy-haired toss of his head when he laughs in his free and easy way, I feel ashamed. Of my antipathy. My desire for Tosh to mete out her love in tiny, measured doses. I no longer wonder whether he loved her as well as she did him, for it no longer matters. Never did. How I hate myself for wishing that she would stop loving him. Stop risking herself.

Blake is making small talk. A congenial attempt to flush away unpleasant thoughts and return us to easy collegiality before he departs. He is telling me about the American soldiers at the Base Hospital where he will be stationed for the rest of the war. 'Mumps, measles, chicken-pox, diphtheria. County boys exposed to infection for the first time. There's hernias and hemorrhoids, bad backs, hammer toes... I don't know what kinda medicals they're given 'em back home, but some a these folks got no business over here. One skinny kid with a mitral sternosis – I reckon he weighs less than his marching kit.'

My tray arrives. Beef stew, hot tea, buttered roll. After a flurry of *m'am*s and *much obliged*s and a good deal of cap-tipping, Blake Tyler departs. From beyond the screens I can hear him chatting with the convalescent officers, promising to send a some discs for the gramophone down from Camiers. 'Got a pile of real good stuff before shippin out. Scot Joplin, King Oliver, Louie Armstrong...' His confident drawl rings out across the ward, drowning out the hushed voices of officers who have spent four long years getting sniped, mortared, gunned, and shelled in places whose names they cannot even pronounce. Reems, Abe, Wipers, and Pop. One of them makes the mistake of saying 'Yank' and gets an earful. 'Now, boys, I don't mind bein called a Sammy. But Yankee? Well, I won't sit quiet for that. My daddy fought under General Lee, and his brother Joe, he died with a Union bayonet in his gut.'

Blake Tyler's voice fades away, and from beyond the screen comes nothing but a clatter of metal trays and clinking spoons. My throat tightens. I tell myself that Tosh died for her beloved 'cause': to prove that women can do everything men can – including, it would seem, dying a wretched useless death. Yet how can her death be useless if this war must be fought, invaders repulsed, France kept free of Prussian militarism? I do not know. But I cannot help feeling that Tosh's death is a crime. That at some unknown moment we reached a tipping point and went hurtling past, blundering far beyond that terrible threshold when *l'impôt du sang* became too high. But bargain struck, there was nothing for it but to go on. To keep piling cash on the barrelhead as Madam Blair would surely say. Cash on the barrelhead: Tosh, Pierre, and countless others.

I take up my spoon. Stir the hot stew. Then push the bowl away, untouched. Images of Blake and Tosh, together, rise before me. The way he bent over her that day by the *camion*, his lips touching the crown of her head, eyes closed, breathing in her scent. How she fretted in the dug-out the night before she died, despairing over the possibility of a future without Blake Tyler. Imagining how it would feel to have him subtracted from her life.

Face wet with unwiped tears, I think of Blake. Camille. Myself. The men beyond the screens who are eating their stew and sipping their tea. All of us muddling on through our diminished world. Never knowing what might have been. What a world inhabited by Tosh and Pierre and countless others might look like. If Tosh would have become Blake Tyler's wife, borne his children. If the Archduke's driver had taken a different route, or if the diplomats had done a better job of forging a peace back in that languid summer of 1914. Or, if all those years ago, I'd taken that room Josie offered me, been more careful the night of the Bisbee Massacre execution – lit a lamp before undressing, checked my room. If Will Keane had agreed to marry me in Tucson; or if those glorious nights in the casita had produced a child.

I imagine myself seated beside him after all these years, weathered hand in mine as the sun sinks below the horizon and we watch that burning ember pulse and flare through an ashy haze of sky, everything gilded with fire. What if I had never fled to New Orleans, met Louis, come to Paris? I subtract these things from my life and what I see is Tosh. Alone on that bombed out road, not having to halt for anyone. Racing with all her might toward that sliver of woodland, running on and on without pause as fast as her youthful legs can carry her.

Chapter 27

One day Camille arrives. Her voice reaches me through the walls of the *baraque* where I sit on a camp-stool, wearing a faded VAD uniform that's a size too big. My elbow rests on a desk covered with memoranda, shift-schedules, and leave requests. And here, under my left hand, are my discharge papers.

The door opens and Camille hurries over, hands outstretched. I rise. She clasps my wrists, kisses both cheeks. Wrinkling her pert little nose, she fingers my sleeve then pulls a tucked silk dress from her valise and spreads it lovingly across a chair. My willingness to wear unflattering clothes seems to trouble her far more than my silence. But the staff could hardly dress me in the lousy officer's uniform I was wearing on arrival.

Outside, a soft fine rain is falling. Camille has brought me a light summer coat that I have not worn in years. It smells of camphor. The pockets contain a worn scrap of paper, some pebbles. Withdrawing them I find they are not stones, but sugar-coated almonds. *Draguées.* Left over from a trip Louis and I took to Verdun six years ago. We were visiting one of his old army friends, Major Pinault, who teased Louis for owning a motor-car and then refused to ride in it. So we spent two cloudless afternoons exploring the surrounding countryside on horseback.

Looking back on those bright September days, I realise they were among the most contented we ever passed together. Each one ended with a leisurely dinner, during which Louis and his friend would reminisce while I conversed with the Major's wife. At some point, I must have slipped three *draguées* into my pocket and here they have sat, untouched, for all these years. One is pocked with tiny holes; the others are smooth and unblemished. I raise one to my lips then bite down, but it is hard as a rock and I almost break a tooth.

Camille takes charge of my papers, stows the bags, converses with officials, offers up *cartes d'identité* and our *laissez-passer* on demand. I keep expecting her to force me to fend for myself. But nothing is ever asked of me, nothing required. She treats me like a tantrum-prone child whose misbehavior is best ignored.

Back in Paris life goes on. Which is to say, the war goes on. Meatless days. Sugar-cards. Bread tickets. High prices. Rationing policies that make no sense (restrictions on hard cheese, but not soft?). Sudden shortages. First milk, then eggs. Queues. Black crepe. Mourning armbands. Papered windows. Sand-bags. *Alertes* that are far more unnerving than the raids themselves. A cacophony of guns, trumpets, sirens. Damp cellars full of mould. Ventilators cemented over in compliance with official warnings about mustard-gas, which thankfully never arrives. Notes of *La Berloque* ring through the streets to signal the all-clear. *Sing a song of safety, nothing in the sky.*

With the arrival of summer, combining our coal rations is no longer necessary, but Camille continues to occupy my guest quarters and act as *maîtresse de maison*. After all, prices remain high and two household allowances, pooled under one roof, allow for economies that would be impossible were each of us to live alone. Still, it surprises me. Camille is a practical clear-headed woman, who has little tolerance for my refusal to speak, my listless ways. She does not say as much, but I can sense it. In the pressed-lip sighs that shoot from her nose, in the sharp scrape-back of her chair after supper. Everyone has lost loved ones. Some women have suffered the death of three, even four sons. Others a son and a husband. And me? I have lost a friend of less than a year and suffered a burn on my neck. A scar easily covered by a carefully arranged scarf, or the kind of high-collared blouse Sadie Blair used to favour. Who am I to indulge such an immoderate *cafard*?

And yet, Camille indulges me too. By living under my roof

and continuing to take charge of the house-keeping, she spares me any need to act or speak. She admits that she ought to move out and force me fend for myself, but a lifetime of austerity is not so easily cast aside. And so Camille stays on, indulging and upbraiding me in every breath. 'If faut tenir, Vera,' she will tut in that piquant tone of hers, while handing money, coupons, and *cartes* to Marie-Rose for the day's shopping. Once the war ends, she remonstrates, *on doît continuer toute seule*.

But until that time, her inborn thrift relieves me of every burden. Decisions are made and I submit, surrendering to acts I once refused to countenance – like eating an illicit fillet on meatless days, or selling our sugar ration to one of the neighbours. Every morning Camille issues instructions to Marie-Rose before bustling off to the pharmacy she has managed to keep going all these years – through the war, Pierre's mobilisation, her husband's death. And once she has hurried off to her shop full of ampoules, powders, and vials, I am free to drift and drowse.

I have spent entire days wandering from room to room. I'll run a hand along my rosewood bed then stare out over the rooftops of Paris, until I grow restless and find myself dragging through the paneled drawing room then down the winding stair and out into the garden. In each room I pause to finger tapestries, lift china figurines, examine paintings. Like an archaeologist studying potsherds. Who was the woman who used to dine at this lacquered table? What has become of that contented creature who liked to stroll down the Rue des Près, searching out small treasures for a pittance? Will these napkin rings she once purchased provide a clue? Lead me back to her?

As the days pass Marie-Rose becomes agitated by my aimless wanderings, convinced I ought be in bed like a proper invalid. To escape her suffocating expressions of worry and constant offers of tea, I take to the streets and find that the city enchants as never before. The boulevards, purged of cars, are all sky and sunlit stone. The faint of heart fled when the Germans reached Noyon and Paris was declared part of the *zone d'armée*. The city now affords the same heady thrill as a ship on rough seas, decks given over to those hardy few who remain unbowed before the storm. Our faces betray us. Everyone you pass on the street wears the same look of complaisance, like passengers who never fall sea-sick no matter how rough the crossing.

The weather, however, has not been the least bit stormy. The sun shines on and on, as June unfolds. All around us the city shimmers and endures, although it is hardly the same city that greeted me eighteen years ago when I stepped from the train at the *Gare du Nord*, searching the platform for Louis' face. Louis. I think of him whenever I find myself in the Bois. How he loved tearing down the Avenue de Acacias in his motor-car. His passion for motor-travel was surprising in a man of such conventional tastes. His cellar was always restocked with the same unsurprising, venerable clarets and white Burgundies. His decanter always contained the same brandy his father used to favour. And, just like *père Auguste*, Louis' table was renowned for its traditional fare and old-fashioned menus.

Yet alongside this unshakable regard for convention, there blazed a passion for modern gadgetry. A boyish enthusiasm for moveable parts Louis could dissemble and tinker with. Rifles, clocks, photographic cameras. And, in the last ten years of his life, his great passion was for motor-cars. Before his heart gave way, he enjoyed nothing more than rolling up at my door, unannounced, to whisk me off on one of his beloved *randonnées*.

Once a windscreen had been installed and we could shed those beastly goggles, I enjoyed our spontaneous jaunts to Chârtres, Versailles, Beauvais, Fontainebleau. Freed from the strictures of Parisian society, and the asphyxiating press of people Louis liked but whose anti-Dreyfusard sentiments I could not overlook, we were able to relax and enjoy one another's company. Travel, as always, seemed to carry us back to the way we used to be. In New Orleans. In those European cities we visited before the war. But once back in Paris, all the irritants, abrasions, and subtle hurts would resurface, despite our closeness mere hours before as we sat huddled under a wool-throw in a speeding motor-car.

Walking down the Avenue des Acacias, I take a deep breath of fresh clean air. No petrol-fumes, no screeching brakes, no tooting horns. Were Louis still alive, this, too, would have become a source of tension – for he would be yearning for his requisitioned Lion-Peugeot, while I delight in this motor-less quiet that now reigns over the Bois. Or perhaps I am wrong. Perhaps the war would have tempered and recast our relations in ways I cannot imagine. Strolling among the cyclists and horse-carts, I put the question to myself and find that I haven't a clue how Louis might feel – what he would do, think, or say – if he were by my side right now. In what ways would the ordeal of living in wartime Paris have changed him? Altered the way we treated one another? How do you spend over twenty years with a man and not know such things?

My chest tightens and it occurs to me that Louis' death was all too swiftly buried by the outbreak of war. Every day brought a fresh avalanche of distractions and disasters, from the drama of mobilisation to the petty hassles of convincing one *fonctionaire* after the next that my papers were, in fact, in order. My recent marriage to Louis meant I was no longer a resident alien and did not need this or that *visé* from the American Consulate, but good luck convincing officious *commandants* and war-rattled *gendarmes* of this fact. Then came Pierre's death and Camille's grief. Which left no time to mourn a man who had led a long, happy life. One who slipped from this world an hour after confessing his sins and receiving extreme unction, dying in the comfort of his own home with the wife he had loved as well as he knew how by his side. Three weeks later came the flood of refugees, the threat of invasion, the evening papers with their daily lists of the dead. And in a city thronged with mothers, sisters, and wives all veiled in black crepe of what account is the death of a prosperous old man whose heart ceased to beat at the age of seventy?

But his loss was of great account to me.

I depart from the avenue, letting quiet tears roll down my cheeks. Trees receive me into their leafy shade, and as the path dips and winds beneath the rustling boughs I allow myself to remember. The early years. Our European travels. Our shared enthusiasm for whizzing down country roads in an open car. His reluctant smile and patient nod. The way he used to pause, mid-conversation, to tap ash from his cigar before launching some clever *riposte*. His consistent, straight-forward desires. A good cigar, a glass of brandy, an evening of lively conversation with a woman by his side. Sometimes that woman was me, other times not. For Louis was incapable of being alone.

I walk on beneath the chestnuts and magnolias, and beneath the fullness of their shade the thought comes to me that our love was always partial. A place of refuge where we could escape our own individual loneliness. For all those years each of us held something back, then blamed the other for failing to seek out it out. Unearth and cherish it. And I perceive, for the first time, the long shadow cast by Star Mansion. How it has stretched across the years and the miles molding and shaping my choices, my fears. Dampening joy, fueling doubt.

When the tears subside I find myself on the edge of the Bois, wandering among trees whose branches have been sawed off for firewood. The stubby trunks have been scored with pen-knives, and I cast a glance over the designs, names, messages… "Boche no bon!" "Jim + Natalie." And on a tree near Porte Dauphine, a large crooked heart has been carved out of the bark and left empty.

One night I jolt awake, aware of a low unceasing rumble. I brace for the *alerte* but none comes. Just the clamour of a ringing telephone, followed by Camille's slippered footsteps. Then her voice, sharp and clear, shouting into the receiver. *Oui, oui! Je l'ai entendu. Qu'est ce que c'est, ce bruit?* Light hems the edges of the curtain. I rise from bed and peek out the window. The sky is a sickly yellow, shot through with streamers of light. Can it be?

Camille raps at the door, then enters. She tells me to come away from the window. We must repair to the cellar with Marie-Rose. But I am pinned in place by what I hear. That rolling heave and pound. A sound I know well. Light from the hall pours into the room from the open door. Camille tugs at the sleeve of my night-dress and gestures at my cellar clothes, which lie ready and waiting on the stool of my dressing table. She stares at me with pursed lips, her mouth small and pale as a rose. My hesitation sends her into a rage. She flings the clothes at me and shouts. 'Ça t'enerve? Eh? Ça, t'enerve, Vera?'

Face flushed, she fires away at me in rapid staccato bursts. Her tirade is littered with words I do not understand. A memory surfaces. Of Pierre. Confiding to me that, as a boy, he always knew when he'd done something unforgivably naughty, because his mother would *dit ses jorons en yiddish. Pauvre Maman*, Pierre had sighed, a Jew only when angry.

Lifting my cellar-clothes from the floor, I perceive that somewhere in the murk that has spawned this outburst lies the answer to Tosh's question. The one she posed on that raw January morning as we stood by the fountain of the old château. *Why are you here, Vera?* And as Camille unleashes another Yiddish-studded onslaught (cursing my wordless passivity, my selfishness and *egoïsme*), the answer becomes obvious: because it was a way to wrest myself free. To escape Camille's insatiable need for solace, her demand for far more than any friend can ever provide. Because in becoming a volunteer nurse, I'd found the one unassailable way to leave her behind.

I clear my throat. 'L'attaque a commencée.'

The shock of hearing me speak registers on her face. She has gone quiet, only the distant roar of the guns remains.

'L'attaque des Alliés.' My voice is hoarse, odd sounding. It sounded different in my head. And the words... they strain my mouth, scrape at my throat. I had forgotten the feel of speaking French. The half-swallowed syllables, that gagging sensation. 'Ce bruit. C'est la front qu'on entend.'

At the news, Camille bursts into tears.

'Madame!' Marie-Rose cries from the hall. 'S'il vous-plaît, Madame. Faut venir au-dessous.'

I take up Camille's hand and usher her into the corridor where Marie-Rose stands waiting. Apronned and bonneted. As a girl, she lived through the siege of Paris and tends to make light of our recent hardships. But when I tell her what is happening, the candle in her hand wavers. We come upon the concierge hovering midway down the cellar-steps, and Marie-Rose cannot contain herself. She blurts out what Madame knows. The allied offensive has begun! He bows his head at the news.

A *communiqué* confirms it the following day. Newspapers report a thousand German prisoners. September arrives. The big gun is driven back. Each day the black line on the front page of every newspaper moves farther from Paris. The city is no longer in the *zone d'armée*. We hesitate. Then, one afternoon in October, Camille and I descend to the cellar and clear away the mouldering candles and musty camp-chairs. Victory, Clemenceau announces, is in sight. But it is only when I see workers removing the blue paint from our street-lamps that I dare to believe it. The nights draw in. Gas-lamps along my cobbled street, unveiled for the first time in four years, give off a soft buttery glow. The sight amazes me.

By day, refugees fill the Rue de Rivoli, trying to discover whether their native *départements* have been liberated. Yesterday, the sign *Lille Interdit* came down. Beside us, a woman let out a warbled cry and clutched two small children to her breast. The children looked frightened. Too young to have any memories of life outside wartime Paris, they know nothing but dingy hostels and refugee nurseries where they are sent while Maman knits socks or makes lace in a work house.

Their mother's fierce caresses stun and upset them, and the youngest one, a blue-eyed boy with curly hair, begins to cry. Camille sees it and turns away. Swiftly I usher her into the Place de la Concorde, where we stroll beside captured guns. She tells me it was all she could do to keep from going down on one knee to console the weeping boy. Her eyes glisten and I squeeze her hand tight, as we continue down the gravel path beneath the monstrous snout of a howitzer.

One evening, Camille attends a séance. She says nothing but I can see it in her face when she returns. Eyes alight, slightly hazy. A dazed, peaceful look that reflects the stunned incomprehension that engulfs me now the end is in sight. Whatever emotion 'victory' ought to inspire seems beyond me. In this, I am not alone. Why else would we indulge in these fits of petty outrage over items in the newspaper? We are guilty of greed as well. Neighbours pause in the streets and under *porte cochères* to whisper about our shared and selfish fear: *what if a peace is signed before the Americans reach Sedan?* It is while poring over yet another speculative article on allied progress in the East that I hear the bell ring. It is late. I am expecting no one. Marie-Rose has retired. Camille, still bustling about in the vestibule after returning from her *clairvoyante*, answers the door. Moments later she flutters into the library and announces, face aglow, that there is a gentleman to see me. *Un anglais.* Her eye gleams, and the hopeful lift to her brow tells me he is *très beau.* Before I can protest, she is leading him in through the door.

He speaks beautifully accented French, to which Camille nips out lively responses. Whatever pleasantries they are exchanging wash over me, unheard, for the very instant I lay eyes on this man, I want to flee.

'Albert MacNeil.' His voice is deep and quietly upright.

I force myself to rise, extend a hand, introduce myself, scrambling all the while for some pretext. An excuse to withdraw that will not offend.

327

'It is a great pleasure to meet you.'

I nod in agreement. But I am not pleased. No, I am not pleased at all.

My discomfort does not go unnoticed. In a gracious display of discretion, Tosh's father returns his attention to Camille in order that I might compose myself. Standing by the curtained window, he inquires idly about the view. It is, he speculates, south facing? Camille dives into a rapid discourse on the merits of such a room during coal shortages, followed by a gushing description of the garden in summer, how the scent of lilacs rises up through the open window. He nods politely, eye falling to the framed photographs on my writing table. He seems to take an undue interest in them, until I recall one of Tosh's offhand remarks about her father dabbling in photography, a garden shed that had been converted to a dark-room...

He lifts one of the frames, squinting at the photograph with a clinical eye. And there in that face, pinched with concentration, is Tosh. My chest tightens. I am about to offer my excuse *(une migraine, vraiment affreuse)* when a familiar look darkens Camille's brow. Then she lifts her chin and utters the word, 'Verdun.'

She is gesturing at the photograph in Albert MacNeil's hand. It is a picture of me and Louis beside a small stone church. Louis' friend, Major Pirault, snapped it on that distant day when we rode out beyond the garrison walls into a village whose name escapes me. A day during which I slipped three *draguées* into the pocket of a coat that would get shoved to the back of a wardrobe upon our return to Paris and remain there for six years.

Camille, dry-eyed, says it again. 'C'est Verdun, Vera, n'est -pas?'

I nod. There is no possibility of excusing myself now.

Sensing her upset, Albert has busied himself with the other photographs. Tall and lanky with a long face and prominent eyes, he does not resemble Tosh except in profile. But when the slope of his brow and the angular lines of his nose and jaw come together, they form an eerie echo of the face that used to greet me in the surgical theatre, bent over a suture or an amputation. My eyes dart away, and in a flash the name comes to me. 'No, it was not Verdun,' I say, speaking in English for some reason. 'That photograph was taken in Ornes. A little village on the right bank of the Meuse.'

'Ornes?' says Camille, a strange uplift in her voice. She repeats the name, as if saying it twice might dissolve the acid taste of the other. Her gaze meets mine, eyes pleading with me to go on – to smother this unexpected burst of pain beneath some trivial patter. So I try. I describe the village. Tell them about the autumnal celebration that was underway when we arrived. Music and dancing in the streets, villagers selling fruit from willow baskets. I talk of the church's walls, moss thick and green between the chalk-white stones. Of the creek that ran alongside the cotton mill, where we sought shade and ate fruit purchased from a stern-faced woman. How Louis regaled me with a long lecture about Calvinist troops fighting the Duke of Lorraine on this very spot four hundred years before, his words mingling with the airy murmur of the creek like some consolatory undercurrent to my own thoughts, which were few and lazily contented.

My gaze drifts back to Camille. With a perfunctory nod she bids us both good night, leaving me alone with Tosh's father.

I gesture at a pair of upholstered armchairs by the fire.

He takes a seat and, for a long moment, we do not speak. In former years I might have filled this well-mannered pause with talk, but now I simply let the silence gather. His leather case stands propped against a chair and I wonder that he has not left it in the vestibule with his hat. He clears his throat as if to speak then says nothing.

'Would you like a cup of tea?' I offer.

'Do not trouble yourself.'

'It's no trouble.'

He gives me a doubtful look. 'I find French servants become extraordinarily surly when rung at such a late hour.'

I suppress a smile. His remark puts me in mind of Tosh. How mystified she always seemed when possessions did not find their way back to suitcases and night-stands of their own accord, for in her amply servanted youth they always had.

'I should be able to manage a pot of tea,' I say, rising from my chair. 'But if I fail to return, send out a patrol.'

I descend to the kitchen, aware that my hand is trembling. I have always known this moment would arrive. A day when someone from Tosh's family would call on me to ask the same question Blake Tyler had. A last word? Some thought of us at the very end? But this time it would be worse. Far worse. Blake Tyler was a doctor. He had seen enough of death to know that certain facts were best left unspoken. He knew not to seek reassurance that her death had been peaceful. Calm. Painless.

Carrying the tray upstairs I resolve to lie. I shall look him in the eye and lie. Never will a person who loved her, nursed her, ushered her into this world, hear of the grisly way she was ripped from it.

Back in the library Albert has placed the tea-table between our chairs. I set down the tray and busy myself pouring and straining. I hand him a cup and he thanks me, helping himself to sugar. His fingers, long and thin with pronounced knuckles, move with the same graceful dexterity that Tosh's did.

'My daughter,' he says evenly, 'took a strong liking to you.'

His headlong plunge catches me off-guard. I was expecting more small-talk. 'She was a dear friend,' I manage to say. 'I felt her loss keenly.' Then I clear my throat and go on. 'Her work was universally admired. The training hospital earned praise from the highest quarters. Just before – that is… back in March, our unit was awarded a special citation by the French Army. She saved the lives of many men and devoted considerable energy to training other doctors to do the same.' I am tempted to tell of her exploits at the *poste*, how she wanted to remain with her patients even at the risk of being captured. But at the thought of that day, I find I cannot go on.

The fire cracks and settles in the grate. I do not dare lift my eyes, for I can feel him struggling to gather his courage – a last word? she died peacefully? – and I am suddenly loath to deceive this man. Condolences should be offered, but accommodating my grief to such conventional forms seems to dishonour Tosh and the phrases die on my lips.

'I must ask—' he falters, then gathers himself and goes on. 'I must ask if there is anything that might be of some comfort to my wife. She is distraught.'

Out of the corner of my eye I can see his hands, flexing then collapsing into fists. I consider mustering the courage to tell him of the aid-post, but what comfort would such exploits be to a mother? My thoughts fall to Camille and what has haunted her most about Pierre's death.

Then I draw breath and meet his gaze. 'Your daughter did not die alone. I held her in my arms to the last.'

His head drops, chin falling to his chest, then he lifts his gaze back to the fire and whispers, 'Thank you.'

In the hush that follows, I expect him to finish his tea and depart. But he does not. I permit myself a sidelong glance and find him lost in thought. Whatever impressions and sensations might be stirring within I cannot begin to guess, although I sense something held in abeyance for many years. A deep vein of grief of which Tosh's death is only a part.

Rousing himself he stretches his legs towards the fire and sips his tea. 'I must tell you, Mrs Palmer, it is a pleasure to find myself in a proper home. Since crossing last week, my days have been given over to meetings and formal dinners. I find hotels tiresome even in the best of times, which these most certainly are not.'

'You are visiting Paris in an official capacity?'

He nods.

So. It is as I thought. He is here with the Foreign Secretary, negotiating the armistice. 'A diplomat who dislikes hotels? Perhaps you are in the wrong line of work.'

He laughs, softly. 'My wife often says as much.'

At the mention of his wife, Tosh's story comes back to me. In an effort to do or say nothing that will betray me, I take up the iron poker for the fire.

He reaches over and clasps the rod, lifting it gently but insistently from my hand. 'You may serve me tea, but I shall not have you stirring the fire.' His thick dark hair has been combed and pomaded, but as he prods the coals, a lone strand breaks loose and drops down onto his smooth pale brow. 'The staff in Boulogne said you arrived on horseback, dressed in a French officer's uniform and riding astride like a man. They told me to expect a wild-haired madwoman. One chap swore you were an Indian.'

'What kind?'

A confused look crosses his face.

'Dot or feather?'

He pauses, then smiles. A restrained, gentle smile that pleases me. 'Feather,' he says at last. 'Like Pocahontas.'

I smile back and feel his gaze fall to the scar on my neck, then skitter away. Taking up his leather case, he rests it on his lap and withdraws a stack of papers. His brown, expressive eyes have become grave again, and I steel myself for more questions about Tosh.

'One day a box arrived. Long after—' He clears his throat and continues. 'Her things were inside. Her uniform. A necklace I had once given her.' Here his voice breaks. I reach for his hand, but he is busily pulling something from his leather case. A packet wrapped in brown paper. He passes it to me and I take it.

'Forgive me.' He clutches at his breast-pocket and his apology pains me. His reserve. His shame at weeping. At the sight of him fumbling for a handkerchief, I feel a sudden rush of tenderness – perceiving, once again, something long stifled now interlaced with Tosh's death.

He gestures at the packet in my lap, which I unwrap expecting a gift from the family. Some token of appreciation for bringing her body to a place where it might be buried, her remains properly memorialised. Instead, a blood-soaked bundle falls into my lap. At the sight of those tattered pages bound by a sallow ribbon, a cry breaks from my lips.

'They are yours?' he asks.

Hand over my mouth, all I can do is nod.

'Please forgive the intrusion. I'm afraid we read some of them. The bits we could make out, given the damage they have suffered. We thought they belonged to our daughter. The moment we realised our mistake, we laid them aside.'

I do not answer at once. My fingers are stroking the frayed ribbon that binds the letters, pages stiff and black with Tosh's blood. Of all the things to survive this war. Of all the things. I find my voice and thank him.

Albert MacNeil rises to take his leave and I accompany him to the front door. The short walk down the corridor allows me to compose myself. Camille has left a light on in the vestibule, and at the sight of his hat and stick on the table, I find myself sad to see him go.

'I apologise for the lateness of the hour,' he says, slipping into his frock-coat. 'It was my earliest opportunity.'

'I doubt the concierge was pleased, but as for me…' I give a dismissive wave. 'Feel free to call anytime.'

'Thank you,' he says in that soft baritone, a voice that hints at a capacity for frank expressions of feeling that even a lifetime of constraint has not eclipsed. He adjusts his hat, consulting his reflection in the mirror, and in the bright light of the vestibule, I grow conscious of my burn scar. When he turns to take his leave, I can feel him struggling not to stare at it.

'You will come again,' I break out.

He gives a little bow, but it is a very polite, English bow, and I find myself pressing the point. 'If not now, then on some future visit to Paris. Promise me.'

My insistence seems to take him by surprise.

'And please,' I add hurriedly, 'be sure to bring your wife next time.'

'Perhaps,' he temporises. 'She dislikes going abroad, and at the moment, with the present difficulties…'

'Of course.' I force a smile, gripped by a strange reluctance to see him go. 'And your son?' I blurt out. 'Peter. He is well?'

Albert nods. 'Wounded on the Italian front two months ago, he is now safely ensconced at a convalescent hospital in London. Well on his way to a full recovery.'

'I am glad to hear it.' I am about to say how fond Tosh was of her brother, how much she relished his letters, but manage to stop myself. He is their father. Of course he knows. Far better than I do.

After closing the door behind him, I extinguish the lamp and make my way back to the library. On the armchair sits the packet of letters. I take them up and begin to fold back the pages. The uppermost letters are nothing but a hard brick of dried blood, pulp, and ink. But beneath them lie several that are merely splattered or a bit stained. A few are entirely unharmed. I draw them out and touch the faded ink, tracing the bold sweep of Will Keane's hand. My eye catches at bits then darts ahead. *My Dearest Vera… unable to sleep, I find I must take up a pen and write…to be swept up in a cataclysm of emotion whose ferocity shakes me to the very core… a state of affairs that both frightens and emboldens me… your consoling presence… I have passed a particularly toilsome day, and now in the quiet of my rooms, my thoughts fly to you… those lovely hours we spent beneath the shade of a cottonwood tree… from this day forward, whenever my eye lights on that bright ribbon of green stretched along the river, I shall think of you and of those delicious hours we spent beneath their leafy shade… that particular shade of green which shall always be ours and ours alone…* until I come to the very last scrap of paper, an empty envelope that reached me nine months after leaving the Territory. I recall the day Monsieur Lebrun placed it on my desk at the Cotton Exchange atop a pile of invoices. At the sight of Will Keane's hand-writing, I tore it open. Inside were three pieces of paper: a cheque from Tombstone Mill and Mining for eight hundred and fifty-seven dollars. A Bill of Sale, detailing my lawyer's percentage, which had been deducted along with a nominal fee for the cost of replacing the window in his office (see attached invoice). There was no note.

I sit for a long time with the letters in my lap. The coals turn to ash and the room grows cold. But still I sit, thoughts drifting back that day in the *camion* when I handed the letters to Tosh, desperate to lift her spirits and keep hope alive. As if loss of faith – in love and in Blake and in happy endings – were the gravest danger she faced.

I think of our flight from the *poste*. Of Simon hurling her helmet after us. Of Pierre playing the piano in my music room and how he used to fling open the doors in summer to let the notes mingle with the song of the lark who lived in the lilac tree. I think of that poor boy dying of chest wounds in the *poste*, each word shuddering forth from his chest like a bird struggling to take flight on broken wings. Of Louis and the day we rode on horseback to Ornes. Of my vanished pre-war self, that woman who stands beside him in the photograph, smiling away on his arm. Of the girl who once loved Will Keane, surrendering herself with a bold assurance that would desert me in years to come. I look back upon the avid simplicity with which I once loved and am amazed. Unable to recognise myself in the young woman to whom these letters are addressed. Who was she? Where did she go?

I rise from my chair and shuffle down the darkened corridor – joints stiff, back aching – and it occurs to me that unlike Tosh and Pierre and that poor boy in the *poste* who could scarcely wheeze words from his collapsing chest, I have grown old.

Chapter 28

At the Gare de L'Est, Camille leaves me with her *valise* as she hurries off to fetch a porter. The sight of her hulking, unwieldy case annoys me. There will be no *porteurs* at our destination and I have visions of wrestling the damn thing over rubble-heaps and shell-holes.

I have agreed to accompany Camille to Verdun, although I do not like the idea and have said so. She will find no trace of Pierre and scouring the battlefields is sure to trigger fresh paroxysms of grief. But Camille insists. Several women who attend Madame Ropaski's *séances* have made the journey and they speak of a great peace descending over them afterwards.

So here we are, embarking on a trip that would have been unthinkable a few months ago. Twice I have patted my breast-pocket in an instinctive check for my thick wad of *permis* only to be seized by a momentary panic. Until I remember. Peacetime. We need but one slim ticket which anyone is free to purchase at the *guichet*. The fact is a marvel.

A demobilised soldier with one arm strolls past. He is selling pencils from an old army pouch. I finger the coins in my pocket, counting them by feel. I never risk a purchase without the exact amount. Too often they cannot give change and become downcast and apologetic. Angry, even. Last week I came across a *mutilé* whose wooden leg had become stuck between cobblestones. Rain poured down as I helped wrest his leg free, but when I tried to buy a cigar from the box round his neck, he refused. 'Moux!' he shouted, shooing me away. 'Tous sont moux!'

The soldier circles back across the *gare* and draws near. He wears a faded blue coat that bears the lanyard of the Legion of Honour. I ask for three pencils, which he fishes from the bag with his good arm, and when he takes my coins our fingers scarcely touch. Walking away, I fall prey to a terrible melancholy. It happens every time. Whenever I approach a *mutilé* , I feel a swell of anticipation. A desire, perhaps, for something deeper to pass between us. Some acknowledgement of our former intimacy. Of how lovingly I once bathed those shattered bodies, stroked their foreheads, slid needles into their pale flesh. And what relief my morphine piqures used to bring. And now? Look at us. Strangers reduced to a dry exchange of coins.

A balmy breeze floats in from the street, fluttering the *tricoleurs* that sag from the rafters. This morning we awoke to rain-scrubbed skies and the scent of damp trees wafting in from the garden. I can scarcely believe that we are about to tuck ourselves inside a railcar for the first unmixedly joyful spring day in years. Except that our joy is not unmixed. Workers, demobilised soldiers, shop-keepers, and domestic servants keep taking to the streets to protest inflation and unemployment and every other injustice peace seems to have wrought, and who can blame them? Since the Conference began Paris has been overrun with foreigners, diplomats, secretaries, and under-secretaries all snapping up taxis, lodgings, and restaurant tables. Petrol costs double what it did before the war. Bread is still rationed. Butter: triple the price, despite the tax being lifted. Yesterday Marie-Rose informed me that the cost of celery-root has increased 900% since last year. I replied that we ought to refrain from eating it – a remark which was meant to be amicable, but it made Marie-Rose indignant. There is what Marie-Rose says and what she means. She speaks of celery-root but she means that, in the interests of frugality, I ought to restrict my evening entertainments.

But I have no intention of doing so. Why shouldn't a wealthy widow open her home to those who have come to Paris to forge a lasting peace? Scarcely a night goes by without several members of the British delegation gathering in my salon, and I have Tosh's father to thank for it. Back in January, when Albert returned for the peace talks, he paid me another visit and made a passing remark about the dreadful food at his hotel. After hosting a few small, informal dinners, I grew to know the delegates and their wives and began to keep an open house. Every Saturday throngs of bright amusing people crowd the stairs and the corridors, spilling out from the salon and the music room where Albert likes to take an occasional turn at the piano.

A quiet friendship has sprung up between us. An intimacy I cherish deeply. But I must take care. Last week Albert alluded to certain 'unhappy facts' about his marriage. The remark was in keeping with the frank, easy way we have come to speak with one another, but it was also an invitation. One delivered so lightly and discretely that it could be deflected by a mere change of topic. Which I did. Only to lie awake far into the night, thinking of the way he looks at me sometimes, the watchful silences and warm gusts of feeling that sweep over me in his presence.

'Viens,' says Camille, as a *porteur* whisks away our bags. I hurry after him to reclaim mine. Camille shakes her head, mystified that I should prefer to carry my own bag when a perfectly capable young man might do it for me. But I have grown accustomed to keeping my kit with me at all times and feel a jolt of panic when I see it carted away.

Newsboys are selling the morning papers and I buy a copy of each. *Le Figaro, Libération, The Times, The New York Herald.* All except *The Daily Mail* whose shrill denunciations of the British delegation rankle me. Threading her way through the crowd, Camille glances back at me with an impatient flick of her head. All morning there has been an air of petulance about her, an angularity to her movements that feels like a reproach. In the taxi I wanted to catch up her hand and say something kind, but her manner put me off. Glowering out the window at the red banners calling strikers to the streets, she spent the entire ride ticking off the ways their demands would damage her pharmacy. So I have resolved to make myself small and unobtrusive. My presence, I have learnt, is comfort enough.

I step from the tunnel into bright sunshine pouring through the domed glass onto the *quais*. Above the platform, victory bunting lifts and sags. A festoon of *tricoleurs* now rimed with coal-smoke. We dart through the crowd and install ourselves in an empty compartment. Seated across from me Camille flips through her copy of *La Vie Parisienne*, staring down at each frivolous page with a grave face. I shuffle through the papers in my lap. Montenegro has deposed their king, voting for union with Yugoslavia. Beyond that nobody agrees on what today's news is. *Libération* devotes its entire front page to the most recent spat between Pichon and the Unified Socialists, while *Le Figaro* offers up quaint little maps illustrating the progress of Bolshevism. And *The Times*? Riots in Punjab, more unrest in Ireland.

With a sharp jerk the train pulls away from the station. I take up *The Herald* and leaf idly through its pages. A horse named 'Sir Barton' is favored to win the Kentucky Derby. US Marines have been sent to Haiti. And on page 5, above an advertisement for something called 'deodorant cream' that is meant to prevent 'armpit perspiration odor', a headline catches my eye:

ARIZONA SENATOR DEAD.
Frontier Lawyer Turned Politician Dies at 62.

The death of Senator William R. Keane of Arizona last Tuesday removes from national politics one of its newest and most colorful figures. Senator Keane was taken ill after a social gathering given by his wife, a prominent Washington hostess, at their home in Georgetown. He was rushed to Veterans Memorial Hospital but died twenty minutes after arrival. Heart disease, aggravated by an attack of gastritis, was given as the cause of his death.

Senator Keane, who had been active in territorial politics for many years, rose to national prominence in 1912 when Arizona became the nation's 48th state and he was subsequently elected to Congress on the Democratic ticket. He had been instrumental in gaining statehood for a territory once infamous for its violent outlaws and savage Indians. As Attorney General to the territory, he brought corruption under control and supervised the peaceful resettlement of Arizona's native populations onto reservations. His final term was marred by the 'Simeon Six' scandal, in which a few territorial appointees were arraigned for taking bribes from Southern Pacific Railroad executives. He was ultimately cleared of any wrong doing, but three of his subordinates were found guilty of fraud and sentenced to two years in federal prison.

In Congress, Senator Keane was best known for his blunt speeches denouncing Poncho Villa and demanding a full-scale invasion of Mexico after the raid on Texas in 1916. As co-sponsor of the Indian Allotment Act, he fought to give the federal government authority to divide reservation tribal lands into farms so that Indians could own property and grow cash crops. Outside the chamber, his colleagues delighted in his wry sense of humor and rough-edged, frontier charm. His talent as a raconteur was legendary and social gatherings in the capital were often enlivened by Senator Keane's raucous tales from his early days in the 'wild west.' The genial senator was also a gracious host and the parties he and his wife threw were renowned for their colourful guest lists and genteel hospitality. Invitations to the Keane residence were among the most sought-after in Washington.

Born in Richmond, Virginia, he moved to Arizona in 1881 to practice law and married Abigail Davis, grand-niece of Jefferson Davis, in 1884. In 1893 he bought up cattle-ranches bankrupted by drought and his company, San Pedro Cattle, soon became the second largest in Arizona. In addition to banks and mines, in which he has been owner or part owner, he was also a partner in the firm of Hudson, Steinem, & Co. at 32 Wall Street.

Senator Keane is survived by Abigail Keane, his wife of 33 years, and their four children, Mrs Rosa Childress, 31, Mr Alexander Keane, 30, Mrs Mary Aguilar, 27, and Lieutenant Marcus Keane, 21, currently serving with the United States Air Service, and eight grand-children.

I withdraw a pair of nail-scissors from my bag and cut out the obituary, trimming the edges just so. Then I place the scissors and the clipping in my bag and stow my bag in the net. But it is no good. The words are inside me now, wheedling their way into fissures and cracks.

Abigail Davis. Prominent Washing hostess. Genteel hospitality. I did not expect him to remain alone. There was bound to be a wife, children. But they were abstract creatures, lacking names and without histories. Four children. Eight grandchildren. His life went on, packed with births, marriages, baptisms. Familial joys and sorrows of which I know so very little. Politics. Wealth. In Washington. What had become of the man who began each day riding alone through the desert and loved to lie in silence beneath the shade of a cottonwood tree? The man who passed nights in a sheetless bed, ate meals cooked on an open fire. What happened to the deep longing he felt for life on a ranch?

I stare at the window as if some answer might float up from the grey-bellied clouds and mist-bound hills, the bombed out villages and untilled fields rolling past. At Suippes, two lace-capped women with bulging parcels bustle into our

341

compartment. Pleasantries exchanged and boxes stowed, they fall mercifully silent as the train continues on its clattery way and my thoughts come to rest on the last contact I ever had with Will Keane – which was vicarious and transpired long after our parting.

New Orleans, 1900. Louis and I are attending an agricultural exposition. Everyone in the cotton business is there: shippers, buyers, factors, growers, traders... and while Louis is busy deal-making, I wander among the stalls. All afternoon he has been pressing me to move to Paris. Two years have passed since his wife's death and he is lonely. A dollar, he urges, goes so much farther in France. You could live like a Queen, *ma chérie*. It is the same every time he visits. The gentle pleading, the subtle guilt. His loneliness. My reluctance. And lately, I have begun to notice things that trouble me. A cool skillfulness to his devotions. A hint of calculation I never sensed before. As if he were extremely pleased with himself for satisfying a woman fifteen years younger. Is it this pleasure, rather than anything particular about me, that constitutes my appeal?

These are my thoughts as I move through the exhibition hall, aware, suddenly, of a familiar face coming towards me through the crowd. Small-featured, dark complexion. Genial. Only when I hear him speaking Spanish to his companion do I recognise the man as Rafael Cruillo. My chest constricts, but some force draws me to him. I approach and introduce myself.

His face breaks into a smile. He is here, he informs me, to promote Arizona's newly irrigated land to cotton growers. They have dammed the Salt River. Built canals. Last year a man in Tempe grew 3,000 pounds of cotton on five acres. And land costs only fifteen dollars an acre! His voice drips with wry amusement. Rafael has the air of a man who is perfectly content to spread the gospel of cheap land, but who is by no means a true believer. I listen, questions multiplying in my head until one manages to shape itself. 'And our mutual friend?'

But before Rafael can answer, Louis arrives by my side

linking his arm through mine. Introductions are soon underway and it occurs to me that this encounter will be reported back to Will Keane. Following swiftly on the heels of this thought comes another: certain facts must not reach him. Will must not learn that I am still working for M. Lebrun. He cannot know that I am still tallying sums in the same office where his own good graces (or simple guilt) landed me a job sixteen years ago. So when the conversation reverts to me, I smile widely and declare, 'How fortunate that we chanced to meet, Señor Cruillo. For I shall soon be leaving the country.'

A look of surprise crosses his face.

'I sail for France next month.'

And Louis, to his infinite credit, brings it off beautifully. He betrays no surprise and leaves me to respond to Rafael's queries, which are swiftly concluded.

'My dear Miss Palmer,' Rafael declares, upon hearing that my move to Paris is a permanent one. 'I always took you for a free-thinker. And as for our mutual friend,' he adds, expression softening in a way that reveals he never thought ill of me. 'I see William very rarely nowadays.'

'I am sorry to hear that. And surprised. He admired you tremendously.'

Rafael receives the compliment with a gracious smile. 'As I did him.' He lingers a moment longer, clasping and unclasping his stick.

'You'll give him my best, won't you?' I force my lips into a smile.

'Of course.'

And with that, Louis and I stroll away between the stalls, basking in the afterglow of my declaration. With Louis feeling triumphant, I can let my attention drift and soon find myself dwelling on Rafael's use of the past tense. As I *did* him.

At Verdun the station swarms with canteen workers, troops,

civilians, and Russian *prisoniers libres*. About Camille's beastly valise I needn't have worried, for the moment we descend, a khaki-clad American soldier offers to help, and after heaving our bags into the back of a shiny AEF vehicle, he drives us into town with alarming speed, given the dreadful state of the roads.

At the Collège Buvignier, two wings have been converted to dormitories for '*pèlegrins*' coming to search the battlefields. The rest of the building houses aid workers and returning *evacuées*. The *patron*, who used to run a hotel that is now in ruins, gives us a hearty greeting and offers to show us the 'roof garden' – a gaping hole where a 380mm shell landed. We follow him down a corridor bathed in sallow light, every window covered with oiled paper. The building served as a hospital throughout the war and the smell of eusol and idioform still clings to the walls. Our room contains a pair of iron cots, wool blankets, and a wash-stand. Water, the *patron* informs us, is carried by pail from the town faucet. We are requested to use it sparingly and told to empty our chamber pots into pit-toilets at the back. Dinner is at six in the *cantine*. Then, with a jaunty twirl of his cane, our host withdraws.

Camille sets to work installing the contents of her enormous valise on the room's only shelf. Opening the drawer of a metal table, I find an empty glass ampoule and three rolls of gauze. Ordinarily, this would depress me. Its sterility, the tepid daylight seeping through its papered window, the faint hospital stink. But after the shock of Will Keane's obituary, a haze of numb disbelief has settled over me. Still, this is no place to spend a bright spring afternoon. I ask Camille to join me for a walk but she declines, preferring to lie down and rest.

So I take to the streets alone, striding down narrow lanes carved through the rubble. Verdun is crawling with people, which surprises me. I'd expected a solitary stroll through an empty wasteland, but troops, aid workers, residents, and children without any school to attend all clog the slender paths. French soldiers who have been put to work hauling water, chopping wood, and delivering bread keep stepping aside, flattening themselves against blackened walls as I pass.

I approach the ancient convent whose bombed out walls are being repaired by workers with 'PG' emblazoned on their backs. I stop for a moment to watch them mix cement and heave stones, before continuing up the steep-pitched slope. When the lane plateaus, a vista of rubble-heaps and roofless houses opens up below. The view across the Meuse, which I recall so fondly, is nothing but a cross-hatch of black electric wires strung across ruins. Fury rips through me. I try to pin it on the Germans, but the vision of those stooped *prisoniers de guerre* shambling about the convent hauling stones makes this impossible. No, I cannot blame them. Will Keane. He is responsible for this inner havoc. Because he died in ignorance. Never knowing what happened the night of the Bisbee Massacre. What that day was like. Mayhem in the streets. The drunken shouts, the fist fights, the gunfire. He died ignorant of the terror that came over me as I glimpsed Texas Lil asleep in my bed. Lips parted, face pale. Peaceful as a child. How preoccupied I was upon entering my darkened bedroom. Exhausted, rattled. After all I had heard and seen that day. In the barroom, the streets. Evie's bedroom.

He died ignorant of the panic that gripped me when I glimpsed those men pulling the blankets off Texas Lil. Asleep in my bed. Exposed. Drugged. Unaware of the sheet being drawn back, the hands shoving up her shift and fondling her breasts, pale in the glow of the streetlamps. Those men, ready to do to her what had been done to Evie. But before I could decide, think, cry out… a hot sweaty hand claps itself over my mouth. A struggle to gather my wits, to breathe. Panic punctured by Gypsie's voice. Gypsie bragging one night at supper about how she'd disarmed a rough john with a strip-tease, undoing his braces, then, when his trousers were down at his ankles – go for the door. Si, Contessa had said. You let the *pendejos* think you want it, then *hasta la vista*. What else to do but try? Flick my tongue against the hand crushing my mouth. Fingers sour with chewing tobacco and dirt. And it works. It works. The hand slides away, gropes at me. I wriggle my hips, slither free from his grasp and slip my arms from the dressing gown. Distract them from Texas Lil – lying there all the while, exposed, bleeding, shivering – yes, I distract them with a clumsy joke of a strip-tease. Jackson's shouts reach me from the backlot. He is busy tackling those drunken brutes taking pot-shoot at the dogs. He cannot help me. Not yet. What choice do I have but to keep the charade going? Buy time doing what the whores do. Moan that I haven't had any for so long… whisper in their ears as I lower their trousers. First one, then the other. Repeat my offer. *Two for the price of one*, I titter sauntering towards the door. Then I fling it open and run. Down the hall, naked and screaming. Crying out for Jackson. *Get the hell up here, Jackson, help…*

I stumble over a pile of broken masonry and look up. A door to my left bears a sign. *We are back. Verbidden to get in.* I walk on. More heaps of stone, bombed out buildings, roofless houses. I try to hew my thoughts to the present, but find myself immune to it all. How many smashed-up villages have I seen? How many rubble-piles? Shattered buildings? And on this scale… it is as if every shattered village and bombed-out building in France were gathering round me, rising to such a terrible crescendo of destruction that all I can do is stop up my ears.

I wander down to the spot where a quaint foot-bridge used to span a moat, carrying pedestrians into town from the Porte St Paul. The footbridge is gone, of course. Nothing is as I remember, except for the clock ringing out over the ruined citadel every quarter of an hour. I listen to the deep, clear chime and gaze down into the chalky green water. I am waiting. For a suitable sensation to grip me. Some upset or stab of pain at the sight of the empty expanse where the footbridge used to be. But I feel nothing. Nothing but shame and anger at the futile course of my meditations. Did Rafael ever tell Will of my glamorous, cosmopolitan life? Did the message I had so hoped he would receive ever arrive? *She is married to a dashing Frenchman. They live in Paris.* Or did I remove myself to France in a useless fit of pique? What kind of woman does such a thing?

I linger a moment longer at the water's edge, watching the green-grey river eddy and swirl. Men are repairing a building nearby and their shouts rise from the site, along with a clatter of metal tools. Clap of stone against stone. The air is hazy with brick-dust. I catch sight of a woman in black crepe, tramping beneath the Porte Chaussée. Trench-mud spatters the hem of her skirts. This, I remind myself, is what awaits us. Days spent traipsing across battlefields, searching in vain. I must banish Will Keane from my thoughts so that I am equal to the task.

I turn on my heel and nearly collide with a workman. White with pulverised stone, he backs away, apologizing. There is something familiar in the rolling gait, a stride that puts me in mind of Jackson. He apologises again, then his eyes widen. 'Soeur Palmer,' he breathes.

His hair is stiff and white, but beneath the stone-dust that covers him like flour, I recognise the face. Thinner. Cheek bones sharper, nose more prominent.

A cart trundles past. Then another.

'C'est moi. Simon.'

I nod and burst into tears.

Placing an arm across my shoulder, Simon tells me that his work is finished for the day. He was just leaving. He apologises again for the dust on my clothes, then gestures for me to follow. He leads me down a backstreet where feral cats dart out from behind chunks of stone, broken-off facades covered in bird droppings. There is a faint smell of sewers.

We walk along a path that leads beyond the rubble-clogged town onto an open riverbank. Underfoot, the ground is broken and uneven. Each step feels strange. Spongy. As if the soil has not been properly tamped down. Metal bits stick up in odd places and over it all grows a thin dusting of grass. Simon leads me to a grove of splintered trees where over-turned munitions boxes have been arranged into a seat. A gentle wind riffles the water, as we sit on the make-shift bench and lapse into silence. His presence calms me, and for the first time since morning, my inner commotion ceases. At our feet daisies shiver in the breeze. He draws a fishing line from his bag. After baiting and dropping it into the river, he tells me what happened after Tosh and I left the *poste*.

Just after dark, he heard voices followed by the hiss of a flamethrower. Simon shouted up in German to let them know there were wounded. An officer appeared, pistol raised. He told Simon to care for the men until they could be evacuated to a German hospital. That night, French artillery pummeled them, sending plaster and debris crashing down onto the wounded men. Simon spent the entire night brushing rubble off the patients with his bare hands. There was one canteen of water and a few raw potatoes courtesy of the German officer. The wounded men lay in puddles of their own urine and feces, for Simon could spare no water to wash them. By morning two patients had died. The rest spent the following day at the *poste*, still waiting to be evacuated. The second night, when the artillery started up again, the boy with the broken ribs who had wheezed out his plea for Tosh to leave stuck a rifle in his mouth and used a bayonet to pull the trigger, spattering the other patients with brains, hair, blood. Simon wiped them clean with wads of gauze.

Here Simon pauses, muscle in his face twitching.

The following day they were evacuated to a German field hospital. It was a charnel house. Not from lack of care, but due to shortages. There were no beds, no sheets. Just a dirt floor and useless bandages made of crepe paper that disintegrated when wet. Anesthetic gas was rationed. Some amputations did not even merit it. Pus and maggots were everywhere. Wagons creaked for lack of grease, tyres were worn to threads. No motor ambulances, just carts pulled by emaciated ponies. Bread was made of ground turnips and sawdust, stews of horsemeat and nettles. After six weeks at the hospital, where Simon was put to work hauling stretchers, they packed him into a boxcar full of prisoners and sent them to a disused factory where he stayed until the end of the war. Only one patient from the *poste* survived.

He lifts his brow and gives a quick head-shake. 'Et la Mademoiselle MacNeil?'

For a long moment, I say nothing. I just sit and watch as he casts his line into the water again. Then it all comes pouring out and when my story reaches the moment of her death, I do not flinch but carry on to the end. It is easier, somehow, to tell it in French. Simon listens, eyes trained on his fishing line all the while, and once I have finished we both fall quiet. The day has begun to wane. A chill steals into the air, shadows thickening. Simon draws his fishing line from the water.

'Chaque jour j'essaie.' He gestures at the empty line, then rolls it up and stows it away in his bag. He will never catch anything here, he says. Not for a long time.

We walk back across the broken ground, and I inquire after his family. They are struggling, he tells me. Until the government decides whether ruined businesses must be rebuilt on the exact spot they occupied before the war, his father can do nothing. And if he cannot rebuild his sawmill on another site, all will be lost. For it lies in a forest that no longer exists, the trees having been blown to bits. Nothing grows there now. It is just a churned up patch of chalky dirt.

I think of Albert and his colleagues negotiating back in Paris. Of Parisians' constant speculations about what formula the delegates will use to calculate damages. As if it were simply a matter of arriving at the proper sum. When no amount of reparations, levied and paid, can salvage our diminished world.

When we reach the *collège*, Simon and I linger at the gate. These days a shadowy sense of dread surrounds every leave-taking, and for a long moment neither of us speaks. But farewell it must be and I cannot fool myself into believing that

I shall ever see this man again. We embrace. Simon clasps my forearms just as the *Directrice* did on that morning when Tosh and I left the château. And at this echo of that other *adieu*, I begin to feel unsteady. But it does not last, for as I rush to accommodate all the old sorrows, their mute ache begins to fade and I let it pass.

Soldiers guard the gate through which Simon now departs, their low-voiced conversation mingling with the strike of bootheels on bare stone. And as I stand in the darkening courtyard listening to his steps die away, I feel something warm and unexpected nestle down inside. A kind of gladness. That Simon is alive. That I am here. That Camille is waiting for me in the *cantine*. At one of the folding tin tables, hair upswept, chin lifted. *Pichet* of wine with two glasses set out on the table.

I must tell her what has happened. The obituary. Will Keane. Star Mansion and Sadie Blair and the night of the Bisbee Massacre Execution when two men hid themselves in my room, skulking in the shadows by the bed where Texas Lil lay sleeping. How I proctected her with a strip-tease. Myself, too. But from what? Those men were stumbling drunk. *Too soused to shoot*, as Gypsie would surely have said. Yes. This time I shall tell it straight. To Camille. From start to finish. No suppressions, no elisions.

A chill settles over the courtyard, but I am not ready to retreat indoors. Tepid light falls across the walls, each oil-papered window shining out like sallow eyes. A lone star flames through the twilight. Venus. I think about the time Tosh and I walked back to the field hospital and glimpsed it high above the serried black of the pines. About those evenings at the casita when its fiery glint pierced the dark above the foothills. The night we stumbled outside to secure a flapping clothesline and found the sky aswarm with stars. How Will pulled me close and pointed out the constellations. Orion. Aries. Cassiopeia. Fixing a story to each one. The ram that led Bacchus through the desert. An African Queen banished to the edge of the galaxy.

I stand in the gathering dark and remember him that way. Radiant and alive. Body pressed to mine as we gaze upwards at the heavens, drawing lines between the stars.

Epilogue

I awake to a room suffused with light. Beyond my window stretches the dull sky of a Parisian winter. Overcast and touched with blue. Morning, to judge from the quality of light, though it is hard to be sure. We are perched so high on the curve of the earth that the sun struggles in winter.

I do not ring for Marie-Rose, but lie curled on my side and stare at this patch of sky. The gentle wash of light soothing in its constancy.

The war is over, the peace signed. Albert and the other delegates have all gone home. What sprang up between us was inevitable, I suppose. Necessary, even. The tenderness, the intimate revelations over supper, the calm intensities of feeling. We laughed, we talked, we ate and drank together, sharing confidences and fears and long-forgotten dreams – chaste companions to the end.

After he left I found myself shifting about in a melancholy haze. But my sorrow soon ebbed, for in those brilliant summer days after his departure, what I felt was not the raw agony of youthful loss, but a quiet mournfulness. The same calm, sober feeling that accompanies the onset of winter. When the rich fruit of the harvest has been reaped and the leafy boughs of the trees are still touched with fire. Still, I miss him. Our walks along the Seine as we browsed the book-stalls, chatting away and sifting through those slim volumes bound by *mutilés* that now fill an entire shelf of my library. During those hours of easy conversation, something within me gave way. In Albert's presence I ceased to wait. Ceased to want. Instead, I simply lived. And into that life I now bring every ounce of self. Every scrap of memory, wisp of breath, and pulse of feeling.

Sorrow still seizes me. When I lay eyes on the photograph of me and Louis in Ornes. Or move through these empty music rooms and feel the weight of their silence, bereft of Pierre's music. When I remember Tosh's vehement expressions, the youthful vigour of her voice, her husky unrestrained laugh. I do not savour every moment, nor even every day. I am too flawed for that. But I am here. At home. In Paris. Walking its narrow alleys and *grands boulevards*, visiting its cafés and its gardens, enjoying the bustle of its shops. Windows that remained shuttered for years have been thrown open. Placards proclaiming *Fermé pour cause de mobilisation, 2 Août '14* or *Le Patron les personnel sont sous les drapeaux* have all vanished. And every time I pass a shop-window where one used to hang, its penciled words fading away as the war ground on and on, I stand amazed.

Camille complains about the prices, the crowds of tourists. But I find the city's jaunty, stubborn return to life miraculous. And yet, 'return' is not quite right. This isn't the same city that went to war six years ago. Nor is it the place Louis and I inhabited before the war. That place is gone. And Louis with it. Some days, I miss him dearly. In a way I never did during the war. Still, I am glad he was spared the ordeal of his beloved *pays* reduced to rubble. Ornes wiped from the map. Lush hills outside Verdun that we once crossed on horseback now flattened by bombs, fields where we'd glimpsed a young boy gathering snails on the *glacis* now littered with corpses and shrapnel. When Camille and I trod that ruined *paysage* I was gripped by a terrible intensity of feeling. A sensation akin heart-break or homesickness. Yet far more powerful.

People claim those fields are so full of gas and unexploded bombs they will not be tillable for generations. And so, through its comparatively swift revival, Paris has resumed its customary place as a country unto itself. A city that exists, as in former days, oddly outside the rest of France. Yet we are still a city in mourning. You can see it in the pale faces of the shop-girls thronging the *laiteries*. In *les vielles* shuffling off to mass in black crepe and all the young, unmarried women with their pushed-up black veils. In the *mutilés* begging on street corners, navigating cobbles on crutches, struggling down from trams with their wares slung about their necks. My writing desk is full of pencils, matchboxes, and cigars, and whenever Marie-Rose sees me open that drawer to add another, she shakes her head. Not from sorrow at their plight but with disapproval at my profligacy, which is incomprehensible to her.

If you know where to look, you can see shrapnel lodged in walls around the city. A few canons remain on display in the Champs Elysées, and down the Rue de Rivoli, far beyond where it is fashionable to go, you will see the shell of a building surrounded by charred rubble, where a tenement collapsed under a bomb burying everyone alive who sat huddled in its cellar. There is talk of leaving it this way, as a monument. But to what? It will never happen. The land is too valuable, people's memories too short. No, that is not true. Desire may be fickle, but memory is a tough unruly creature. We need no pile of rubble on the rue de Rivoli to remind us of all we have lost.

The patch of sky beyond the *jalousie* has turned a soft pale blue. People are filling the streets. On their way to work, to school, to church and soon I shall join this quick-footed throng, for I must make my way up to an atelier in Montmartre where I work three afternoons a week. Stretching canvasses, preparing pigments, mixing plaster for an artist who survived Verdun, the Somme, northern Italy. Léon served with an artillery battery without ever being wounded, though he suffered from typhus and trench foot and now walks with a limp. Before the war, he was stationed in Morocco and it was there he began to paint. Léon has become renowned for his masks. *Mutilés de guerre* travel from all over France to have Léon cast their faces and create a mask to hide their mutilated chins and missing eyes, their stove-in cheekbones. At the sight of their raw, fire-scarred flesh, I do not flinch. I simply mix the plaster and hand Léon what he needs. Knives, clay, spatula, gauze.

Last week, he pointed to the scar on my neck and asked what had happened. So I told him. About Tosh and Simon and the *poste de secours* and although, for some strange reason, you feel bound up in it all... I have said nothing of all that. Perhaps I shall speak of it all one day. Tell Léon about my time at Star Mansion, those nights at Rafael's casita. Evoke the beauty of those foothills, smell of the desert after rain, fiery astral excess of its skies. Describe for him those irrepressible shards of light that lack any myth to give them meaning but flame up nonetheless, nameless and on fire. If our talk ever drifts to such things.

Or perhaps it would be best to let silence fall across what once was but is no more. Telling Camille was hard enough. She pressed me about Texas Lil, Contessa, Jackson... their respective fates. Of which I know nothing, towards whom I have cast so little thought for decades. Unbearable images began washing back through me... the trusting look in Lil's eyes as she'd gulped down the laudanum-laced milk I gave her the night I stole the money. Memory of her soft pale hands clasping the glass, her grin as she'd set it down, empty, on the night-table then snuggled down deep into the bedclothes... never sparing a thought for how my flight might have affected her. Not once all these years.

But for all the pain they caused me, these confidences healed our friendship. Brought Camille and me close again. Of course, she has her own view of it all: that Will Keane pined for me all his life, that he married a young woman with no past, no history that could ever pain him, but all the while, he longed for something deeper, more passionate. For me. Well. I have my doubts. But let her make of it what she will. After all, some women seem to favour the sentimental motive. And why not?

Camille suggested I travel back. To glimpse once more that wild extravagance of light, the eerie beauty of those cactus-clad hills. To walk again beneath the violent blue of its skies. But the desert, I suspect, would seem as foreign to me as post-war France would feel to Louis. And just as empty. A place as unrecognisable as the man you became. Besides, I am much more than the history of those bygone days.

Sitting up in bed, I swing my legs over the side and take your letters from the drawer of my night-table. Uppermost sheets stiff and black with blood. I cross the room and stare at the coal piled high in the scuttle. Its presence, too, seems miraculous. During the war, a jeweller on the Rue de Rivoli placed a huge black lump of it in his window with diamonds massed around it. Passers-by stopped and stared, while a guard made sure no harm came to it.

I strike a match. The fire leaps to life in the grate. I hold the pages covered with your blue script, corners crusted with Tosh's blood, and bend down before the flames. But something within me recoils and I step away, unable to destroy a thing that has survived such a bizarre and violent journey. And against such odds. I carry the fragile pages down the hall and place them in the drawer stuffed with matches and cigars. Faint noises drift up from the courtyard. My neighbours have begun to stir. Soon the air will be heavy with the smell of bread and coffee, coal-smoke, petrol fumes. The city, resurgent, awaits.

Wrapper pulled tight, I return to my room. A bright blaze fills my *chambre* with heat and light. I strip away my wrapper and night-dress and stand naked before the fire, watching the flames dance over that once precious coal, feeling the heat soak my skin. A heat I shall never again take for granted. I stand before the rippling flames and close my eyes. Roll that knob of flesh beneath my fingers and think of the night in Châlons when Tosh examined it. Of the way she looked as she died in my arms, terrified and wild. Of the water rolling down my flesh that night in the casita all those years ago. Of your body, once so beloved, in a distant desert grave.

My fingers press the knob of flesh harder, and with every dull familiar ache I know. The way that newborn baby Camille held in the cellar one night during a bombing raid knew its mother. Blind, three days old, eyes still shut. Still it knew. The way an infant knows how to suckle. How to smile.

I roll this knot against my rib and know that some piece of you is here. Inside me. Mingled with those sun-soaked hills and pitiless skies, the fire and the rain. The man I remember and once loved, couched safe within all these years. A tiny pearl on the cage around my heart.

Acknowledgements

Countless debts have accumulated during the writing of this book. I would like to acknowledge the editors of *Superstition Review* and *Edinburgh Review* who published earlier versions of chapters one and two respectively. Residencies at Hawthornden Castle, Tyrone Guthrie Centre, and Chateau de Lesvault provided me with precious stretches of unbroken time during which to write. I am also deeply indebted to Melissa Pritchard, Jay Boyer, Ron Carlson, and Alberto Ríos for their unrivaled instruction (your lessons continue to accrue and resonate down the years). A million thanks to the entire staff at Freight Books for their unstinting support, especially Adrian, Rodge, and Fiona.

I am also grateful to Colette Korry-Hatrick and Ankhra Laan Ra who nurtured my work in ways they do not even realise, as did Kat Shaw, Karen Breneman, and Sarah Hatcher (namaste).

Thanks are also due to Alan Gillis for his sanity and good humour; to Aaron Kelly for lugging a heavy bag of books through the streets of Belfast during a heat wave; to Valerie Acuff, Zena and Gilles, Steve and Marty Kessler, and Kate Nichol for giving me shelter and sustenance on various occasions; to AW for his generosity and *savoir faire*; to Ruth Burnnett for her friendship and editorial savvy; to Susan Thomas, George Wrangham, and Tony Morinelli for sparking my initial passion for literature and history; to Susan Ziemak for her expertise in all things equestrian (you are deeply missed); to all my students and academic colleagues throughout the years; to Nichola, Georgia, and Jane for taking such marvelous care of my children while I wrote; to those magnificent people in my life whom I'm blessed to call friends (you know who you are!); to my siblings and parents for their love; to Nicole and Callum; and above all to Thomas Legendre, who has been forced to read more drafts of this novel than any sane individual should have to endure. Without his patience, love, and endless encouragement, this book would never have been written.